The Pomegranate RING

The Pomegranate RING

Simon Brian Cartlidge

Copyright © 2016 Simon Brian Cartlidge

The moral right of the author has been asserted.

Apart from any fair dealing for the purposes of research or private study, or criticism or review, as permitted under the Copyright, Designs and Patents Act 1988, this publication may only be reproduced, stored or transmitted, in any form or by any means, with the prior permission in writing of the publishers, or in the case of reprographic reproduction in accordance with the terms of licences issued by the Copyright Licensing Agency. Enquiries concerning reproduction outside those terms should be sent to the publishers.

Matador
9 Priory Business Park,
Wistow Road, Kibworth Beauchamp,
Leicestershire. LE8 0RX
Tel: (+44) 116 279 2299
Fax: (+44) 116 279 2277
Email: books@troubador.co.uk
Web: www.troubador.co.uk/matador

ISBN 978 1785890 130

British Library Cataloguing in Publication Data.
A catalogue record for this book is available from the British Library.

Printed and bound by CPI Group (UK) Ltd, Croydon, CR0 4YY
Typeset in 10.5pt Bembo by Troubador Publishing Ltd, Leicester, UK

Matador is an imprint of Troubador Publishing Ltd

For Rebecca and Flynn.
For my family.
For all my students past, present and future.
And for Shay, Sean and Tabatha and the heat, steam and abandon
of the southern Portuguese coast.

"Oh my son, my sorrow, why did I ever bear you?"
The Iliad

PROLOGUE

The Greek had sailed through the night and walked endlessly through the caramel canyons of Thera. The morning fog made her shiver as she carried the child to the temple. Twice she had lost her way stumbling down dark ravines and slipping on the serpentine stone of the island. And now the light cloud was devoured by the morning sun and the essence of lemon trees and olives became stronger. The man was waiting at the temple gate. He stared and frowned. His clothes were ill fitting and bedraggled, a poor man's tunic barely covered his drum like chest. His natural enmity towards the traveller was cooled by the smile on the woman's face. He gave the old greeting and the woman responded. All the same he determined to cleanse himself of this unworthy Greek whore when he had the chance.

"This is the child?"

"Yes. You have your payment and you are clear?"

"Questions need to be asked."

"They will not be answered."

"Then why is the infant to be protected?"

The woman passed over the child. The fog was still lifting. The volcanic ash of Perissa beach glinted ebony black with the first light. The volcano murmured his greeting to Eos the Goddess of the dawn and she embraced him.

"And it's name?"

The Greek woman smiled,

"You decide."

1

The Greek sun, red as Greek suns often are, sank with a sigh behind Lesbos and into the western Aegean. Its dying rays caught the island in its path and the upper rim had power enough to turn the bobbing boats in the harbour at Eresos to gamboge. The island of Lesbos was beguiling in all her moods; from the morning when Apollo rides westwards over the Anatolian plains past the walls of Troy to the evening when the shadows lengthen and bless his temple with a rosy hue.

It was to the temple of Apollo that Lyria made her way hurriedly. It lay in a valley protected by cypress trees a good hours walk from her parents' home in the small village of Nape. Apollo was her favourite God as he protected young men and was gifted in music and poetry. He would know what to do. Had he not lost his love Hyacinthus murdered by the jealous Zephyrus? Did not Hestia forsake him vowing eternal chastity? She knew she didn't have much time before her mother would notice she was gone. An ibis that pitched and shrieked above her head told her that bad weather was on its way. She remembered a poem taught to her by her mother and shuddered,

> "Sing bird rise storm
> Ship ashore before morn"

The sun set deeper, the rays dancing through her red hair as she climbed the steps into the temple. Kneeling before the altar she clenched her hands, closed her eyes and began to speak the prayer she had been rehearsing all day,

"Dearest Apollo, brother of Artemis son of Zeus and protector of the young. Please guide my brother through the storm and bring him safely home to his family. Dearest Nereids, please speak to my brother Philon in his dreams and comfort him. Please keep him safe in the night and let him know that his sister prays for him."

She paused for a moment and looked up. Apollo, handsome and serene returned her gaze with a calm dignity,

"Darling brother, I will pray for you every night till you return."

Lyria gently laid the laurel, sacred to Apollo, at his feet. Darkness began to creep over the temple as the young God reined his chariot over the horizon. The air was suddenly fresher as she turned and rushed down the steps and out through the avenue of cypress trees. Behind the altar Cyrene the temple guardian gently placed the laurel to her breast, smiled to herself and returned to her duties.

2

Lyria was excited. It was the time of the summer festival, the first of the season to honour Demeter. It was a hot day and the corn gleamed gold on the furrowed land. The bales sat squat with the sun warming in their bellies. All work had stopped and Lyria had spent the morning putting wreaths and bouquets of flowers on the oxen and plough and all the farm tools. The oxen had stood dutifully whilst they were adorned and prepared. Lyria was pleased with her work,

"How beautiful you look."

Like her mother she was known for her love of nature and colours. The girls called her Lyria the dreamer. But they loved her for it and were mindful of the gifts the Gods had given her, her powers of reflection and speech and poetry, her loyalty and love, her prowess in the water; so they chided her only gently when she tied ribbons to the horns of the valley goats and hung hyacinth pots around the stable yards. They were aware of the strange manner the muses often bestow their gifts. Along the dry paths of the vineyards and fields the men walked slowly and shouted out the name of Demeter thanking her for a fertile harvest. The oxen followed bejeweled with summer garlands. The women danced and recited the words of the mysteries from Eleusis whose meaning they had long ago forgotten,

"Welcome Demeter. Clean of speech and hand. Free of blood guilt."

It was Lyria's first festival and she walked trippingly behind her mother carrying the baskets of plums, figs and apricot they had picked that morning. She held back and stroked Persephone her favourite Ox,

"I will share this fruit with you later Persephone. Where do you think we are going?"

Some men carried wine, their gait and manner as controlled and temperate as the breezes that touched their faces. Others carried herbs, rosemary and basil to flavour the meats. The women danced gaily around the men teasing and laughing as was the tradition. Lyria looked around in wonder at the profusion of life and colour, smells and sounds. And so the rituals of Demeter continued. As the gentle, slow winds stirred the cornfields so Lyria's thoughts stirred in her mind and for the first time since her mother Danae had announced that she would let her take part in the rituals she was unsure. That night as she lay in bed in her mind she was still in the procession watching helplessly as Persephone was spiked, her blood caught. Helpless and dying she had looked at Lyria. And Lyria wept as the words of the priestess resonated,

"Happy is she who has seen these things."

But Lyria was not happy. Her devotion to all living things had been imprinted at an early age. For two days she took no solace in food or sleep. Then she went to the market and carefully opened the cages of all the imprisoned creatures and watched as they scurried or flew away delighted with their freedom. Her father had scolded her, her mother shouted. The traders had to be recompensed. But it ended her nightmares. That night she slept the deep sleep that only a child can sleep untainted and warm where the dreams were softly drawn just as Persephone had once pulled the plough. Thus the early girlhood of Lyria passed sweetly, disposed to contemplation rather than action, her behavior at the market a rare exception; a childhood richly veined with equal aspects of love and delight both imagined and real. A spirit of meditation grew within her as anyone could see as they saw her collecting wild lavender or sweeping the temple floor with a ready smile.

3

Above the low strung streets of Larissa in central Thessaly the sky was perfectly calm. The last few stars had faded in the west and in the east the sun sat ready to rise. The town began to stir. A deep orange light brought vividly to life the hues and tones of the buildings and farms that were now the colour of owls' eyes. But then the long shadows shrank and died and Larissa opened like a flower, the traders turning to the light. The voices from the various quarters were joined by the cattle bells and the hiss from the smithy's furnace. So the smoke and sounds floated upwards to greet the sun and the river was a ribbon of silver that cuddled the village with a liquid arm. The traders began bartering for wine and oils. The Thessalians were genuine Greeks with their distinctive approach to life, their unhurried stoic ways brought from the plains of Argos far to the south or, further still, from the noisy streets of Corinth with its pot bellied vendors. Cool winters, hot summers and ample rainfall provided Thessaly with the most fertile, arable land of any on the mainland. Lush grasslands where herds of horses and cattle could thrive were the envy of all Greece where rocky barren land was the norm brought on by the fierce unforgiving suns that cursed the southern Peloponnese and the islands. Its vast northern plains were crossed by rivers and surrounded by mountains providing natural frontiers to shield them from Macedonia to the north, Epiros to the west and the ever threatening Phocicians and Myceneans to the south led by Agamemnon.

Peleus the priest king, the *myrmidon* and ruler of Thessaly mused on these blessings as he wandered first through the markets of Larissa then past the clusters of mud huts that formed part of the hundreds of farming communities worked by the *Periokoi*, the free Thessalians. He was a stout man with thinning brown hair a small nose and dark black eyes. Pausing he looked to the horizon. Peleus loved Thessaly, loved her ochre valleys and the gleams of gold and green when the evening sun caught the cedars and willows. He loved to see the sun warming the backs of the horses, the Magnetian and Thessalian stallions renowned for their speed and mild temper. A pensive man by nature he liked to muse on the short lived gnats on the wooded paths or watch the ox and plough as it sliced and flopped over the black ash of the fertile fields of Tricca, Dodona and Larissa. He watched enthralled as the traders and craftsmen went about their business.

Leonides the wheelwright examined the ash wood that he would spend the morning coaxing and bending for Acaius who needed two new wheels for his chariot. He noticed the wood was darker. 'From Mesopotamia the land east of Babylon' thought Acaius.

"I told him the wood was stronger from that region. Hmm, and pricier too" he muttered. "We'll see."

A short distance further on Dion the blacksmith prepared his furnace. Ever since Agamemnon's men had moved west toward Delphi he had been busy with swords, spears and axes. He set to work quickly. Looking up he saw a man approaching. He immediately recognised Peleus and bowed. Picking up a sword he handed it to him,

"Here, for you to see."

The sword had exquisite balance, bronze bladed and double edged. Peleus took it, expertly testing its weight and character.

"My fourth this week" said Dion who was the son and grandson of blacksmiths.

"You work swiftly and expertly Dion. Your father would be proud."

Peleus took his hand,

"I have a special task for you Dion."

"Thank you Lord. It is my life to serve Thessaly."

Peleus noticed the gnarled hands of the blacksmith and wondered how many hours of distraction they had given him. All the thinking they had saved him. A short time later he walked back to the palace fording the Peneius where it ran shallow. In his eyes now the sadness of a man who saw the future but could do little to prevent it. He must meet with his generals and listen to the reports on Agamemnon.

4

Lyria watched as her parents checked on the amphorae stored in the cellar. 'There must be a hundred' thought Lyria. 'Each one as big as me with enough wine to last a household a month.' She knew that the wines came from as far as Lemnos to the east or as south as Thera where the island smokes and rumbles,

"This year we will have a good harvest. Better even than last, Dionysus blesses us" said Parmenion as he stroked his beard. Lyria recognised the gesture as her father always stroked his beard when he was pleased. He had spent the morning overseeing the production of a promising wine. The grapes had been crushed into a must by the local children who'd had their feet perfumed with coriander and anise. Eratos's idea. Parmenion smiled. He knew it was the size of the *pithoi* that mattered, the large jars where the must is fermented, not fancy herbs and spices. But he was happy with the quality of the amphorae when the must was eventually transferred – they were lined with a good quality resin and sealed with a pitch and cork stopper,

"I hope Philon gets a good price in Crete. Sometimes he can be erratic, just like Mandrakos."

"I hope so too father."

Lyria knew that her father was holding a drinking party that evening and it was important that everyone made a good impression. Her father's close friend Eratos was coming. The women weren't allowed to be at the meeting and were there only as servants. But Orpheus was coming to help with the preparation. Orpheus would often walk with Lyria to the fig orchard and listen attentively as she spoke of her ideas on the Gods or recited her latest poem. They were best friends. Later in the afternoon Danae called for her daughter.

"You must wear your best tunic Lyria and be ready to serve your fathers' friends. Remember a good hostess always provides for her guests' needs."

Danae tried once again to impose some kind of order on Lyria's unruly red locks.

"But mother, why can't I listen to what they say? Why can't I sit in the corner? I promise I'll be quiet."

Danae gently tugged at her daughter's forelock which immediately sprang back into a curl,

"It's your job to help in the kitchen."

Lyria was careful not to test her mother's patience too far incase she left. Sometimes a sickness of the mind would overcome her and she would need to be alone, begging her husband to leave her whilst she disappeared, sometimes for months. Danae as a young woman had spent ten years searching for herself as the virgin grew inside her, sacrificing the carnal world on the altar of chastity because of a certain psychic intolerance, a childhood scar, her father's misplaced affection. Parmenion never questioned her, his love for her allowing her time to recover with friends and family on Seraphos her childhood home.

5

Lyria had served at many of her father's symposiums. As a wine dealer Parmenion was never short of willing guests and invitations were rarely turned down. She remembered the *Anthesteria* last winter, a festival in honour of Dionysus where new wines were tested. It had seemed like the whole of Lesbos had turned up to try the wine from their cellars, six amphorae had been drunk. Parmenion was known to have the best wines and Danae was an excellent cook. First tonight there would be the *komos,* the collection of guests arriving noisily at the door. Danae would let them in and guide them to the dining room where the *deipnon,* the main meal, would take place. Offerings would be made and libations poured in honour of Dionysus and Aphrodite. Lyria knew of all the Gods from her mother. It was Zeus who sent the lightning and Hephaestus the blacksmith who brought the thunder as he fashioned the armour of the Gods. After the libations the men would continue drinking in the *androcrites,* her father's special room where male guests talked of women and boys but more often of politics and the Pisistratids. Lyria mistrusted the rulers on Lesbos. The Pisistratids were a powerful family who were supported by Agamemnon. Orestes was the main landowner on the island who received money and support from the mainland. Agamemnon ruled Lesbos through Orestes. Lyria knew that a good deal of the talk at the symposium would be taken up with him especially after the wine had been drunk. 'My father argues too much' thought Lyria. 'Sometimes his face contorts and grows red when he criticises Agamemnon.'

6

Later that evening there was a knock on the door. Danae dressed in her best white tunic opened the door to reveal Eratos, her husband's best friend. Eratos stood tall and had short cropped brown hair with large dark eyes set in a bright lively face. Parmenion valued his friendship believing it brought him closer to the Gods. Eratos was known for his piety and the deference he showed to Apollo. Although he was of an age he was yet to grow a beard for which Parmenion teased him endlessly. Lyria liked Eratos the best as he would often bring her gifts, carved figures of her favourite Gods or flat peaches from his orchards. She didn't like the way her father teased him but knew it was because he loved him. Eratos gave a little bow,

"May Zeus bless all those in this dwelling."

"And may your deeds dance wildly in a golden bay" replied Parmenion giving his favourite greeting. He stood and welcomed Eratos,

"May my humble dwelling meet your honoured needs."

Parmenion turned to Lyria and gave a little wink,

"Now Eratos, have you forgotten your beard again?"

"Ah, how clumsy of me my dear Parmenion. It was with me yesterday but I believe the muses stole it in the night."

"Again?" Parmenion rose his eyebrows in mock wonder, "these Muses must be watched. Perhaps we will drink with them later."

Eratos turned to Lyria who was hovering at the kitchen entrance,

"Well, I've forgotten my beard but I haven't forgotten my favourite girl. Here, try this for size."

Eratos reached into his dark blue chiton and produced a small bracelet made from seashells finely strung together. Lyria squealed and ran to hug Eratos who was nearly knocked over,

"Thank you, thank you. Can I wear it now?"

Her mother nodded,

"Yes, I don't know how I would stop you. Eratos you spoil her. But what of Orpheus? Have you seen him?"

The question went unanswered. The rest of the party soon arrived. Acastus and Agathon, two polite but rather serious brothers who were known to despise Agamemnon and the hold he had on the island. They always surprised Parmenion with the quality of the wines they brought with them. They handed their latest offering to Danae,

"Here, from Cos. It is nearly a year old. It contains seawater to preserve it – and some honey and chalk has been added to the amphorae to balance the flavour and bring out the sweetness."

Then came Copreus who was obsessed with plumbing. At the last symposium he had described in detail the king's *megaron* at Sparta, a seat above a drain where ten times a day the servants emptied water to flush it clean. He worked for the *koprologoi*, a recognised trade on the island, cleaning out cesspits and removing the contents for disposal. Then came Demophon, Periphetes and finally Pylades who had made a small fortune trading in obsidian from Melos. All trusted friends of Parmenion. Lyria had known them all her life. She liked all her father's friends apart from Copreus. He seemed to always avoid Lyria and never looked at her directly. And then sometimes she would find him staring at her. He never brought her gifts like Eratos. When all the guests had arrived Lyria helped her mother prepare the food then serve the guests. Danae then wandered down to the stream to wash some clothes. Lyria, inquisitive as ever crept up to the door and listened to the men. She could hear her father's deep, clear voice. He spoke slowly and quietly but everyone always seemed to listen,

"It was the Aeolians who farmed this land first. This is well known. Peleus is the true ruler of Lesbos."

"I agree Parmenion." Lyria recognised the voice of Copreus. She imagined him speaking with his head bent forward avoiding any eye contact,

"Metcar settled here with his daughter Lesbos."

"Not forgetting Terpander of Antissa. Only Arion of Methymna can match him. Both islanders" said Demophon proudly.

Lyria knew of Terpander. He had invented the seven string lyre and founded the *Carnea* at Sparta a summer festival held every year in honour of Carneus the God of flocks and herds. Her father had been known to send upwards of two hundred amphorae to the festival. One year Philon had taken part in the festivities. Dressed as a priest he had been pursued by four unmarried youths all holding garlands of grapes. If he was caught it ensured prosperity for the region. Parmenion had had much difficulty in persuading Philon that he must at all costs make sure he was caught. Lyria smiled at the memory. How she missed her brother. Her father continued,

"We have the best wine, the sweetest olive oil. And we have to pay tribute to that tyrant over the water. He envies our rainfall and wheat crop. Agamemnon can grow nothing in Mycenae. The earth is as dry as his women. And now I hear he plans to desecrate Delphi. Everyone knows why Agamemnon values this island. We are the stopover, a link between the Lydian east and the Greek mainland. As long as he holds us he holds the trade. But for him the Corinthian merchant ships would trade here instead of sailing to the Troad. Orestes enforces his rule and if anyone disobeys him his garrison will deal with them. Did you hear of Pitticus? He spoke in the *Agora* against Agamemnon. Now no one has seen him for a week."

There was a pause before Periphetes spoke with his high pitched voice,

"They say he is buried outside Arisbe. I have heard the soldiers at night."

"And so Orestes the puppeteer gets richer along with his enforcers whilst we get poorer. But not for much longer."

"What are you going to do Parmenion?"

The group huddled close around their host. The wine fuelled their excitement. What could they do? At that moment they were all willing to follow him to Hades itself.

"I will organise a revolt. I will not stop until all men of Lesbos can count themselves free men. I will speak tomorrow at the *Agora*."

"Is that wise Parmenion? Think of Orestes."

"We need action. Subterfuge and backstreet plots are for the beardless lads – they never work and take too long. Do I have your support?"

Eratos was the first to stand and embrace Parmenion, "Of course you have our support."

Eratos turned to the others,

"Put the word around that Parmenion speaks at the *agora*. We will be rid of Orestes finally."

Lyria quickly moved away from the door. She was scared. What if Orestes heard her father speak? What would he do? Look at what had happened to Pitticus. She was puzzled and frightened. She left the courtyard and walked to the beach as she always did when she was tired or upset. She remembered her father carrying her when she was very young. She had hung onto his back as he carried the unsold wine back from the markets. The leather had bitten into his skin and she had kissed his shoulders to make them better. She looked around her mind full of memories. Spotting the mollusc shells and crabs in the small pools that formed in the rocky outcroppings was a comfort to her. Here the surfaces were slippery and the concentration she needed took her young mind from the words she had heard. The shells here were good but Lyria knew the best ones were to be had near the water line at Mytilene. Her father would take her there and watch her swim whilst he was waiting for a shipment of fine wines from Gargora or even Troy. Lyria had heard such wonderful stories of Troy. Ruled by a young king Priam the walls were said to be as high as a mountain and made of rose quartz so the city shone pink when the sun set and white when the moon was full. It was rumoured the golden hinges of the Scaean gate were forged by Apollo himself. Lyria wondered again about her father's plans. And where was Orpheus? It wasn't like him to not turn up. Was he poorly? Lyria determined to seek out her friend first thing in the morning.

7

Orpheus had woken early. He was a slender boy with fair hair and smiling eyes. His long lashes leant his face a kindly, feminine affectation that revealed itself in a purity and grace that served him well although he was too often crippled by shyness. Quiet by nature his father mistook his silence for idiocy and had kept him hidden, passed over him. Even more so when it became clear that he could not run like the Gods or uproot trees like Hercules. On warm spring mornings Orpheus liked to linger by the fruit walls smelling the scent from the overhanging apricots as they started to warm in the morning sunshine and then in summer moving on to the pear orchard to see them falling heavy and ripe. On this morning he filled his basket then walked through to the kitchen to prepare breakfast. Hearing a noise he looked out into the courtyard and saw his father Icarius the priest stood in front of a young boy. Orpheus recognised him as the boy who cleaned out the stables and tended to the horses. He liked him and would have befriended him had it not been for his natural reticence. His name was Acristes and Orpheus knew his family were poor and related to the Chaones on the mainland. Acristes was usually full of energy but this morning he had his head bowed and moved his feet uneasily before Icarius who smiled and placed his hand on the young boys head. Orpheus recognised this gesture and his heart froze,

"Master Icarius. I swear by Almighty Zeus it is not a lie."

Icarius replied slowly and gently as was his manner,

"Then where is the new saddle?"

"I don't know. I am not lying."

Icarius turned away and muttered casually,

"Why do you treat me with such disrespect?"

Acristes didn't speak. Orpheus looked at his father's face, his black eyes and leathered skin. He feared for Acristes. Icarius then took out a long thin knife from his robe. Acristes fell to his knees and cried out. Icarius pulled his head back and cut off his earlobe so blood poured down the boy's neck. He then took his knife and wiped it clean with the boy's hair cutting a lock so that Acristes cried out in terror and pain. Orpheus was sickened and turned away.

"Now all will know you are a thief."

Acristes ran from the courtyard holding his ear and crying out. Orpheus had half a mind to follow and comfort him but looking up suddenly he saw his father stood over him. He raised his arm and Orpheus cowered. This seemed to please Icarius who smiled and left the room. Orpheus summoned his courage and ran out after Acristes.

8

A short time later Orpheus sat in the stable. The oak woods and deep rift valleys of Lesbos were waking from their rest. Hearing a noise he sat up straight only to be bowled over by a force of fur and saliva. The animal jumped with joy and began to circle Orpheus barking,

"Cerebus! Haha. Lyria must be on her way."

A Lydian mastiff with a deep powerful chest and dribbling jowls Cerebus was an immensely strong animal but soft and placid in the company of the children. He loved the children but Lyria was his favourite. He now jumped high in the air raising his paw and gently butted his old friend. Orpheus was nearly knocked off his feet. Then he heard whistling and his heart leapt. Lyria! She always whistles. Sure enough Lyria appeared at the stable door smiling. He remembered the first time he'd seen her. Sent on an errand he had opened the courtyard door to see a young girl about his own age. She was quite tall with bright red curly hair and green eyes with a pale white skin and hundreds of freckles. He had never seen a girl with such brightly coloured hair and he stood there dumbly. Lyria grinned,

"Hello tufty."

Orpheus shyly put his hand up to touch the piece of hair at the front of his head that no amount of brushing or coaxing could tame. Lyria, still smiling, spoke again,

"Have you come to see my father about the wine?"

Lyria rather liked the look of the boy. 'He has a kind face' she thought. Orpheus, struck by his usual inability to speak around strangers continued to stare before shaking himself,

"Yes, my father would like the Scopelian wine for the rituals. I'm to give the message to Parmenion."

"I can tell him."

Lyria looked at Orpheus then took his hand and whispered, "Do you want to see my own private summer house? There is an owl's nest."

From then on Orpheus had warmed to her and they had become close friends, sharing secrets, walking in the hills, looking for herbs and talking of the things that all children talk of.

"Here, let me show you my favourite things."

Lyria opened a small chest. Inside were sea shells, a scarab from Kush and a pebble worn smooth. Orpheus noticed an old scent bottle and a ring. He took it and examined it. A small oval seal stone ring. On its face was engraved a pomegranate exquisitely detailed.

"That's my pomegranate ring. My father gave it to me. I wear it on special occasions. He told me when I'm ready I should give it to someone I love. I don't know what he means but you are my best friend so I'll give it to you. And may your deeds dance wildly in a golden bay."

Orpheus looked confused. Lyria giggled,

"That's what my father always says."

To start with the idea that anyone could take any interest in him filled him with a dizzy delight and he followed Lyria like a lap dog, treating her piquant moods and vibrancy with both equanimity and wonder, simply grateful that anyone knew he existed. He felt freer and lighter than he'd ever done before. No longer the dull, bastard boy backward and slow. A giddiness overtook him. In a world where once there had been many voices there was now just one. He listened to her poetry and song, watched her dance and in return she called him her prince and friend and the little bird in his breast grew wings. Those early days were full of sunshine and jewels, a friendly intimacy that in years to come Orpheus would treasure. In short Orpheus had found a salvation in Lyria and he yielded gladly to her whims and caprices. But now she looked a little troubled. She told Orpheus about the symposium and what she had heard. They walked to the storehouses and sat in the granary on piles of dry corn. The wide wooden doors were open and let the sun in so it seemed to Lyria they were sat on piles of gold.

"But my father will say too much."

Orpheus pondered,

"But everyone agrees with him so he will be safe."

Lyria suddenly jumped up and ran to the yard pleased with what Orpheus had said. She shouted,

"What treasures do you have?"

Orpheus followed her laughing. It was an old game they played,

"I have ostrich eggs from Egypt."

"I have ivory from Syria."

"I have dyes from Crete and copper from Kypria."

"I have gold from Kush."

"May your deeds dance wildly in a golden bay!"

Her vivacity was so potent that Orpheus like many people was drawn to her, drawn to the light she gave out, wanting to bathe in its warmth. Just as he left the granary he noticed a glint of metal from behind a stray bale. It was the new saddle placed there earlier by the saddler for which Acristes had lost his ear. Lyria turned excitedly to Orpheus and took his hand,

"Let's go and see Aphrodite."

9

It was still morning but there was a sudden unexpected heat so the sea's surface ran smooth in the gulf of Pyrrha turning the sullen and silent water cobalt blue. A short walk inland at Mesa stood the temple of Aphrodite. Lyria and Orpheus sat in obeyance before the shrine. The Goddess was dressed in a cloak of braided gold fringed and tempered with Meliboean crimson. A veil covered her face. Lyria bowed her head and knelt filled as she was with awe and reverence. Offerings and incense surrounded them. In the air the sweet, acrid smell of dried blood. The image was alive there was no doubt of that. Lyria knew her. The priestesses spoke but their voices were far away. A corona of light now surrounded her like a Hesperidean fire and Lyria felt herself rise. Is she speaking to me? Her lips trembled and she gripped the hand of Orpheus and felt calm again, soothed by the press of his palm,

"Did you hear her?"

Orpheus shook his head.

"No Lyria. But she is beautiful" he stuttered, "and you are too."

They walked outside still holding hands. On the beach at Brisa the sea licked the shore and the soft breezes carried the smell of olives and hay up the gulf and into the stone valleys.

10

Once a month when the full moon began to wane Lyria was allowed to ride around the island. On the eastern shore at Mytilene she would gallop along the beach holding one hand high in tribute to the lantern moon as her shadow swung and waved back at her. Then she would harness the horse and swim out and dive for shells. Lyria was known for being a strong swimmer, the strongest by far for a girl her age. Even though still a child there was a balance and harmony about her which her father noted as he watched his daughter's progress from a safe distance. He turned and began to make his way home in his mind rehearsing the words he would speak at the *agora*. Lyria, exhilarated and thrilled after her swim climbed back onto her horse and rode on unaware as always that her father had been watching her. She liked to imagine herself a messenger of the Gods, a maid of Apollo cutting through the clouds to deliver her divine message. Tonight was extra special for as she turned into the wind she thought she smelt the summer again. She looked up to the sky. Who but Apollo moves the sun across the sky? He rests in the evening when Selene nudges him gently out of the heavens. Does Selene sleep in the day? Lyria wondered,

"You are almost full tonight bless you with your finest ivory dress."

Just as she spoke the words a cloud covered the moon and the darkness surged around her. Lyria shivered and turned to home.

The sound of the horn on the high walls of Mytilene signified a change of the watch. Inside the citadel Orestes looked west towards the mainland where his lord and master Agamemnon made his plans,

"Parmenion speaks tomorrow your spies tell you?"

Mandacles, his advisor, nodded his head,

"They say he has much anger in his heart."

Orestes nodded,

"Anger is always the last passion to die in a man."

11

Parmenion woke to the sound of the cockerel and after checking on the wine stores walked through the cellar to his daughter's bedroom. Lyria lay asleep on her side. Her father gazed in awe and thanked the Gods again for his wife's beauty,

"For where else would Lyria acquire such provenance?" he mused, "certainly not my looks" he chuckled to himself. He leaned over his daughter and whispered,

"Lyria, wake up."

She didn't stir. A little louder,

"Lyria daughter, quickly."

Lyria, half dressed and half awake followed her father in the half light stumbling and puzzled but obedient and curious. Outside it grew lighter although the scarlet flush of dawn was not yet etched on the sky. Lyria turned and saw her mother stood at the doorway with a look on her face that she didn't recognise. Parmenion led his daughter out of their home through the orchard and into the valley. This was an adventure and Lyria felt excited. She felt the dew seep through her sandals. The sun rose but they were hidden from its warmth as they walked west in the shadow of the valley to where the island became bare and rocky. Lyria now sensed her father's earnest mood and dutifully followed at his heels like an eager pup.

"Never count your days away, make your days count. One day you will cross the river."

Although young she knew he spoke more to himself than

to her. Now climbing up the side of the valley the ground was arid, rocky and precipitous. Parmenion paused at the foot of a stone overhang which concealed a small opening. Scrambling through they came into a vast cave. Immediately their voices and movements became amplified as Parmenion lit a torch and beckoned his daughter to see the graves and tombs that lay before them.

"These are your ancestors my daughter, your heritage. Never forget you are Thessalian, Aeolian, born in the shadow of Mount Olympus in the Gulf of Pagasae. You are descended from the Aleuadae family forced to flee from the Athenian ruling family the Pisistratids." Parmenion paused to spit,

"Never bow down to any other authority, stand firm."

Lyria, scared but fascinated was acutely aware of her father's anger but it was her fragile mortality that overcame her as she stared at the decaying tombs of her ancestors. And yet for the first time in her life she felt as if her entire body were breathing.

"I feel strange."

Parmenion laughed then, sensing the integrity of his daughters words placed his hand on her shoulder,

"This place has that effect on people" said Parmenion, "some say it is haunted by the harpies. But these tombs will always have the last word and one day men will sneer at us like dust on the breeze when we have lost the worlds' delights. Can you smell the mortality in the air?"

Parmenion breathed in deeply. Lyria sniffed too but could only smell old men rotting in darkness. She felt a surge of compassion for these entombed corpses. Didn't they once breathe the air like me? Did they not once roam freely? Who am I to disturb them? Parmenion suddenly raised himself. She noticed the haunted look in his eyes that framed and defined his features. Lyria would never forget his words,

"To change people's lives. To have been a force for good on this island. Do you think some day people will remember us?"

He looked hard at his daughter,
"How would you like to be remembered?"
Lyria thought for a long time before replying,
"Forever."

12

And so at dusk a small collection of men gathered at the *agora*. No women were allowed. A handful at first, a small blot of a crowd so in the half light it seemed as if a part of the twilight had begun to coagulate as they clustered together. The semi darkness added to the expectation, men were bolder, tongues looser, their clandestine thoughts shared as if the darkness would shield their names – revolutions are rarely planned in the guilty sunlight. And then Lyria's father took his stand and began. Parmenion seemed to stand taller as he spoke. Generations later men would remember this night and speak of him and the speech he made; marshalling his words and sending them out into the crowd like soldiers into battle. A lean figure with long arms and huge hands that scythed the air as he pleaded with the islanders to cut their ties and end the tribute to Mycenae. Proudly he spoke of the noble Penthelids, their Thessalian neighbours who had promised men and ships and who with their leader Peleus had refused to bow down to Agamemnon who if the rumours were true even now laid waste to Delphi. Parmenion stood with his fist punching the warm night air and spat the tyrant's name through clenched teeth. But always measured, passion tempered with dignity. The listeners fell silent. Even the richest farmers who reaped the top soil at Mytilene and who had most to lose; and the fisherman who were likely to feel the wrath of Agamemnon first and hardest, they now had no doubts of their grievance. And the young men tasted the sweetness of rebellion on their lips, risking their leaping lives for the island they loved and its pretty golden haired girls. To laugh in the face of Agamemnon and live freely, to see him running ragged from the battle on the beach. Their hearts raced and their mouths cheered, the cosy comfort of numbers and the star strewn spring night strengthening their resolve.

At the back of the crowd Orpheus stood alone. Icarius had abandoned him choosing instead to stand with the furtive Copreus. Icarius looked around, searching for any women who may have inadvertently strayed into the *agora*. Even the animals felt uncomfortable as he moved his tongue between his lips and eyed them lasciviously. If ever he saw a woman he wanted he sent Orpheus into the street to proposition them on his behalf. Many acquiesced, the price was good and as they told their friends afterwards the experience was not wholly unpleasant. But then it was the Greek way to meet virtue and vice with the whimsy of the Gods. But Orpheus hated him for it and comforted his barren mother who grew colder as the days grew hotter. And then Icarius would look at her and recite the same words,

"It is a love not tainted with jealousy. Cold but civilized lust. The greatest love of all." And then he would laugh and fall back in his chair.

"But it is a love that the world has no use for" Orpheus would murmur.

The way that Orpheus had been raised was not one to inspire envy. He had quickly learned to find his own amusements, quietly sinking into a secret world of thought and sentiment, a veiled private world from which he would emerge and peep only occasionally. He hardly spoke especially when in the company of adults. But he would chatter and gossip with Lyria. It was a friendship Icarius approved of; the wine cellar of Parmenion was legendary. But the friendship of Orpheus and Lyria needed no succour for Orpheus loved Lyria and shared his secrets with her. All but one. He kept the stories of his brutal father to himself. At times it was as if a vow of silence came over him, hiding in corners in fear of being noticed. But his taciturn demeanor was sometimes circumscribed, his affection showing in delicate ways, a flower left in his mother's bed or an apple gifted to Lyria in an equally surreptitious manner. He had learned to live on the periphery, to ask questions of himself thus to develop in a most insular way. But his thoughts were pure, virile and true and so he found it difficult to marry the supposed wisdom and asceticism of his priest father with his vile temper and violence. Lyria opened up new worlds and told him tales of the Gods, of Apollo and Hera, of Eros and Psyche. Set in juxtaposition to the poverty of affection he saw between his parents these stories formed the genesis of an idealised love in the boys mind which fed on a flawless beauty and an elevated spirit; something to which he would always return. Lyria drew him out but she was the exception rather than the rule. Hiding in corners he was often party to his father's pious politics and endless plotting. A father who thought him dumb and backward and treated him so thus allowing his most intimate conversations to reach the boys ears. Orpheus turned his head once again to Parmenion. As he looked on the words meant little to him but he followed their tone and rhythms as easily as the wind that touched his cheek. He noticed how the crowds were stirred by his words and he was pleased.

"I will tell Lyria when I see her."

13

Later that night after Parmenion had spoken Orpheus tried unsuccessfully to find Lyria and so returned home and lay in the courtyard. He often slept outside. Tonight the air was still and stifling. Only occasionally did a sweet breath of air caress him bringing a brief scent of magnolia blossom to his nostrils. These dizzying drafts were delicious causing the lanterns to flicker slowly and Orpheus to breathe deeply. He heard his father return and slam the door and walk through the kitchen to the wine stores. Orpheus could picture him taking his pick of the wines in the cellar. He was glad to be outside away from him. He heard his mother speak,

"Do you have to drink every night? At least leave some for the Gods. The boy is outside asleep."

"What do I care for the bastard boy? Thanks to me you have a reputation and a home. I'll do as I please and you'll do as you're told."

Icarius didn't shout the words. They were spoken slowly with malice, his body tense, a thin smile on his lips, a lizard like man but strong with it. Icarius went on,

"Anyway, we have something to celebrate. Soon we will be away from this filthy island."

"Why?"

Icarius took a long drink from his *krater* and licked his lips.

"Parmenion spoke. Everything is in place. He dies tonight."

And so it was that Orpheus heard of the plan to murder Parmenion. The whole world stood still as, faint with fear, he digested what he had heard. For a few moments he was paralysed.

His mind whirled with the nuances of what he'd heard. Had Icarius been joking? Orpheus was old enough to know better, to recognise the true intent of his father's words. Although not disposed to act decisively or quickly he knew what he had to do. Raising himself gently he left the courtyard and took the short track to Lyria's home.

14

Parmenion was excited. He had never shaken so many hands or been cheered so much. Some of the islanders had set him on their shoulders and paraded him around the *agora*. Now he walked home full of excitement. Tomorrow I will form a committee to petition Orestes. All the islanders are behind me. Even Agamemnon will have to yield. And if he doesn't, well. Parmenion half hoped that Agamemnon would send a force to Lesbos. We can last out here indefinitely. It's a war of attrition he can't win. Parmenion thought of his endless wine stores and allowed himself to dream a little. He looked skywards. The stars winked like jewels on a silk cloak. The moon shone brightly and he could just make out a number of circles which circumnavigated the main body of light. They gradually faded as they moved further from the mother moon. Rings around the moon. An omen. Parmenion was glad. Even the Goddess Selene is for our cause. I will be sure to tell Lyria. His thoughts turned to his only daughter. He laughed when he thought of her freeing the animals at the market. He thought about how well she rode and felt proud. And she can swim faster than anyone on the island, man or woman! And then Parmenion fell. His skull gradually emptied and became a vacuum as the voice of his old friend Eratos disintegrated into caverns of inaudible pain,

"Do you like my beard old man? You died like the dog you are."

Orpheus, frozen with fear stayed silent as he watched from the side of the road.

15

To the south of the Peneius river at Phalanna the palace of Peleus rose impressively from the landscape like a giant predatory spider. The walls of the palace were covered in white vine which had spread ravenously as if to devour the building. Isolated and ponderous the palace gave off a menacing architectural quality as it cast its giant shadows over the plains of Thessaly. The plains croaked in the searing heat at noon but at night the dry heat surrendered to the cool moonlight which soothed the sunburnt stone. To the north of the palace the plains were girdled by Mount Olympus and to the east Mount Pelion and it was on the latter that Peleus fixed his gaze as he rose from his throne and stared at the horizon from the limestone balcony. Peleus handed his plumed white crown to Praxos his body servant and turned to his generals. Anexos, a high ranking soldier who served under Meriones was the first to speak,

"Lord, I beg you, every murderer and criminal from Philippi to Ithaca and beyond has gathered at Pagasae. I'm getting reports of a murder every hour. Slaves are rioting and killing their masters. The harbour is chaos. We must restore order."

"Has Meriones been recalled?" asked Peleus. "I need his report. If these murderers as you call them are in favour of the cause then perhaps they would be good men to have in battle."

Prodicus stepped forward,

"But they are undisciplined, untrained your Lordship. They will desert as soon as they confront the enemy."

"Or sooner" added Anexos,

"All we have are rumours of a detachment of men in Delphi. Nothing certain."

The generals looked at each other skeptically.

"I have sent Dion. He has my seal and gifts. He may still persuade Agamemnon."

Peleus considered. Where was Meriones with his report? Probably in a brothel. At that precise moment the great doors were opened and Meriones, leader of the Perrhaebi entered covered with the detritus of a day in the saddle and strode over to the waiting Peleus. Taking his hand in the act of supplication he kneeled and looked up at Peleus,

"I have it from good authority that Agamemnon turns towards Delphi."

"How many men?"

"Two detachments. But Agamemnon is not with them."

"Of course. So he can deny all knowledge. Well he hasn't broken the law. Anexos, tomorrow you will take a thousand men to Pagasae and be sure these men know where their loyalties lie. But tonight I will entertain you. We will have a *choreia* to console us from the miseries of life. The Delphic oracle belongs to Apollo and Apollo loves to dance."

Meriones was doubtful,

"The *Pyrriche* is what we need, a good war dance to invoke Ares."

"Not tonight friend. Tonight we will be moderate to appease the Gods and bring peace. Remember Hippocleides? In Hades there is no song, no dance, no lyre."

Meriones whispered to Anexos,

"Perhaps, but soon there will be plenty of Thessalians if we don't act quickly."

16

Later that night Meriones took his place between Anexos and Peleus in the great hall. As leader of the Perrhaebi tribe he was second only to Peleus in importance, part of a Thessalian alliance that was crucial if Agamemnon was to be kept in check. The banquet displeased him. Did Peleus not realise Agamemnon's intentions? Meriones was a soldier first and a statesman second. At the age of fourteen he had led his troops through the fields of Corinth to fight the advancing Phocicians on the plains of Arcadia. Always brave in battle and generous with his soldiers he kept the rank and file close knowing it to be the beating heart of any army. Only his generals despised him; he was ill tempered and demanding of them so although he stopped short of cruelty he inspired the fear and rigid discipline that other leaders found it difficult to achieve when their backs were turned. The soldiers however loved him. Those showing resilience and fortitude were personally rewarded. So they fought hard for Meriones for the greater glory of themselves, the Perrhaebi and Thessaly. Peleus knew the alliance was precarious; he was merely first among equals so he kept Meriones close and did his best to placate and please him. Tonight I will feast him and show off my beautiful wife. The sound of the music signaled the arrival of Thetis. Peleus turned to his ally,

"You may lead the Perrhaebi Meriones but no woman of yours can match my Thetis."

"And your boy Achilles, does he do you credit yet?"

Meriones knew of Thetis's qualities but he knew the boy was weak and ungainly.

Peleus turned away. He remembered that morning on the Peneius. As Achilles had pulled away in the skiff his oar had hit the water clear before any other boy. His stroke was faster. Peleus grabbed Meriones's arm,

"Achilles is in front, he's started strongly!"

Meriones looked skeptical. As the race wore on Achilles' strength left him and the boys caught up. First one, then another leaving the boy prince in the lower placings. Meriones was pleased. Peleus baulked at the memory. He put the thoughts of his son to one side.

17

The musicians signaled the arrival of the dancers. Young prince Lycomodes from Scyros watched from a distance. He hated these banquets where men spat and swore and talked of their battles. He enjoyed the dances in honour of Dionysus popular on Scyros. It was here he could hide his pock ridden face and mix as an equal. So he always chose the most fantastical and handsome charades and plunged himself into this temporal fantasy where for once appearance and reality were distinct. He hoped to one day speak to Thetis whom he worshipped and loved. It was a secret he held close; he'd rather be eaten by wolves than disclose it. So he wandered amongst the dancers hoping to later meet his idol; the woman to whom he had never spoken. Thetis shimmied into view, the slow drumbeat complimenting the *kithara* and flute. From the moment she shook her hips Lycomodes was lost. Thetis flowed like water as she moved through the tables. Her expression was as calm as prayer and contrasted sharply with the frenzied gyration of her hips. Men stopped eating, some closed their eyes to be alone with their sinful thoughts just as the moon that was rampant raged overhead. But her sexuality was that powerful she danced in their minds with even greater potency. The young prince's head began to spin. All he could think of was Thetis. The black kohl around her eyes matched her ebony tresses which shone and shook. Lycomodes felt his cock stir again as Thetis brushed his leg giving him a fresh broadside of naked eroticism that caused a spasm to run the length of his spine. At the far end of the room a serving eunuch yawned horribly. The music became faster and Thetis responded passing by Peleus and Meriones, her back arcing, her tunic sparking fire. Her femininity let loose its sting and for one gorgeous moment to all in the room she seemed like something sacred. She took off her veil but it was the men she was unveiling. She had come through the rivers and valleys to be with them alone. She knew Lycomodes's whims and desires; they came to her like a doomed dream. And then nothing. The music stopped and the men roared. Only Lycomodes remained silent.

"Thetis, my wife. Come here."

Thetis walked over still breathing heavily. Her beauty was typically Greek, a flawless skin and black hair shaped and curved with olive oil and scented with jasmine. She wore a blue tunic woven with golden thread which marked her out as a woman of importance, the wife of king Peleus, the mother of prince Achilles. A gold necklace set with turquoise and onyx hung around her neck. Full breasted and with a high brow that shadowed the greenest of eyes. She stood tall and calm which only added to her beauty. Peleus took her by the arm and turned her around noting her poise and full hip.

"Thetis, you know Meriones, the leader of the Perrhaebi."

Thetis looked towards Meriones and bowed with an elegance that never failed to please Peleus,

"Thetis, daughter of Nereus. It is an honour."

Thetis turned away awkwardly then took her place at the side of Peleus.

18

After the feast Meriones staggered back to his room in his mind the military machinations of Agamemnon whirled. What were his plans? He felt sure Agamemnon would invade Thessaly sooner rather than later. In a corner of the courtyard some wives cuckolded their husbands. Meriones couldn't quite make out what they said but their clipped dialect placed them in the western islands. Perhaps Seraphos he mused. They grabbed at him as he passed by to draw him in to their sin,

"Come here. We'll show you a good time."

Meriones smiled. For these harpies no one was immune. He turned into his room and shouted into the darkness.

"Wine, wine. Achaean wine."

But one of the courtyard harpies had followed him and now whispered,

"Am I not your wine?"

Thetis put her chin on Meriones's shoulder,

"Drink me."

In the bedchamber she threw off her robes and jewelry and pulled him onto the bed pulling his head into her bosom and kissing him,

"Do I not taste better than wine?"

They slid down the bed as the inebriated Meriones stared drunkenly about him,

"Do I not have a good head on me?"

Later she turned to Meriones,

"Am I just your whore?"

"What does it matter? If you are then you are the only whore. The only woman who has excited me in an age."

Thetis felt empowered. But there was something else, a feeling she was unsure of but she felt it sometimes when she saw an injured soldier or an animal cry out in pain. She hesitated,

"And love?"

Meriones laughed,

"Love?"

"Have you ever loved sir?"

Meriones turned away as he often did when he lied,

"No."

Thetis raised herself from the bed and began to dress,

"I must get back to him."

Thetis knew the destiny of Achilles, her only boy whom she loved. She knew that Peleus would have him train and prepare for an early death. She knew that Meriones was her salvation, would take them away where they could be safe. He was the only man with enough power. All that she had cared about was her son from the very beginning. Against the advice of the priests she had taken him to the oracle before she had taken him to her breast. It was part of the love she bore him. Her mind returned again to her labours and the birth of Achilles.

"My lady I have the crops you asked for."

Thetis carefully placed the wheat and barley into purses of cloth. Then placing it on the hearth she crouched and urinated over them.

"Demeter grant me a child for Peleus and may he be a male child."

Thetis knew that if the wheat sprouted first it would be a boy, if barley then a girl. If neither she would not bear at all. If she gave birth to an heir her position would be strong. A week later the pains began yet she knew they were but pale imitations of the great agonies that would come. At first she felt an icy coldness cover her body; she wrapped herself in robes and cloths. Yet still she shivered. An anger overcame her that a man could cause her pain, but then pride that the boy child would rule Thessaly. But then the pain returned. In the high walled cities to the south or to the east in the Troad she knew there were ways of ending the pain, ways that pierced her body. But she abjured the waves of agony that overcame her though in her dreams she cursed Demeter and urged the Gods to rip out the seed of Peleus. Priests of Apollo were appointed to oversee the birth. Prayers were offered to Asclepius and sacrifices and offerings laid at his temple. Peleus oversaw all details including the wet nurse,

"She must be wise, tall, of good complexion and smell sweet."

Peleus knew of the existence of good and bad quality seed and his failure to produce any offspring had raised doubts and threatened political stability. Good seed meant a strong spine and bones, the child will inherit flesh and blood from the mother and bones and heart from the father.

Thetis had first felt a twinge after washing in her room and leaning over to reach for a robe. She was immediately rushed to the adjoining chamber where the servants of Apollo were ready for her. Ivory images of Asclepius filled the room, the air was heavy with incense. At Thetis's insistence a wax image of Demeter was burned and whilst sitting on a birth stool she let the incense enter her womb to 'smoke out' any curse. Messengers were ready to ride to all corners of Thessaly to announce that Peleus had an heir. He knew that this would please his people and provide stability for the region ensuring the bloodline of the Aleudae. As word spread that an heir was imminent the atmosphere in the palace and surrounding farms became jubilant. Torch bearers, matrons, serving girls and men at arms all crowded near the antechamber to be the first to see the new boy. On the second day of the labour, as instructed, Peleus was woken before dawn but told that the birth was delayed. Despite this he went to Thetis's side and laid on his back groaning so as to invoke the pity of the Gods and share the pain. Peleus was assured by the priests that this would ensure a boy was born. Thetis was draped in the traditional birth gown of the Aleudae blessed by Demeter the Goddess of fertility who was said to have worn it when she gave birth. It didn't help. For the first hour she lay back and cursed the Gods and Peleus. She turned to her handservant,

"Have you brought the knife?"

Aristaya looked uncertain. She was a young girl who had worked hard to rise and serve the inner circle of the court of Peleus. Thetis screamed,

"Have you brought the knife?"

"Yes, yes."

"Is it under the bed?"

"Yes madam."

Thetis was glad for she knew that with the blade under the bed it would cut the pain in half. Peleus was less sure. He noted the bloodless lips of Thetis and her colourless complexion.

"Here girl, eat this."

With his own hand he daubed her mouth with wine soaked bread and comforted her. Time passed. Thetis became weaker and still no sign of the child. Peleus refused all company and prayed for an end to her pain. An heir was utmost in his mind but at what cost? It seemed almost certain that Thetis would not survive. Peleus knew the answer to the question he asked himself over and over – he would sacrifice the girl for a son. He felt a hand on his shoulder,

"I will bleed her again and add herbs to her water. Then it is in the hands of the Gods."

"But what of the child?"

But the priest had already left to offer his own prayers. Dawn came and Peleus sat hunched, his heart and soul heavy. Thetis slipped out of consciousness, her breath laboured. Peleus went to his room exhausted and resigned to the death of both Thetis and his heir. Collapsing in his private chambers he was soon in a dreary grey dreamscape where a voice spoke to him from the darkness,

"Peleus you have an heir."

"I have nothing."

"You have a son."

Still only half awake he rose suddenly strong,

"A son? And Thetis?"

"She lives. I have sacrificed a goat to Demeter who blessed us. The goat was flayed alive and I wrapped her in its coat. She shivers but she will live."

The priest shuffled off to tell his family the good news. On his way home through the palace he purchased some date wine and practiced the story he would tell his young wife and son; how Demeter had blessed him personally and granted him the birth. His place within the palace was secured. Aristaya watched as he left the birth chamber then crept up to where Thetis lay. Cupping her breast she squeezed Thetis's nipple gently and placed the drops in a small cup. Her mother had instructed her that morning,

"If she gives birth to a boy mix mint with the milk then sell it to a woman with child. She will then have a boy child."

And then the same day before Achilles had opened his eyes.

"I am ready."

The servant bowed and closed the door and the priestess waited nervously. The offerings for Apollo had been steadily arriving all morning, silver armour and copper ingots, ahmeni peaches, jasmine and jewelry. Outside the chamber the priests performed their oratories and salutations bearing their incense and lustral waters whilst whispering their prayers to Asclepius,

"Preserve me from sickness and imbue my body with such a measure of health that I may pass my days unhindered."

The priestess heard the key turn and looked to the door nervously,

"This is the boy Achilles. Tell me of his destiny."

Thetis herself walked into the chamber. The sleeping Achilles was carried in by a serving girl immediately behind her. Thetis took her place kneeling at the feet of the priestess.

"Tell me of my son."

The young priestess pulled back her shoulders and spoke proudly,

"I am Chione, the *klawiphorus*, the key bearer and servant to the sun God…"

Thetis cut in,

"I am aware of your position. Tell me what I came for."

Thetis had surprised herself. But she was tired and her love and concern for her son overrode any proclamation of power or rank. Later she carried Achilles back to the palace. Looking westward she saw the sun pierced and spill its colour over the horizon. And then the wind had cleared the sky and soothed the sore with precious night.

Thetis had watched the signs as the time had passed and the child kicked and grew as the moon waxed then waned. The prophets and soothsayers were called yearly,

"A man who will rule wisely" said one.

"A philosopher, a great thinker" said another. But it was the words of a diviner from Babylonia when Achilles had entered his fifth year that stayed with Thetis. His deep blue eyes moved her as he touched her heart with his fingertips then spoke deeply and slowly before rising and leaving,

"*Aristos Achaion*. Greater than his father. The greatest of all warriors. Doomed to win battles."

This prophecy above all others returned to her as she ran through the palace from the bed of Meriones. In the sky the moon was cosseted and warm swathed as it was in the robes of the night that unfurled like a dark blue curtain. As his unfaithful wife hurried back to his bedchamber Peleus dreamt of a vast field of ambrosia in a land where the sun never set. He was strong. Then he saw Thetis and his fields were fallow and the night endless. The next day he gave orders for his wife to be banished,

"You will leave. You will speak to no one. You will never see your son again."

19

The preparations for the funeral were exact and followed all the formalities. The body was carefully washed and perfumed with cassis, smoothed with oils then wrapped in the finest linen shroud before being sprinkled with geraniums and herbs from the valley. As a prominent public figure the body of Parmenion was to be displayed in the *prothesis*. On the second day the mourners gathered in the early morning outside their home singing dirges, beating their breasts and tearing at their hair. Lyria had seen these mourners at other funerals. It puzzled her. They didn't know my father. Why are they crying? But she knew that to neglect the proper duties would mean imprisonment and punishment. On the third day was the *Ekphora*, the burial. Before the sun rose the body was taken to be burned. An individual cremation was afforded Parmenion and Danae and the young Lyria were mindful of the honour. During the days of preparation Orpheus withdrew. Icarius put it down to his son's backward nature. But Orpheus was scared. He knew his knowledge was a dangerous thing. He knew his father was involved in the death. He knew the name of the murderer. He knew a good many things. But thoughts of Lyria gave him conviction and he knew what he must do.

20

Danae held the hand of the two children and wept as the mourners passed silently. Copreus walked by and spoke to Danae, Lyria noticed his quick, awkward movements as once again he avoided any eye contact. Then Eratos approached with his head bowed. He took the hand of Danae and slowly kissed it before placing it on his heart, an old Aeolian tradition discouraged by Orestes. To the onlookers Eratos was taking a risk. Orpheus knew better. He looked away filled with disgust. It was twilight when the three set off home. A distillation of night smells fermented the air as the cold of the night clashed with the stored up warmth of the flowers and the earth, the earth that now had the sun warming in its belly and the scattered ashes of Parmenion for a blanket.

"We must try and get word to Philon" said Danae, "he is the head of the household now and will find who killed your father."

Lyria looked up at the mention of her beloved brother. Danae smiled and leaning down kissed her on the forehead.

"There's no need for that" said Orpheus, "I saw who did it."

21

It was a relief for Orpheus to unburden himself. Grownups always seemed to know what to do. His lips trembled as he recounted everything he'd heard Icarius say and the murder of Parmenion at the hands of Eratos. Lyria took his hand as he spoke. Danae acted quickly. Even before Orpheus had finished she had prepared salted fish and goat's milk and then led the children out into the thyme scented night.

"Are we going to the old tombs mother?"

Danae looked down sharply.

"Yes, and you must stay there till the morning. You will be safe. Keep this lantern and take this food. Someone will come for you."

The children were left alone in the large cave and huddled together for warmth. Danae set off at a good pace and was soon home. Without stopping she continued walking down the lane where her husband had been struck down. Turning into a courtyard she knocked at a large wooden door. Icarius answered. Behind him Danae recognised the face of Eratos,

"They know. Orpheus heard you and saw Eratos."

Icarius turned to Eratos,

"You fool. You were seen. Where are they now?"

"They are safely hidden in the old tombs. Parmenion always thought he was the only man on the island who knew the hiding place."

"Good. Let's go. Eratos, bring your sword. No witnesses this time."

22

Dion as well as being the royal blacksmith was *Periokoi*, a freeman of Thessaly and able to work his own land. A skilled diplomat with the common touch he had been used by Peleus before to settle land disputes with the *Hestiaeotis*. He was pleased that Peleus had entrusted him with this delicate mission. He thought about Agamemnon and the task ahead. 'I should be in Pharsalus by tomorrow evening. Agamemnon's border guards should escort me from there.' Dion carried treasures and the seal of Peleus. He wondered what lay inside the saddlebags. It must be expensive judging by the half dozen guards who accompanied him. They followed at a discreet distance fully armed. Dion certainly felt safe. He followed the Peneius south out of Larissa, the valley was steep in places so the river flowed quickly. A while later as they left Larissa behind it slowed and Dion decided to rest. He ate some herbed bread and salted fish that his wife had prepared that morning. His thoughts turned to more mundane matters at home. There was still much land for him to work in Larissa. He had chosen his land well in a shallow raised area south facing to squeeze out the last winter rays. It was a rich strip with olives and corn land and pastures for the sheep and vine. He had been working hard lately. Chryseis his daughter was eighteen and he wished to buy her a silver necklace and an ornate statue of Hermes whom she loved. He knew if the negotiations went well Peleus would reward him, perhaps Agamemnon too. He patted the saddlebags and once again wondered at their contents.

23

"Look there's an oil jar."

Orpheus trimmed the wick then lit it breathing orange life into the tombs that now flickered with flame and shadow. Lyria shrieked as she looked into the corner of the cave.

"Who are you?"

They didn't recognise the figure that was half turned away from them his head covered in a hood.

"It doesn't matter. If you come with me you will stay alive."

The bewildered children had little choice as they were half dragged in the direction of the harbour. Lyria detected a faint scent of cyperus and sage, a perfume her mother sometimes used and thought it odd a man should choose this scent. Finally in the harbour laying at anchor was a double decked galley fashioned from red oak, twenty oars for each deck, a sight rarely seen at the tiny harbour of Lesbos. Lyria quickly looked up at the white sails held closely to the mast and breathed a little easier. 'The ship is a trader' she thought. She remembered her father saying it was only the ogre Agamemnon who could afford to waste expensive dye on purple sails. Walking up the gangplank they were taken to the back of the ship,

"Here, under these rugs."

They obeyed. Orpheus peeped out to see the hooded figure speaking in earnest to a large red faced man who seemed to disagree with him. The man then took out a purse and passed it over. This placated him and he nodded and looked over to where he lay. Orpheus quickly hid his head again.

24

It was dark when the boat lost its moorings and began its journey. The large man barked out his orders and the men pulled at the oars as the vessel eased its way out of the harbour. Lyria didn't dare raise her head and cried quietly to herself. Where are we going? Where is my mother? But it was the betrayal of Eratos that most disturbed her. These thoughts were so overwhelming that she didn't notice the red faced man lean down and pull back the rugs and awning that hid her. Lyria looked up. The man had no hair and piercings in both ears like the pirates she'd heard of. He smiled. It was a kindly smile as his eyes seemed to twinkle as he spoke,

"You must be Lyria and Orpheus. I know about you. I've been paid to see you on your way."

Lyria stopped her crying as her curiosity overtook her,

"Who are you? And who was the man who brought us here? Where are we going? Where is my mother?"

The man laughed so his face became even redder and his earrings bounced as his huge shoulders heaved.

"My name is Otus. I'm the captain of this ship and will see that you are looked after. You are going to Thessaly. As for the other questions, I can't answer you. Here, eat this. And don't worry about the crew. They won't harm you."

Otus handed her some fresh bread and cheese and a flagon of water. Lyria took it and watched as Otus returned to the helm of the ship. Thessaly. The land of my ancestors! Lyria remembered her father speak so fondly of this place. In her mind it had acquired a magical quality. But who will I meet there? Who will know me? She gazed at the sleepy ocean, midnight blue and restful. Looking around her the crew were all hard at work so none of them noticed the moon float from behind a cloud so that a string of temple pillars on the shore was lit up like a procession. She saw and heard the gentle waves softly kiss the shore. And then suddenly a large dog ran along the beach. Its moonlit shadow jumped and ran beside it. Lyria recognised Cerebus. But then the moon hid her face and the world was dark again. But the crew heard the loud splash as Cerebus launched himself into the water. He was a strong swimmer and using his tail as a rudder was soon level with the boat. It took three sailors to haul him aboard but they didn't mind – the animal would bring luck. Cerebus jumped and barked in glee to see Lyria and Orpheus. But the children were tired. So, overcome with weariness and grief they lay down their heads. Lyria dreamed of the boy kings far to the south where the rivers flowed with honey and gold. Orpheus dreamt of a golden lyre and Cerebus just snored.

25

In its enclosed entirety the palatial citadel of Mycenae would have impressed any traveller descending south from the port of Corinth with its high class whores or north from Tiryns home of the wise and brave Nestor. And even at night when no one saw her but the stars her graceful sloping walls formed a mighty defence. These walls dazzled in the midnight hour coated as they were in white Tura limestone mined from the valleys of the pharaohs. It fed Agamemnon's vanity to think that this self same stone that coated the giant pyramids now gave him the same protection. The walls of Agamemnon's palace were surmounted by a mud brick super structure so from the stone base to the summit it rose some forty cubits. Towers placed every thirty cubits added to its presence; numerous stone ramps led to passages and thoroughfares in and out of the city. Visitors could not fail to be awed by the great stone lionesses, the Lion's Gate, two exquisitely carved statues that guarded the entrance to the palace complex. Below the main thrust of these ramparts lay the courtiers houses and the sanctuaries and tombs of Agamemnon's court. Still further stretching to the nearby hill of Panayitsa where Atreus lay buried the outer structures were home to some six thousand people ready to fight for Agamemnon. They feared their king but respected him for the wealth he had brought them. Every woman must bear three sons to keep the army strong. Mycenae was now a major power, a muscular warrior culture.

Aerope had named her first son Agamemnon meaning 'steadfast' after giving birth to the huge baby boy. He had grown quickly. Solitary and aloof he had refused to talk, only agreeing to speak to his younger brother Menelaus at official functions. If he wanted something he took it by force which was easily done as his strength was formidable. Even as a boy he could match the guards in feats of strength and wrestling; his power and fury coupled with his guile making him a ferocious opponent. So he was feared and hated in equal measure by his peers. But this was of no concern to Agamemnon for it was the guards with whom he liked to pass his time pleading with the captain of the guard Aegisthus to let him 'interrogate' a thief or watch when the more gruesome executions were carried out; executions that even the hardiest guards would baulk at. For Agamemnon compassion was a weakness. His father Atreus encouraged him and was proud of his fighting skills but even he wondered at his savagery. He was still in the grip of boyhood when he had the first of his 'urges' to kill. Walking the endless passageways of the palace he had come across an old dog and assuaged his bloodlust by throttling it then skinning the flesh from its bones and setting them to dry in the sun. No one had questioned the son of Atreus. He began to venture out when the moon was thin and spiteful laying on her back and scratching at the stars. But dogs and chickens were not enough. Late one night he made his way into the fields where the sacred bulls grazed and slit the throats of half a dozen – then a week later he watched with no emotion as his friend Aegisthus was executed for the crime. Soon after whilst trawling the drinking dens of Mycenae he came across a sleeping drunk and strangled him with his bare hands. The warring factions and feudal politics of Mycenae didn't interest him. The prostitutes were easy game stumbling over their fleshy chattels, never missed. But Agamemnon never raped them, to kill was his sole purpose. It was only natural that at the age of fifteen he be entered for the boys *Pankration*. He trained under Alpheos. Discipline was hard but Agamemnon responded well, happy with his vinegar and blood soup whilst the other boys had their families smuggle in salted bread and cheese. His urges could now be channeled into destroying his sparring partners often beating them half to death before being pulled off by Alpheos who, too scared to cross Atreus, stuck with the prince. As he grew and came to power his administrative acumen also grew as did his political ambition. He divided Mycenae into sixteen districts each governed by the *Korete*. He knew the importance of structure and hierarchy and had rewarded his people according to their trade. At the top were the bronzesmiths essential for weapon production; highly skilled and entitled to tax rebates. Agriculture and livestock were all highly organised and accounted for so wheat, barley, oil and wool were produced in great quantities. Wool in particular was produced in great surplus and exported in return for copper ingots, oxhide and metals to fuel the war machine. Everything was recorded, taxes levied and duly paid. No exceptions. Carding, spinning and weaving were left to the women. The army needed roads and chariots were needed for effective trade between Mycenae and Corinth in the north and Sparta, the kingdom of Menelaus, in the south. So two roads linking the city states had been built passing through Tegea, Argos, Nemea and finally Corinth. He built bridges on the causeway on the road to Berbate and east of Nauplia near the fort of Kasarmi. He hired specialists from Egypt who showed him corbelled arches to make the royal tombs – then had them murdered. Agamemnon would serve Greece and Greece in turn would reward him. His greed and ambition were without limit.

26

The *Megaron* lay at the centre of Agamemnon's palace fortress. Access here was strictly limited to the *Hequetaria*, the warrior elite and *Klawiphorus*. The walls were decorated with frescoes, the floors of variegated marble. Eight columns rose in a circle around the central fire, each one covered in lapis lazuli from the mountains of Mysia. The room sparkled with light. It ran from the coloured marble walls and reflected onto the mosaic floors then wandered and flirted with the statues that lined the rooms and outlaying corridors. And such statues! In one Zeus shared a moment of ecstasy with a muse, in another Apollo stood naked applauding the denizens of Hades. Agamemnon was happy to hunt quail and dove and risk the wrath of Aphrodite. Even as a child he had derided the older guards for whom years of war and death had brought on a dreadful lassitude. But it was his vanity rather than any moral prescient that exhorted him to forge his own destiny in the face of any fanciful fates.

"Peleus worships the Gods like the old fool he is. I'll forge my own destiny, not guess it from the entrails of chickens."

Agamemnon enjoyed his luxuries and saw them as useful trinkets; as heralds to pronounce his greatness, his just reward for another hard campaign. When he rested his feet they lay on ebony footstools. He ate from silver plates. Even his servants drank from bronze cups. He made sure all emissaries were made aware of this. His House of Shields was crammed with tables of stone and ivory inlaid with kuanos and gold. In his House of Sphinxes columns were decorated with rosettes and ivy leaf and carved with images of palms and dolphins. Many of his treasures were 'borrowed' from Crete. Agamemnon reflected. The palace at Crete had never been fortified. Did these Cretans think they were protected by the Gods? The arrogance! The Gods protect the strong. Taking Crete had been the easiest thing he had ever done. Agamemnon worshipped strength and knew that everything flowed from it. Nothing survives without it. He smiled mirthlessly,

"This is why the Gods protect me. Just two years ago we paid tribute to these Cretans. Now they send me gold. Our mother kneels before us."

His power extended as far south as Sparta ruled by his brother Menelaus and as far west as Pylos where taxes were levied in the name of Poseidon but paid to him. In the east Lesbos paid tribute and all the islands. Orestes had done well. Now only Troy lay unconquered. But it was the north and Thessaly that concerned him now. Troy could wait. He paused to look into a mirror taken from the Opeans in his last campaign. Agamemnon's was not a handsome face especially when he was deep in thought as he was today. His features lacked order as if they were in two halves. One half seemed more alive, a furtive left eye as black as an olive scrutinizing everything and surrounded by a maze of wrinkles. In contrast the right side was calmer, smoother and more relaxed. It's as if there were two men living in his features. A vain man by nature he insisted that courtiers and generals approached him from the right to catch his 'noble profile' as he called it. He was uneasy as he always was when there wasn't a battle imminent, a race to subjugate, a foe to conquer. If the Thessalians could be subdued it opened the way to the north and the kingdoms of Macedonia. Agamemnon knew that Peleus' people would fight like savages for they hated life when it was separated from freedom. But they would fight without discipline and order just as the Arcadians had done and before them the Opeans and Phocicians. He grinned so his wrinkles became suddenly more pronounced. The Thessalians are as likely to kill each other in battle as the enemy. With his hands on his hips he stared to the west and Mount Elias which stood guard over his kingdom. When Peleus and Thessaly bowed to his rule he would light fires at its summit announcing his victory just as he had done with the Arcadians and Opeans.

"Bravery is nothing without unity and order. My soldiers are better organised. They may not love me but as long as they fear me that is enough."

The great oak doors were opened,

"Dion of Thessaly my lord. An emissary of Peleus."

Agamemnon strode towards Dion his arms outstretched,

"Dion. How is your daughter Chryseis? Tell me of Thessaly and my good friend Peleus."

27

Lyria looked out over the deep expanse of the Aegean. It was early morning and Orpheus still slept. The decks were empty apart from one lookout who snoozed sporadically. Cerebus snored and his jowels quivered. Lyria hoped she might see dolphins. Her mother had told her they were the carriers for the Gods. In legend the young sea God Arion had been captured by pirates who let him sing one last song after which he jumped overboard and was saved by the dolphins attracted by the music. Lyria spent most mornings at the helm of the boat staring ahead at the empty ocean. It was cooler in the morning and she enjoyed feeling the fresh breeze on her face. Sometimes the captain would join her.

"When will we reach Thessaly sir? It's a long time since I saw any land. Will we pass many islands?"

The captain, who had grown fond of this well spoken polite girl put his arm around Lyria and pointed to the distance,

"The islands are a gift from the Gods. They made them stepping stones. As soon as you leave one behind the next appears in front of you. In that way the Gods guide us through the Greek seas. We will soon be in sight of Lemnos where the Argonauts landed. Then we'll sail south to Scopolos."

Lyria became excited,

"Do we pass near Seraphos? It is where my mother was born."

The captain looked down sharply at Lyria. He was about to speak but stopped himself. Otus always had time for the children. He taught them the parts of the ships, the stern, the halyard, of the mighty triremes used in battle. He told them of Agamemnon's huge ships with their bronze rigging, purple sails and jeweled prows.

"We must be cautious and watch for pirates."

Otus pointed to the top of the rigging where a lookout was positioned.

"Who are the pirates? Where are they from?" asked Lyria.

"Agamemnon finances them to make coastal raids around the Argolian peninsula to Epidaurus and Cannakale at Troy. They capture ships carrying alabaster and tin, silver and gold. He takes a tithe from the pirates and forces the owners to pay yet more tribute. So the Lord of Mycenae makes money raiding his own ships. Greece is in his palm and has taken his bribes. Most of Greece fears him and despises him. All but Peleus. Only he can save us. And the Gods."

"Do you believe in the Gods sir?"

"All sailors believe in the Gods" replied the captain. "Why shouldn't we? We spend our lives surrounded by eternity. We live with the stars. We are the music makers, the greatest philosophers."

Otus looked to the prow and yelled out,

"Westward. Oars in."

So Otus raised the oars making the sea foam under the sky which was bright blue and sprinkled with pearls of cloud. He turned away leaving Lyria staring ahead into the empty ocean. The captain's words somehow reminded her of her brother Philon. Perhaps he was near these waters? Her mind drifted.

Philon sat beneath the acacia and watched the ibis. The bird swooped and dived picking at the gnats and flies that formed frantic clouds above him. Lyria laid her head on his faithless arm. She held a jar of lemon perfume fashioned in palmetto silver. Around her neck a garland of amethyst, carnelian and amber which complimented the blood and the bones and the flame of her hair,

"Do you like my necklace brother?"

Philon, dreaming of a Nubian water bearer answered without looking,

"Your eyes are the only jewels you'll ever need Lyria."

The night air became sweetened by the scent of the sea. Beyond the valley in the fields of Nape the colours were fading as the sun slowly sank. Lyria could see her brother was far away. She loved this about him,

"Where are you Philon?"

There was a silence before Philon replied,

"Part of me is with you sister. The other part is away from here standing on the deck of a ship bound for Troy, catching the trade winds and tasting the sea salt."

28

Philon loathed the bustle of the Cretan markets. He preferred the mountains and forests of his home on Lesbos or even better the easy swells of the empty sea. But his soul was malleable and shifted shape. In battle strong and quick witted but on the ocean eternal and mellow like the setting sun stretching out his broken hands in the blind gutters. He was tired. The wine trader's route was often precarious. East to Seraphos, pick up the wine, south to Cythera to avoid the tolls at the Isthmus then north with the grain so the islands could eat. But too often the journey was threatened by the hazardous Ionian sea, known for its storms. He longed to wander the beaches with his sister Lyria again and teach her the names of the shells or pick herbs from the rocky outcroppings of Nape his boyhood village. He worried for her and his father Parmenion always challenging authority, looking to speak his mind in the square at Mytilene and invoking the wrath of the ruling family, Orestes and the Pisistratids. One day his father would say too much. Just one more trip, he mused, and he could pay for them all to move to the mainland, away from the petty politics of Lesbos, as beautiful as it was, and back to their Aeolian ancestors in Thessaly. But first he must barter with this tiresome Cypriot who thought he knew about wine. Philon listened as he had before to the stories of the great kings to the south of Crete in the land of Kush,

"They build houses of eternity where they place their dead kings. They are shaped like your wheat cakes Philon."

"*Pyramidius?*"

"Yes and as high as a mountain. Gold is like sand there, they cover their kings in it and call them Gods. Their boy kings are worshipped and carried everywhere."

"But what of their wine Crixus?" replied Philon, "good wine is the mark of any civilized society."

Philon always judged a people by their cultivation and treatment of the grape. The savagery of the Babylonian and Scythian tribes was symbolised by their drunkenness and preference for beer. Wine must be diluted in a *krater* with water, not gorged and swilled as the drunken Cyclops did. The aim of wine drinking was not to lose control but to promote bonding in a civilized manner. For Philon, in common with all Greeks, drunkenness was as unforgivable as abstaining. Crixus went on,

"I was told of an old King Ramses who fathered two hundred children, a great warrior king who defeated the Hittites at Kadesh."

Philon had heard of this battle and suspected like many that it had been less of a victory than this Cypriot believed. But he was becoming increasingly impatient,

"And the wine?"

"Ah! The wine." The trader kissed his hand in a gesture of affection and looked to the sky as if to invoke the Gods themselves.

"This is not wine for the masses Philon. Beer and date wine is for the peasants. Here is a wine to impress your Pramnian and Ismaric palates or even your island of Lesbos."

Philon raised a doubtful eyebrow as Crixus after decanting the wine through a strainer to remove the 'lees' carefully poured a measure from the *oinochoe* into a small cup.

Philon gave a start,

"But it's white."

"Yes, rare indeed and sweet on the tongue. They say the boy king Tutankhamun had fifty amphorae buried with him. One day I'll find his tomb. Your island wines are all well and good Philon but they are like Corinthian whores – used and drunk by many but no real quality. Only the best wines like mine can sustain ageing. Here, try this. It's a year old. The resin has flavoured the wine to perfection."

The trader handed the drink to Philon and as he did so the sleeve on his chiton snagged. Philon noticed the forearms of the trader were scarified with images of battle. Peasant. I bet he's circumcised too like all these barbarians. He lifted the wine to his nose then tasted it. The taste was unfamiliar to him but not unpleasant reminding him of the moderate Thasian wine to the north of his homeland. Crixus watched closely. Philon was impressed with its mild aroma and sweet taste.

"I don't like it. I can't help you Crixus."

Crixus shifted his weight uneasily. Was this impudent islander bluffing? He had five hundred amphorae stored and waiting to be sold. A sale to Philon would ease his worries and enable him to appease his master and pay some of his gambling debts. Philon was the best known trader on the island and if he bought the wine others would follow. He couldn't afford to lose the sale but couldn't afford to let Philon bargain him down.

"But my dear Philon, you can double your returns in the northern islands. Seraphos alone will take a hundred amphorae for the rituals."

Philon who had played out this scene many times recognised the signs in Crixus's earnest tone and paused to rub his chin before speaking,

"But what of the transport Crixus? That costs money, and will the wine keep for the voyage? The Carian pirates are well known on this route. I cannot risk it at the price you want."

Crixus knew his options were limited. Philon turned to leave. He felt the air leave his body before he hit the ground and struggling for breath he looked up at Crixus who had his blade drawn,

"I could have killed you when we first met, I could kill you now Greek scum. Your life will be the price you pay unless you make this purchase and seal it with the contract."

29

"Peleus will attack the Myceneans. The Gods have willed it" said the bearded man.

"Peleus needs to relax. He should be taking temple maidens. He's too old to be fighting" said another.

"And too ugly" said a short fat man who was evidently more interested in appearance than politics. The bearded man continued,

"The Thessalian armies are gathering under Peleus. The tribes have pledged their allegiance. Meriones and the Perrhaebi are for him."

"It's time the Pisistratids were put in their place."

Phoenix stood at the periphery of the group that was gathered at Archanes market. Archanes was the lesser of the Cretan markets situated as it was five miles south of Knossos near the gypsum mines and dealing in the inferior furs of the Assyrians or the cast off pots of Platanus west of the Asterousia mountains. The market conversation had followed predictable patterns, ignorance and bravado speaking out loudly leaving facts and certainties far behind. It was all the Cretans had spoken of for weeks, the possibility of war. And so the free men of Thessaly and the tribes were coming together. Thessaly was a major power controlling the Delphic alliance that centred around this sacred site. And now Agamemnon's aggression and posturing threatened this precarious peace. Phoenix had learned nothing new from this latest installment. He was a tall and slender young man of some twenty years, sanguine, of good handsome features, his boyish looks and litheness masking a keen strength and stamina. Sold in the slave markets of Thessaly to a Libyan trader who had stroked his cheek and smiled at him his childhood was lost long ago. The Libyan had him bathed and powdered then brutalized him for ten years. He had him starved and beaten if he were insolent, and starved and beaten if he wasn't. His master had groaned with pleasure when he had first rubbed his paunch with honey and lime to assuage his whims and guilt. Never allowed love he thrived on hate and the layers became deeper, his heart and soul dreaming of what might be, of what would be. And now the armies were gathering. That night he stared at the waning moon that hung like a pendant behind Mount Juktus. The stars were clear and as bright as the Tropics as he slit the Libyan's throat then headed north for the sanctuary and escape that Thessaly and the army of Peleus offered.

30

The Cretan harbour at Amnisos was only eight miles north of his old masters house at Phourni. From here cypress, juniper wood and evergreen oak used for beams were exported north across the Sea of Crete to Thera and then onwards to Naxos, Kea and the mainland. Wines were taken west to the growing Cretan colonies where Agamemnon roamed and plundered. It was this self same route Phoenix had travelled at his masters pleasure trading Tyrian purple dye; an exclusive but lucrative market for the imperial palaces of Mycenae. Phoenix knew the routes well. He lengthened his stride and his heart began to swell. It was an unfamiliar feeling for Phoenix. Laughing, he ran for a herd of goats that scattered before him,

"Now I know I'm free." His heart swaggered and the newness of it, the exhilaration almost made him weep,

"I must be dreaming."

Drawing his sword he cut himself so as he might awake but the blood ran freely as the goats steadied and stared. Travelling through the night he wore a brown wolfskin blanket which blended with the rugged terrain of northern Crete. He made his way quickly through the limestone landscape and raised upland plains. Although the moon was sick and waning Phoenix scolded her vile light which produced the clumsy shadow that mirrored his every move. Resting briefly he remembered his master's eyes as they had bled crimson confusion and then rolled over white. The gurgle and pain of his breaths had disturbed him and Phoenix had shivered as he had hauled him to the clay pits to the rear of the house. The Libyan's blood had blended with the sandstone outbuildings which gave all the architecture in the region south and west of Malia their reddish tint. As he rested under the tamarisk he fed on figs and onions, drank honey mead and was careful to leave no trace. His caution was born of fear of the inevitable execution if he were discovered. But deep down in his heart Phoenix knew that execution was preferable to the continued abuse of the Libyan. He sat for a moment and pondered Mount Juktas as it loomed in the darkness to the south. At its summit legend had it lay the tomb of Zeus himself which labelled all Cretans liars. Phoenix whispered,

"For all the Gods are immortal are they not?"

From the top of his tunic there emerged a tiny nose. Phoenix smiled. The mouse was one of his many pets. He had always loved all animals for their innocence and they in turn loved him back and were drawn to him. From beetles to thoroughbreds they fell under his spell. He lifted his hand and touched the small creature's head. Its nose seemed to twitch faster. He never forced any animal to stay with him. They were all free to leave but none ever did. Phoenix slept. Later the smell of the sea salt brought him fresh reverie and he picked at the moon that was now setting. He calculated he had at least two days before the Libyans absence was considered in the least bit unusual. Phoenix wasn't to know that as he lay staring at the stars his Libyan master fought for his life, discovered by his neighbour a short time after Phoenix had left and that even now soldiers pursued him.

31

Phoenix lay dreaming of freedom and one God of fire. He was woken with a sword at his throat. He knew his mortality was cheap and yet he was curious,
"Who are you?" asked the man with the sword.
"Phoenix, a slave."
Phoenix considered the man above him. His ill fitting clothes told him he had a master; older, square jawed and bearded his eyes were a window to despair. Phoenix stared at him and saw the bone beneath the skin, the warrior's gait. But he felt no fear in his heart because for slaves death is a kind of freedom,
"Where are you heading?" he asked.
The man considered Phoenix before he answered as if weighing in his mind the possibility of butchery or mercy,
"I sail to the mainland to defend the oracle at Delphi. Agamemnon will forfeit, he is the scourge." He leered and his eyes danced as he spoke and Phoenix knew he had the madness he'd heard men speak of. He smiled a vacuous smile.
"Let's slit their throats together" said Phoenix, "that is where I am heading."
The slave released his sword from the throat of Phoenix. He talked as they progressed
"I am Titus, I sailed and pirated in the Iberian peninsular. What is the name of your God?"
"No matter" said Phoenix who wasn't sure he knew the answer. He began to warm to this pirate as he heard his familiar tale.
"So how did you end up here, how did you escape?"

"I have almonds and figs, what do you have" asked Titus who seemed unwilling to answer.

"Just some wine and oils."

"I am hungry" said Titus, "I'll show you something."

The pair sat shaded from the sun as it was a day of bright brilliance with skies of purest blue blown from Zeus's palm. Titus removed his cloak and showed the weals and boils on his back, infected and scarred,

"My back was scarred too often so I escaped the scream of the lash."

Phoenix nodded and told of his life with the Libyan tyrant. He showed the scar on his groin which indicated the mark of the eunuch.

"An extra gift from my beloved master."

Phoenix and Titus ate sparingly. Titus out of humility and habit bred from a lifetime of servitude, Phoenix because of the castration. His mutilation had affected all his appetites. All his lusts taken by the hot knife, pale ghosts of the hungers he had once known. Titus stared longingly at Mount Juktus.

"When I was young my father would take me to Mount Juktus. We'd hunt and fish and at night sleep under the stars."

They sat under an old citrus tree and talked until the night turned cold. And then when the stars shone they embraced, the joyful catharsis of mutual souls unburdening themselves. They caressed without desire but from a conglomerate of sympathy, affection and gentleness which left no mark, didn't bruise their hearts, only nursed them. As the moon wheeled higher the glint of metal alerted Titus,

"Soldiers!"

The voice of the lead soldier travelled quickly through the cold air.

"A quick death if you surrender now slaves."

Titus laughed and taking a clay pellet from his shoulder bag released the missile from its sling. The soldier hit full on the cheek fell to the floor his jaw broken and teeth shattered. Titus cackled, spat and reloaded his sling. The remaining soldier threw his spear then turned and fled. The spasms of agony brought Titus sanity and clarity as he gripped the spear and the hand of Phoenix,

"Am I to die a slave?"

Memories of his home came to him as he reeled and puked. Looking up at Phoenix his eyes danced as his body tightened. And Phoenix knew he was dying and the anger in his heart grew stronger.

32

Crixus stood over Philon, his blade held tightly, his eyes wide with malice and anger. Philon, still disorientated looked up and saw a shadow fall over the face of Crixus and a thud before his body fell forward. Shielding his eyes from the sun he could just make out the outline of a man whom he did not recognise. The man leaned forward to help him,

"Thank you, thank you."

"Are you well friend? I turned the corner and saw you in trouble."

Philon began to gather his senses and stood. His head felt bruised. He looked at the man who had helped him. He liked what he saw. A tall, young man, lithe and athletic.

"I am indebted to you sir. What is your name?"

The man smiled and took Philon's hand.

"Phoenix."

Philon noticed the seal ring on the hand of Phoenix. Ornamented with milk stone it singled him out as a slave as they were often worn as a seal script. Phoenix saw Philon looking at his hand and remembered the ring. He had lost count of the times he had affixed his masters seal into the soft clay to confirm ownership of figs and oils. Not only did the ring confirm his lowly status it also linked him to the Libyan and he instinctively covered it,

"Who is your master? Perhaps I can thank him?"

This was the last thing Phoenix wanted. He now regretted getting involved in this side street argument but it had been his natural instinct to help this man. He turned to Crixus who lay prostrate on the floor. Phoenix knelt down and put his ear to the man's mouth. Then slowly looking up at Philon he spoke with fear in his voice,

"He's dead. I killed him."

Phoenix's situation hadn't improved or worsened. He faced execution anyway. Philon's response was decisive and quick and put Phoenix at ease,

"No. We killed him. Quick, help me with the body. Then we need to leave this island."

"You have a boat?"

"Of course. Take his legs."

Phoenix did as he was told. A boat? Perhaps saving this man was a good thing after all.

33

Lyria leaned on the rails of the ship and looked ahead. Orpheus, missing his friend, joined her. It was early evening and as the night crept in from the east they watched the sea change from yellow gold to a gentle orange and then a deep crimson. The sunset faded and died and then the stars appeared, just one or two to start with and then hundreds, countless and clear shining in the celestial ocean. The *auloi* players regulated the rowing and Orpheus knew he was sailing with the Gods in a musical paradise. The night whispered its harmonies to him. Darkness fell and the boat was a dark silhouette against the sky. The water whispered noiselessly chiming her assent with the pale night sun. It was a ceaseless low key murmuring which acted as a sedative and he was stirred gently to sleep to dream of drifting melodies. Much later Lyria awoke with her head in his lap. For a while she listened to the sound of the waves and then her own tears before falling to sleep. Otus looked to the sail and prayed for wind.

34

"I was trading in Egypt."

Philon answered the question Phoenix had posed without turning, busy as he was with the sail trying to turn it to the wind. Phoenix knew of Egypt and had learned much from studying their medicinal practices and listening to the 'Priests of Sekhmet', those who master the scorpions. They had occasionally visited Crete and he had watched them work. For him Egypt was a land of fabulous treasures and mystery.

"I hear the sun shines so bright there that it can weave a cloak of solid gold from thin air. The buildings dazzle in the moonlight and blind you in the daylight."

Phoenix as a slave had often begged his Libyan overlord to let him travel to the land of the Pharaoh but the Libyan had always refused and more often than not had him beaten for the mere suggestion. If Philon had travelled to this land he wanted to know more.

"Are their buildings as high as mountains as they say?"

Philon gave up on the sail and turned to sit by Phoenix,

"Yes, and coated with a living skin of white. Their kings ascend to heaven through them."

Phoenix looked to the horizon and imagined once again this magnificent place as if he expected the king of Egypt to appear from the waves. Philon sensed the awe in Phoenix and placed his arm around his shoulder and whispered,

"But they are savages friend who worship an abstraction. The sun God, the Aten they call it. Their temples are empty of food. Pharaoh follows the one God. Pah! His priests are in revolt. They say his wife does not come to his bed. One God. Ha, there are many."

Phoenix wasn't so sure,

"Perhaps there is just one God in all of us who is unnamed."

Philon looked hard at Phoenix then continued his battle with the sail. Way in the distance now the blue haze and shimmering peaks of the Cretan landscape.

"So where are you heading?"

"Thessaly. Agamemnon threatens again."

"Again? He has never stopped. Never will."

Three years had now passed since he last fought the Mycenean tyrant. Philon remembered the agonising night marches he had taken from Athens to Megara and then Corinth, driven on and deluded by hunger. The feelings of mortality common to all soldiers loomed and shaped every valley and hill; the horses collapsing and the men drinking from poisoned wells at Isthmia. The mocking cattle of the enemy were always out of reach like Tantalus stretching for his fruit. As the enemy retreated they knew the land was theirs without a battle being fought for what did Philon and his sweat ridden soldiers know? Only the hunger, the frozen sandals in the night and the stinking bodies of the day. Does an army possess a territory merely by entering it? Their skin was sore and their lungs filled with dust. Villages were burned, the women raped and sometimes the men. Philon had been shocked to see these men had genitals just like his and had stared. Their bodies were the same and the fear too as the generals slit their throats and made the women watch as their husbands inhaled and drowned in their own blood. He knew his youth had ended that day. And then the winter came at Isthmia and with it the dark blue storm clouds sailing across the sky at Tiryns. And the waves broke and the leaves scattered turning the earth to cold death making it as colourless as air; the cold kills everything eventually. So Philon had bent double and shivered with this cold and looked to the tents and the women for warmth. But the women were the dead flowers of the conquered valleys, barren with their dour faces and dry greetings, dreaming of the stripped flesh of their captors. Sometimes the snowflakes paraded and whirled around their heads in the dark blue night, like a thousand voiceless spirits restless and searching for shelter. Then the fires of the camps were pools of gold in which men fretted and stared unblinking into a lost dream of victory. The Greeks always fought as families, his father his commander. He remembered the crude orders of Parmenion, "kill the enemy and not your own men!" Even this had been disobeyed. Philon had returned home triumphant but sad and his sister had noticed the change, even Parmenion eased his anger as he taught and tutored his only son in the ways of the vine and the profitable trading routes. No longer the boy he had carried on his back and gently chided. Now the man, now the heir.

The long slopes of Mount Pentelicus were draped in darkness then drenched in moonlight. The wolf lay still. Just her stomach spasmed. She looked down expectantly her large black head straining to see. All her previous litters were born dead; endless tidbits brought for ghostly cubs that never were. Then her body convulsed and she had her cubs, just two, mewling in a sack of blood and water. She set about licking them dry from nose to tail; ceaseless until the dawn parted the dipping cloud. A week later they opened their eyes and chased their tails till their heads span and the world with it. She led them slowly east for food, past Megara towards Mycenae wary of the smell of hot tar and tally men, the two legged creatures.

35

Philon lay on his back on the prow of the boat and stared at the night sky that was now a blue meadow sprouting stars. Have I done the right thing? Who is this Phoenix? Can he be trusted? He thought of his sister Lyria waiting for him on Lesbos and smiled. Looking westwards through the purple night the moon threw a silver blanket of light over the quiet ocean. A gull swung low by the boat to take a closer look at Philon. Unimpressed she flew onwards. He watched her for as long as he could before the night swallowed her whole. It was these solitary moments that Philon never tired of despite his many voyages,

"Now I know the Gods are listening to me. Mighty Apollo, grant me immortality through my deeds and through my battles. Let me be remembered and let my deeds shine."

It was an old prayer he had recited many times. Did the Gods listen? Well, I'm still alive aren't I? Thanks to this fellow. He sat up. The light from the torch that hung from the stern showed him that Phoenix was asleep. He lay back again. The breeze blew suddenly fresher on his face and he smiled. He knew they were in the grip of the northern Etesian wind which if he let it would take them past Thera where the island smoked then Icaria and Chios and finally the Troad where the young King Priam reigned. But first Lesbos.

Phoenix wasn't asleep but like Philon he was restful and content. He reflected on the past two days. At a stroke gone his old life. No more than a memory now that would feed his nightmares, a crepuscular thought on the dusty stair behind him, a spider's web. In his heart he knew that something inordinately brutal had vanished. Phoenix was still too young to know that his dreams and delusions were the same. After years of abuse and obeisance he expected adventure. Now my destiny has leaped out at me. I will cross the Aegean. I will fight for Peleus. I will find my mother. I am mutilated but I will sleep with the sunset and stroke the rust red hours. He lay back and stared at the moon. Far to the north under that same moon Meriones, leader of the Perrhaebi lay with Chione the priestess and *Klawiphorus*. He wondered once again how and why the moon changed shape. As for Chione she knew the answers but was long past caring.

36

It was the second night and there was no wind. Just the black ebony stillness of the ocean its surface now pitted with stars. Nothing moved in the water,

"It's the girl. She brings bad luck" said Guraxes a tall thin man who had sailed all his life.

"And the boy too. Look, like a pond."

Otus walked over to Guraxes and spoke quietly in his ear,

"Silence sailor or I will have your tongue."

He then stood back and gave the order. The men pulled at their oars and secretly wondered if they'd ever see land again or be rid of the taste of the salt from their cracked lips.

"I expect the wind soon" said one.

"From your backside?"

"Will you bet your dagger's hilt?"

"Done."

"Fool. The hilt is mine. Look at that candle. As straight as Dionysus's cock."

But the wind did come and Otus breathed easier and the daggers hilt was lost.

"Tack her in then. Let Hera kiss the sails. She has delivered us."

37

On the boat the days passed, the islands came and went; stopping to refill the many water pots that lay cool in the bowels of the ship. Night then day, sun and moon. And then changing direction, the tacking prow, the listless sway of the mordant water. Sat still in the pregnant darkness waiting for the birth of the dawn. Then slowly she heaved herself into view giving the mind's eye a sense of time and place after the void of night. The sun rising bringing life and light to the sea; numberless points of light sparkling on the surface as cormorants fished for breakfast. Forgetting her troubles and dreaming of the adventures and love she'd find in Thessaly. But suddenly her heart would sink as she thought of her mother and what she had left behind. And so too with Orpheus whose heart pitched and tossed like the water that lay around him. But one morning there came the clatter of the docks and the pitched shrill of the gulls. The captain yelled,

"Pagasae!"

Lyria sensed the relief in his voice.

38

To the south and east of Mycenae on the banks of the Eurotas river between the eastern Parnon and Taygetus range lay Sparta ruled by Menelaus, brother of Agamemnon. His loyalty to his older sibling was born of fear and he provided Agamemnon with troops and materials. The abundant rainfall on the western slopes of the Taygetus made for excellent fire timber and marble which Agamemnon put to good use. He also supplied women to grace the court of his older brother. Of these Helen was by far the most beautiful. It was Menelaus who first saw her potential. He had been inspecting his stables when he had seen a girl sweeping the yard. He watched for a few moments then turned to Samis his body servant,

"Who is that girl? Is she a whore?"

"Aren't all women? Let us say she is well schooled in the beatitudes of love."

Samis laughed. He knew the girl well, the daughter of Leda now out of favour, her father banished. Menelaus nodded and Samis was pleased.

"She could be sir. Theseus knows her well." He winked. "She is young and clean, a hive in the summer with all her honey locked in. They say she swims like Aphrodite herself and can dance. And she is in trouble financially. Many debts. A woman like that is good to know. Her name is Helen."

"Hey girl! Over here."

His belly trembled as he shouted. Helen, ambitious and brazen walked slowly over to Menelaus. Her plan was working. Already she knew the power she held over men. Menelaus had something she needed. Menelaus was thinking the same as he looked her up and down. He stood and smiled. Helen took a long look at him, his swarthy features, the powerful head with almost no neck. She noted his large ears with exaggerated lobes, his dry colourless lips and the small half opened mouth,

"Perhaps if you please me you can be my *Hetairai*."

Helen knew what that meant. She would become a 'companion' of Menelaus. A high class whore a cut above the flute girls and the half naked *Pornais* who hung around the street corners of Corinth with their garish make up and transparent tunics. The *Hetairai* were untouchable and well respected with their veils and robes. They were always attached to men of note and could amass a considerable fortune. It was said that Klepsydra ruled Troy through Priam. She had been called the water clock – she stopped 'performing' when it emptied. Helen bowed pleased at the opportunity this gave her. Menelaus then pulled her onto him. His breath smelt of old cheese; a small price to pay for her sudden promotion.

"When I've finished with you I shall send you to Agamemnon."

39

The journey overland took two days. The children were packed on a horse by Otus who said his farewells and gave clear instructions to the guide,

"Guard them well Acorges or I will hear of it. Present them to Peleus and tell their story."

Otus then took Acorges to one side and spoke to him out of earshot. So the small party headed east through Pherae and Pharsalus. They stopped sporadically to pick flowers at Lyria's insistence; some Lyria had never seen as the horses took them higher along winding tracks through the high scented pines that gave her a giddy feeling as she breathed in the aromas. At Pharsalus a festival was taking place. Lyria and Orpheus watched with interest, Lyria wary lest any animals were harmed. Acorges took the children to one side,

"Pharsalus is known for its religious festivals. We are safe but be careful not to interfere."

Lyria watched enthralled. First came the attendants of Aphrodite dressed in white robes scattering flowers. Ivory combs adorned their hair which they used to pamper each other in mimicry of her preparations. Other women carried great mirrors of gold and silver so her beauty was reflected and magnified. The men and women followed dressed in their best linen plucking the lyre or rattling the drum. Orpheus took note of the exquisite instruments. The priests followed somberly carrying the symbols of Aphrodite, sparrows eggs, doves and fruit which they held above their heads. Some knelt as they passed and made to kiss the priests hands in acquiescence and adoration. Cerebus cocked his head inquisitively but stayed silent knowing the men weren't threatening. Orpheus and Lyria looked at each other when the procession had passed, their minds racing, discordant, questioning. Lyria was thrilled at the literal truth of what she beheld but Orpheus wondered if there was a simpler explanation of the world he saw around him; man being the measure of all things was a self evident truth for the boy although he didn't yet know it. He wanted to speak to Lyria about the Gods and the fish in the sea, a dozen different things but Acorges, mindful of a long days travel bade them to sleep. For a moment above Pharsalus the sky was a splendid aorta of deep reds until the colours curdled. Salmon pink then puce and crimson, the jeweled breast of a queen. And now night.

40

Achilles was bored. He had escaped his morning duties and now lay in a small hollow in the hillside just outside Larissa staring at the sky. The hollow was filled with burdocks and daisies in summer and dead leaves in winter. Hearing a noise he lay flat and lifted his gaze over the lip to see two children being led by a man. They stopped a short distance away. The boy sat down whilst the girl sat to pick flowers. Achilles watched the girl. He liked the tint and sparkle of her green eyes and her red hair and fringe that she was forever tossing behind her. He liked the way her lips fluttered as she spoke and her bright lively face. Encouraged he stood and walked over to the group. Acorges reached for the hilt of his dagger but relaxed when he saw just a young boy.

"Can I walk with you?" Achilles asked simply.

"If you can lead us to Larissa and Peleus then you can gladly join us" replied Acorges.

Achilles took the bridle of the horse and nodded,

"Of course. It's only a short way now."

Achilles thought it best to keep his identity from the group,

"What is your business with Peleus?"

"That is for his ears only young man."

Achilles nodded but all the same his interest was piqued and he decided he wanted to find out more about this young girl and her companions.

"I shall strive to be worthy of your sense of loyalty sir."

Acorges looked sharply at Achilles. This boy spoke very well. Too well.

"And your name?"
Achilles replied quickly,
"Ixion."
And then,
"I'm in charge of stores."
Lyria liked this polite young man,
"Ixion? Descended from the river God Peneius?" she asked
Achilles pointed,
"Yes, this very river. I am descended from the centaurs."

Achilles was glad he had chosen a name whose provenance he knew. This girl seemed well educated. Shortly they came to the mud huts and small holdings on the outskirts of Larissa.

"You are welcome to spend the night in my home."

Achilles knew of a deserted hut with a few provisions,

"Tomorrow I can take you to Phalanna and the palace of Peleus."

Acorges decided to accept the hospitality of this well bred young man. They were tired and it would give them time to rest and eat before meeting with the Thessalian leader. After eating and lighting a small fire they fell to sleep. That night Lyria dreamt of her father. His kind eyes stared at her through the dark folds of the night. The fields and roads they had wandered on Lesbos became a geography of despair. She saw him young and strong in the market selling wine and her heart beat faster as she reached out in her sleep. And then from her closed eyes two tears running seamlessly down her cheeks creating two glistening and symmetrical paths of moisture making their way over her flawless face freckled with fire. Orpheus reached out and took her hand and squeezed it and Lyria felt safe. Achilles watched. He decided he liked Lyria and Orpheus.

41

As they walked to the palace Achilles explained to Acorges the procedures that morning,

"Every two moons servants are brought before Peleus for inspection and to air any grievance. The kitchen workers are to be seen today."

He promised Acorges he could procure an audience with Peleus. Acorges didn't doubt it. He was becoming increasingly impressed with this helpful young man. As they entered the great hall Lyria and Orpheus were instructed to wait with the other servants whilst Achilles took Acorges to the antechamber behind the hall. Acorges was astonished as the guards bowed their heads,

"Prince Achilles."

"Father. This is Acorges. He wishes to speak to you about Lyria and Orpheus of Lesbos."

At the front of the hall the servants waited patiently. Lyria was frightened her nerves would get the better of her as she bowed her head. Peleus then arrived with a flourish wearing a tunic of gold and ivory. He carried a stick made from yew inlaid with amber. The grip was made from the skin of a lion. There were many guards with him and Orpheus thought this was strange. Behind him walked Achilles. Orpheus nudged Lyria,

"Look, Ixion."

Lyria looked up. What was Ixion doing? He was too young to be a guard. The herald made everything clear,

"Lord Achilles."

Achilles looked over towards them and smiled. Lyria felt a sudden warmth that puzzled her. It was a feeling she had never felt before. Peleus too smiled at his servants. It was a smile of easy complicity and always put the servants at ease. It was a gift he had whether speaking to kings or beggars. Although past his prime he was still a handsome man but his beauty was increasingly rendered from his fragility like a rare bird or butterfly; his gnarled phthisic hands spoke of wisdom but still possessed a keen strength. As she crouched in obeyance Lyria noticed the blue veins that crossed on his legs. Peleus walked along the line of servants to where Lyria knelt. He stopped and gazed at her placing his hand gently on her head,

"Lyria, I remember your father Parmenion. A brave man. We will miss him."

"I, I…" Lyria was unsure what to say. Should I answer she wondered?

"I will too sir."

Achilles smiled too and Lyria felt as if the air was being sucked from her body. Why doesn't he move on? The room seemed to spin before Peleus spoke again.

"We can always provide work and shelter for the daughter of Parmenion."

He looked towards Orpheus,

"And her friend too."

After Peleus had left Achilles came running up,

"I'm sorry for my little deception. I was bored."

Orpheus and Lyria looked at each other still a little puzzled. Orpheus made to bow but Achilles stopped him,

"Father says he has jobs for you. Come, I'll show you both around the stores. You may be asked to bring supplies for a feast or ritual."

So the three of them set off. The stores were well guarded but Achilles was allowed access. Peleus encouraged agriculture knowing its importance in time of war. If Agamemnon laid siege he could last a year possibly two. The farmers grew lettuce, celery, onions and garlic. Flax was cultivated to make clothes. Saffron was harvested for medicines. Even the olive stones were kept and burnt for fuel; collected from the floors in large jars by palace workers at the end of every day. Lyria stared in wonder. Every type of foodstuff was here.

"Enough to last the whole of Thessaly a year" grinned Achilles.

Lyria gazed at the huge jars of figs, almonds and pistachios. Further along more jars filled with peas and quince. Sacks full of hazelnuts, yet more filled with oats. Sometime later the children parted ways. Lyria couldn't help herself,

"Will we see you soon Ixion?" she grinned.

"I hope so."

With that Achilles turned and left them. After a few strides he began to run. He seemed to run with liquid ease and such grace that both Orpheus and Lyria watched him till he had all but disappeared. Lyria raised her eyebrow to regain some control of a new emotion that, like a bird, was beating its wings in her breast.

42

Agamemnon loved to hunt wolves. After dark accompanied by his torch bearers sometimes riding home alone in the early hours. Some say he had killed all the wolves in Mycenae. He had been known to kill a dozen in a day, trapping and stalking, sometimes killing with an arrow, other times a spear which he threw with great precision. But there was one wolf which evaded his arrows and dagger. A she-wolf with a black head that he had tried to kill many times. The stories surrounding her were plentiful. Anubis had eaten women and children and dragged off beautiful shepherdesses. She had brought down warriors at the gallop and injured countless hunters. Because of her black head he had named her Anubis in reverence to the jackal, the black headed God of the Pharaoh kings over the water whose power and influence he so admired. Now the heat was high so the scent was preserved. On cold mornings it was harder to pick up. The hounds had been chosen, the slaves set, the nets ready for the beaters to lure and lead the prey. But today Agamemnon was furious. All morning they had ridden. At first the light had whitened and then turned gold as they passed wild valleys thick with dry swamps as the summer took hold. But then the mists had risen early and the sun was now strong so the beaters and stragglers limped and the dogs panted and howled. It was Danius who, beating the bushes, came across her shivering in fear protecting her two cubs. Now threatened she stood, her eyes ice blue, her black withers sleek. With hackles high she leaped at Danius who cried out as her teeth easily bit through his leather grieves into his calf. Agamemnon turned and smiled on hearing the screams of his servant,

"Ah, Anubis. And now she is vulnerable with two cubs to protect."

The king offered no aid to Danius who lay bleeding and clutching his leg. The cubs had now scattered and Anubis howled as Agamemnon gained ground on her children. One of the cubs, the youngest ran into a gulley and turned to see Agamemnon closing. Shaking with fright he yelped for his mother as he slowly backed into a bank of willows which surrounded him and offered no hope of escape. Agamemnon, seeing the cub was alone eased his mount into the grove. Reaching slowly for his whip he raised his arm as the frantic cub sprinted forward under the hooves of his ride. Anubis in a blind panic had her other cub in her mouth and set him safely in a raised crag. She turned and ran toward the willow grove where she had heard her child cry out. She saw Agamemnon's raised arm; his long whip lengthened slowly in the air and then became rigid with a dull thud. The wood became silent. Agamemnon dismounted to take a closer look at the mutilated cub, its innards still warm and spilled over the ground. Reaching down for its entrails he smeared his face with blood then left the tiny corpse where it lay and rode to rejoin his party to show his bloodied hands. 'I will tell them I have killed the mother with my bare hands' he thought. He was at a good distance when Anubis arrived by the willows and, exhausted, lay down still by her dead child and gently licked his face one last time.

43

It was the pride of Peleus and the Penthelids that the prince was never pampered. Achilles was encouraged to play with his peers, to grapple in the stables and skiff across the Peneius in makeshift boats. And for the boys who ran about the palace they knew that Achilles would one day rule them but they were wise enough to know that for now they were equals. Because for young boys the future is the afternoon's racing or tomorrow's sword play in the forest. For boys now is all there is. So Achilles ran and scraped his knees with the rest of them and when he was insolent he was punished. At night in the cramped dorms the boys dreamt of armour and arrows. As for Achilles he learned to read the sleep of the guards – the snoring, the intermittent coughs, wheezes and mutterings that rose and reared their heads. They indicated to Achilles how deeply the guard slept. It was silence that Achilles was wary of for it was then, he knew, that the guard stared coldly into the unblinking darkness. But the guards were more often asleep so Achilles would slip by them. On these nocturnal wanderings he would check on the horses speaking in low whispers whilst Thessaly slumbered. Sometimes he would fish in the moon bathed river watched over by the songless owls who stared unmoved as he returned to his rest in the darkened dorm.

But this night he left the fish and the horses and wandered to the outbuildings where he knew Lyria and Orpheus slept. Perhaps they lay awake. We could go fishing or ride the horses. But, pursuing a strange whim, he decided to leave his friends. He walked through the apricot grove and breathed in deeply.

The moon sprinkled the upper branches with silver light and beyond as she followed the curve of the valley that squeezed and coaxed the river westwards. Turning towards the kitchens he hesitated as he could make out a hunched figure sat alone. It was Orpheus who was sat under the acacia. He couldn't sleep and had left his bed and was now listening with interest to the ibis above his head. Although he couldn't see it the bird sang sweetly as it picked at the gnats and flies. In the corner of the torch-lit courtyard a lyre lay on its side. 'Most probably left behind by a drunken musician' Orpheus thought. He had seen his father play at symposiums and rituals but had always been silenced and ignored when he had even attempted to pick it up. Icarius had not wanted to add musical incompetence to his long list of faults. Thinking he was alone he walked over to the corner of the yard. The instrument was dusty but Orpheus could see and feel the quality of workmanship as he ran his fingers over the carved wood and tortoiseshell inlaid with gold. The strings were made from sheep gut, tightly wound they seemed to sing even before he touched them. Dare I pick it up? I'll be punished if I'm found. But at this hour everyone is asleep. Despite this Orpheus turned away and made to leave but looked over his shoulder to give one last look at the lyre. The strings were taut and hummed in the night mimicking the drowsy breezes. The music resonated with the boy and yet there was something wrong. Instinctively he reached for a peg and turned it two full turns and then another two turning them each back a quarter turn. He hardly knew what he was doing.

"Hey you, leave that alone." Nixion, an off duty sentry was tired and making his way home after guarding the palace storerooms. He had seen Orpheus, the backward and timid boy who had just arrived from Lesbos. Nixion needed someone to shout at.

"Im… Im sorry" stuttered Orpheus, "I was tuning it."

"Ha! It takes years to learn how to even hold the lyre. And you think you can tune it in one sitting? Away boy."

Orpheus scurried out and Nixion set off home. He'd been gifted some wine by a secret admirer. I'll drink the wine then seek her out. Achilles who had watched from the kitchen waited till the guard had left. He then stooped to put the lyre back in its chest but not before he strummed the strings; he had been taught the lyre by his mother but hadn't kept it up. He was surprised at how the lyre played, every string perfectly pitched, tuned and harmonious. He turned and shouted,

"Orpheus. Hey."

But Orpheus had long since fled. Achilles took the lyre. He had an idea and the next morning when Orpheus awoke he was astonished to see it resting by his bed.

44

Phoenix let the boat drift as they partook of a breakfast of leavened bread. And then onwards drifting peacefully or catching the wind. Watching for the quick grey flash of a dolphin's back. Sometimes a lazy swell would carry them; lying on the bottom of the boat to see the high blue sky. At night the strange sounds and the luminous waters that shone red. Phoenix listened to the whispering water and wondered. What is the love I feel for this place? Something was being satisfied. A seascape, a woman in a deep blue dress she carried them and when the sun set scarlet and silver falling like a wounded Amazon. Blood on the water. Philon looked at Phoenix and knew his mood,

"The sea is a whore, she kisses everyone. She'll lie with you but we'll all pay the price."

"What do you mean?"

"I mean it's a long lonely affair with only brief moments of joy."

"She's the only love I know" replied Phoenix wistfully and then remembering his shame, "will ever know."

Like many slaves Phoenix loved the sea before he even saw it. Born to land, then sold to toil in the sweating hearts of towns he had dreamed of the sea and sought her out as a man searches for love. And she didn't disappoint for she gave him the infinite, the dread, the vitality and the beauty as all women should. He had seen men fall to their knees and kiss the sweet sand offering themselves in awestruck devotion. For when the sweet sea salt sighs men forget everything, they lose everything. Her waves die, fall back but another enters, ceaseless. These rhythms are ancient and fixed and pull a man's soul towards its centre. 'She will take me' Phoenix thought 'and when I am tired she will whisper and sing to me like my mother.' His soul he knew was irrevocably warped but the sea offered indescribable blessings and promised eternity.

"And you Philon?"

"It was infatuation. I only skirted the edges at first; looked into her eyes from a distance and traced my fingers over her horizons."

He lifted his head and smelled the air. Excitedly he turned to Phoenix,

"Lesbos."

45

Whilst the ship sailed slowly into the harbour they furled the sails and stored them in the hold. A short time later Philon anchored the vessel and jumped ashore eager to feel solid ground after days and nights of drifting; the familiar smell of fish, seaweed and hot tar invigorated him. Phoenix however laid a while in the ship savouring the anchored silence that was only broken by the creak and sway of the deep easy roll of the boat. Philon left him to his reverie and surveyed the scene before him. The bay looped around with an assortment of fishing boats steady in the soft waters and beyond the sway of the hills with smoke rising from the occasional settlement – it was a relaxed landscape that had always pleased Philon. A dozen cats were scattered around in various states of feline lethargy. Some were laid belly upwards as if drinking in the sunshine through their fur. The cats were plentiful; sacred as they were to Poseidon they were left alone. The faint smell of citrus and meats tickled his nose. It was early in the afternoon so indolent bodies lay sprawled in the shade to avoid the fierce heat. But some listless bodies lay submerged in sunlight as if freshly washed up by the sun; wheelwrights and boatswains, net menders and carpenters taking their meat and wine. Bronze sheets were placed over fires to cook the flat breads and heat the stews. Then honey and strange pointed sweet breads that were a favourite of the islanders were passed around. Phoenix had now joined his friend.

"*Pyramadius* cakes" said Philon. "The Pharaoh kings bury their dead in giant mountains shaped like our cakes – we call them pyramids."

46

Phoenix noted a change in Philon as they walked along the beach with its fine sand and black shale. Philon pointed out his family's vineyards hidden behind high stone walls. The crickets sang and the air was fused with the scent of limes. The citrus from the bursting vineyards produced a perfume so intoxicating that he paused sensing a boyhood friend had tapped him on the shoulder,

"Here is the best wine in Greece Phoenix, protected by the highest walls. We pour lime on the grapes to stop passers by eating them. Makes them taste sour but doesn't harm the wine. Clever eh?"

Phoenix nodded his appreciation but he had no interest in hearing how wine was produced, just in drinking it. As a slave most of his life the opportunities to taste fine wine had been rare. Further on they approached two wheelwrights who were doing excellent business heating up the big copper tyres for the broken wheels of the islanders. Philon smiled as he heard their conversation,

"A face like a decrepit old wineskin."

His friend nodded agreement as he heaved the giant wheel into place,

"And you'd have to be as drunk as Dionysus to take her."

The man who had uttered the remark looked up and almost dropped the wheel in amazement,

"Philon."

Philon smiled as both men stood and embraced. Phoenix noticed a reluctance in the man who embraced Philon. Philon

felt it. The man stepped away from his friend and looked down in the sand. There was a pause before Philon spoke,
 "What is the matter Agathon? What news?"

47

"Your beloved son has returned."

Eratos whittled the branch idly with his blade and looked up at Danae.

"It seems that Crixus failed."

"And what do you suggest?" replied Danae.

"Be rid of him. Spin him a tale. Cry with grief and send him on his way. Tell him anything."

Danae nodded. Outside it was suddenly cold. The ashes of the old fires were raked. The braziers full, the old carob gnarled. A strong breeze blew through the yard as she placed a shawl around her shoulders. A lantern that hung from a beam provided a moving cone of light in which two moths fought a frantic duel.

"A storm is coming." Eratos grinned.

Danae hurried back home. Looking up to the hills she saw the esculent oak forest moving with the wind that blew east from Mytilene to Eresos.

48

The red dawn embraced then swallowed the night. The moon was hideous. On the desolate beach at Antissa Philon sat by the shrine he'd built many years before with his sister to honour Ares the God of war. Lyria had prayed there every day for her brother to return safely from the war against Agamemnon. And now he was home but where was she? Phoenix by his side dreamt of his old master. Sent early to the gloom of Hades the Libyan stood by his side his jaw gaping and his head rolling cut by Phoenix's knife. Phoenix awoke and shuddered ridden with sweat and guilt. He wasn't to know that the Libyan trader lived confident that Phoenix would be found and killed. Philon could not sleep. His every bone yearned for revenge, his mind considering all the possibilities that would provide this end.

He turned to his friend,

"What are you thinking of Phoenix?"

"I'm thinking of the man I killed. He haunts me."

"He cannot harm you."

"But maybe the *Erinyes* will have me."

Philon shook his head. The *Erinyes* were the viperous witches of vengeance sent from Hades to avenge the dead.

"Do you really believe that? You are free, he deserved his fate and now you can please the Gods by fighting for Peleus. You can return to your homeland."

"And what of you Philon?"

Philon didn't answer. His hand moved toward his friend. His thoughts were suddenly far away. He remembered a time when he had satisfied all his lusts the same. Uncouth in all his appetites he had fed at the trough and had his fill of brothels as he traded from Melos to Scopolos. Then in Corinth he had called for another slave girl to bring life to his tired carcass before taking the boat back to Lesbos and his beloved sister. So Demera was brought in. Already at twelve years she had known rape and the tears of her mother when Agamemnon's hordes had marched through Argolis to Tegea. Philon envisaged her fate. Sent to the slave market after he had had his way then on to the Phoenician traders where she would infect the locals who would pay a pittance for her favours. Diseased and terrified she shook as she lay beside Philon who, struck with a sudden emptiness and desolation, had turned from her and wept as his fickle friends laughed and jested. His heart had still been heavy that night when he had placed the gold in the captain's hand and put her on the night boat to Lemnos where her family waited. He turned to Phoenix,

"I will come with you to Thessaly."

49

Agamemnon always avoided the midday heat and as the sun shone hotter he made his way to the courtyard at the rear of the palace where he knew the cypress trees offered shade and respite. The water coolers, ever present for fear of the whip stood straighter as they saw the king approach averting their eyes and wishing for anonymity from this man who could as easily punish as promote on a whim or fancy. He washed then stood whilst a servant rubbed him down then draped him in a fine crimson cloak dyed with the hot blood of eagles. He then lay back and summoned the nearest slave who ran immediately to his side and kneeled,

"Fetch Helen to me."

Helen, daughter of Leda, could serve Agamemnon in his bed and in his politics. She knew his deepest desires although his hairy arms and broad back disgusted her. But she was thankful to the king. After the fall of her parents it was he who had taken her in from the court of Sparta after the recommendation of Menelaus. Her cunning and guile had been set in motion by the need to survive in the mercurial power shifts that always threatened her and had led to the demise of her mother Leda at the court of Tyndareus and Sparta. At twelve years old she had been exquisite. At fourteen her hair like yellow sunlight fell in tresses and ringlets across her white shoulders; eyes like lamps of heaven that danced gold and green when the sunlight caught them. And now at sixteen her cheekbones carved from rose and ivory led the eye to her flawless full lips leaving words unspoken. A physical beauty sickening in its scope. But for all this a grisly beauty in its self awareness and vanity. A beauty framed in ice. She knew the effect she had on men and wielded her sexuality with a crude perfection. Men would prostrate themselves offering their verses and their hearts whilst Helen, ghastly and gorgeous, painted her nails. The grace of the dancers or the touch of the lyre did not move Helen's heart. She could not remember a time when men had not looked at her. Even as a child of ten, acutely self confident she had squirmed coyly, a slip of a girl rubbing against the bed post framing her loosely covered limbs by the central fire of the *agora* mimicking the provocative Minoan dancers with their twirls and graces; dancing naked in the foothills of Mount Amiclae where the land was fertile and teeming with game. She knew that the heralds quivered as she brushed by them. She desired the luxuries she had known before her parents fall from power, the servants and silver brooches, the golden necklaces. Helen needed to be surrounded by extravagances. Decorative vases filled her quarters at the palace. A tundra of animal skins covered the floor so her guest's feet were neither hot nor cold. Ceilings were touched with ebony and the intricate red gold tapestries of the Opeans thus denying them of their only treasure.

"Achilles is to be wooed by you Helen and in turn spied upon. You are to make him fall in love with you. Like all men this will be easy." Agamemnon smiled, "and you do have a habit of enjoying your work. These people are savages. They will be subdued. Offer them anything, everything, as long as they submit to my will. And remember with these peasants it's easier for them to believe a big lie over a small one."

"I will do what you say sire." Helen paused. Even she was anxious at what she was about to say, "if you can assist me."

Agamemnon turned surprised.

"Why should I assist you in anything?"

"For the good of Mycenae?"

Agamemnon paused and Helen seeing this pushed her advantage,

"For the good of Mycenae make me *Klawiphorus*, the key

bearer. The land that is set aside for the Gods. Put me in charge of it, in charge of religious duties. Then when I am in Thessaly I will have their protection and I will be feared. Better able to carry out your wishes."

It took Agamemnon an instant to decide. Secretly he was impressed by her nerve. The petty, political vicissitudes of the priestesses bored him. Chione would be slighted but what did he care for religious titles? If this cunning child could use this title then why not? Helen knew that as key bearer she would oversee all the religious rituals. This would place her nearer the *Hequetai*, the advisors to the king. All the imported slaves from Knidos and Lesbos were now at her disposal to do with as she pleased. Even Chione would have to bow to her.

"And what of Chione? You will have to persuade her to relinquish her position."

"I will arrange it."

50

Helen remembered the words of her king as she brushed her hair and looked with lifeless eyes at her pitiless reflection. She had heard of this boy Achilles, this saviour of the Greeks. It would be an easy task to spy on him, perhaps even enjoyable. She had been told he was weak and a disappointment to Peleus. Bored and restless she made her way to the *Megaron*, the beating heart at the centre of the palace complex. As she left her rooms a short shrill scream made her turn and question the guard on duty,

"It is the eels madam."

The guard bowed not daring to look at Helen whom he knew to be powerful and therefore dangerous. Licking her lips with anticipation she left the palace through the lion's gate eager to see Agamemnon's latest execution. It was a favourite pastime of the king to feed the eels live bait; chickens or even goats. But the most satisfying were slaves, innocent or guilty, who happened to displease him. He would move his face as near as he could to the victim to breathe in their dying breaths as if it sustained him, an elixir. Agamemnon loved how the creatures sensed it was time to eat as soon as his great shadow crossed the water. Their hulking backs breaking the coiling surface. Helen had even seen him speak to the beasts and stroke their backs, whispering to them with affectionate tones. The extended labyrinth of tunnels at Mycenae had been flooded many generations before and no one knew how many monsters lurked in the bowels of the palace, perhaps many thousands. His father Atreus had bred them and had his favourite, a skulking freakishly large beast he had named

Collosses who twisted and thrived in the dark corners of the old tunnels with the strength to crush a man's bones and tear the lips from his face. Agamemnon had had the tail of Collosses pierced with solid gold rings – two men had died attaching them. Helen watched nonchalantly as the man was dragged under the frothing waters.

51

Later that afternoon Agamemnon met his brother Menelaus at the rear of the palace then they both rode northwest beyond the small holdings and past Medea where the earth could not be farmed, a no man's land of fallow earth between Cleonae and Nemea. Menelaus became more puzzled as they rode further from familiar Mycenean territory, he became wary too for he feared his brother and knew what he was capable of,

"Where are we going brother? No man ever passes here."

"That is why we are here."

Agamemnon stopped and dismounted taking an old goatskin water carrier from his horse,

"Something I need to leave behind" he said grinning at his brother. Agamemnon emptied its contents and a human head landed with a thud on the hard ground, the eyes leered through the skin that was drawn away from the black ghoulish grin, ripped apart by the eels. Menelaus gasped and balked drawing in his reins. He recognised Dion, the emissary of Peleus,

"So peace talks don't interest you?"

Agamemnon laughed so for a moment Menelaus thought him half mad and worried for him. Agamemnon kicked the head hard so it rolled over the ground, the eyes loosened and the black teeth scattered. Menelaus knew well the malevolent smile of his older brother,

"Not now, not ever."

"And where is the rest of our friend?"

"In the bowels of Collosses."

52

As the days passed in Larissa Orpheus, Lyria and Achilles became firm friends. The days moved forward and the seasons leaned on each other with a terrible inevitability. Tides of brilliant colour washed over each other. Spring hesitated before bringing parity and pouncing with her green and yellow light. Summer swelled with a fecund pride then brought her fire inland. After their chores the mornings were spent skimming stones in the Peneius river, six, seven, eight jumps. Cerebus barked and swam out after the stones. Then as the sun grew hotter climbing the slippery cliffs where the river ran through the valley glad of their leather sandals to grip the precarious rocks. The capricious visions of earthly love had not yet taken hold of Lyria's thoughts but her whims and fancies, unbeknown to her, were being pulled towards a half conscious heart indescribably sweet. A masculine heart that beat strongly lay waiting very near. As the sun fell in the west the three stared into the horizon. They watched as the sun drenched the trees around them with its dying light so the ground was dappled and stitched with royal gold. And yet only a league away a dead ox lay bloated and stinking in the sun covered with a canopy of flies.

"Apollo has spun a beautiful robe tonight" said Lyria.

Achilles grunted,

"Maybe it's the God of war who is angry."

Lyria smiled to herself. Why do boys talk of war? There are so many more worthwhile things. She scratched the head of Cerebus who looked up adoringly. They sat for what seemed like an age so now the moonlight soaked the ground casting her awkward shadows on the river bank. And then later still a rippling circle of ivory on the river.

"What are you thinking Achilles?"

"I'm standing with Hercules on the bough of a ship. The deep sea salt water is shining red. I can see the dolphins jump and guide our boat; each one the soul of a dead sailor."

"And where are we going?"

"We're sailing with the souls of dead soldiers. Sailing with the wind to Tiryns where Agamemnon hides. He's cowering behind his women."

Achilles turned to Orpheus,

"Are you with us Orpheus?"

But Orpheus was having dreams of his own, fifty fathoms down he dwelt with divine musicians and played for the Muses.

"He's asleep. Come Achilles. Let's swim."

Lyria stepped towards the river but Achilles paused and looked down rather sheepishly,

"I, I'm not a great swimmer."

Lyria was surprised,

"Has no one taught you? Have you never dived for shells?"

Achilles said nothing. Lyria quickly took his hand,

"I can teach you to dive for pearls and shells. To swim."

Achilles felt foolish. What could a girl teach him? Lyria sensed his unease.

"Perhaps there are things you could teach me."

"I am to be a great warrior so the oracles say. I don't feel like a great fighter."

Lyria's heart warmed to him,

"Well, to be a great warrior you must be a great swimmer. Tomorrow we can go to the lake. After the morning chores are done."

Achilles reluctantly agreed.

Lyria raced through the palace grounds under a timid sun that hung in an empty sky. As she ran her shadow ran with her rippling unevenly over the cobbled courtyards then upright alongside her as the candlelit walls threw back their pallid light. This shadow was even in hue and tone but still it seemed to possess the vital qualities of the body that cast it as it slid and screamed silently into the heart of the palace. Until finally with no light to speak of the shadow merged and formed seamlessly into an invisible tear of darkness and died. Lyria sat amongst the discarded amphorae, a hidden arbour she had claimed for her own where she could speak and think unhindered. Lyria liked to speak to herself; fragments of words and songs she put together which helped her understand her heart and feelings. Sometimes she thought for a long time before the words would tumble out and chime their meaning to the walls. Often she would see snakes curling inside the jars, it was a lucky omen to be visited by a snake so Lyria would smile. But now her thoughts and words tripped over each other like the pool crabs she would collect on Lesbos. Achilles. Alone. Lyria was unsure as to whether she shook with fear or excitement.

53

Soon they passed through some low hills and in the distance saw a flash of water. The guide pointed and Lyria broke into a canter,

"Lake Karla."

Formed by the floodwaters of the Peneius Lake Karla lay adjacent to Mount Mavrouni its gentle slopes covered in oak forests descending into the Aegean. Near the waters beech and chestnut flourished and where the streams reached out poplars, elders and willow. Reed huts were scattered by the shore. The air was fresh and so clear that their senses were flooded with all the myriad colours and smells of sky and water. The world sparkled. On the bank the fishermen secured their nets and counted their catch. A small statue of Poseidon watched over them as they worked, an ancient carving polished and revered daily to bring health and prosperity. After speaking to one of the fishermen they secured a boat and were soon out on the water. It was hard work. Sweat appeared on the brow of Achilles. Drops of sunshine fell like rain beading his forehead with pearls of moisture. Lyria wiped his face with her tunic. The small boat swayed and bobbed as she moved but Achilles kept a good rhythm. He felt he wanted to impress Lyria. When he leaned forward with the oars he noticed her twinkling green eyes and snub nose. Her lips were full and her curly red hair although unruly and salt ridden had a wild magnificence about it. He noticed her teeth were bright white like the island girls his father had told him about. Her hands were rough and had seen hard work, her fingernails broken from washing and carrying. 'You can always tell by the fingernails' thought Achilles. 'The servants of Apollo always have smooth hands and skin.' But in that moment when she had wiped his brow it hadn't mattered to Achilles. This simple act had touched him. He was now desperately tired although he was determined not to show it. They were a good way out and the boat rose with the swells. Achilles could see other boats dotted around all with the same purpose,

"This seems a good place. I will dive first. Keep counting Achilles at this speed."

She tapped her heart slowly,

"The speed of your heartbeat. Count fifty times then pull me up or if you feel me tug then pull straight away."

Before Achilles had time to respond Lyria was gone, her body leaving hardly a ripple as if the lake itself had opened up for her. Achilles fed out the rope fast feeding it through the bronze ring that was well oiled. His other hand he kept on his neck counting his heartbeat. One, two, three. How far down was she now? Achilles looked anxiously over the side. Forty three, forty four. It seemed an age since she had dived over. He had held his breath as soon as she had disappeared but had long since exhaled. And then he felt a tug on the rope and he began to haul in the line with both hands wanting to see Lyria was safe. She emerged, water sliding from her skin, her red hair swept from her face and cascading down her back. Drops of water hung from her hair like pearl pendants set in fire. She grabbed the side of the boat and smiled up at Achilles. She felt confident in the water much more so than on land. She knew she could swim and dive well, perhaps better than anyone, certainly better than the priestesses and maidens that Achilles would be used to. She expertly pulled herself over the side of the boat. Achilles helped her and didn't fail to notice her flat stomach and small pert breasts although he tried to look away. She had collected two shells which she showed proudly to Achilles. She regained her breath and before Achilles could say anything she was off over the side again. He quickly fumbled for the rope clumsily trying to find his pulse with his left hand. Two dives, three then four, Achilles wondered at the fitness of Lyria. By the sixth dive she had collected some twenty shells,

"They will receive a good price in the market. I can exchange them for food and oils."

Lyria looked around,

"We have drifted some way out – you had better start rowing."

Achilles obeyed marvelling at her. Was this the same timid girl he played with and teased on land? But now it was his turn. Although his first dives were clumsy he soon felt strong and his confidence grew. After all if a young girl can do it why can't I? Later as they approached Larissa Achilles thought about the day. He looked down at his arms and legs. Yes I can run fast but what use is that? At that moment as he looked at Lyria he devoutly wished to be raised to manhood. Eager to be rid of the boy as a snake sheds its skin, an old cloak to be thrown off. There would be no sentiment. The folly of a child would not be endured, would not be missed.

"Lyria. Why do you think girls can't run fast?"

Her nose wrinkled and her eyes danced with such an infectious exuberance that Achilles laughed but Lyria had had enough of Achilles' gentle teasing.

"I can" she said and sped off down the river bank. Achilles was after her in an instant. He easily caught her but was surprised at her athleticism, the grace and symmetry with which she ran and for a few seconds he paced at her heels watching the movement of her supple legs under her tunic. Lyria, exhausted fell to the sand panting whilst Achilles stood over her laughing. Despite herself Lyria looked up into Achilles' face. Her mouth was dry and the night seemed hotter than usual. She knew she was blushing and felt confused. An age seemed to pass before Achilles knelt and sat beside her. For all his speed Achilles felt suddenly clumsy as he reached out and touched her hair. As if in a trance he followed the line of her neck with his finger. Lyria, flushed and thrilled turned to Achilles,

"What are you thinking now?"

She found her words came from parched lips and a dry throat. She wished she was sophisticated and beautiful like the priestesses. She wished she were wearing her best chiton and sandals. She wished for a lot of things as her mind seemed to race.

Achilles as if suddenly aware of what he'd done stood abruptly. Turning from her he ran off at pace.

54

"The journey will take three days. East to Lemnos then south east to Scopolos and Pagasae."

Phoenix nodded as he unfurled the sail. Any plan that took him near Thessaly was a good one. He placed his hand on Philon's shoulder,

"We may hear of your sister. Someone will know something."

Philon seemed doubtful,

"It is Agamemnon's men who are responsible. My father too. The least I can do is offer allegiance to Peleus. There's little for me here now."

"And your mother Danae?"

"She blesses me."

Philon looked longingly at his home. He remembered the shrine he had built with his sister a mile inland from Mytilene. A fresh spring had burst from the ground drenching them both,

"A shrine to Aphrodite" Lyria had shouted excitedly

"No. Ares, the God of war!" Philon had laughed.

He looked back on the familiar territories of Lesbos as the boat pitched its wake out of Eresos. For a long time he gazed as Phoenix heaved the patched sail into the wind; the high walls of the fortress, the broken roofs and farmsteads, the sleepy valleys resplendent with wild olives and oak and the dusty road from Arisbe to Nape, his childhood home. He remembered how he had planted a palm and a fig. A spring was channeled and tamed. As the years passed he had dreamed of building a courtyard around the spring paved with marble and sandstone from Lydia. Stables would house his horses which would graze in the shade as the palms and figs grew and spread. Perhaps even melon beds such as he had seen in Nubia where the wine flowed in rivers and the gold grew from the desert sands. Store rooms for the finest wines from Seraphos. Living rooms where he would meet his trading partners from Chios and Icaria. Thick rugs from Babylonia would warm his toes in winter as he watched the flames in the giant hearth and then in summer listening to the chorus of horses, waves and women – the snorting and stamping of his beloved mares. Spending the spring coaxing the vines and sniffing the limes. His heart yawned and he wept as his dreams fell away and the island disappeared. And now the dark ocean blue of the early hour had given rise to a deathly grey so the landscape of Lesbos was a penumbra of savage hues and dark shadows. Phoenix knew it was a time for silence and sat unblinking. Men without tongues.

55

On the first day the sea was a dark blue mirror, still and restful breathing heavily under the hot, hirsute sky. On the second day there was a deep swell so Phoenix threw up his meal and groaned through his chores. The wind blew harder bruising the sails and bending them like bows. A dormouse hidden in Phoenix's tunic appeared and looked around uneasily. Philon looked to the sky,

"It is Boreas the north wind."

On the third day within sight of the mainland the storm came bringing its grinding, bellowing intercourse of rain, cloud and thunder. A storm so fierce that every horse in Greece shied and stamped as the world shivered on the cusp of madness. In the sky the clouds converged in battle. They crashed and swore changing shape and colour in an orgasm of deathly greys; the darkest reds lit by a lording sun malevolent and mischievous that turned their boat turtle. Phoenix walked the beach for three days treading the slack water and bracing the neap tide but there was no sign of Philon.

"Great Poseidon, God of the waters. Grant him dry land."

With his heart and soul heavy he bowed his head and turned to Thessaly. He would find Lyria and tell her of her brother, of his good companionship, how he had saved him. His old dreams gradually returned to him and he was emboldened. After a few days Phoenix found his spirits returning. He felt invincible, his stride effortless and arrogant, his muscles in perfect physical unison so the swaggering miles glided by in perpetuity with little strain. And when sleep came it came suddenly, even the stoniest furrow blessing him with sun scented dreams. In those dreams he outran stags and flew with eagles.

56

Peleus often let his prudence give way to his passions and so it was on this morning he was joined by Meriones (who hated the hunt but had seen the carnage caused by the creature) and a handful of huntsmen as he made his way south with the dogs on the trail of a dangerous sounder boar who had attacked, maimed and killed cattle in the area. The morning mist was gossamer thin and they were soon galloping on the heels of the hounds who took up the scent quickly cornering the beast on a marshy piece of ground fronted by a brace of willows. Peleus now well ahead with his blood up rode up to the fearsome beast that snarled and spitted at the dogs. He released his spear just as his horse shied and whinnied throwing him to the ground where he lay still.

The young man watched from a thicket. Instinctively he ran to put himself between the animal and the motionless Peleus. The other riders held back seeing the danger and fearful of provoking the boar further or of releasing their spears and harming the king. The spear thrown by Peleus had hit its target but had seemed to bounce off the boar neither wounding or disabling it. He advanced slowly on the boar naked blade in hand trying to draw him away from Peleus who had begun to stir and having gained enough clarity to read the situation, thought it best to stay still. The boar drew away from the dogs and now made to charge at this new human foe. This was what he wanted, he knew the speed and momentum of the creature would hasten its end if he held his blade true. He would have one chance. The others held their breath as the two stalked and circled each other waiting for the moment.

57

Phoenix had no idea that the man whose life he had saved had been the King of Thessaly but now he knew the truth he was happy to accept his hospitality and favour. Peleus listened patiently to his story and his background,

"Your master had you educated and trained?"

"I was schooled in medicine, military tactics and combat" and then he added smiling,

"and I can cook."

"You can ride and master a horse?"

"Of course."

"Then I have a work for you Phoenix. The man who saved the king of Thessaly deserves no less."

58

The days passed as the sun never set, a ceaseless song, swimming in the Penieus, racing skiffs, skimming stones. Laughter. Thirteen summers now lay flush on Lyria's cheek and the girl searched for the woman as spring looks for summer. Orpheus and Achilles were suddenly taller, the curve of the leg more pronounced and firmer, the voice deeper. The much prized beard began to show on the chin of Achilles. Lyria would hear him giggling and talking of the serving girls who waited on the nobly born. Clandestine meetings and groans from the boys' quarters. Was Achilles taking women to his bed? It was the way of things. Expected. He is a prince and heir. Half the girls in my quarters talk of the handsome Achilles. She knew all this. The girls too giggled and chatted. And yet often at night as the cicadas fell silent all that was left was the sound of her tears. Lyria found herself watching for him, listening for him, turning at the opening of every door or the mention of his name. She followed the paths he had trodden, sat in the seat where she'd spied him eating, picked up objects she knew he had handled and dumbly caressed them. When he visited the kitchen with Peleus she would catch the scent of pomegranates and olives which she knew were rubbed into his legs to make them supple. She would sit by and watch him with Orpheus juggling or wrestling and for a moment it seemed as if her eyes were fixed, locked and frozen into the pale blue ice of his eyes. She would panic; feel a redness in her cheek. As for Achilles she couldn't guess. Did he seem to turn away? Sometimes it was too much for her and she would run, ashamed, angry and confused hiding between the sacks of grain and barley in the vast storeroom beneath the palace.

59

Peleus had sent for his son.

"You are to meet him at the stables."

This had been the only instruction from the surly guard who had thought this straightforward message was beneath him. Why couldn't they send a kitchen boy? I am a soldier not a messenger. Achilles decided to take the long road by the Penieus. To his right the river twinkled blue and silver bright. 'This is the river that will flow into the western ocean' thought Achilles, 'the home of Odysseus the peacemaker.' The air grew warmer as he walked, the woods thicker and the fruit trees more luxuriant. What does my father want? Achilles was aware of an expectation. He saw it in the eyes of the people who bowed and spoke in whispers as he passed. He knew of the inevitability of war, of the threat of Agamemnon. But still he didn't feel like a true fighter though sometimes he dreamt of a fighter who had no thought of himself – no thought of victory or defeat. Achilles arrived at the stables just as dawn with her rosy fingers parted the crimson clouds. The king was stood alone whilst four or five horses stood around him and nuzzled him affectionately. Achilles gasped. They were all magnificent. But one horse stood apart, a black amongst so many greys and browns he stood proud with a graceful lean head. 'A horse for Zeus himself' Achilles thought as he watched him whinny and nudge his friends playfully. Peleus beckoned Achilles over as the horses gathered around glad to make a new friend.

"If you have an unbroken colt Achilles you must test his body. Firstly and most importantly look at his feet. I don't care about his height or colour, his muscular flanks. If he has bad feet he is good for nothing. Thick horn is better than thin."

Peleus lifted the bent leg of the animal which didn't seem to care about being handled,

"We want a high and hollow hoof. A low hoof Achilles and he will walk like your bandy legged grandmother. Listen, the good hollow hoof will sound like a high drum when it hits the ground."

He led the horse around the stable and sure enough the sound on the stone was sharp and true. Achilles marvelled at how the beast followed Peleus's every command watching and waiting for him, man and beast in unison.

"Now look below the fetlock, if they are straight up and down they will make for uncomfortable riding, no spring. Look for a stout shank boy as this will support the body but no excess fat or veins. Veins will swell over a long campaign and spread to the back creating lameness. Your life may forfeit."

"I want the strongest horse sir with the broadest chest."

"But always in proportion Achilles. The broad chest will set the legs well apart so they don't cross each other and stumble. See how his nostrils are wide?"

Achilles stepped forward and noted the hand width between the nostrils.

"Why does that matter?"

"It makes for easier breathing and a stronger disposition to unnerve the enemy. And see how the small ears are set well apart too, it leaves a large poll."

At last Achilles heard the words he was longing to hear,

"Sit on him Achilles."

With the help of his father Achilles was soon sat on the back of the horse surprised at how comfortable he felt. How high I am! It's the first time I have ever looked down on the king. Peleus stood back and breathed in as he always did when he was about to say something of note,

"Achilles, listen hard. This is a Bucephalian, bred on the

plains of Thessaly for hundreds of generations, no other horse is swifter, stronger or as loyal. This horse is coveted by kings and princes. And Xanthos is the best of them. Look at his small jaw so his eyes can see better; he can see what lies below, beyond and around. He does not need to stretch his neck or arch for want of sight. He was a gift from the seabound Carian king. They are a race far to the south Achilles. They are known for their strong navy and talented bowmen."

"I love him."

"That's good. He is yours. But you must never ride him alone. Not till you are ready. I will have Phoenix tutor you."

Phoenix, watching from a distance smiled and returned to his rooms.

60

That night Achilles, breathless with excitement crept past Leucippus the old guard who was slumped on his haunches after another night of indulgence in his favourite nut brown ale. Achilles kept to the shadows as the moon was high throwing its black and silver shadows over the courtyard and stables. The night air was as soft as a bridal embrace as he mounted the beast. Xanthos, upright and fractious was surprised as Achilles unbridled him and snorted. But he remembered the boy.

"Quiet Xanthos, we will ride out."

With his beautiful black flanks and Achilles sat strong and proud their figures were carved from metal and moonlight as they cantered out of the stables turning left onto the path that led to the river. The night air was scented by the vineyards as the blushing moon searched in vain for cover – it was the clearest of nights. A rabbit that appeared on the path in front of them seemed transfixed for a moment before it scurried out of view. This was enough for the usually stoic Xanthos who bolted ahead as Achilles hung around his neck with a deathlike grip. The tighter he held the faster he sped so in an instant they were by the Peneius leaping over dunes and dips on the fringe of the river. Becoming vaguely aware of a horse galloping on his right hand side Achilles glimpsed the grim visage of Phoenix his body barely visible amongst the hooves, mud and debris that both horses were now throwing up. Achilles was now only a length ahead of the rapidly gaining Phoenix,

"Almighty Zeus, stop him!"

Achilles with his arms wrapped around the neck of the stallion could feel the beating heart of the horse as his head pressed against his powerful neck. He clung tighter but the tighter he held the faster Xanthos sprinted ahead. And then in an instant he saw Phoenix's riderless horse overtake him and felt the breath of his master and mentor on his own neck,

"Don't turn around."

Xanthos turned to the river, whinnied then cantered as Phoenix dug his heels and thighs into his flanks with an inhuman strength. Xanthos trotted, shook his head then cooled his hooves in the shallow moonlit waters of the Peneius that ran smooth and clear.

"That's twice I've saved Thessaly. The king and his heir. They should make me ruler."

When they returned to the stables Achilles was expecting a reprimand, shouting, threats or worse but Phoenix surprised him.

"This is Xanthos, a gift at your father's wedding. He needs washing every evening. He is calmer in the moonlight. Wash from the fetlocks down."

Phoenix bowed and left. Achilles decided he liked him.

61

Achilles didn't yet know if he was brave or what true courage was. But he knew he was swift.

"Let's race to the bend in the river."

"But that's too far" complained Orpheus

"Then just to the first rock."

"But…."

"Go!"

Before Orpheus had time to complain Achilles set off at a pace his quick feet racing along the bank. Orpheus ran hard after his friend but it was no good.

"You cheated."

"How?"

"I'm faster than you anyway Achilles. I could beat Hermes in a foot race."

The boys sat panting. Lyria dangled her feet in the river and smiled to herself. Even though it was early the sun was still hot on their backs.

"One day I will beat you Achilles."

"I will make a pact with you. You teach me the lyre and I will teach you to run."

Orpheus often brought his lyre and played whilst they talked and laughed. Now he began playing at speed,

"My fingers move faster than your feet Achilles."

Achilles nodded. Even in the crib Orpheus had delighted in making rattles from pods and dried seeds and as he grew, drums of stretched skin on hollowed logs, gongs from beaten bronze and pipes from hollow bones and hollowed out horns that his mother made for him. But his father took them away and buried them, disappointed that his boy took more interest in feminine pursuits. He thrust a spear in his hand and replaced the drum with the shield and Orpheus turned inward and sullen till his father thought him backward and beat him.

"What you can do is truly beautiful" said Achilles, "any fool can throw a spear Orpheus. But you. Your gift. You can make the trees bend their branches. Apollo said the lyre and the curved bow shall be his special care. You see Orpheus, together we make both halves of Apollo. Play for us now."

It was true that a stillness surrounded Orpheus as he played. The moon would freeze and the willow stooped to hear. Lyria sighed as the notes reached out and placed their arms around her. Achilles relaxed but deep inside he was troubled. Why does everyone assume I can fight? I don't feel strong or brave. Orpheus placed his lyre aside.

"But I want to fight like you Achilles. I have to attend military training. It's compulsory. I have my first induction soon."

"I will come and watch." Achilles stood quickly,

"What? What is it?" asked Lyria.

"Can't you hear?"

Lyria and Orpheus shook their heads. Then they saw. In the distance two soldiers approached on horseback at speed. Very soon they halted before Achilles. Dressed in full battle dress they were formal, fearsome,

"We are asked to take you before the king prince Achilles. And you too Lyria."

"But we are happy here." He turned to Lyria pleased with himself.

The guards looked awkwardly at one another and then back to Achilles.

"We have our orders prince." He prepared to dismount but the other soldier raised his hand and bade him stay where he was. Achilles recognised him, it was Parentos. He had played dice with him before. He was one of the king's most trusted soldiers. He dismounted and walked over to Achilles and gently placed his hand on his shoulder. A short time later Achilles and Lyria were galloping across the fields with the two men.

62

"If you are to leave us Helen we must recompense Pipituna the Goddess of love and fertility."

The *Klawiphorus* Chione stood before Helen. She wore a skirt in the Cretan style, no strophian, hair dyed, tied and patterned with buckweed and herbs. Her breasts were bare and fully displayed. A necklace of gold fashioned as a serpent with amber eyes rested on the curve of her bosom. Secretly she was pleased Helen was leaving. She would miss her body but not her ambition. Around her stood the old statues of Peragia and the demi-gods now all but forgotten by the Greeks. Chione stood tall, even Agamemnon himself was said to fear her. The rumour in Mycenae was she was an Amazon and had deserted her tribe to avoid the ritual cauterization and removal of her left breast; the fate awaiting all Amazons to aid them in combat and make the drawing of the bow more efficient. The smell of poppy seeds was strong and the temple was filled with a curious blue haze left by the burning of the raw opium. It was a smell Helen knew well. She knelt before the priestess,

"You are the new moon Helen. We wax and wane, hunt and kill. Did you know that all things grow as the moon waxes and freeze when it wanes? The only boy born to me is the sun. We must tear his body and mix it with the seed so we have a strong harvest. When I was first initiated I companied with five men. The children I bore were all boys so were thrown back to the earth."

Helen gazed up at Chione,
"When?"

"Tonight."

"Where?"

"By the elm grove and the cypress, the tree of the dark Gods. Where the river turns."

Helen bowed and left to prepare.

63

Tonight the *Megaron* was reserved for the religious rituals. Helen stood in the centre of the room with her arms held high whilst her servants sluiced her with scented water. The water cascaded off her slightly tanned skin and full breasts. She was shaven all over as was the Spartan way. The light, blonde down on her arms and legs softened with hot walnut shells. The walls were decorated with elaborate frescoes, the floor made of coloured marble and lapis lazuli. Eight columns rose in a circle around the central fire and it was here that Ashia the mistress of the water gently tipped the contents of the jug over Helen. The fragrant liquid was perfumed with roses and jasmine and gave off a delicious scent. Five priestesses surrounded Helen as she walked to the anointing chamber their eyes focused on the floor. Helen, naked, enjoyed the touch of the shaven headed acolytes as they smeared her body with rich oils made from honey and bitter almonds. The salve was scented with cinnamon, lilies and terebinth resin which gave the skin around her thighs and buttocks a smoother feel. Ashia crouched in front of Helen who nodded her approval as she licked and teased her,

"A woman's body is a sacred altar Helen. And pleasure is a pathway to Peragia and the doves."

Helen lay back enjoying the attentions of this servant of Pipituna. Nearby stood a maidservant holding in her hand a bottle of kohl mined and crushed then fetched from the mountains of the Red Sea. With infinite care the kohl was applied around each eye with an ivory brush. Crimson for the lips, white lead for the complexion and henna powder; a combination of potions so potent that after the application she often had to be revived with a mixture of rare white and pink lotus blossoms. Finally as the sun sank deeper into the horizon and with a garland of irises and jasmine held at her bosom she was ready to meet the Priestess. Chione, who had watched her preparations through a carefully constructed peephole with lascivious delight, scurried to the river to await her arrival.

64

The sun was almost out of view as Helen left the palace and walked through the outbuildings and smallholdings to the crook of the river. Although the darkness was falling quickly she felt safe. If any man were to even look at her he risked a meeting with the eels. Helen smiled to herself. The execution had been an interesting one. The Thessalian spy had died well. Perhaps Achilles was just as brave. Well, I will find out. What was the name of the man who died? Helen couldn't remember. Her skin now shone white gleaming like a polished pearl in the moonlight as she made her way slowly to meet with Chione and her servants. Her hair had been curled and shaped with a bow comb from Sparta and sparkled with olive oil so it hung in long ringlets around her shoulders. She knew what to expect. Helen was the last to arrive. The twelve girls were sat within the circle of small statues of the old Gods by the bend in the river. As Helen took her place Chione stood and spoke. She was dressed in a white robe held with a silver sash. Her hair was tightly bound and scraped from her head, jet black and shining with oil. As she looked at the girls each one seemed to melt – a look as beguiling as sleep or death. They were at once fearful yet drawn to her. The wind died down as she whispered, the girls already enraptured,

"Goddess, my heart is seized with desire. For hearing a new song in this chorus of girls in lovely melody will leave me to sweet sleep where I'll be tossing my black hair. A dance of delicate feet with limb loosening desire."

Her voice rose as she finished. She then paused and raised

her arms. Looking to the sky her eyes caught the moonlight. She then walked a few steps to the trunk of an elm tree that stood strong and erect. The sweet wind gently kissed its upper boughs so they trembled slightly as Chione approached. She beckoned for the girls to follow. Slowly they rose and stood around her. Helen licked her lips in anticipation. Warily she looked to her left at the young girls who would one day be priestesses – some may even serve the oracle. But for the moment all Helen saw was the full bosom and rounded thighs of her peers as they stood transfixed. For some it would be their first time. Taking a flagon of oil she threw it over the bark so it fell in rivulets, slowly making its way to the base. Walking around Chione poured the oil.

"Helen."

Helen followed her and kneeling down began to massage the bark slowly. She threw her arms around the base using her chest to spread the oil. Then stepping back she lay on the ground as Chione knelt over her and shouted for the young virgins to follow Helen,

"Revere me. I am Helen's tree. We shall be the first to plait for you a wreath of ground loving clover. And we shall be the first to make an offering of gleaming oil dripped from our silver flasks under this tree's shade. In its bark we shall write this message. Respect me. I am Helen's tree!"

The girls now repeated the words, some howled them to the night sky rubbing themselves against the elm and each other,

"Revere me. Helen's beauty is like the return of spring."

The girls were now all lost as they laughed and held hands, dancing in the midnight blue river. As the opium took hold nothing mattered to Helen. It was a torrent of talk where words were sent out into the darkness. They chased and collided. Helen knew that real power came from beauty and death.

"Don't be afraid. With death comes freedom."

She jabbed the knife quickly through the ribs, then twisted and thrust upwards as Chione screamed and the girls cackled and caught the blood in bowls. Then with that sudden clarity that comes to all on the cusp of oblivion she spoke clearly and firmly,

"Build her a beehive tomb. Bury her jawbone and naval string to remind her that she was born of a woman. Burn the rest. I am *Klawiphorus*."

65

Peleus walked through the great oak door to visit the temple built by his father Aeacus to honour Ares the God of war. Outwardly he paid homage to the Gods but inwardly he doubted their credence. Wisely he kept his own counsel on this conveying the outward appearance of a reverent and obsequious servant of Olympus. Standing before the statue, legs astride it was his habit to speak at the God telling him of his plans. But a gentle knock on the temple door made him turn around. A soldier entered.

"Yes?"

"Lyria and prince Achilles. They say you sent for them."

"I did. Thank you Demosthenes."

Demosthenes, an overzealous guard who was keen to be promoted bowed and left. Peleus walked to greet Lyria and placed his arm around her shoulder.

"Your father told me you are a great swimmer. He was proud of you. The swiftest on the island, boy or girl."

Lyria blushed.

"You are blessed. I have been told of everything your father did for me and what you have done for my son."

There was a pause whilst Peleus looked hard at Lyria. She appeared a little small to him. He shrugged,

"Helen of Mycenae is arriving tomorrow. She is *Klawiphorus*, high priestess. Come to spy no doubt but don't let that worry you. You are to attend to her Lyria. Give her everything she requires. Report to the bedchambers where you will be given further instruction. Serve her well Lyria. Now leave us."

Lyria left the room with a mixture of emotions; excited but nervous about her new role. Peleus and Achilles were left alone. He turned to his son,

"You are to leave with Phoenix."

Peleus turned away and continued,

"You are to spend time with him, to be educated by him, far from here. I trust him with your safety just as I trusted him with mine. He saved my life."

The words had a curious effect on Achilles. It was no surprise that he was to be tutored. That was expected of a prince of Thessaly. It was that his father had never openly taken an interest in his education. He had always been civil, never hurt his feelings. He has always respected my independence. But he has never let me close to him. Achilles loved his father, knew he could talk with him, was full of wisdom. But then just as quickly he would abandon him, dismiss him with a word. His great hand would push him aside.

"Yes sir."

There was a short silence. Achilles looked to the ground uncomfortably.

"Take this sword Achilles."

Peleus lifted a fleece that was covering an exquisite sword. Its handle was silver bronze leading to a blade that even now almost blinded Achilles as it caught the sunlight. Peleus handed it to his son. Achilles was amazed at its lightness, how it had a life and balance all of its own. Peleus smiled,

"It was of great use to me when I sailed with Jason for the fleece. All swords are forged from the earth Achilles. They have come from the earth and will one day return to it just like us. They are only borrowed like our lives which are a brief flash of light between two eternal darknesses. But you will blaze and run Achilles like a star that shoots across the sky."

Achilles stood silently, overwhelmed by his father's words and the beauty of the sword. Eventually he spoke,

"Shall I leave, is there anything else father?" And then he added,

"When?"

Peleus thought for a moment before replying,

"Soon. I will give word."

As an afterthought he continued,

"Have you noticed Alope? She serves in the great hall and works in the stable. Pretty. They say she watches for you."

He dismissed his son curtly and then searched absently for his favourite cloak. He heard the door shut and then finally turned, his eyes full of tears. He looked to the hills. There was a knock on the great door and Meriones entered. Without turning to face his ally Peleus spoke.

"It is time to unravel this Mycenean. Dion is clearly dead. Take a detachment to Delphi. Tell me of any irregularities. Any sign of his posturing report to me."

Meriones left quickly. At last, some decisive action from this hesitant king.

66

Achilles hid and watched from the dark of the olive grove. The flares lit up the barracks. Phoenix was stood instructing the boys. Many families put forward their boys for military training to instill discipline and perhaps get them a head start in a military career which could be lucrative. Some came from as far as Thrace and Messenia to receive expert instruction. Achilles could see from his stiff back and gait that Phoenix was speaking sternly to the new recruits. He suddenly spotted Orpheus stood in line with the others. As he was now officially a citizen of Thessaly he was expected to attend military classes once a month and more as he grew older. Achilles chuckled to himself. The other boys were well developed and muscular for their age. Orpheus looked out of place. Phoenix looked hard at the boys rubbed his chin and sighed. Why had Peleus put him in charge of new recruits? He approached a boy on the front row who seemed a little more alert and eager than the rest of the group.

"What is your name boy and where are you from?"

"I am Polites servant of Priam from the harbour of Troy in Anatolia."

Phoenix was impressed. Troy was well known for its tough fighters.

"Does King Priam not have an army for you to serve?"

"He is idealistic master Phoenix. I will fight for Hector when he comes to the throne of Troy. Until then I will seek my fortune elsewhere."

Phoenix ordered them to run barefoot around the courtyard

with a heavy sack of sand on their backs. He then disappeared into the makeshift barrack room. Very soon the boys became fatigued until one by one they dropped their heavy burden. Orpheus was one of the first. Achilles laughed to himself and watched as one of the other recruits stood over him,

"Call yourself a soldier? Why don't you leave the fighting to the men? Go and play your lyre! See how far that will get you in battle."

The boy named Solon then kicked Orpheus as he lay on the ground. This was too much for Achilles who ran at him with his head down and pushed him to the ground. Solon, badly winded stood up shocked. The rest of the recruits gathered round. Phoenix was still busy in the barracks,

"So, prince Achilles. Come to protect your lover perhaps? Are you ready for a beating? Everyone has seen you started this."

The two circled each other slowly. Achilles noticed how big the boy was, brawny and sinewy. Solon suddenly lurched at Achilles. Achilles stepped to the side as Solon careered past him. He was surprised how easy it was to evade his attack. Again Solon threw a punch and missed. Achilles was making this opponent look comical. Solon was incensed. He threw himself at Achilles and caught his leg taking him to the ground but Achilles managed to break free and kicked Solon in the chest as he rose. This seemed to take the fight out of him but by now Phoenix had appeared. The fight was over. Achilles' stock had risen considerably,

"Did you see how swiftly the young prince moved?"

The recruits never forgot what they saw that day.

67

Achilles took a closer look at her, her beautiful olive skin like that of the southern islanders, her brown shoulder length hair that she tossed behind her. For a moment she reminded him of a young thoroughbred mare, the flowing hair and her gaminesque, ingenuous grace. He remembered the words of a priestess,

"The man who avoids dance, wine and women remains a fool all his life."

They had now reached the riverside and the night held its breath. How had they got here? Achilles didn't know and realised suddenly he didn't care. Nothing made sense to Achilles at that moment. Nothing but this beautiful girl. Her dress was in the Cretan style, coloured and open to the waist. She began to undress giggling. For Achilles it was infinitely sensual, almost too much and he drew back. Alope looked to the sky,

"Look, I can see Andromeda."

Achilles couldn't bear to take his eyes from her. She looked at him and smiled. It was a faultless smile and his virginity was lost in a single glance. He suddenly felt the blood draining from his face. He knew exactly where it was heading.

"I'm told you watch for me."

Achilles could think of nothing else to say. He knew it was expected of him that he should take women but he hadn't expected this. They both stood and faced each other. A little nervous laughter. Achilles reached out as Alope spoke,

"Don't be afraid to love me."

Achilles dared to catch a glimpse of her secret breasts. An

amethyst which rested on her chest caught his eye. Achilles decided he liked her hair. But the lust would always come through for it is a powerful beast, all conquering and quick to the battle. And then there was the moonlight bathing the contours of her face and the irregular shadows provided by their dancing limbs as they stuttered and swam then fell to the floor and began to drown. Her embrace is warm. I like her arms around me. Let me roll my tongue around her breasts like golden apples and kiss her honey hair. Oh comforting dust…

68

The word spread quickly that Achilles had taken a lover. Lyria was teased.
"Achilles is a man. Did you know Lyria?"
"I hear he is a big boy."
'He may sleep with others but they mean nothing to him' she thought. She hated him but she knew that hate was only love in waiting. He is faithful to me with his heart and mind. And so the sophistries of sweet love sustained her. Lyria was now in her fourteenth year and she was a flame. As such all eyes were drawn towards her. Like the jewel she was she shone. Her unkempt hair reflected the sun with a million iridescent rays, the moon on the water, her face timid white; the moon staggering and leaning low with a whisper. All men wanted to embrace the fire of her. All but one it seemed. From her still deep sleep Lyria turned and sighed as Achilles appeared thus her waking and sleeping hours became one long lament. In the day the tone and hue of her dreams would remain, a taste on her tongue, a tug on her heart as she walked, her longing as relentless as the tides just as his hair rose and fell through her fingers, the moonstruck miles winding and wooing. Lyria whispered her affections on the cusp of sleep then shimmered in his arms dancing and singing strange songs in coloured lights. But always she would wake up alone. Lyria knew that to speak with anyone would open her to ridicule. Prince Achilles? Forget him Lyria. I've heard Leodes the stable hand speak your name. What's wrong with him? So it was her own private despair and she would have been torn limb from limb rather than disclose it even though it was clear to all who knew her. But still the dreams continued.

69

Meriones, leader of the Perrhaebi tribe followed the sandy track eastwards as darkness fell over an unremarkable landscape. They could just make out a dark mass in the distance. As the wind turned a sound emerged in the purple twilight; a high pitched moan. Like a note from a musical instrument it hung on the air. Some of the men gripped each other in fright. Meriones spoke,

"It is the singing statue. It always makes the same noise when the wind blows. It's not to be feared."

In this eerie manner the gigantic Delphic oracle on the slopes of Mount Parnassus lumbered towards them. Their pace quickened as the air became suddenly charged with atmosphere.

"The priestess must be found and brought to me."

The men spread out and advanced nervously. The Delphic oracle. Shrine to Apollo. The very centre of the world! Zeus had released two eagles in opposite directions and here was where they'd crossed. As the men edged nearer the outer perimeters of the temple they gasped in fear, some fell to their knees and wept in disbelief. The ground was strewn with bodies, lifeless, put to the sword in this holiest of places. Meriones, filled with anger ran to the main shrine stumbling in the darkness;

"Phthia?"

In the inner sanctum he lit his torch and saw the upended spear with the head of the Pythoness Phthia the priestess attached staring with sightless eyes. Her ears and nose had been hacked off. He dropped his torch to the ground and was sick where he stood.

"Agamemnon."

70

Every year Antigonus of Tricca a farmer of middle years avoided the fallowing where the land was ploughed to break up the soil and destroy the weeds. This time it was the green fallowing. Anciles, his son, needed to plough the barley under to build up the soil then let the flocks graze to make it rich again. It was back breaking work and Antigonus's illnesses and neuroses always coincided neatly.

"If I sweat I may die" he said solemnly.

As the hired helots toiled he took to his bed with a new ailment each one more severe than the last. But even by his standards his latest malady was extreme. Antigonus was seized with a disease of the chest. His self delusion was that great he knew he was to die. With no thought of an offering to Asclepius he spoke to his eldest son Anciles,

"Build me a grave."

Anciles wept but obeyed digging the grave by the wayside on the outside of their boundary farm, a privilege afforded all *Periokoi* and freemen of Thessaly. Antigonus, certain of a quick death yet mindful of a lingering one (he packed wine, cheese and bread) lay in it. His dog Hermes lay by his side and barked at the moon.

71

Antigonus, two weeks now in his 'grave' ate his dinner whilst his wife Claryta, with child for two moons, looked on with her son.

"The end is soon dear wife. Where is the wine?"

Claryta folded her arms and turned to Anciles,

"It is his mind that is sick. Not his body. He was always lazy. Why can't he just say he hates farming? This happens every year before the harvest – an illness or injury. He will recover."

She had married him because he had made her laugh and women prize laughter above all things but passion. But now as the years passed she could disregard the passion and humour as long as the ox was yolked and the fields farmed. They left him for another night. Later he was woken by a low growl from Hermes, a sure sign that someone was approaching. Antigonus leaned forward and looked down the dusty track over the cusp of his grave to see a man laden with armour, sword and shield striding through the blue twilight.

"Can you tell me the way to Larissa?"

The man bent on one knee to address Antigonus who gave him his answer. The man, keeping his counsel despite his urge to ask Antigonus why he lay in a hole in the ground with his dog, strode on.

"Wait. Who do you fight for and why?"

"For Peleus of course. There is to be a war in the south."

"Against whom?"

"Against the Mycenean tyrant."

Macedon, an escaped slave from the Troad, continued onwards until the silence surged back and the only sound was the goat bells ringing in the hills in nearby Tricca.

72

Claryta rushed back to the house still carrying her husband's breakfast,

"Anciles! Anciles! He has gone. Come quickly."

Anciles, who had already set the men to work and was about to start his breakfast rose disgruntled from his meal and followed his hysterical mother down to Antigonus's 'grave.' He was the shrewdest and wisest of Antigonus's sons and wasn't in the least surprised. They both looked down at the empty hole in ground. No sign of Antigonus. Hermes attached to a post looked mournful.

"If only you could speak Hermes. Perhaps the Gods took him."

Anciles was doubtful but comforted his mother as they returned to their home. He had a shrewd idea of where his father would be but now was not the time to mention it to his distraught mother. She would recover sooner than she knew.

73

As *Klawiphorus* it was easy for Helen to gain access to information concerning the whereabouts of Achilles at any given time, his princely duties, when he was most likely to be alone. As a priestess she was feared. Helen knew she must flatter him, show deference and charming acquiescence to his status, she must light the fires that had burned so brightly in her previous victims. They must meet accidently and to her best advantage. He must learn that only in her, Helen of Sparta and *Klawiphorus*, could he confide. She must appear loyal to Thessaly in word and deed. In truth Helen was glad to be rid of the stink of Mycenae with its military drills and regimented days, its male prostitutes with their oiled bodies and scarifications; she despised their long black hair and painted lips. She looked in the mirror and gazed at herself, her saturnine features showing no emotion. The strophian supported her breasts. Her himation was properly arranged, the solid gold plates sewn into the borders reflecting her good breeding, her veil lowered. She had chosen a light scent of cyperus and sage with a hint of olive oil. Her silver rings were Minoan and engraved with great skill, her long hair curled in front of her ear. A single necklace of carnelian and amber hung around her neck. She was ready. Helen knew that Achilles would walk the hills on an evening. It was one of the few times he was left alone. It wasn't long before their paths crossed. It was early evening and the sun, tired with her day's work sank to her knees with her arms outstretched across the entire horizon. Achilles in his brazen manner simply stared,

"You" he started "are beautiful."

It was nothing less than Helen had heard a hundred times before. She expected it. She demanded it. Achilles continued,

"You are the Mycenean. Helenaise? Something tells me you have a face that means trouble."

In the cold subterranean chasms of her consciousness Helen congratulated him on his insight. From a young age she had dealt in subterfuge and lies, at first to survive but then because she liked it and knew nothing else. It was a second skin. The truth was another land, a fruit she had rarely tasted. And now she had spat the seed so far away that even if she spent a whole lifetime looking for it she would never find it or even recognise it if she did.

"You dance and skip and tease the young men. All are left panting. That's what I hear. All waiting a moon's length for a smile, a word."

"Do you believe everything you hear prince of Thessaly?"

"No."

Achilles sat down and as he did so reached out bringing Helen with him. His liaisons with the voluptuous Alope had given him confidence. They now lay side by side on a bed of basil. Above their heads a bee busied itself searching for its next flower. Achilles, with the arrogance of a prince moved to kiss her. She looked at Achilles and paused. For once in her life her sexual allure wasn't enough. She wanted all of Achilles, to be loved by him. And to give in so easily would spell doom for her plans.

"Is that all you want from me? Just the act? Sex is so cheap."

"What else could I want from you Helen? What else could I give you?"

Achilles was ready to leave, to forget her. For every girl that rebuked him he now knew there were many more who would take him in their arms. Helen raged although her appearance remained demure, always controlled. How could he simply want my body and nothing else? Doesn't he worship me like all the others? Doesn't he love me? The strange irony twisted her heart, that it was she who had rejected him and yet it felt like just the opposite. This boy was prepared to brush her to one side, to humble her. She knew she was in the presence of royalty, a royalty that seemed eternal, not the gaudy crown the sons of Atreus had stolen. A line of blood that stretched back to the Gods themselves. And Achilles was the newest bloom, the living incarnate of the Penthelid dynasty. Helen had never met anyone who didn't want her completely. She was the ultimate trophy and here was someone with blood so much bluer than her own but equally someone she could not punish with her blatant infidelities. Someone who didn't care? Helen's heart beat faster. So now the huntress was disarmed, Artemis without her arrows! If she couldn't have his heart and soul she would have his life. The thought of his death excited her as he entered her and pulled her desire towards its darkest heart; her mind fed on these solicitudes, those most secret and sybaritic thoughts that are a part of every sexual act. If she couldn't have his love she would have his life. She cared nothing now for the orders of Agamemnon. She only wanted revenge though her honeyed eyes still gazed upon him adoringly. Suddenly his kisses weren't perfunctory, they thrilled her and fuelled her ardour. She ran her tongue slowly along her lips and smiled. If Achilles had seen that smile he would surely have been scared.

74

Not for the first time she gazed in wonder at the bee that furrowed and buried itself in the flower at her feet. Lyria knew the bee was the creature that bridged the natural world with the underworld.

"Your honey is a gift from heaven, the food of the Gods and a symbol of knowledge and wisdom. The priestess at Delphi drank the honey before she chewed the laurel leaf of Apollo."

Crouching she stared intently at the temporal perfection of its exquisitely formed wings that whispered,

"I gave Apollo the gift of prophecy."

And now she rested so the sun flecked her transluscent wings with patterns of gold and yellows that complemented her body like a perfect cloak. If only I had a garment so beautiful. It reminded Lyria of the cloaks spun far to the south on the banks of the Nile by the priestesses of Isis, five moons in the making. And yet this perfect balance of beauty was here for her to see, this miracle of nature. She reached forward to touch the creature only for its wings to spring to life. It rose unsteadily heavy with its drink and flew towards the orchards then the low hills beyond. Her sharp eyes followed it until it became the tiniest of specks. Lyria wondered. Does she feel the pain that I sometimes feel? Is there something it is like to be her? What secrets does she have? These questions returned to the child again and again as she wandered the countryside. As yet she had found no answers that satisfied her. She was wearing her favourite chiton recently imported from Mysia. She had bought it with the shells she had dived for with Achilles. It was full length linen with wide billowing sleeves.

She felt very grand. She began walking towards the olive groves through the scattered farms; the vines hung gracefully from the low trellises, heavy and rich, full of seed, soothed by the songs of the crickets. Lyria smiled as she thought of Achilles and Orpheus whittling sticks to make cages for the insects. She always made sure they escaped to the boys' annoyance. The river ran narrow as she left Larissa. A recent rainstorm made the air pungent with odours. The oleanders and sweet pea perfumed the air with a bitter scent their pink blossoms scattered at her feet. The only sound now was a drowsy bee that seemed to follow Lyria. Was it the same one she had seen earlier? Lyria liked to think so. It hung in front of her now as if leading her to a secret destination. But then an unfamiliar sound halted her. A sound like a boar or snuffling pig. It seemed to be coming from a short distance away from behind some thick undergrowth just by the road. As she drew nearer the creature breathed heavily. As always her curiosity overcame her fear and she crept nearer looking beyond the bush. The blood drained from her so she felt faint and cold. She turned away taking a few light steps then ran down the dusty path her new chiton dragging and snaring, the tears running down her face.

75

Helen turned to Lyria who was busy arranging the bedding,

"You will brush my hair whilst I sit."

To Helen all servants were objects, less than human. Lyria turned and looked up unsure as to whether Helen was speaking to her. Helen wasn't pleased with her hesitation,

"Girl, do you know who I am? I am an emissary of Agamemnon."

Lyria knew exactly who she was and what she had been doing that afternoon. She looked at her and was struck by her piercing eyes and shining golden hair. Her smell was sharp and sweet reminding her of the citrus vines on Lesbos,

"Of course my lady. I will put these blankets away."

Lyria wasn't ready for what happened next. Without warning Helen rose from her chair and struck out at Lyria with her open hand. Lyria fell and cowered, the laundry scattered over the floor. She could feel her cheek burning. She instinctively raised her arms to protect herself,

"Do you not hear me you bitch slave?"

Lyria looked up. Helen had her fist clenched and spoke slowly through clenched teeth. Her face was suddenly not so beautiful. At the doorway Helen's companion Eurypylos smiled,

"You…will…brush…my…hair…now."

Lyria was too scared to speak or even move. She looked again at Helen and noticed her features suddenly soften. Eurypylos stood to one side and Achilles entered. 'That is why her face has changed' thought Lyria recognising with alarm the leg and dress of Achilles.

"What has happened here? Let me help you Lyria."

Lyria, still startled, rose. Helen bent down to help her with the laundry,

"Oh dear, we are clumsy aren't we. No harm. Now Lyria dear, if you could plait my hair tonight I would be grateful."

Helen smiled benignly. Lyria was amazed. This woman had attacked her only seconds before. A small part of her felt like warning Achilles. She felt more protective of him than of herself. But what could she say? So she merely bowed and left taking a deep breath as she left the room. She glanced at Achilles and he smiled at her. She could smell pomegranates and oil. She felt suddenly weak but wasn't sure if it was fear of Helen or excitement at seeing Achilles that made her heart beat faster. Her cheek still blushed red.

"Lyria, I'd like to talk with you later. Can I see you?"

"I'm working."

"I'll come and find you."

Helen noted the gentleness in his voice as he spoke to Lyria and didn't like it.

76

Antigonus and Macedon strode on,
"Larissa is where Peleus holds court."
"But if we fight we sail from Pagasae" said Antigonus, "so let's get a head start. And we will need to conscript."

Macedon looked doubtful,

"Conscript? If you are *Perioikoi* then that will be enough, and you can second me."

"Well I might need to know a little more about you." Antigonus was only half joking.

"There's not a lot to tell. Do you want to hear?"

Antigonus nodded, "it will pass the time."

Macedon shrugged.

"I stowed with my brother Cratylus from Eretria across the blue water to Delium then north through Boeotia hiding in the hot days. We were slaves to a gentile family in Troy who served the young Priam. I heard them speak of the desecration of Agamemnon at Delphi. So we forced our way to the master's apartments and tickled his ribs for the keys. I hid in the cellars of the merchants and grabbed at the rats for food before I escaped Troy. My brother was captured. And so I came to the army of Peleus, his wages they say are good, his cause loved by Apollo."

Macedon sighed and slowed his pace, tired with his monologue. Antigonus was unsure whether he sighed for his lost brother but his answer had impressed him. Perhaps these eastern slaves can be trusted after all. They lay silent now waiting for sleep and staring at a starless sky,

"What happened to your parents Macedon?"

"They were slaves. Cretagenous. My mother was sold as a breeder, reared on a slave farm to add wealth to the estate of the Pisistratids. Then Atreus was victorious so games were held. They were old and so were cast to the dogs to amuse their masters. My father tried to protect my mother. He fought the dogs for a long time but he fell and was eaten alive whilst my mother howled,

"You saw this?"

"I was held and made to watch. This son of Atreus who we fight. He smiled at me and made me clear the bones away."

77

Lyria worked alone in the kitchen grinding the wheat for the morning bread. Later she would add dates and honey for sweetness. She spoke softly to herself as she worked,
"Why should I be upset? Why should I be angry?"
"Talking to yourself again Lyria? You can get help for that."
Achilles stood before her,
"I have to go to learn my trade. To fight. That's what my father wanted me for."
He paused,
"I don't feel much like a fighter."
Lyria turned to him. Desire and disgust rose in her equally. She saw Achilles on his back with Helen laid at his side, her white skin exposed, her legs apart, her dress pulled up to her waist, her arm reaching out and holding him, her beautiful breasts full in the sunlight. Achilles eyes were closed. Lyria's eyes were sorry and sad and gave her away. She tried to speak casually without emotion but it was too much for her,
"Don't go Achilles. Be a prince, a merciful ruler."
"If I lead I must lead by example. I must fight."
"Why?" Lyria drew herself up. "Why not lead through love and forgiveness?"
Achilles looked at her with incredulity,
"Like Agamemnon?"
It was hot. He pulled off his chiton. Lyria could not look away. Like sandstone, she thought. His skin looked warm and smooth. Again the images she couldn't control invaded her thoughts, thoughts of Achilles, of the two of them together. Why

must men fight? Why can't they love like we love? Receive love as well as give?

"I must serve Thessaly."

Lyria could feel herself getting angrier,

"Thessaly? What is that? Is it the birds that fly over the trees? The hives? There are trees and land beyond the seas so I am told with different names. What matters to me is people. The people I love. I hope if I'm faced with the choice of betraying land or someone I love I will have the heart and guts to choose my friend!"

She couldn't help herself. She had to say it,

"And what of Alope and Helen? Won't they miss you?"

Achilles looked away and blushed. Lyria realised she was angry and this was of no use to Achilles or herself. He took a step towards her and leaning forward bent to kiss her on the forehead. As he kissed her he seemed to look past her to a darkness that lay beyond. Lyria, overcome, turned away. She heard him walking away but didn't bother to turn. Achilles was gone.

78

So Lyria took to her tasks with a new vigour. Her friends noted how hard she worked preparing the meals for the great hall, collecting the herbs in the hills. She avoided Achilles and Orpheus, wandering the valley to give her heart some respite but her thoughts always returned to him, again and again she recounted the conversations; innuendo and desire tempered with hope. Each day the desire grew stronger grasping and squeezing the breath from her so she would bend double and reach out at a branch or building. But there was to be no reprieve. Once again Lyria lay in her room and gazed sightlessly with the blindness of all lovers who only see a vision of fevered perfection. The next morning she was up first as usual. She washed in the courtyard before the other servants awoke. She knew very soon her privacy would be over and her daily chores would begin and the tiresome gossip that went with it. It was a perishingly cold morning, grey, with the wind blowing the mist low from Mount Pelium. The wind piped and gusted and the only colour was a faded glow of orange to the east where the sky wore the first kiss of dawn. Lyria decided to sit in the old rose garden. She loved the garden with its unkempt wisteria beds and brambled winding paths where she could lose herself. It was really for the disused amphorae but Lyria had claimed it. These pots have been here for so long. They will probably be here when I'm gone she pondered. What will happen to me when I am old? Will I be remembered? Will anyone speak my name? She looked up on hearing a sound. It was early even for the herders and farm hands so Lyria, puzzled, walked through the yard and saw Achilles and Phoenix heading from the palace leading their laden horses. Unable to help herself she ran to catch them.

79

On the right side of the Peneius the lush plains spread for miles to the horizon, a green and lush landscape in summer and autumn but callow and ill bred in winter as the cold winds gathered to rush and race over the exposed land. On this morning the clouds glowered and spread a sad purple hue so the horses in the stable stamped, fractious and anxious. And on the plains the occasional cicada and fir and the twisting roads that led east to Epiros and then north to the fighting tribes of Macedonia. Achilles greeted Xanthos who with his keen eye had recognised him. He turned him towards the storm that promised to arch the cypress trees like bows. It was a cheerless prospect. All the same it was a breathing landscape and one that Achilles loved. They led their horses laden with provisions and tools, medicines and pots out upon a dawn that had weaved a light blue mist upon the river which had spread up and over the banks. It curled around their ankles as they trod a route Achilles had followed many times. There was a frost on the exposed ground and the air was crisp and fresh as Xanthos snorted and whinnied, excited at seeing his new master. Phoenix heard the cry first and looked behind to see Lyria running to catch them. Phoenix didn't hesitate,

"Come boy, we must reach Tricca before the storm."

He gathered the reins and galloped ahead. Achilles, his heart heavy, his head confused followed after one last glance at Lyria. Lyria stood alone watching the figures disappear into the dark grey of the morning. She thought she saw Achilles turn and look once again; something seemed to drop from his saddle. Without hesitation she ran to warn the pair, perhaps it was something important. She reached the spot and bent forward picking up the flower from the cold ground. She knew it immediately – the wild virgin lily common to Epiros. Her eyes were so sparkling and bright that a tear that appeared on her eyelash seemed like a pearl cast carelessly on a green ocean.

80

"If anyone finds out about this I will be whipped."

"I will keep my word" replied Achilles.

He gently opened the door and stepping over the threshold peered into the darkness and called out,

"Mother?"

Thetis sat seated and smiling. If it wasn't for the change in attire he would have feared she had never moved since his last secret visit. But since the banishment he had visited and it was a game between them to ignore the time in between as if it had been short; that he had never left her side as she painted and weaved her wounds.

"How is your father?"

She always began with this but today there was an extra sharpness brought on by the smudges of an unrealised regret that had long ago congealed into a willing cessation of passions. Achilles was to go. Achilles is to fight. Her beauty was fading though still only young; stolen from her by a malignant plague that pocked and hollowed her skin leaving her face in ruins. Gone the magnificent eyes now hidden by a veil. Now she was without the will to face the world that had talked of her beauty in wonder and hushed whispers. Now she was only glimpsed at a distance in the cool morning hours and talked about when the brooks ran dry in the summer heat. She tolerated no objects of beauty or ornamentation, no mirrors or jaded combs were permitted. But in the small hours she lifted the lid of her ivory box and took out the kohl mined from the red mountains and remembered a time when men fought for her favours and risked their leaping lives for a glance. She touched her eyes again applying the kohl in different shades, looking left, looking right to tempt the guile and seductions of her youthful graces as if a formula could be found that would reignite her lost beauty.

"I'm here to say goodbye mother."

"Bless you for this news."

Thetis didn't look up as Achilles stood before her. She bit her thumb and looked to the distance wrestling with her own voices. Finally she turned to her son and cupping his face in her hands whispered,

"Do you see the sun that shines today Achilles? It is a spring sun, an easy companion unlike the golden brilliance of the summer sun or the cold and wan winter sun whose every ray bids you farewell. It is a Greek sun, a sun that greets you full of hope. You are this sun Achilles. My son. You are the rebirth and the hope. Your bright armour rises above the horizon and its first rays are your fiery arrows. And your armour and sword will strike hope for the Greeks. And they will look to you as they look to the heavens and know there is order and hope."

Achilles bowed his head,

"I will come and see you. Always."

Thetis knowing this would never happen wrung her hands and turned away muttering.

81

Achilles was seeing at first hand the land he would inherit. They passed through remote farms and tiny settlements that relied on a small herd and a plough to yield strong crops from the land. But they were few, these farms and on the whole unwelcoming. Although the farmers themselves were friendly enough they were, Achilles thought, glad to see them on their way. No effort was made to improve the tracks that connected these small villages, the inhabitants encouraging the rifts and boundaries which surrounded them making as they did natural defences. They left the boy with a feeling of unease and indicated to him the lack of trust between his people engendered by these fortifications. A gloom overcame him which he found hard to shake off.

As the mornings grew old the clouds would disperse and the patches of blue grow wider and frequent so the sun shone hot on their backs. But then just as suddenly a heavy shower passed over them moving seaward over the marshes so ever changing patterns of light and shade accompanied them. Columns of smoke from the occasional farmer's huts were the only distractions over the flatlands they crossed.

They came to the outskirts of Tricca and the town itself where they rested. The village was named after the fountain nymph Tricca the daughter of the river God Peneius. Machaon, the town's ruler was said to be a descendant of Asclepius himself. The temple of Asclepius that stood there was visited by the sick from all over Greece who hoped for divine help. It was here they took their rest. It was late afternoon and to the northeast beyond the mud huts Phoenix could make out the flat expanse of the plains that rolled out into the foothills of Olympus,

"Three days travel."

Phoenix had been impressed at the stoicism of his charge. Achilles had ridden without complaint. He had been expecting more demands for rest and food. But the boy had been dutiful following the whims and plans of his new lord and master. Phoenix looked hard at Achilles. Perhaps there is a great warrior here after all. But he had to be honest with himself and admit that it still seemed unlikely.

82

Lyria knew Eurypylos was deaf but really he should know that is wrong. But he seemed to have no shame as he continued urinating in the yard whilst smiling and staring at Lyria. She turned but in the periphery of her vision Eurypylos was still stood. Alarmed she ran back into the house. That night as she lay in bed she thought about Eurypylos. She tried to put it from her mind but the more she tried the more difficult it was to forget. Lyria only knew how to love one way; completely. Her heart was a deep sea that hung onto its treasures tightly so the daily wrack and flotsam of affections never swayed her loyalties. But all the same Lyria was entering a world of impulses and doubts, currents and eddies that terrified her but left her wanting more, half remembered images excited her but filled her with fear and guilt. Seeing a body in the mirror that she didn't recognise, a longing running through her veins. The exquisite spiral of fire that spread from her thighs now bewildered her, shattered her world but now dominated it. She was unprepared for it, incapable of understanding it. It was her own terrible burden. But still every night her hand would move slowly down.

Now she sat on her bed and stared at the walls of her room listening to the silence. She missed the sound of the ocean. Her first memories were wrapped in the sea; seeing it from her window and tasting it on her lips as her mother walked with her along the beach; seeing the seagulls sewing the white waves to the edges of the sky. Or at night staring as the moon danced with the waves throwing up flints and shards of silver spray. And now just the sparse torchlight of the grey dark walls of the servants' quarters. But Lyria was by no means unhappy with her lot. She knew she was lucky and enjoyed her work but for the pain of what she knew now to be love, unrequited and unfulfilled. She fell asleep and dreamt of wave after wave passing over her but it was a happy dream. She was woken from her watery reverie by a sound she didn't recognise, a high pitched yelping that came from the palace courtyard. Quickly slipping on her tunic and sandals she scurried through the kitchen. Again the pitiful sound came but this time accompanied by a human voice,

"That will teach you, dirty smelly dog."

Lyria ran into the open courtyard and by the light of the torches she could make out Helen stood over old Cerebus. She was kicking him and yelling at him. The sound that Cerebus made pierced her heart and she threw herself between Helen and the poor creature,

"Stop it. Stop it. Why would you do this?"

Perhaps Helen could see the look in Lyria's eyes but without saying a word she simply turned and walked slowly away. Lyria turned her attentions to Cerebus. It was clear he was hurt. His tongue bled where he had bitten down. His eyes were half open and he had a cut on his head,

"She has thrown things at you." Lyria could see the stones that lay on the floor some almost the size of her clenched fist,

"You are too weak and too old to fight back. It's not in your nature."

Lyria cradled poor Cerebus in her arms,

"Dear Cerebus, why would she do this to you?"

Despite his injuries he tried to wag his tail and rise to his feet but his back legs collapsed and he fell to the floor,

"The old dog has fleas and tried to enter my bedchamber."

Helen stood on the balcony looking out over the courtyard. The flickering torchlight meant her face was half in shadow. These shadows leant a sterner aspect to her features, her words now even colder and impassive,

"I chased him and punished him."

"He used to sleep in that room to escape the heat before you arrived. He meant no harm."

"Be careful what you say Lyria. You serve me."

Helen then raised her arm and pointed to the ground.

"Get down on your knees before your mistress."

Lyria's main concern was for Cerebus and she knew that the quicker she appeased Helen the quicker she could attend to him although she balked at the thought of this new humiliation. So in the half shadows of the courtyard with Helen looking on Lyria bowed her head and knelt forward.

"Good."

Lyria looked up. Helen had already disappeared back into her chamber. Lyria rushed to the kitchen where she collected some water and linen to dress Cerebus' injuries. She bent over and picked him up as a shepherd holds a poor sheep and staggering with the weight placed him under the torchlight where she began cleaning his wounds. But it was clear from his shallow breathing that Cerebus was struggling.

"Don't worry dear Cerebus. I will stay with you."

She stroked his face and cupped some water dripping it onto his mouth then whetted his head. He lay still on his side. He had stopped whimpering but he was so exhausted all he could do was follow Lyria with his eyes.

"You will feel better soon Cerebus. Dear boy. You are my friend and I will care for you."

"Here, let me help you."

Leodes the stable boy knelt down beside her and began to gently stroke Cerebus.

"Oh." Lyria started. She had thought she was alone and seeing Leodes was a shock. She remembered how some of the other girls had teased her saying that Leodes watched for her and asked after her. He is big and strong Lyria! Imagine his arms around you! Or your legs around him! Lyria had blushed. She found it all too easy to imagine someone's arms around her. But they were the arms of Achilles not Leodes handsome as he was. Leodes was not yet fourteen but swarthy and muscular for his age with the beginnings of a strong beard. Lyria noticed his smell when he knelt beside her. A slightly musky smell that all boys seemed to have. It reminded her of her brother.

"Thank you. Helen beat him."

"Why?"

Leodes worked night and day with the horses and found it difficult to conceive how anyone could harm any animal. For him all animals, especially horses were better than people.

"He's old but handsome." Leodes smiled as he continued,

"Animals are better than you or I Lyria. Cerebus has spirit. When he was younger he had strength but humility. He is everything your mistress isn't."

Lyria was amazed at these words which seemed to come from someone much older and wiser,

"Cerebus is my favourite" she said. "I feed him every day and he follows and watches over me like the Gods."

Leodes stood up and made to leave,

"You're Lyria aren't you? I'm Leodes." He extended his arm.

"I'd like to see you again some time."

Lyria felt unable to reply but eventually she stood,

"It was good of you to help me Leodes. Thank you." She took his hand and Leodes sensing her hesitation smiled, turned and returned to his stables. Lyria watched him leave and noticed his strong calves that flexed as he walked across the courtyard. He reminded her of Achilles, moving with the grace of a muse but purposeful with a symmetry of poise and movement, the unique execution of all physical action that belongs to boys teetering on the verge of young manhood. She turned away slowly and returned her attentions back to Cerebus.

83

The boy Achilles and his mentor rode onwards. Sometimes the ground was hard and tensile, sometimes they traipsed slowly through water, dead and stagnant, the lifeless pools splashing the feet and legs of the travellers; edged by crusts of salt mud that told Phoenix they were nearing the coast. The mud was encrusted and stank as the hooves broke the surface and buzzed the flies and mosquitoes that thrived in the putrid air so even the horses seemed to hold their breath. But when the ground hardened and the spaces opened the horses would gallop sensing their freedom, the saddle leather groaning, their manes tossing with Achilles and Phoenix both laughing at the wild sky. And still onwards through valleys where wild flowers bloomed and butterflies skitted and then a day of dark horizons with prickly scrubs and shale underfoot so the horses skidded and the two travellers dismounted to guide them. But just as quickly a green pasture with lush streams of sunlight telling Achilles that his land was one of many moods; always pushing westwards until the sun set before them so to look up was to see a vista of gold and orange. Sometimes Achilles would trot ahead and turn to see the dark silhouette of Phoenix set fast against an indigo sky. The last rays often turned their shadows to purple in the hidden bowels of the landscape. Then a hush would drift between them filling the voiding valleys with silence but for the distant howling of wolves, the clatter of the hooves over the harder ground and the vile ululations of the waning moon.

84

The next day Lyria rose early to prepare breakfast. It was a part of the day she enjoyed as she knew she would be alone. Helen would still be asleep or having her face made up with white lead and kohl. She was still tired after having slept uncomfortably next to Cerebus who thankfully had now managed to stand up. She had taken him some old bones that he delighted in even though his teeth were old and broken.

"I'll take my breakfast in bed."

Lyria jumped and looked around. Helen was stood at the kitchen doorway looking stunning as usual in a crisp blue chiton freshly laundered. Around her neck was a single gold necklace inlaid with faience. Lyria carried on preparing the figs that needed to be cut and washed. What happened next amazed Lyria. Helen walked over and stood by her,

"Lyria, I'm sorry about what happened yesterday. Can we be friends?"

Lyria was astonished. How could she be so brazen? Does she think I can forgive her like that? Lyria was so stupefied she couldn't speak. Helen took her silence as acquiescence,

"Im glad" she said before walking to the door. Before leaving she turned and smiled,

"I think we can help each other."

Lyria wasn't fooled by her mistress. Does she think she can mistreat Cerebus and then expect me to forgive her? Helen walked back to her rooms. She felt ill at ease in the company of this girl Lyria. If she had searched deeper she would have known it was the coldness of her soul so juxtaposed as it was to the visceral heart of this simple girl from the islands. Her very existence antagonized her throwing open her own insecurities. She felt threatened just as a cold frost shrinks from the morning sun. She despised Lyria with her fanciful worship of the new Gods. She revelled in her own heritage, so much better than any here at the court of Peleus.

"I am the daughter of Leda! A Spartan princess trained to ride and throw spears. Fed on lizard's gizzards not the warm tales of Aphrodite. I am descended from Amazons and I have killed!"

Helen had been proud to run home and tell her mother of her first kill, a meaningless sacrifice under the guise of priestess. The boy had died poorly. She would be happy to do the same with Lyria. But first she may be of some use. There was a knock on the door. Eurypylos answered as Helen turned,

"Ah, the brave and handsome Leodes. Come in."

85

After her morning jobs Lyria walked out through the back entrance of the kitchen and past the old outbuildings used for storing the huge pots that held the olive reserves. She often walked this way for here the flowers and the trees ran wild. This morning she noticed how the walls caught the sun and shone a deep orange, a colour she loved. Despite being early the air was already close and tight so the heat rose in waves from the quince and herb beds as she passed by. But the delicious fragrance could not alter the fact that Achilles was gone. There it was. There was nothing to soften that blow for Lyria as she walked barefoot to the orchard. She continued walking for some time barely conscious of her surroundings. The sun was well up now and sweating across the sky. The dry earth crunched and bit into her feet but she barely noticed so deep was she in reverie. Her love for Achilles was all encompassing and dwarfed her. But it was a misery tainted with ecstasy. A sickening sweetness expected of Gods not mere mortals. Lyria continued walking westwards through the grove to the river where Achilles had ridden. Soon she was by the Peneius where the air was cooler. The cypress trees provided a natural avenue for her as they embraced seductively over her head so the sun dappled the ground with fists of gold. She loved how the river changed colour with the seasons. From the blue brightness of spring to the smooth dull grey of winter. Opaque and calm at summers height so the tench and bream choked and sweated in the narrow banks till Autumn came and cleansed the water with her gold and yellow fire. 'It's a cycle of birth and death' thought Lyria. 'Nothing ever dies, the land just sleeps.' Lyria then stood still startled.

"Who is that?"

She had heard a noise like a grunt and although it was daylight she felt scared,

"Don't worry Lyria."

This voice had no body which perturbed Lyria even more. She looked around, just the river bank and the trees. Then a laugh that came from above her head. Is it the Gods laughing at me?

"Look above you Lyria."

Lyria looked up shielding the sun from her eyes. Leodes was sat on a branch looking down and smiling,

"I'm sorry if I startled you. I'm picking plums for the horses. Here catch."

He lowered down a huge basket of plums which Lyria took from him and placed at the foot of the tree. There was a part of Lyria that was pleased to see Leodes. But he always seemed to appear when she least expected it. Almost as if he knows where I am!

"Hello Leodes. What are you doing here?" Lyria felt slightly ridiculous. Leodes had already answered that question.

"I can go where I like can't I? Are you my keeper? Would you have me in the stables all day stinking of horses?" Lyria looked sharply at Leodes as he hung from the lowest branch and dropped before her. The muscles in his legs bulged as he landed. They were already covered in black hair like a grown mans. But it was the tone in his voice that she didn't like. He now stood before her his hands on his hips. His eyes had a look which she didn't understand but she had seen it on the faces of men she had served when they were drunk and staring at the dancing girls. Was Leodes drunk?

"And how is our friend Cerebus?"

"He is better today thank you Leodes."

Lyria made to pass Leodes but he blocked her way. Despite

his previous gentleness she felt she didn't trust him anymore. All traces of kindness had gone from his manner.

"You don't seem very pleased to see me. Is that the thanks I get for helping you yesterday?"

"No, of course I am grateful."

'What does he want from me?' Lyria thought.

"You should be a little more kind. I've heard the women talk. They all say you watch for me, that you stare at me from a distance. Well I'm here now, you can stare as much as you like."

Lyria was astonished. Who had said these things?

"I'm thankful for your help sir. But I must be on my way." Lyria made to walk past again but Leodes grabbed her by the waist,

"Sometimes thank you isn't enough, you can show your thanks in other ways."

"Please Leodes."

"I know you want me. You are ready. I bet I'm not the first either. That's what I've heard."

Even though the sun was well up the dawn's vapours lay still on the river's surface. It was broad daylight but there was no one around to help her even if she screamed,

"I know you want me. I can see it in your eyes."

Leodes laughed and reaching down put his hand under Lyria's tunic hitching it up so her thighs were exposed,

"You see? You're a woman and you didn't even know it."

Lyria felt nauseous. Leodes was so powerful. She could feel the strength in his arms. His fingers dug into her like iron. I must escape. I must. She kicked out but her legs swung impotently missing their target. This took all her energy and Lyria fell to the floor exhausted,

"That's better. You never know, you might enjoy this. Apollo says virginity is dangerous for young girls."

"Please leave me alone. I won't tell anyone. I'm sorry if I gave you the wrong message. I didn't mean it."

"Whores like you don't deserve a man like me. You should

think yourself lucky. If you please me enough I may not kill you but don't count on it."

There was a part of Lyria that wanted to die now before he continued. Please kill me now. Please, please. Leodes took off his tunic and placed it neatly on the floor. In the folds Lyria could clearly see a long blade with a bone handle. She had seen him use it when shoeing and preparing the horses. A great shadow then passed over her but before she fell unconscious she saw the face of Leodes contort slowly and horribly and a figure wearing a cloak stood above her whose face she couldn't make out. And then once again the slightest hint of cyperus before her eyes closed.

86

That evening Helen walked the same route that Lyria had taken that morning. She looked at the river and saw nothing but a dull stretch of water. Under a tree she saw a basket of plums and picked one out. But it was too young and not yet ready so she tossed it in the river and walked on. Where was Achilles? That bitch Lyria will know. It was well known that he was being tutored by Phoenix but where? Helen knew of Phoenix the eunuch and smiled. In Sparta she had witnessed castrations and amused herself by parading naked whilst they looked at her with their sad eyes. Some had cried whilst she had laughed and brushed her breast against their faces and danced provocatively. But then she had felt a disgust at these creatures who were less than men and who dared to look at her with their dull, lifeless faces. And so, bored, she had had them whipped and sent away. But where was Phoenix now? Helen was confident she would soon have the answers.

87

Deeper they travelled into Epiros through the valleys that formed the entrance to Mount Pindus. Achilles noted how well cultivated the land was in the few farms they passed, this was the prized top soil loose and free from stones. Further on the hills welcomed them in an unbroken ridge; a backbone running south east from Ossa to Pelion which looks across the sea to Troy and the young king Priam. They crossed the rougher parts of this mountainous land with its oak forests and small isolated valleys where the wolf now found its home, hiding from the creatures that would eventually see its extinction in the western and southern lands thanks in no small part to the work of Agamemnon's hunting parties. The Epirot and Thesprotian tribes feared the wolves especially in winter when their hunger drove the packs nearer to their villages; dragging the corpses of elders from still smouldering pyres or worse, children who roamed too far. Phoenix didn't expect to be troubled by wolves in the day. Feeling a sudden movement in the sleeve of his tunic he caught sight of the twitching nose of a fieldmouse he had picked up earlier. All animals loved Phoenix and he loved them back but there was more to Phoenix's devotion than mere affection and husbandry. Following the guidance and instruction of the priests of Sekhmet whom the Libyan had invited to his home he had studied the medicines sought out by sick animals – the bark the crow chose when ministering to its young, the junipers the squirrels stored to toughen their skin for the harsh winters. Animals can teach us so much more than merely strength and forbearance.

88

Orpheus understood why his best friend was leaving but was aggrieved that he wasn't going with her,
"It's something I have to do on my own Orphy. I'm telling you so you won't worry."

Lyria knew that to have Orpheus along with her would implicate him in the disappearance of Leodes. This was now her own private burden which she knew she would have to come to terms with, her journey would give her that opportunity. She wasn't ready to speak to Orpheus about what had happened. One day I will tell him but not now. I need to be away from here. Orpheus smiled at his oldest and closest friend. He took a ring from his finger and taking Lyria's hand placed it in her palm,

"You gave me this when we were small children."

"The pomegranate ring!"

"To be given to someone you love. Dear Lyria. May your deeds dance wildly in a golden bay."

They embraced then Lyria turned and was away. Returning to the stables she heard a small bark and saw Cerebus looking up expectantly,

"Are you sure you want to come with me? It's a long way Cerebus."

Lyria knew there was nothing she could do to dissuade him. Cerebus had made up his mind. It was a bright day when Lyria began her journey. The sun shone keenly on the shallow boats coursing the Penieus as it widened on its way to Tricca and the tributaries at Dordona. And further still the isolated mountains of Epiros and its vast forests of holm oak with their curious toothed leaves. This is where Achilles would be found. As for what she would do when she found him she wasn't sure. She looked over the wide expanse of the river. In the early morning stillness its ebony surface reflected the trees and foliage fringing the banks like soft flames of green and orange fire. Her heart was glad. She could hear a fisherman singing as he tapped out a rhythm on the prow of his boat and beyond that the sounds of the village, the wheelwrights and blacksmiths. The women churned the butter in the goatskins that hung from the trees. Then a hundred yards further on she was overcome by the smell of damp earth and lingering wood smoke as Galathis the water bearer threw leaves onto the dull glow of a fire, an invisible wall of scent that knocked Lyria flat, more so than any club or shield. It was a happy coincidence of things that started to move her, the chance to leave the putrid air of Thessaly behind her which for her still stank of the foul Leodes. A place where laughing eyes did not follow her. A place nearer the sea. As the ideas and dreams swelled in her brain the implications became trivial. The sheer joy of her decision made her weep and her breath come quicker. But mostly it was the anticipation of finding Achilles which made her heart beat faster. The road now forked, the northern road leading to Mount Olympus, the western road to Epiros. Her eyes followed this road and she started down it dreaming of what lay ahead.

"Lyria has gone mistress Helen."

Helen turned to Eurypylos,

"Gone where?"

"No one knows my lady. She is not to be found."

"Leave me."

Helen returned to the mirror and smiled. It would not take long to find her,

"She has played in to my hands. My loving brothers will find her."

Helen left her rooms and ordered the stable boy to prepare her horse.

89

That first night she slept with Cerebus at her feet. The first few days merged quickly following a pattern of sun and moon, silver and gold, hunger and tiredness along high valleys and narrow paths and brown pebbled streams where Cerebus cooled his paws and drank. Then shaded orchards and forests of fig and oak, verdurous valleys, plum and willow and acres of bloodied poppy fields. In this way Lyria travelled onwards through the great plains and valleys of central Greece. North of Pharsalus she came to a small village and rested. She noticed a change in the few people she saw; the women looked sallow and disagreeable, their complexions spoke of toil and pain, the children no better grimacing and crying. A young man helped his mother light a fire under a great pot of vegetables. She seemed sad to Lyria but as she bent over the broth she turned and smiled and bade Lyria come and eat. Lyria hesitated but soon joined them and asked her name,

"Claryta, wife of Antigonus. We are here to buy hides from the market at Pharsalus."

The woman spoke of her hard life, the baby she had lost and her fears of war,

"It will come soon. Agamemnon covets this land, he will have it and demand even more taxes. There's nothing anyone can do."

The sun fell quicker the further west she travelled setting the marshland and valleys into a sudden dusky relief. The lilac afterglow was always too brief, the colours delighted Lyria before they were captured by a pitiless alluvial darkness Then the quicksilver canvas showed her the way. At night she recited the same prayer to help her through the dark hours,

"Send me a shimmering light, a path for me to follow sweet Selene. Lift your eyes to me and be gracious. Let not the wolves or the boars devour me. Let Endymion have a heart to love me tonight; be my sweet love."

Sometimes Cerebus would halt and growl and it was then that Lyria was most scared holding her breath as if the jaws of the night lay waiting to swallow her whole.

90

Castor and Pollux had been imprisoned in a remote storage cellar in the depths of the Spartan palace for a year ever since they had witnessed their sister strangle and suffocate a small child for some minor transgression. Helen could think of no other way of ensuring their silence, dumb and backward as they were. So for a year now they had been told through furtive and dramatic meetings that they and they alone were the sole survivors of a plague that had ravaged Sparta and that they must stay hidden until she deemed it safe for them to leave. So they must be indebted to her, thank her, grovel at her feet. Search parties organised by Helen herself had been sent all over Laconia and north to Thessaly after Helen's traumatic recollection of the night she saw them ambushed and taken away. She had recognised the dialect of the abductors, northern, probably Thessalian. Now she took great delight in bringing her brothers the latest death counts until even Menelaus lay dying in his bed. The twins, ever grateful to their loving sister became obsessed with cleanliness. Both wrung their hands and washed them repeatedly so the skin would peel from their palms leaving red blisters. On hearing of their father's imminent demise they argued pathetically over sovereignty and who would rule. The store room they called home was never visited containing as it did overripe produce, barley pearls and corn husks as well as their sisters conscience. Even the servants never ventured near as its walls were moist, the air dank and toxic, a rats lair. Helen let it be known through well placed whispers that it was a place of ill omen and anyone venturing near would incur the displeasure of her and the Gods she served. Only Eurypylos would come, throwing in meat on the orders of Helen every new moon. So the twins lay undiscovered and would have died had Helen not derived such pleasure from the power she exercised over them; their obsequiousness pleased her as they kissed her hands and placed themselves utterly at her mercy. Their servility knew no bounds. Helen knew this and now the time had come to set them to their work. Such was the time they had spent together that through a bizarre osmosis each had morphed into the other, sharing one idea, one mouth, one mind. Though they rarely spoke when they did they often finished each others sentences. Or even stranger they spoke simultaneously, their bloodless lips moving in unison, their bland intonations and whispers lost in their disease ridden cell. Only the rats could hear them and see them but they stayed hidden from the hungry pair watching them as they moved in perfect symmetry. Even their dreams were the same as they slept in each other's arms. And now their beloved sister was here with her final instruction. But first always the same question from the twins,

"Who"

"Has"

"Died"

"Today?"

For once Helen ignored the question and repeated the mantra she had spelled out to them over the last year,

"You will never speak of what you saw that day. You will speak to no one for everyone is unclean. To speak to anyone but me is to risk the plague."

Disinherited from the sun they plunged deeper into the littorals of their black souls. Unloved, unleashed, their cannibalism now defined them. The more they fed the more they crowed. Only Helen could rule them as she led them on a rope under a trembling moon for her own private murders. Her instructions were now complete and the twins stood silently nodding.

91

The old servant was tired and gave Orpheus a cursory look before rising and opening the great oak doors. Despite the old man's frailty Orpheus was genuinely taken aback by the strength of his voice as he announced his entrance,

"Orpheus of…" he turned and spoke softly, "where are you from pisspot and what is your purpose?"

Orpheus, somewhat aggrieved replied,

"I am Orpheus of Lesbos and I am here for the linen."

The bellowing voice returned,

"Orpheus the Lesbian linen boy!"

He entered the rooms through the grand oak doors decorated in gilded bronze. The room was large with high windows which circulated the air keeping the room cool. Orpheus noted the intricate tapestries in red and gold adorning the wall. There were mirrors everywhere so the room appeared larger. In the corner sat Helen. Orpheus bowed,

"I am here for the linen."

"So I hear. Do not take offence at old Tantios. He once did a favour for my father."

Helen stayed sat down staring straight ahead,

"Please sit down young man."

Finally she turned to Orpheus,

"How young you look, how old are you?"

Orpheus paused and stood a little straighter,

"I have twelve years, almost thirteen."

"Almost a man then." She smiled.

"I have seen you around the palace young man. What is your name?"

Helen knew his name, knew his character, his weaknesses, but mostly she knew he was a friend of Achilles and Lyria.

"Orpheus."

"I will call you Orphy."

Helen looked at Orpheus closely, her head on one side, a playful smile on her lips,

"Will you let me call you Orphy?"

Her voice caused Orpheus to shiver. Helen noticed this and smiled to herself,

"P…p..please, lady Helenius."

"You know my name then?"

"Yes, I've seen you and…"

Orpheus paused,

"And?" asked Helen

"I enquired after you."

"How sweet, and here you are."

Orpheus stood, unsure of what to say or what to do. Helen could see his discomfort and let him stand.

"I will allow you to call me Helen. Would you like to help me wind this flaxen?"

Orpheus nodded and followed her. Later when he ran the scene through in his mind he was scarcely able to remember anything about the room. Helen sat down, undid the skein and laid it across the palms of Orpheus. She wound the wool in with an amused look on her face, her lips slightly parted. Occasionally she would look up at Orpheus with a face of such indescribable pulchritude that Orpheus averted his gaze not daring to move. He suddenly wished there were a thousand skeins to unwind. He never wanted to leave. Helen was satisfied, she knew that Orpheus was being wound in as surely as the wool.

"Now listen Orphy. I like you. I have a feeling that we will be friends. Would you like that?"

Orpheus nodded.

"But I am a little older than you. And I know a little bit more. So you must always tell me the truth. Do you have many friends?"

Orpheus was at a loss. Dare he mention the prince as a friend? And there was Pellason the stable hand – and Lyria of course.

"Come now Orphy. How long have you been friendly with Achilles?"

"Since I came here. We play together."

Orpheus bit his lip and immediately regretted what he'd said,

"Erm, that is, we speak of things and sometimes fight."

"And what do you speak of?"

Helen lowered her eyes so they once again shone sweetly upon him. Orpheus paused unsure of how to respond,

"No matter, perhaps one day you could bring your friends here and we could play together. Would that please you Orphy?"

"Yes, Lady Helenius, I remain at your service."

Orpheus was flattered and overcome by the attentions of Helen and wished more than anything to prove to her that he was more than a mere boy,

"I'm glad, I can see that you are grown up."

Helen now stood sideways on so Orpheus had the chance to raise his eyes and scrutinize her features. She seemed even more lovely in profile. Her delicate features spoke of charm and elegance. It was now early evening so the sunlight shed a soft light on her face and hair, her swan like neck and breast. 'How dear she is' thought Orpheus. He suddenly realised that she was looking at him through the mirror,

"Do you like to stare at me?"

Orpheus, deeply embarrassed said nothing.

"Come and see me again tomorrow."

Orpheus blushed. I must be totally transparent to her. She knows what I am thinking. She knows everything about me; his thoughts fell over one another. He turned to leave although he struggled to take his eyes off her. Helen was alone and looked out at the green Thessalian landscape. The stillness was palpable as her adamantine body finally lost its rigidity; her face relaxed and twisted into the macabre visage that no one ever saw. Even her thoughts shed themselves; they fell away like scales as she stared blankly at the countless mirrors. Thus her serpentine soul was revealed. Agamemnon had seen it once and it had chilled his blood.

92

It gradually began to dawn on Lyria that she would not reach Epiros in one or two days. Beyond the instruction to follow the river she had no idea how long it would take. Each night as the sun set and the night closed in the drone of the cicadas and insects disappeared to be replaced with new sounds that the young girl was unfamiliar with. Her ears became more sensitive, her green eyes keener. She whistled to keep up her spirits trying to imitate the high chirrup of the swallows and the guttural call of the wood owls hunting for mice. The pipistrelles flew and flitted across her face so that she shrieked and waved her arms. Eventually she tethered her horse and wrapping herself in a blanket tried to sleep. At her feet Cerebus twitched his paw, locked as he was in the cat strewn dungeons of his dreams. Above her the moon, around her the still night and in the distance the amethyst coloured mountains.

93

One morning before the sun had fully risen Achilles spied a small settlement in the distance set against the grey dawn. A stone brick structure and what looked like stalls for the cattle. Curious he set off at a gallop but Phoenix, ever wary, called him back. So it was that Phoenix approached the buildings first only to find they were burnt out, a charred ruin, empty and deserted,

"What happened here?"

Phoenix said nothing but his face was grim. They carried on a little further. Just beyond a small wood they came upon another building again ruinous and deserted with no sign of life. A goat's corpse lay sprawled covered in a shroud of flies. He stood by it. Dead only a short time, an expression of serenity lay on its features like a sleeping boy who slumbered after a struggle with a mortal enemy. He marked it taking in every part of what he saw so that when the time came and Agamemnon asked for forgiveness none would be granted. Inside him a nausea, more than if the corpses had been merely human. His outrage was rounded with pity and shame that he should belong to the same species that committed this murder. Men can fight their way to Hades. But animals? And to what end?

"Not even offered to the Gods" he whispered quietly.

What he saw troubled him but he didn't want the boy to see. Privately he wondered what had happened to the honest workers who toiled on this land. There were no human remains. Had they fled or been forced to become foot soldiers for Agamemnon? A sound made him look sharply towards the building. A soft bleating barely audible. Phoenix dismounted and walked slowly towards the broken down building. There, cowering in a corner lay a kid, its withers matted with blood. Its small tail had been cut off. It bleated gently when it saw Phoenix approach. It was clearly scared and orphaned judging by the animal corpses that lay before it. The kid was licking his dead mother,

"And so these are your parents little one? Murdered like your owner I bet. If only you could tell us what you saw."

Phoenix then made a curious noise. Achilles instantly recognised it. He had heard him use the same noise when speaking to any number of animals. The kid turned its head and looked up. It got to its feet unsteadily and gazed at Phoenix. He made the noise again and then the kid ran and jumped into his arms. Phoenix chuckled and held the kid tight whilst it covered him in licks. Pleased he stroked its head affectionately,

"Now, what shall we call you?"

He looked around and thought hard but as soon as he turned his head away the kid bleated and purred so loudly it sounded like a small lion.

"You purr like a wild beast. Ah, that's it. Purdy, so that's your name then. Now if you could just let me put you down."

But Purdy had no intention of being left and butted and bleated till Phoenix picked him up again. Achilles looked on and marvelled at the power his mentor held over animals. It really was wonderful to see. Achilles crouched and beckoned him over. He came timidly but it was clear he had only one master. Even Xanthos was smitten and bent his head to nuzzle the small animal. Xanthos was besotted and for the rest of the journey would sidle over to Purdy whenever he got the chance. There was no question that Purdy was going to join them. But first Phoenix bathed Purdy's wound with a honey and carrot based salve. Eventually they set off, Purdy gamboling at the feet of Xanthos. Phoenix took one last look at the settlement still puzzling over the charred ruins of the barn; but more than that, the bite marks in the flanks of the dead goats. Thankfully the boy hadn't noticed them. Phoenix thought hard. 'Bites. The only ones I saw like this were once during the plague at Seraphos. The rats got to the bodies before we could dress them. But these? They were human…'

94

Lyria raised herself in the saddle and shook the night from her limbs. Her linen frock was damp and she shivered under her loose fitting cloak. She remembered the words of her mother as she rode. 'A woman's love will always be stronger, it's the way of things. Don't suffocate him or he will wish to escape. Don't hold the bird too tightly or you will squeeze out the life.' Lyria thought about Achilles and in her mind she spoke to him.

'The act of love is in the heart too. All those couples lay alone with nothing to hold onto but their grief. They grunt and stumble through the stagnant pools of their affections. They go through their lives not knowing if they've ever lived. But not us Achilles. I want there to be nobody like us.' So Lyria dreamed of a complete love as she rode, one that fed on understanding, a circle that never ended like the precious pomegranate ring.

95

Orpheus left Helen tired but happier than he'd ever been. Helen had smiled and kissed his forehead. The air tasted sweet as he walked home. He welcomed the breeze which fanned his brow. Looking up he noticed the dark clouds moving slowly across the sky and beyond them the winking pinpoints of light. As the wind blew the trees they shook as if preparing for battle. And then far beyond the sound of Zeus's thunder as he chided his children. Without undressing he laid on his bed staring as if enchanted at the ceiling. As the storm gathered outside so his breath grew heavy as the images of Helen filtered in and out of his mind's eye and he reached down. Helen gazed at him, held him, kissed him. Orpheus lay still, he was unwilling to move, to even turn his head in case the night's events should be rendered obsolete, a passing fancy, a dream that never was. He looked out of his room and beyond Mount Ossa to the east where Zeus now threw down his spears in anger. They flashed and trembled like the dying notes on a lyre as the music of the night continued. The moon sank and watched Orpheus. The blue night gave way to red and gold. The notes quivered and died finally muted so Orpheus lay dumbly watching the secret fires of the morning that spoke of the new passions within him.

96

One week now into her journey. Lyria's bread and dates were long finished. She found a few wild grapes still hard and green and balked at their sour taste. Further on the remains of a patch of beans provided some food. But her hunger began to overwhelm her, her thoughts wandered and she knew she must eat soon or die. But she kept moving, her hunger never once sullied her resolve. Rather it feasted on what it lacked, the thought of seeing him again, this was the meat and drink that fed her resolution. She emerged from another wood with the river still to her left as it had been for the entire journey. But she decided to follow a tributary which after a short time led her to a vale sparsely populated with small clusters of hazel and elders. Some strong oaks stood alone at the base of the hillside to her right. Lyria noted the trees seemed greener and taller. Perhaps there is more rain here, all these streams must feed the Peneius. Seeing a slight overhang that provided some shade she led her horse towards it and tethered it to a large rock. Cerebus settled quickly gazing up at Lyria who lay down resting her head against the huge bulk of her horse's belly. She was soon asleep. She awoke a short time later as the moon moved through her silent world. She flooded the earth casting a rare beauty on the landscape so nature herself seemed hushed reflecting on her own divine provenance. But there was more. Lyria stiffened as she saw two helmeted figures side by side disappear into the forest noiselessly. The woods held their breath as the two men walked by in perfect unison. Lyria stayed perfectly still. Something told her the men were not friendly. Only when young dawn softly whispered for the stars to leave did she move.

97

The small procession wound around a collection of large rocks where they came upon a spring that gushed down the hillside. Phoenix dismounted,
"Let's drink."

Achilles nodded. The water was clear and clean and they drank deeply. Achilles splashed his face and body and felt much fresher. Purdy looked at him confused then jumped into the stream on all fours. Xanthos watched patiently. Phoenix looked around. The valley was steep in parts. A wood further down the valley would provide fuel and game. Looking further Mount Pindus glowered down its jagged summit partially hidden by clouds. Phoenix remounted and they ventured further. The sweet pea perfumed the air as Achilles cantered at the side of a weary Phoenix. The river ran narrow but would eventually run its course into the eastern ocean home of Odysseus the peacemaker. Achilles looked around. It was a beautiful valley. He had never seen such tall mountains, so tall that they broke through the clouds. Occasionally the clouds drifted to reveal the snow peaked caps. Both paused for a moment gazing at the scenery around them, the huge mountain range somehow seemed to hem them in. Achilles had an uneasy feeling that he was trapped. The whole place despite its beauty had a lonely feel as if something terrible had happened. But there was something else that perturbed the boy as he looked around but as yet he couldn't quite work out what it was.

"This is where we will stay. We have travelled far enough east. The Epirotes will already know we are here."

98

Phoenix appeared jovial but the truth was he too felt uneasy. He kept his thoughts to himself so as not to upset the boy. The small holdings had become sparser the further they had travelled. The terrain was drier with the owners perhaps too old to work the land. But was that all? He had seen many old buildings fallen and disused as if some great calamity had struck. Only tamarisks and carob had been hardy enough to survive.

The two of them hunted around for a place to make camp. Phoenix knew from the salt scented air they were less than half a day from the coastline. Secretly he expected this to be their final camp; the ground was lush fed by the many underground springs and the nearby wood full of herbs for medicines and oak for fire and splints. He dismounted and looked around;

"A cave would be ideal. We can light a fire at the entrance to keep away the wolves."

Phoenix shot a glance at Achilles to see his reaction and seeing the look on his face smiled broadly,

"Don't worry boy. There haven't been wolves in this region for generations. Hunted down by the Epirot tribes."

Achilles was relieved. Fighting wolves was for true heroes like Hercules. I am still a boy!

"Water the horses Achilles whilst I take a look around."

Phoenix walked up the slopes of the valley with just Purdy for company. He followed him everywhere and like all animals was devoted to his new master.

"Purdy, you are sure footed and agile. I'm looking for shelter of some kind. Can you help me?"

He cocked his head inquisitively for all the world looking as if he understood Phoenix perfectly. He trotted on ahead. The valley became very steep in parts and Phoenix found himself slipping more than once. Purdy was quite happy leaping from rock to rock. Phoenix eyed him jealously as once again he lost his footing.

"I wish I was as agile as you my friend. Hey, can't you give me a leg up?"

Purdy was now stood on a rock above his head. Phoenix watched as he suddenly turned and to his amazement seemed to disappear. Intrigued he dragged himself up to see where the young goat had gone. There must be some kind of overhang. Excited he finally pulled himself up to where he had last seen the kid. All he saw were some thick ferns which hung like a curtain. He was about to continue upwards when he heard a noise which seemed to come from behind the ivy curtain. He reached out and pulled at the green fronds and gasped in amazement.

"So this is where you are. And what have you found?"

Behind the curtain was a cave protected by the protruding rock and hidden by the ivy. "This must be virtually impossible to see from the valley floor. It will do fine for us. There's even a curtain of ferns to protect the entrance."

Phoenix heard a sudden movement and instinctively reached to his hip for his knife. He relaxed as soon as he saw Purdy emerge from the back of the cave which was of a good length with a dry mossy floor. Although the ceiling was low it was high enough. The stone on the walls was dark with a slight sheen and smooth to the touch. Really it was the perfect hideaway only to be discovered by luck and stealth.

"I'd have never found this without you. You showed me the way. Come here."

Purdy was only too happy to lie at the feet of Phoenix whilst he petted him and thanked him. The only problem Phoenix saw was getting the supplies and equipment up the side of the valley. But it could be done. He thanked the Gods for showing him the cave. But privately he knew it was Purdy who deserved the credit.

99

Meanwhile Achilles had become bored waiting for Phoenix and decided to do some exploring of his own. In the distance he could hear a sound which was unfamiliar. He lay on his stomach putting his ear to the ground as he'd seen Phoenix do many times. As he concentrated the sound amplified, it had a musical quality to it. Achilles thought of Orpheus and smiled. He followed the noise climbing higher up the valley which became steeper and stonier but Achilles persevered. Surely whatever was making the tumult of noise would be around the next corner. Still higher Achilles rounded a rock and found himself stood on a makeshift stone platform. He gazed in wonder at the source of the noise; the biggest waterfall he had ever seen falling from a great height. It seemed to fall from the sky itself far above him and sent out a mist and spray that whetted the face of the boy; he licked his lips savouring its taste. Inside the waterfall points of light shone and sparkled like blue and white jewels. Achilles stood motionless aghast and astounded at the beauty of what he saw. All his senses seemed heightened by this mighty mass of water which thundered to the ground just in front of him. Far above his head he could just make out a ledge of stone that lay behind the waterfall itself. Achilles considered trying to get to it – what a view! But it would be impossible, the rocks too precipitous, the climb too slippy. He looked down and saw the water join the river which curved calmly away through the centre of the valley. Achilles stood mesmerised for some time before shaking himself from his reverie; Phoenix will be wondering where I am. He slipped and slid down the valley eager to tell Phoenix of his find.

100

Lyria was now choosing to travel at night as the sun burned a hole in her soul and laughed at her slow progress. Her freedom which only a few days ago had seemed like salvation was now a burden. She yearned for Lesbos, her real home, helping her mother with her chores, the smell of citrus in her nostrils. She thought back to the hills above Methymna staring over the waters to Phrygia and Troy. Every aspect she remembered so clearly; in her mind's eye filling in the faded cracks like an artist touching up his mural; the bright green grass shining like a lizard's eye, the sunlight on the gulf of Adramyttia, then the great gulches of moonlight that smudged the waters, the softest winds flavoured by the apricot groves. But mindful even as a child of the transience of this beauty, the bitter cold of winter betraying summers kiss, but still her hidden faith beneath the snow. Winter brought reflection to Lyria but with summer came exhilaration and purpose in patterns of blue, wearing the colours of the day on her face. And now her questions were of a different kind. What has become of my mother? Who is the man in the cloak who helps me? Who are these soldiers who wander the woods? Her choices which only a few days ago had seemed simple were now limitless – the dizziness of her freedom made her afraid. She thought about the men she had seen by the woods. She had heard stories of slaves forming gangs that preyed on lone travellers, capturing them and selling them to the chattels of Nemea and Sicyon. In the dark she could make little out. Far away an owl whickered. Her horse stepped forward gingerly then snorted at the moon which raged up the river.

"Where are you dear Endymion? Come for me tonight."

Lyria began to shake with a sudden fear. Cerebus growled. She was sure she had heard a step, a sound out of sorts for a forest. Too frightened to gallop ahead yet too scared to stay still Lyria shivered. Her eyes trained on a bloom of yarrow plants that formed a clumsy shadow directly in front of her. And then it rose and moved toward her with great speed and her breath left her body and her body left her horse. She screamed but the air was so thin that the sound was stillborn, strangled by the night. Giving in to the pain and the force of what she felt she closed her eyes expecting death. She heard Cerebus spit and snarl and then a high pitched scream. Her last sight was of the half moon resting on its back as she lost consciousness.

101

Before long the cave felt familiar and was filled with the many tools, weapons and instruments they'd need. Phoenix had arranged the weapons neatly, the bows and shields, scimitars, axes and blades of differing sizes some of which the boy had never seen. There were *kitharas* and lyres and flutes made of bone and wood. They reminded him of Orpheus. How he would love it here. Then towards the back of the cave arranged neatly from the smallest to the largest a series of pots for cooking and preparation. These were the tools for making the many medicines and ointments that Phoenix delighted in mixing. Phoenix had been instructed by the Libyan and had a good knowledge of medicine. He prided himself on being *Iatros*, a healer. His knowledge had been collected in Crete from the Libyan whose grotesque array of warts and skin diseases coupled with his innate morbidity had meant the house had been full of herbalists, root cutters, bonesetters and surgeons. He had been proud of his collection of medicines. He had heard of a magical potion from the land of Kush that could cure headaches, it came from the bark of trees and was said to relieve pain. Achilles could not believe the amount of potions, ointments, herbs and pomades. Of all the treasures in the cave it was these that Phoenix coveted most. Very soon Achilles learned to leave them alone but he was most eager to learn,

"What do they all do?"

"In time Achilles."

But Achilles was impatient and picked up some leafy herbs and what looked like tree bark.

"What about these?"

"Headaches and fever."

"And these ears of wheat?"

"Skin problems."

"Black figs?"

"Impotence."

Achilles looked confused.

"I will tell you another time."

Phoenix had decided it was far too early in the day to discuss such matters. Achilles would never forget the meal they ate that first night. A simple vegetable stew with leavened bread. Phoenix only ate meat sparingly when necessary. They drank water from the spring that gurgled not far from mouth of the cave, the sky was clear and fresh, the whole vault of the heavens clear and exalted. As they sat and stared Phoenix felt something brush lightly over his skin. Looking down he saw a tiny lizard looking up at him,

"You're a pretty fellow. Now, can you tell me anything about this place?"

The lizard stared back unblinking. Reaching down Phoenix picked up the tiny creature by its neck,

"If I pick it up by its tail it will break and run off."

Achilles could not believe it and stared amazed at the tiny creature with its brown markings on its back and its tiny exquisitely formed feet one of which appeared a little crooked,

"Will it stay with you sir?"

"Well let's see" replied Phoenix who secretly hoped it would.

Holding the small creature in his open palm the lizard seemed quite content to stay where it was. It began to slowly make its way up the arm of Phoenix with a slight limp.

"If you live with a cripple you will learn to limp."

"How?"

"Never mind. I have a new pet. She's so beautiful. Look at those green eyes! Lizards are faithful creatures. What shall I call her?"

Without a moment's hesitation and without really knowing why Achilles replied,

"Lyria."

102

Orpheus walked down the northern passages near the great hall; he knew this was the part of the palace where Helen would often walk. He tried desperately to think of an excuse for why he should be there but none came to mind. It was too late anyway for suddenly without warning she appeared. Orpheus immediately turned into the first room, an armoury. Shields and stiff leather greaves bound with silver lace were arranged in rank order. The smell of metal and leather was strong. The great ashen spear of Peleus was secured to the wall. Peeled and polished it shone like a yellow flame. It was said only he had the strength to throw it. It had been a wedding gift from Idomeneus of Crete. Orpheus watched Helen walk by seemingly deep in thought. Seeing her walk away was more than he could bear and he coughed. This didn't seem to startle Helen who turned, smiled benignly then continued. In truth she had known of Orpheus all along. His eyes followed her watching her graceful steps, her gilded robe complimenting her hair as it soundlessly brushed the stone passage. Suddenly he became aware of footsteps behind him. Turning around he saw Peleus who was inspecting the weaponry,

"Young Orpheus isn't it? Spying again eh? And who is it this time. Is that the young Helenaise?"

It was foolish to deny it so Orpheus answered lamely,
"Yes."

"And are you in love with her like most men in the palace?"

Orpheus blushed as Peleus suddenly placed a hand on his face and slowly stroked his hair. Orpheus stayed silent and Peleus laughed.

"You are friends with my son and Lyria. I know. I hear you have a gift for the lyre."

In common with many men of noble rank and with a cultured heritage Peleus had a liking for boys particularly musicians. Now he turned his eye to Orpheus. Orpheus for his part was not so naïve as to misunderstand his motives.

"Music is a gift from the Gods Orpheus. The Gods bestow gifts on those who honour them with music. Report to me. You shall play for me and if you please me you shall be my body servant."

Peleus then walked in the direction of Helen. Drawing level with her he offered her his hand. Peleus always dressed well but it seemed to Orpheus he had never looked so gallant and handsome despite his years. Or perhaps it was because of them. His olive skin and keen eyes had a new vitality. He watched as Helen followed him with her eyes. Orpheus instinctively moved towards Helen but he checked himself and turned away. However, she suddenly turned and walked towards him and whispered secretly,

"Tomorrow, after sunset, in my rooms."

103

At Pagasae Antigonus watched as the men ate. Oak trestles were dragged and assembled, then a procession of dead animals seemed to appear from nowhere; a headless pig dripping fat and blood was hauled and spiked followed by two goats. The corpses were covered in salt and turned slowly whilst another man threw a sizeable chunk of meat onto the fire which sizzled and spat.

"For the Gods."

He didn't know which he hated more – the sight of the burning flesh or its sickly sweet aroma. He looked at the man who had sacrificed the meat. His hands and arms were covered in thick black hair which seemed to compliment his bestial features. His swagger and gait easily betrayed his inebriated state. He recognised him,

"Look Macedon, that is Meriones, leader of the Perrhaebi, second in command to Peleus. He is a brave man but his idleness and appetites are legendary. Rumour has it he never bathes and if it moves he will bed it. Even the eunuchs are not safe."

Macedon watched him closely as he ate. Even this seemed an effort. The sweat swam around him in rivers as he swigged wine by the bucket. His belly trembled as he laughed.

"I'd kill for his armour" mused Macedon, "silver and copper, handmade and engraved. Worth a tidy sum."

Twenty thousand men now awaited the orders of Peleus to march on Mycenae. Some had travelled for weeks just to get to the Thessalian harbour. One hundred ships waited his command in the gulf of Pagasae. Two thousand horses, sheep, goats wine and fruit sat waiting to be loaded. He regretted the day he had signed the treaty with the Myceneans. But he had made a pact with Agamemnon which the Mycenean lord had broken. To not act would render him a coward. Agamemnon had stolen the oracle, taken it for a prize and killed the servants of Apollo. He lifted his arms to the sky as Orpheus fitted his body armour. Another servant held his grieves. Peleus pondered his appearance as he looked in the mirror. In his forty eighth year he wondered if his fighting days were over. But there was no grey in his hair which he wore in the old style, tied at the nape with a decorative silver clasp. And there was the problem of Achilles. Was Phoenix preparing him well? Should I recall him? Prodicus, leader of the Petthali ruled over the plains that stretched from Tricca to Dordona in the west. Like Meriones he had sworn allegiance to Peleus who had forfeited these lands so that they would enforce his will. Peleus knew his position was precarious.

"Is your mind made up Peleus?"

"What choice do I have? The oracle at Delphi is for all men to worship, not the glory of one man. Agamemnon forgets this. Even now he builds at the temple, refuses entry to the weak, he has murdered the servants of Apollo, defiled the priestesses. Am I to invite Hubris on my people? I am Peleus ruler of the Aleudae and Penthelids, the noblest of all the families of Thessaly descended from Aleusa himself the son of Heracles. This is the blood that runs through my veins. I have sworn an oath with Asclepius to protect the oracle. I will not invoke Nemesis. I will not violate the laws of the Gods. My ships and lineage will be a curse on Agamemnon and the Pisistratids. Ares will protect us."

Peleus turned once again to the distant mountains,

"We move against Mycenae."

104

Even before the door was opened by the irascible old Tantios Orpheus could hear the sound of excitable voices from within. When the door was finally opened he was amazed at what he saw. All the young men and women were dressed elegantly. Orpheus looked down rather shamefully at his own clothes, rather scruffy sandals and an old robe that Achilles had gifted him. The *Komos* was underway as the men reclined on drinking couches and passed the communal *krater*. Some ate from a trestle table that was covered in the most delectable foods. As well as the basted lamb Orpheus noticed the honey cakes and spelt wafers. Jujube, peaches and apricots were scattered carelessly over the table and floor. Scented myrtle, privet flowers and camomile blossoms gave the room a delicious aroma that easily overpowered the copious libations that had already been spilt. Baskets filled with sultana oranges, ahmani peaches, lemons and autumn cucumbers were hung from the walls. Orpheus loved sultana oranges. Helen knew this and had sent for them that morning. In the corner of the room two men sat each playing a lyre. Orpheus could tell instantly that the man playing the smaller instrument was out of key. Helen once again was the centre of attention as the young men played around her. One in particular seemed transfixed as he never left her side. Orpheus watched him as he stood on the threshold of the room unseen. He was a blonde curly haired youth with a narrow face and bright blue eyes. As he watched the antics it felt to Orpheus like the room was small, as if it was closing in on him. And yet the room was infact large, a privilege afforded an emissary and *Klawiphorus*. Helen saw Orpheus standing nervously at the door,

"Ahh, here is our guest of honour. Orpheus."

Orpheus, who had never been a guest of honour or indeed a guest, paused.

"Come, come. Do plover's eggs tempt you on a bed of moss? Or quails? Let me introduce my friends. What fun we shall have. Now, here is Eurypylos."

The blonde boy so obviously enamoured of Helen stared at Orpheus without offering any greeting,

"You will get used to Eurypylos, he's a little sullen. He cannot speak and he cannot hear so he is my most intimate acquaintance. Now this is Acastus, brother of Erachton the poet no less. And this is Phegaras the musician son of Dares from Ithaka."

"Where the musicians have the finest ear and the wine is the sweetest in all of Greece" interjected Phegeras whose flushed red cheeks were already paying homage to his love of the vine. Despite himself Orpheus soon became intoxicated with the laughter and gaiety that surrounded him. Helen clearly favoured him and the dark looks he received particularly from Acastus did little to discourage him. Orpheus laughed more than he had done since his friends had left and he took every opportunity to gaze and take his fill of Helen's beauty. It was the music of her voice that most moved him. Her words sang creating a parallel meaning, a perfect pitch of charm and chime, a melodious parity. The truth was he missed his friends but now once again he dined on ambrosia. The laughter took hold like a strong wine and Orpheus, intoxicated, laughed out loud; the glory of sudden laughter rising from deep within him shaking the cobwebs of his stilted mirth. Lyria was gone. Achilles too. Now it was Helen that shone. Her fragrance was the sound of the sunset. She opened a secret door and Orpheus stared at the treasures therein. Gradually and with infinite guile he was being led into a state of mind where his whole world was hers.

He believed in her implicitly, he obeyed her without question. Finally, at the end of the evening Helen once more took centre stage for the final game,

"Now, you must all have secrets. Think hard what they are. Then I will choose one of you to share it with me."

Helen gazed deliciously at the boys who were all thinking hard. Orpheus was struggling to come up with anything that would serve to impress Helen. It was with an equal measure of hope and fear that he waited for Helen's choice.

"I choose Orpheus. Now, come Orphy we must hide under this robe so the others cannot hear."

In an instant Orpheus found himself knelt on the floor facing Helen. The world faded from sight; this was another world, a close and intimate, perfumed world. Orpheus noticed how even in the darkness her eyes shone. He felt her breath on his cheek, Helen blew in his ear and whispered deliciously,

"Tell me, tell me Orpheus."

Her hair fell in ringlets over her shoulders as she embraced him. Orpheus remained silent, struck dumb by her beauty and closeness. To speak at all would have been impossible for him. He was sure his blushes would ignite the room, that his heartbeat could be heard through all Thessaly. Here was the dumbness his father had spoken of.

"Speak Orpheus. I hear you are body servant."

Without knowing how or why Orpheus suddenly remembered the conversation between Peleus and Prodicus earlier that evening. Orpheus repeated this to Helen. Her face hardened as he spoke the words nervously. And then the world returned; the robe was lifted. Acastus was gone, only Eurypylos remained, glowering in a corner. Orpheus left and Helen turned to the supposedly deaf and mute soldier who raised one eyebrow,

"Well?" he said.

"It is good."

105

"Today we begin your diaita, a strict routine of diet, exercise and bathing."

Achilles sighed. He didn't know which he dreaded the most,

"Do we have to bathe often?"

"Yes. And swim"

Achilles thought of Lyria, her lithe body diving into Lake Karla. 'I wonder what she is doing right now?'

"You must maintain the proper balance of hot and cold and wet and dry. Women are wetter than men Achilles. That is why they must bleed every month to prevent a build up of fluid. Roast foods are dry, boiled foods are moist. We shall mix them. If you are hot you will cool off. If you are tired lay down. If you are hungry eat."

Achilles laid down and grinned up at Phoenix,

"I'm hungry sir."

Phoenix smiled,

"Then let's cook. I shall teach you."

"But when do I learn to fight properly? To use the sword?"

Phoenix looked at Achilles,

"It's a terrible thing to have knowledge without power Achilles but much worse to have power without knowledge."

"What do you mean?"

"You'll see."

106

In the mornings Purdy would come to the mouth of the cave where Achilles would pet him. Then after collecting the pheasants' eggs he would hunt for berries and herbs, again following his mentors instruction, clover for pain relief, mint for avoiding infection. Achilles enjoyed these moments of solitude away from the sweat and the leather. Phoenix knew that the early mornings were important for Achilles. He could reflect on the previous day's training and look forward to the day ahead. But just as important was his understanding of herbs and medicines and to be able to collect and cook food. These were skills that may one day save his life and if nothing else would teach wisdom and more importantly humility to the young prince of Thessaly. Achilles spent the afternoons grappling with Phoenix, practicing holds and locks that would gain him advantage in the 'in-fighting' as Phoenix called it.

"If weapons are damaged it may come down to hand to hand fighting. If this is so then eye gouging will win a fight or any attack to the groin. Aim for the temple to concuss an opponent. It will gain you valuable time. Can you feel here where the skull feels softer?"

Phoenix touched Achilles on the side of his head – he could feel the area was vulnerable.

"A punch or strike here will disorientate your opponent. A further punch against the line of the jaw will break it easily. Now try it on me."

Achilles had long since learned to not hold back in attacking Phoenix as it only angered him so with Phoenix holding out his chin he threw his fist full force in a round arc. Phoenix quickly raised his right arm blocking the punch and in the same motion swung his body around so his left elbow missed Achilles' chin by a hair's breadth.

"A spinning elbow or fist will always surprise your enemy and the momentum of the spin will add power to the strike. Now you try."

And so the boy learned day after day. Phoenix told him of the Hyksos, a tribe to the south of the pharaohs who used bronze tools in battle, bows, scimitars and drawn chariots,

"They charge at the enemy with an archer and a driver. Before them chariots were just a means of transporting soldiers to the front line. At Quadesh they became a weapon."

Achilles listened fascinated,

"They say Egypt is the mother of all civilized societies. Women own property, they have specialized schools to train healers and they dilute their wine like us."

Phoenix paused and putting his hand on his head ran his fingers through his slightly thinning hair,

"They have a cure for baldness." He sighed wistfully and reaching behind produced a small jar that contained an evil smelling ointment,

"Crocodile, lion and hippo fat."

"Does it work?"

"I've never had the courage to rub it in."

107

Achilles enjoyed the nights the most when the instruction was done and the fire was set at the mouth of the cave to ward off the wild boars. Then the two would stare into the night sky or at the purple peaks of Mount Pelion that glowered in the distance,

"That is where the centaurs roam Achilles."

"What are they?"

Achilles had heard the kitchen boys and courtiers speak of strange beasts on the slopes of the mountains to the north but had dismissed the talk,

"Powerful creatures with the body of a man mounted on a Magnetian stallion – they will deprive you of your reason and strip the flesh from your bones."

Achilles, wide eyed with excitement looked to the hills,

"Ixion was an ancient king of Thessaly, the first man to commit murder. Madness overcame him and Zeus forgave him and cured him. Ixion repaid his kindness by raping Hera. Zeus would not believe this and so fashioned a likeness of Hera from cloud and placed it in Ixion's bed. Ixion ravished it and Zeus punished him by crucifying him on an eternal wheel of fire. And yet the cloud produced a child which mated with the Thessalian thoroughbreds on Mount Pelion. Thus the race of centaurs was created."

"Why are men such fools with women?" Achilles spoke more to himself than to his mentor but Phoenix heard him and laughed throwing a stout olive branch onto the fire,

"If I knew the answer to that Achilles I would hold the

secrets of the world and have my own berth on Olympus."

Achilles for the hundredth time determined he would never let himself be led astray by any woman.

108

"Now a sword is just a sword. A bow is just a bow. This won't always be so. A sword becomes more than a thing of metal, the bow the same. But then one day you will master the art of fighting and a sword once again will just be a sword. You will be able to overcome ten men single handedly. This means an army of one hundred can overcome a thousand, an army of a thousand, ten thousand. A hundred *myrmidons*."

"What are they?"

"Elite warriors like your father. He sailed with Jason."

Achilles knew that his father had searched for the fleece but Peleus had never confided in him or sat him on his knee to tell him tales. Phoenix continued,

"It is important you have the right sword in a battlefield situation, one with a good temperament and stamina."

"I like the sword sir."

Phoenix stepped nearer to Achilles and placing both hands on his shoulders pulled him closer fixing him with a strong stare,

"I don't want to hear that Achilles. I don't want to hear that you like the sword, the bow or the club. You must be practical for one day you will find yourself with your least favourite weapon on a field of battle. Your enemies may know this and it will give them strength. You might as well say I prefer my arm to my leg. All are needed, all are extensions of you. Fighting is a trade Achilles. Everything I say you must consider and absorb. Think through. A Greek warrior is not a piece of meat but a thinking spirit with strong convictions. But reign in your emotions, temper them just as the blacksmith hones his weapons. You need discipline in the mind and endurance in the body. It takes real judgement to handle these precious qualities."

Achilles nodded.

109

Achilles woke with the malodorous smell of herbs and unguents in his nostrils as Phoenix worked busily at the back of the cave on his many concoctions and mixtures. Stretching out his stiff limbs he sat up and stared for a few moments at his mentor admiring his dedication to his craft. How long has he been working? All night? Phoenix without turning spoke,

"Fetch some water boy. I need to dilute this mixture."

Achilles put on his tunic and sandals grabbed a handful of dates and clambered down the valley side enjoying the warmth of the sun on his skin. He headed for a hollowed out rock near the waterfall where he knew there would be plenty of fresh rainwater. He often drank from it after a gruelling training session. When he returned Phoenix was stood well outside the cave. The smell of his latest ointment was so overpowering he had had to leave.

"My apologies boy, it seems the whole valley now reeks of goat shit."

Achilles began to laugh and Phoenix despite himself laughed too. Phoenix seldom laughed knowing it gave away his shame, the high pitched laughter of the half man, the mutilated. He put his arm around Achilles as they walked,

"Fighting encompasses all the senses and more. First you will sense your enemy. It may be a silence, a break in the natural order, a hawk that swoops too near the wind. Then you will smell him, then hear him and see him before you taste his mettle and finally in death you will embrace him."

Achilles thought for a few moments,

"What's for breakfast?"

110

Later that morning when the sun was well up Phoenix called for Achilles,

"I need you to wash my back."

Achilles dutifully fetched some more water from the stream. "Here, take this."

Phoenix took off his chlaina, a short woolen cloak that was draped over his shoulders and tied with a pin across his chest. A small fieldmouse caught in the folds emerged and twitched at the morning breeze. Phoenix paused and looked at Achilles who sensed his nervousness. He turned and spoke with his back to the boy. Closing his eyes he cursed the Libyan for the thousandth time, the man who'd taken his appetites,

"Remember to arrange your clothes well boy, a good chiton or himation well wrapped reflects good breeding. Never lower your standards and let it drag. And never spend too long in the sun, it will tan your skin. You are not a farmer."

Phoenix knew the time was coming when he would have to turn and reveal his shame,

"That cloak, it helped me through the Cretan winters. The coldest winter I ever…"

Achilles suddenly spoke,

"Sir I know."

Phoenix froze and looked upwards,

"Did you see the sunset last night boy? Did you see the drama? A wounded lion limped across the sky bleeding and broken, his mane melted and then in the upper reaches the eye of a lizard,"

"Sir please. You can show me."

And so they embraced and Phoenix wept whilst Achilles washed his mentor. Later Phoenix recounted the agonies of the knife as casually as if he were dictating a recipe,

"I miss the lusts Achilles. Don't take them for granted. Lust is a kind of love, it can overpower you."

Achilles wasn't sure he understood and thought it a strange thing to say.

111

"Sire, I have a slave here for your perusal. Says she has always wanted to meet you. From the slave cargo that arrived yesterday."

Palantes knew that Agamemnon would never turn a woman away. Young or old it didn't matter. It was his job to keep the king satiated with a never ending supply. Agamemnon would perform regardless of looks or age, his sexual mores and appetites knew no limits. Women, whores, children and, it was rumoured, goats and cattle.

"Well Palantes? Be my eyes and ears, I need details."

"Quite exceptional in her appearance sir, there is nothing which repels or is disagreeable."

Agamemnon, tired and irritable barely acknowledged his servant but now looked up. Palantes continued,

"Her skin is a little pale sir, however that is because her use of make up is somewhat primitive. Her eyes are not sparkling but neither are they dull, her teeth are all there if a little stained, her hands a little blotchy, her nose the same. This can be put down to the sea voyage."

"And her thighs and breasts?"

"All they should be for a woman of her age. And she speaks well, dances well and is a graceful eater."

"Then I shall take her tonight. Arrange it."

Palantes bowed and left.

"It's your lucky day woman. He wants to take you, not kill you. Do you have a name?"

The woman who had expected nothing less of her employer looked up,

"Danae of Lesbos."

112

Agamemnon walked towards her and cupped her face with his hands,

"Danae. Ever faithful. It's been too long. Palantes wasn't complimentary. Although he did say you were a graceful eater."

"He can please himself. The voyage did me no favours. Those islanders stink of fish and tar and they are full of wine and fat."

"You did well with Parmenion. But Lyria lives. You may live to regret that error. Or die."

"What harm can she do? She's too busy dreaming to be a problem."

"You are sure she knows nothing. Good. Then I think it's time for a tearful reunion. I hear Lyria has friends in high places. She is close to Achilles. Some say they are lovers. It is time to be a doting mother again. Find out what you can. And what of our bastard boy? Don't tell me you still pine for him?"

Danae had dreamed of the child she gave up and saw the shadows of his bones in the flickering twilight and she had groaned so Parmenion had turned in his sleep. She thought of this son now, Agamemnon's heir, and how he would have honoured her and watched the waves at Mytilene. Eileithyia had been summoned to ensure a good delivery but Agamemnon had not countenanced this bastard boy invoking the law of *amphodromia* as he carried the boy around the hearth. And then for Lyria to appear. How she hated her daughter for the epiphany of pain she had caused her, her self control gone, abandoned to the screams of the furies for all to see. How she had screamed. The shame.

The priestesses had brought the poppy, offered incantations and amulets and prayed to Hera and Hecate both venerated birth Goddesses. The final insult to beget a girl, a small, weak, bloodied testament to the pain to which she had conceded. Lyria's love for her was maddening, unbearable. Her aristocratic forefathers on Seraphos pushed her political leanings towards a firm dictatorship, rules that were clear, freedom for those of good stock, of wealth, of lineage, who were intelligent enough to use it wisely – and Agamemnon was the clearest advocate of this inbuilt prejudice. A benevolent, thinking ruling class only leads to anarchy and muddled idealism. What a fool Parmenion was. Impractical, naïve dreamer. And he had paid the price.

"My payment Lord Agamemnon?"

"Your life?"

"The price has gone up."

Agamemnon smiled and walked to a large wooden chest at the rear of the room and opened it. Danae gasped when she looked inside,

"A war chest from Crete. You can take any two items."

Danae left with a leopards hide and a low strung sword belt dripping with jewels that had belonged to Idomeneus.

113

"Tell me about the Gods Phoenix."

Achilles was asking this more and more as his training advanced and his confidence grew. Phoenix guessed the reason for his enquiries. He was empathizing more and more with the pantheon of Olympians as if his training was bringing them nearer to him. As his self awareness increased he began to mature and understand what was expected of him. Phoenix wished Peleus had not put this burden on him. Perhaps it would have been better for Achilles to discover his own destiny in his own way,

"What do you want to know?"

Phoenix had exhausted his knowledge which was extensive. Achilles had heard all the legends from the Titans through to the indiscretions of the Olympians.

"Was there ever a Greek hero who lived long?"

Achilles looked away when he asked and Phoenix felt as if his heart would burst. This young boy had the dreams and hopes of a nation weighing him down. Sitting by Achilles he placed his arm around his shoulders. As they sat by the cave entrance half of Achilles' face was in shadow, the other half lit by the dying sun,

"Many Achilles."

In truth Phoenix was struggling to think of any.

"Tell me."

"First rest, then I will tell you in the morning"

Achilles lay down reluctantly.

"Just as I thought. There are none."

114

Peleus looked out over the Thessalian landscape and at the moon that was tinged red,

"It's a blood moon Orpheus. Soon the the Thessalian witches will roam. They will tempt her down to extract her blood."

He returned to his bed and lay with Orpheus and thought of the days of his youth, the days of his glory. The memory of the journey of the Argonauts was bittersweet but Peleus held it close and treasured it. And now his new lover could hear his tales. Orpheus lay on the bed and listened whilst Peleus reminisced. But he always turned away as if ridden with guilt, unable to look at Orpheus directly.

"Shall I tell you of the eastern journey?"

Orpheus said nothing. He had heard the story many times and was tired of it.

"We sailed from Iolcus to Aea on the Colchian river Phasis. But first Jason had consulted the oracle at Delphi to ask for the blessing and guidance of Pythian Apollo who had told him of the murder and dismemberment of Apsyrtus. We were refused entry to the sea of Marmaris by Troy until heavy tribute had been paid. And when they heard the purpose of the voyage they eased their demands for a share of the gold that would surely follow. Ha! The purple fleece fringed with gold used when the crops failed. I don't blame Phrixus for stealing it. He had to bring the rains or it meant death. But it had to be returned, our sense of doom and foreboding rose every day. Long, long ago when the Gods were sober and refused libations. The treasure never came so with my brother Telemon we ousted king Laomedon and put Priam on the throne."

Peleus smiled when he remembered the young king's look of amazement. But what of swift footed Zetes? Euphemus who could out swim a dolphin? Sharp eyed Phalerus who could place an arrow in any target? The old familiar faces. Poor Nauplius the navigator who had perished with the plague caught from the stinking Hittites. They were barbarians. Peleus's jaw tightened when he thought of the eastern tribes of Nicodemia. May their souls wander endlessly. He remembered how they wrapped their dead in untanned oxhides suspending them from trees away from the city. That's when Nauplius fell sick. Peleus turned to Orpheus,

"Where is the Argo now I wonder? Buried they say at the temple of Poseidon on the isthmus at Corinth. Or at Aphatae on the Pagasean gulf."

Orpheus now knew his masters moods well. He felt sorry for him. He also hated him. Peleus frowned.

"Do you think blood still flows from the Sangarius streams where we slaughtered the cattle in dedication to Apollo? Some good it did us. Sometimes my memory wanders. It seems I am cursed by the Mnemone, by the Lethe and the lotus."

"Because you forget everything master?"

"No, because I remember everything."

115

Helen, wearing her favourite lifeless smile stared at him with loveless eyes. But to Orpheus those eyes were flaming, benign and loving. Helen had spent most of her short life being the sole source of the profoundest misery in others. Women were enemies to be blocked. Men? Lovers or servants to be moulded like soft clay. She shaped them until they stood in line in utter obeyance. Then smashed them. Orpheus was one of many. He like others stood ready to risk his leaping life for that exquisite face that hid the girl he would never know. She knew his mind by now, had watched him. She knew instinctively that this was a boy apt to be moved by the oddest of things. Music, verse, a sunset. Different yes, but a boy all the same and open to the choice cuts of lust, licentiousness and reckless flattery. But the slightest error, a word misplaced and the house would collapse. A strange and complicated creature this one. The barren light of the moon was the meretricious warmth that Helen's soul dined on, but no light was ever reflected. She took two napkins from Eurypylos and sat down cross legged. She bid Orpheus join her and so they both sat whilst their hands were ritually washed with orange water then dried. Orpheus was hungry and he ate his fill of olives, figs and cheese before the cooked meats were brought. Orpheus loved the flat thin cakes of southern Greece which enabled him to mop up the blood and fat of the skewered salted lamb. Helen ate sparingly. And finally the sweetmeats and fruits after which they rinsed their hands in the orange water again.

"It would have been nice if our other friends could have been here."

Orpheus remained silent,

"I wonder where Lyria and Achilles are."

"I couldn't say Lady Helen. I haven't seen Lyria for many weeks" he said truthfully.

His reply displeased her but no trace showed on her exquisite features. But it irked her that she had to wait for news. This boy knows more and I will make him speak. Helen wore her finest nightdress held at the yoke with a gold sash and silver brooch. She loosened the girdle of her robe and let it fall to the ground. As for Orpheus he saw nothing but the heaving bosom, the heavy lips, the painted face and sculpted thighs.

She stood nonchalantly staring at her naked body in the mirror. She untied her blonde hair so it fell over her high breasts. Orpheus was paralysed. Was this the way Mycenean women behaved? Helen, egregious and flagrant seemed oblivious to Orpheus but presently she spoke,

"You will bathe me."

His mind raced but he was too fearful to refuse. He longed for her to speak again. Her words floated gently from her parted lips like petals on the wind. Landing gilt edged on his senses it was paradise on edge, the scent of a rose. Already in his head the music and harmonies of her voice resonated and sang. But in his heart there heaved a sea of sentiment. This was a world he'd never glimpsed or tasted before. A tremulous thing, the sharp fruit of suspense. As for Helen there were no depths she hadn't plummeted, the slow burning incense and animal sacrifices to the old Gods, the crucified wolves, the scalped sluts from Lydia, her virginity never in question, never lost, never tasted. Orpheus stood in the flickering light and watched her step into the marble bath that Eurypylos had prepared. She noted the look on the face of the boy. This was her game, her rules, what chance did he have?

"Bring me the verbena" she whispered sultry as summer. Helen always whispered. It was a way of drawing in her prey. The men leaned close and her skin and perfume would overwhelm

– all the easier to entice and trap. Orpheus moved towards the pot of perfume on the side table glad to have something practical to do. Verbena was an expensive scent used only by royalty. He moved with short timid steps barely audible on the frescoed floor. Helen watched her prey looking for the slightest hint of desire. She took the lanolin and began to remove her make up slowly. She tossed her hair and Orpheus caught a glimpse of her breasts. I will let him wait and wonder. Ha! See how he trembles. Slowly now. Helen lay reclined in the rosemary scented bath,

"Wash my back."

Helen delighted in the tense, awkward movements of her victim. But still the interminable wait,

"Now my breasts and front."

Her breath was palpable and heavy. She took his hand and placed it on her breasts guiding it easily over her stomach and the sweet hollows of her thighs. For Orpheus there was an emotional chaos, his scrotum on fire and ice in his loins. As he leaned towards her Helen pulled away slowly,

"Now tell me about your friends. And what does dear Peleus have planned?"

116

Achilles took most delight in running, taking off his tunic, his sandals slipping slightly as he sprinted by the long stream that ran by the river. Slowly counting in his head as Phoenix had taught him. Ten, eleven. Short rests, his heartbeat barely raised. The morning grown old so the sun now hot on his back. A sudden shower bringing relief moving seaward through the valley, the steam from his body, his heart gently pulsing, one….two…..three. Phoenix had few concerns about his progress. Achilles grew stronger every day, fuller, leaner. Technically he was already a skilled fighter. But still there remained that lack of core belief crucial to all warriors. Phoenix sat at the cave entrance pondering his student's progress. Achilles needed to know that victory was the only possible outcome as he faced his foe. Victory is for the fighter who has no thought of himself. Too much self awareness is the greatest obstacle to all physical action.

"Too much thought will mean his senses lack an edge like a blunt blade."

Phoenix looked down the valley. He sat for a long time whilst Achilles slept behind him. Soon the stars grew out of the sky and the evening whispered her affections. The wind caressed his face and curled into the corners of the cave. Phoenix turned around and looked at Achilles and spoke softly,

"You are still a child."

Achilles kept his eyes closed. He didn't wish Phoenix to know he had heard him. But soon he fell asleep. When he awoke the next morning he was surprised to see that Phoenix hadn't moved and still sat pensively at the mouth of the cave. The dawn broke high behind the blue grey mountain so its slopes leaned towards its splintered summit pulling her shadows back to her bosom. Without turning Phoenix spoke. Achilles was not sure at first if his mentor spoke to him or to himself,

"Think of the great men who have lived and died. Hercules, or Jason who led your father to the fleece, the kings and rulers who came before, the ones who will come after, the philosophers who knitted their brows, the priests of Apollo in search of cures for their lingering patients. They loved and died, and their sons and daughter too. See how short and transient our life is, one day a babe in arms, the next a handful of dust. You came from the earth Achilles and you will return to it. So you must make your mark, be glorious, know where your capacity for greatness lies and grasp it keenly. Die happily like the fruit that falls when it is ready and ripe, with a prayer for the tree that rendered it and the earth that takes it. Know that oblivion awaits and let this drive you, think of the footless chasms of eternity that came before and will surely follow us. Let intrigue and slander occupy lesser men; you will not change their nature; a fig tree will not yield apples. So meet the accolades of men with cool indifference, their fickle applause and judgements do not concern us. Be master of yourself and your name will live forever and you with it."

Achilles was now stood by Phoenix and they stared at the mountain, its summit now hung with the morning draperies of silver grey mist. Phoenix reached out and stroked Achilles' hair and smiled. Achilles in turn drew Phoenix to him and they embraced.

117

Achilles sat idly by the entrance to the cave. Phoenix lay asleep. It was rare that Achilles was up before his mentor. Feeling a slight pressure on his knee he looked down and saw Lyria the lizard staring up at him as if to say 'Phoenix is still asleep. I'll spend some time with you.'

Achilles smiled,

"Come on, let me catch some flies for you."

The lizard seemed to understand and followed Achilles out of the cave where the boy quickly caught two flies and placed them in the palm of his hand. In an instant the flies were gone and Lyria blinked with pleasure before returning to the cave to see if Phoenix was awake. Achilles looked around. There was a stillness to the morning that seemed out of sorts; despite being well wrapped up he trembled. Looking to the mountain ridge a glint caught his eye. Far in the distance two men approached. They appeared to walk in symmetry with each other, each step meticulous and calculated, identical in every respect. Despite descending the mountain they moved easily and swiftly and seemed to glide rather than step. As they got nearer Achilles could just make out that each held a spear and were dressed as if for combat and as they walked a quietness fell around them; the animals hushed themselves, hid and watched. They approached with purpose and great speed and yet their strides seemed slow. Achilles shuddered and closed the ferns. With a child's reasoning a part of him believed that if he couldn't see them then they couldn't see him. When he opened the ferns a short time later they were nowhere to be seen.

118

It seemed as if the entire Greek population had gathered at Pagasae to ready for war. The galleys had been commissioned and prepared. Already boats full of warriors had arrived from the eastern and northern Aegean to wait on Peleus' orders. Amongst them were Macedon and Antigonus. For weeks men had gathered at the port in search of fortunes and adventure. They sat and chatted excitedly rubbing their eyes in disbelief at the mass of humanity around them. Some remembered their families and talked of their home and lands. Their sheer numbers bred confidence and an easy manner. Some gambled or took their chances with the whores who were plying their trade around the harbour. Many spoke of politics, of Agamemnon's blasphemy, greed and treachery, of his thousand ships. Some spoke of Zeus and the revenge the Gods would take on him and his kinsmen. Battle scars were shown and new friendships formed. The hawkers and tradesmen prospered. The wheelwrights did excellent business repairing the copper on the charioteers' wheels. The Thessalians were expert at providing food and wine quickly seemingly from nowhere and everywhere there were tables and carcasses sizzling on spits, libations being poured and the Gods satisfied.

"If this is the best wine I'd hate to taste the bad stuff."

"That's right. But why save the best wine for the Gods?"

Macedon tore at the roasted lamb with a passion,

"Now I know this to be true, I can't be dreaming the sweet taste of this meat. When do we march?"

Pyrrhus of Antioch eyed him and guessed his lowly origins

from his dress and crapulous appetites but knew better than to point it out.

"In two days if the blacksmiths and carpenters finish their work. I for one like to have a sword in my hand when I run at the enemy."

And so the hours passed as the soldiers waited. Anyone observing from the cliffs at Pherae would have been transfixed by the swarm of humanity far below. Copying as it did the swell of the ocean the warriors moved to their own rhythm arriving and departing from the spits and the smoke like bees at the hive. As water finds the easiest route so they moved earnestly in an endless flux of flood and flame and talked till the stars grew out of the air. Macedon and Antigonus sat together as was their habit,

"It is for definite this time my fugitive friend" said Antigonus.

"What is?" replied Macedon.

"The invasion" continued Antigonus, "I know the palace groom and he overheard Peleus saying we sail at first light."

Macedon, bored and restless picked his feet stretched his neck and looked to the stars before replying,

"The sooner the better for me. Thessaly stinks."

And further along Aulos, a small, shy carpenter threw another stick for Aenaes.

"Do you think they'll let me send a message to my wife? She's not too well you see. Going to give birth in the spring."

"Your first?" asked his friend Zeno of Soli.

"Well, no, it's just she's weak."

Zeno turned to his friend,

"What's her name?"

"Chirates, she's my girl."

Macedon cursed,

"The slop pit is full. There's nowhere to shit for miles around."

"Use your shield."

"How about I use your helmet dung breath?"

"Macedon, there is a fine line between untidiness and dirtiness. And you cross it."

Macedon grunted. He understood the concept of hygiene, he just didn't understand how it applied to him. His stinking feet now enjoyed not only a local but an international reputation.

"Your feet are like the cheeses at Miletus – you clear a tent in a heartbeat."

But what did Macedon care? He had seen enough of toil and misery to cast a cold eye on his own mortality never mind unwashed feet. His youth and young manhood had been an endless, execrable twilight searching for Kyprian copper in the pits of Hades. When they surfaced to see the blinking sun or feel the treacherous sea breezes that tempted them it was the dream of one day waking on his own terms that spurred him before returning to sweat out his soul in the belly of the mine. Antigonus continued speaking to the bored Macedon,

"We sail east to Seraphos to meet up with the Argives from Lesbos, and then south to face Agamemnon."

"Which means we will be dead in two weeks" said Macedon, grinning.

Aenaes returned the stick to Antigonus even though it was Aulos who had thrown it. He looked up at his new master waiting for him to throw the stick again.

"Will these winds never stop" Antigonus murmured to himself, "I just want to get going even if we miss Mycenae and sail off the end of the world."

Aenaes, suddenly very tired settled at his feet and slept. The whole harbour now slept pregnant with the dreams of warriors and women. All but Macedon. His thoughts ran deep as he gazed into the star strewn night. 'Where does the sun go at night? Is it possible to count the stars? Why does the wind blow hard then soft?' As for Lysistus the whore wrapped in his arms, she neither knew nor cared.

119

Achilles loved watching Phoenix. He was never sure which creature or insect was about to appear from under his tunic, all were under his spell. Recently a dormouse had taken residence in one of his sandals and only yesterday a caterpillar had appeared on his shoulder,

"Ahh, there you are."

Phoenix had handed the insect to Achilles.

"All animals can teach us lessons. Patience, humility and fortitude. They can see better than you or I. They know the worlds' secrets we seek. They can run faster, hear more acutely and fight better. They have beauty without vanity. But they possess these qualities without the ingratitude of arrogance. Be like the animals Achilles."

The boy put the creature on the back of his hand then lay back and looked at the sky. And the sun flowed down like honey on Achilles, son of Peleus.

120

Peleus was sleeping better than he'd slept for months without the usual despairing dreams that dragged down his days. This young boy Orpheus pleases me. It didn't concern Peleus that every night Orpheus wept as he fanned him to sleep. It was a cool night with a fresh wind that brought the smell of the plains breezing through the palace. Orpheus now slept outside the chamber but was awoken at dawn by the sound of Helen who had crept into Peleus's room and now stood over the sleeping ruler. He watched intently. Helen made no movement except to remove her white tunic which fell silently at her feet affording Orpheus a view of the naked priestess who now lay beside Peleus and pulled him onto her. Peleus awoke and looking at Helen he saw a look he recognised and remembered – the hunger that women had once had for him and he for them. His desires overcame him and he remembered the days when temple maidens had queued at his door. Orpheus watched distraught. How jealousy injects love with a new fervor! He ran from the palace.

121

"From the way he takes his first step, from the way he holds his sword, this will tell you all you need to know to defeat him."

Phoenix stood in the mouth of the cave. The sun had barely risen and Achilles felt tired and hungry. Why can't we have breakfast before we start classes? Achilles was looking at the figs in the corner of the cave that Phoenix had already picked that morning. But he knew how important it was to pay attention or breakfast would be even longer,

"How is that sir? How will I know those things?"

"It is because you will know his rhythms. Antagonise him with rhythms that counter him and confuse him."

"I'm not sure I understand."

Achilles was now on his feet and from the length of the shadow cast by his body realised the earliness of the hour.

"Here, I am the enemy, approach me."

Achilles grabbed his sword and took a step towards his teacher. Remembering what Phoenix had said previously he focused on his eyes trying to watch for any peripheral movement. I see his body. I see his eyes. I am ready. An instant later Achilles lay on the ground holding his shin after Phoenix had kicked him hard.

"There is more to a fight than swords and shields and spears. Be ready for anything."

Achilles, bewildered and bloodied and more than a little angry struggled to his feet,

"But, but you kicked me in the shin!"

"Yes, a kick in the shin, sand in the face, spit in the eye. There are no laws Achilles when a man wants to stay alive. You must be aware of your opponents' weapons but not look at them directly, be aware but not aware. Achilles, you must learn to win on the battlefield just as in politics, in governing Thessaly in winning the peoples' hearts."

Achilles placed his sword back in its sheath and walked back to the cave entrance. Phoenix, sensing his mood followed closely. He secretly sympathised with the boy who only a drum beat ago had dwelt with Hermes, the bringer of dreams.

"Achilles, victory will always be yours but you must have no thought for yourself. And have no thought for your opponent either. He is neither weak nor strong, short or tall."

He placed his hand affectionately on the shoulder of Achilles.

"Be absolute in your application to the art young prince. The smallest grievance, reflection or regret will expose you to your enemies. It will grow like a disease and be visible to other fighters. You are an artisan, this requires great skill and mastery. See me as the needle that guides the thread, you are the thread. Like the tradesman your tools must be whetted, ready to choose a timber free from knots, a blade that is balanced, a shield that is strong but light. But remember having a superior blade is not enough, you must wield it with great skill. And you will. Now, are you hungry?"

To the east the morning grey had dissolved. Above the peak of Mount Ossa the sun rose dispersing the gloom with a shimmery haze.

122

Orpheus kept running. As the darkness enrobed him he ran unseen past the farmer's huts and fields then followed the path of the river as it made its way westwards towards Tricca. The moon blushed as it hung pendant in the velvet soft Greek night. Orpheus reached out and hung it around his neck. He turned away from his usual path and headed towards the woods and groves that he knew lay due north. The red moon stalked him casting her shadows of blood and ivory. Orpheus started. Instinctively he crouched although there was no protection or cover to be had. He was sure he saw a movement in the groves ahead. Who would be in such a desolate spot? Orpheus remembered the words of Peleus,

"Soon the Thessalian witches roam."

Orpheus had thought nothing of it at the time but now he hesitated. There it was again, the quickest flash of white and then nothing. Now on his elbows he edged himself gradually closer to the blackness of the small wood that lay ahead. Closer still, a woman was kneeling, her head turned away from him. Then her voice reached him,

"Three nights have I kneeled before you Selene and now you shine blood red in radiance upon the mortals below. Your hair falls loose and roams the land, even Apollo's chariot grows pale before you. Bless this poison that I might kill my enemies and beat them down. I have been anxious Selene and thirsting for your potency and now your beams drown me as you shower the night and thrill me. Our passionate affair with the stars gives me strength. And your face blushing pink with vice and venom thrills me with corruption and lust, bride of Dionysus inspire me. I am unused so use me."

Orpheus had heard rumours of these female rituals in honour of Dionysus. He knew he was forbidden to witness them but this compelled him even more to keep watching. The woman turned and like all followers of Dionysus sniffed the air – it was her way, the way their kind judged all men and beasts. Beasts that were to be ripped apart and devoured. A smell of any kind was to be hoped for but tonight she smelt more than the pine and overripe olives. If it was a man then so much the worse for him. Danae had been left cold by the politics of her dead husband, despising his devotion to the *agora*. In between his kisses which she endured with a calm patience she longed for her sisters and the abandon she had already known as a young woman in Seraphos. She then looked to the sky so the moon lit up her face and Orpheus gasped in horror. And then he knew he was in danger and he turned and ran. At his back the *Maenads* shrieked and pursued him.

123

It was night and Achilles lay at the foot of the cave and looked upwards. The fern was tied back so he could see the sky. The number of stars overwhelmed him. They seemed brighter than usual like a shock of white flame searing across the heavens. It was difficult to see the spaces between them,

"Why are they so bright? They're brighter than the sky in Thessaly."

Phoenix was at the back of the cave trying to prepare yet another ointment from horse fat and sour wine. He joined Achilles at the mouth of the cave and looked up,

"It's because they're nearer to us here" he said simply. "This region is higher than our home in Thessaly and we are half way up a mountain. It's natural we should see more."

"What do they mean Phoenix? What do they tell us?"

Phoenix placed the old wine on the floor and sat with Achilles.

"They tell us many things. They tell us when to sail and where. They direct our actions, they guide us on the oceans."

Achilles said nothing but continued looking upwards still in awe of what he saw,

"Do you see that cluster of stars there?"

Phoenix pointed to a small group of five or six stars set apart to the east. Achilles nodded,

"Farmers use it. It's called the Pleiades. When it is on the ascendant it means winter is about to begin and the weather will turn colder. The land will die. We will offer prayers to Demeter to ensure its rebirth in the spring. When it is on the descendent, when it wanes, then it's time to plough the land and prepare."

Achilles was hesitant but finally spoke his heart,

"I'm frightened to die Phoenix."

Though his heart ached for the boy he had long expected this question.

"Of course. Your fear is what will keep you alive."

"How?"

"The only time you can judge character is when you see a man in battle. The mask they have worn through their life is ripped off and their true face is revealed. You must fear death Achilles. Find a place for it in your heart. Greatness in battle comes from a love of life, a wish to keep living. Hold the feeling close for nothing makes you more ferocious and grateful of life than the black wings of death, the acute dread of it."

Achilles sat down and lay back until sleep finally overcame him. Phoenix gathered him in his arms and carried him to his bed toward the back of the cave. In these lonely hours he would sit by Achilles listening for his steady breath and wondering where his dreams were taking him. Then he would stand and stare into the darkness sailing his memories of home like ships across the Aegean; watching the sun as it rose in his mother's eyes. In those empty hours he touched a woman scarcely remembered long, long ago. And his jaw set and he wondered at the cold malevolence that had urged her to abandon him. Now he stood in the dumbing purple twilight and stared at a star that shone above Mount Olympus. He knew that a sickness of the mind was close at hand and on this night he was too tired to hold back the flood. So his thoughts ran over themselves and he wept that he would never know love nor feel the hunger for it or see his seed produce a son to honour him. All this taken from him by the Libyan. Though he could give no love he had been happy to receive the affections of any who would offer. A soft spoken merchant perhaps as he traded the dyes at Tiryns. The Libyan of course had had his whores. Any man with a shake of a dice can win a woman and lay in drowsy content this night; drink wine then taste the cutting shards of lust. But not I. Walking outside he laughed at himself and looked upwards but found no solace in the querulous stars. Then walking to the back of the cave he leaned over slowly and kissed Achilles with his mother's lips.

124

Antigonus shook Macedon out of his sleep and pointed. Peleus stood on the deck under the flag in his finest filigree armour. His presence was such that he was able to ensure silence from the hoardes that now turned towards him.

"Men, we have the Gods on our side. They will guide, clothe and feed us and keep our women safe. Take heart then. Agamemnon has murdered and plundered a sacred shrine. The Gods want revenge and we are the instruments of that revenge. It is our time."

Then the hawsers were slung and the black sails hoisted and spread. The soldiers were quiet, the libations over. Only the shouts now of the bulwark crews as they guided the creaking boats slowly south out of the harbour. Orpheus held onto his sword tightly pleased with the anonymity the army now gave him.

125

Achilles couldn't sleep. He lay naked on his blanket. Sometimes if the night was hot and the day had been hard his mind would not slow. It would race as it was now, thinking of fights and foes and the tireless instruction of Phoenix. But more and more as he stared at the dark ceiling he would think of Lyria. What is she doing now as I lay here? Does she ever think of me? It was then that he would feel most alone and far from home. Why am I here? People say I'm to be a warrior, a saviour. Why do they say that? I don't feel very heroic. He listened to the breathing of Phoenix who was clearly deep in slumber. The stream chuckled in the distance. Then his reveries were brought to an end by a noise that made him catch his breath. A snuffling sound just beyond the mouth of the cave and then light steps as if someone were trying to sneak up to the cave entrance. Outside and tethered to the tree Xanthos grunted uneasily and then snorted. Achilles then heard the noise again. He sat up his senses fully alert. A low threatening growl seemed to fill the entire cave. The moon was waning but almost full as he looked towards the horses at the eerily grey and silver landscape. What he saw made his hair stand on end. He remembered Phoenix's story. Had the centaurs returned? But it wasn't centaurs that were gathering slowly. It was wolves! Five or six of them were circling the horses. Some stood still and stared at Achilles. Occasionally they looked up to the moon and he caught the green flash of their eyes.

"Am I dreaming? Phoenix must have been wrong." Achilles felt he must wake his mentor but at the same time he felt rooted to the spot, frozen and transfixed by the wolves that surrounded Xanthos and Balios. He sat for what seemed like an age and yet it was only a few heartbeats. He realised that the horses were in danger and something had to be done. Had the beasts seen the two of them sat in the cave? Surely they must have smelt them. Mustering himself Achilles leaned forward to wake Phoenix but before he moved he felt a tight and powerful grip on his arm,

"I know boy, stay still."

Phoenix was very slowly preparing to burn a bandage that he'd already dripped with oil and wrapped around a long piece of wood. He placed it on the embers of the fire that still glowed near the entrance of the cave. 'So that's why the wolves hadn't entered. They were fearful of the light and heat their dying fire still gave out' thought Achilles. He thanked the Gods that their fire still pulsed and crackled. Phoenix's torch was now lit and with it raised at arms length he opened the ferns and ran naked like a madman towards the wolves who snarled and hackled. This was too much for Xanthos who galloped off into the distance joined by Balios. Achilles watched all this in an incredulous silence until finally the bubble burst and he too also naked joined Phoenix who looked rather sheepish.

"We have lost the horses Achilles. I never meant for that to happen. We must find more tomorrow. We must meet with the Epirotes, they will help us. Meanwhile we must light a fire quickly."

But it was too late. The wolves had started to return. Phoenix thought fast,

"Quick, fetch me the pots of honey from the cave."

Achilles fled without a word whilst Phoenix sat and planted the flame in front of him.

Achilles was soon back and sat with his back to his mentor swinging his torch in front of him. The wolves were wary but their hunger kept them interested. And now they sniffed the air and began to circle as the smell of honey reached their nostrils. At their head was Anubis who had lost her pup to Agamemnon. She was followed by her only cub now a full grown male. The others stayed back and eyed Phoenix suspiciously as he dipped his hand in the huge pot of honey and began to smear it up and down his arm. Achilles watched bewildered and stopped brandishing his lantern. He soon began again when one of the wolves came a little too close. Phoenix then slowly stood and walked toward the beasts dripping the honey as he went. He walked toward Anubis as it was clear she led the pack. Achilles watched ready to spring up and fight if Phoenix was attacked. Phoenix looked over his shoulder and for one moment he saw the man in the boy as the moonlight hinted at the fire in his eyes,

"Keep waving your torch Achilles."

Anubis bared her teeth. Her growl was deep and threatening and Phoenix paused. He then turned and returned to the boy still pouring the honey as he walked. Anubis stopped growling and put her nose in the air. She loved the sweet smell of honey but had been stung so often she was wary of moving closer. But there are no bees! She licked the ground whilst the rest of the pack watched. I haven't been stung yet. And where are the hives? She lapped at the honey Phoenix had poured on the ground. The other wolves followed and began helping themselves to the great pools of honey left by Phoenix. All the wolves were hungry and they forgot about the threat of the flames as they looked around for more food. Eventually Anubis took a few steps nearer to Phoenix. He had put his flame to one side and now held the pot of honey in front of him. Anubis stared ahead whilst the other wolves waited. She backed up again and snarled. Achilles trembled and held his flame tighter. But then Phoenix began to murmur. Achilles couldn't make out the words but it was the same tone he used when speaking to all creatures whether it was Xanthos or Lyria the lizard or the tiny dormouse (who on this night had judiciously chosen to stay in the cave). All animals seemed to respond to it. But wolves? The boy marvelled again at the skill of Phoenix. The ears of Anubis had pricked when he had begun talking and now her head cocked to one side. Achilles for a moment thought of his beloved Cerebus. The wolf took a step nearer to Phoenix who held out his arm that was covered in honey. Anubis hated these creatures with two legs. But she was also hungry and this one smelt good. She moved closer still listening to the rhyme of Phoenix's voice drawn in by his sound and scent. She was ready to strike but instead she lay on her stomach and whined, then, lifting her head began lapping at the honey on the arm of Phoenix. Anubis had made up her mind and this was enough for the pack who crowded around this new leader to get nearer to the delicious honey.

"Take some honey and offer it to them."

Achilles did as he was told and soon the wolves were helping themselves as Achilles stroked them gently with his free hand. The moon now looked down on a strange sight. Two naked men and four wolves enjoying a midnight feast of honey. If she had looked harder she would have also seen two helmeted figures watching silently and malevolently from the edge of the wood. Phoenix eventually rose slowly and made his way to the cave. The wolves seemed untroubled by this and followed obediently. He left the pot of honey outside and the wolves were soon helping themselves whilst Achilles and Phoenix prepared to sleep,

"Shall I light another fire?"

"No need. I have new friends."

Achilles smiled and looked once more at the wolves who were beginning to settle down to sleep right outside their cave. Phoenix thought about the horses. Secretly he was disappointed with Xanthos and Balios and puzzled too. How had they escaped their tether? Had they not been tied to the tree? And if not what or who had untied them?

126

The sun rose slowly the next day flooding the valley with pale gold light. The sky was as smooth as a baby's skin with only the faintest wind that blew in from the south. Achilles remembered the events of the night before and quickly opened the ferns expecting to see the wolves,

"They're gone Phoenix" he said disappointed.

"Of course. They roam. But we may see them again."

Achilles hoped secretly that they would. He wondered at Xanthos and Balios. Why hadn't they returned?

They set off north following the coastal path. Phoenix knew he had to make contact with the Epirot tribes. He now needed horses and as an official emissary of Peleus he was to ensure their loyalties for the inevitable war and reassure them of Thessaly's continued support. So they began their journey. To their right the blue grey Mount Pindar with its lush valleys. To their left the green western sea. In the distance looming from the sea haze Achilles could make out an island. It seemed like a small patch of blue mist gently balanced on the upper rim of the horizon,

"What island is that Phoenix?"

"Corcyra."

Equidistant between themselves and Corcyra was a huge rock that jutted out of the ocean dramatically. The waves crashed at its base seemingly angry at its impertinence but the obstinate rock stood proudly. There was no way a boat could moor there, only the gulls could land which they did in their thousands,

"That is Leucas Petra, the shining rock. Spurned lovers are said to jump to their deaths from there into the Aegean. But how they get on there in the first place must remain a mystery."

Achilles looked out to the high rock. It was well named for its coruscated surface gleamed and shivered as the sun caught it. Phoenix continued,

"Their souls pass over the Styx by the rock then through the gates of the sun into the district of dreams."

Phoenix knew the main tribes in Epiros were the Thesprotians and Chaones. But it was the Molossians he sought out, the largest Epirot tribe and known for their love of the horse. Phoenix had heard their leader Triades was a wise and gentle man; his tribe was a mixture of Illyrian and immigrant blood from the island of Corcyra forced to flee when the paid mercenaries of Agamemnon proved too strong. Achilles ran to the edge of the cliff and peered over. It gave him a queasy feeling to stare at the rocks far below. A short way down he could just make out a flimsy path that was hewn from the sheer face – but the elements had long since worn it away and now the seagulls used it as a perch stretching their wings and gliding on the air currents far below him. He rejoined Phoenix who was now a good way ahead. Phoenix was excited about the Molossian horses,

"I have heard they prize their horses above their women. We will see. The knees should be supple when the colt walks – the same when ridden. Supple knees will add a high price to any colt. They are easier to ride and less likely to stumble."

Achilles listened and nodded. The sun began to wane and still they walked until in the distance they could make out a figure stood by the cliff edge and staring out to sea. They approached cautiously until very soon they were stood behind him. And still he did not turn.

"Corcyra waits for us. Every day I look at her and curse the Mycenean. By helping you then I help my people."

The man finally turned and embraced Phoenix warmly. He was a short man but with a kindly face thought Achilles. He continued,

"I was told to wait for you here. We were told you may come and be in need of us. And this is the boy?"

"Achilles son of Peleus. This is Triades, leader of the Molossians and the Epirot alliance."

Achilles stepped forward to greet the man but before he did the old man knelt to the ground in the age old act of supplication. Achilles watched puzzled as he took a pinch of earth from between his feet. He pressed it into his forehead before taking Achilles' arm and gripping it tightly. It was a greeting typical of the Epirotes passed down from the Aeolian islanders who had first farmed the islands generations before but who now thanks to the greed and ambition of Agamemnon were forced to the mainland. Triades's head was still bowed and his arm still gripped Achilles who turned to Phoenix unsure what to do next. Phoenix winked and made a light tapping motion signaling to the boy who gently touched the old man on his shoulder which was evidently the cue for him to rise. The three then walked toward the Molossian settlement.

"We hear Agamemnon still swaggers and boasts."

"Yes" replied Phoenix, "he wishes nothing more than a kingship with him at the head. All would pay him homage and serve his vanity. Your Epirotes would be expected to bow down. Does the alliance still hold?"

"Pah." Triades spat on the ground in contempt, "there is no alliance. The Thesprotians have deserted us and sided with the Mycenean. The Chaones still resist."

Phoenix thought hard. Agamemnon's influence was spreading all the time. With his pirate ships raiding the Troad and plundering the Phoenician traders it was an easy task to bribe and corrupt the many tribal lords on the mainland.

The three of them took a tacking chalk path that led them east and to the village of Triades,

"I hear that your king Peleus still defies Agamemnon's rule."

Phoenix nodded,

"He has the support of the free Thessalians, the *Periokoi* and the northern villages."

"And he can count us as his friends." Triades smiled, "I may be old but I'm worth any two Myceneans."

Phoenix privately doubted this but admired Triades' spirit. He was pleased that Triades had seen fit to meet them personally. He had been a great fighter and Peleus had always spoken well of him at the battle of Tiryns when he fought against Atreus. Atreus had been forced into a truce which neither side had honoured. It was then that the sons of Atreus, Agamemnon and Menelaus had begun their murderous rise to power. 'The time with Triades will be useful' thought Phoenix. 'I will gather information on the movements of Agamemnon and trade for horses.' Eventually Triades shouted and pointed ahead,

"We are almost there. See where the valley narrows?"

Achilles strained his eyes and in the distance saw a cluster of men and horses grouped together in the shade. Triades' men were waiting to guide them to the tents. The men shouted and chatted as they came nearer. They smiled at Achilles who felt uncomfortable. Their dialect was unfamiliar, their voices rasped and cracked at the edges as if their throats had never known water and when they shouted their voices shrieked short and sharp like Hades unleashed. But they were allies and friends to his father.

127

Eventually they were both shown into a large tent which provided shade. Food had been provided and they were given fresh tunics to wear,

"Now you can both rest" said Triades, "and then when the sun is colder we can talk and you can choose new horses for the prince of Thessaly."

Triades smiled then clapped his hands, the water bearers stood erect waiting to wash the feet of the guests or mop their brows. Triades left.

"It would be a good idea to rest Achilles. I need to gather my strength for the battle ahead."

Achilles lay back and wondered at Phoenix's words. What battle did he mean? The word stuck with him as his eyes closed and he lay back. Not long after a fusion of images gathered together with a terrible clarity and raced through his young mind. In the half light of his nebulous dreams he hung on though his body squirmed and perspired.

Achilles felt safe as he waded into the Scamander. Up to his knees now he was comfortable with the hacked bodies that putrified the river, choked her; a thick bloody broth of worm and flesh as his toes picked out the bodies under his feet. An ethereal blending of faith and stone, brain and bone now surrounded him. As the river swelled and searched for air to breathe so Achilles lifted his head to avoid the stinking sins that floated slowly by him. Half way across up to his waist now the river seemed ready to vomit with the Trojan bodies that stuck in her throat and stymied her progress. Bodies, limbs, horses and shields drained her lifeforce, her search for the sea. So she gathered herself and flew at Achilles ready to drown the man who had poisoned her. And then her friend the wind joined with her, the breathless wind who'd touched the brow of many brave men. No man could challenge Achilles but the river and the wind bore him down; his shield and armour became a sodden dead weight and the river engulfed him. And now the sky and the river were allied in an angry concerto bearing down on him with a hellish triumphalism. Achilles fought, half swam, swung his sword at the waves, its glistening blade for once impotent, yelling and screaming in silence. The river now forced itself upon Achilles from all angles.

"Is this my death then? And Hector still lives?"

So the shield became his shroud and the river his grave as his mouth took in the first gulp of Trojan blood and water, hacked torsos and faces that hours ago laughed and cried now drawn into the Stygian gloom. They spewed at him and Achilles cursed the waves and wished for the breathless sun.

"Mother Thetis, help me and forgive me."

Thetis dreamed of her son. She turned and sighed in her sleep and the wind blew lighter and Achilles knew he was dealing with a woman of many moods as her temporary madness was over. Her rage had abated and she lay back sullen and restful. Achilles, thankless as ever, strode on.

128

Achilles awoke frightened and turned to Phoenix. His head felt heavy, his heart beat fast and unsteady. He wanted to wake Phoenix and tell him his dream. Perhaps it meant something. Outside the tent Triades waited silently. They had slept through the night and most of the day, their night with the wolves taking its toll. The air was fresher when Phoenix awoke. For a moment he was unsure where he was. A part of him thought he had heard laughter. Still only half awake he stood up and acknowledged the water bearers who stood obediently by. The tent flaps opened and Triades entered smiling,

"Have you slept well friend?"

"I heard laughter, yes, I feel rested."

"And are you ready to choose?"

Phoenix nodded and followed Triades from the tent. As they walked to the stables they were followed by an increasing number of Epirot tribesmen, some bringing their wives and children.

"They want to see you tame the horses. They believe you are Thessalian and a master in the saddle."

"I was sold into slavery and tutored by the northern dwellers."

Triades turned to face Phoenix,

"I know this but they expect a show. Your king evidently prizes you."

Triades turned away quickly to hide his face. He continued,

"You won't disappoint will you?" he said half smiling. "Any horse you conquer you can keep. This is my gift to you and Peleus."

Phoenix thanked him and looked around the stable yard. Instinctively he looked around for Achilles,

"And where is the boy? Is he to watch?"

Triades didn't reply. Decaying palms and wisteria bordered the stables providing much shade as the sun had begun its descent. Here Achilles sat and watched Phoenix stride over the still hot sand to inspect the beautiful creatures that were now being paraded before him. There were a small number of colts and thoroughbreds, untamed and excitable, tossing their manes. Inside the stable were still more horses that were hidden but Achilles could hear their whinnies and snorts. It's as if they wanted their chance to test Phoenix too, to be part of the show. Phoenix paused for a moment then gathered himself and began to confidently move amongst the horses walking around them slapping their flanks as they pranced and skipped. Then he stood back with his hands on his hips looking at each horse intently. After a short while he pointed to a dark grey colt that stood on the periphery of the group. Immediately a servant ran up and bridled the horse in a single well practiced movement. Instantly Phoenix mounted the beast. There was a pause during which time the colt seemed to process the calamity which had just befallen it. A saddle! With a cry (which Achilles saw as fear rather than shock) she bolted whilst intermittently kicking her hind legs to try and dislodge both Phoenix and the saddle. But Phoenix was strong and hung on grimly. Somehow the scene puzzled Achilles. He realised it was because he had only seen animals show love to his mentor. To see any creature, even an untamed horse, show anything but utter devotion to him seemed strangely out of sorts. But the young colt couldn't dislodge Phoenix who now leant forward as if to whisper in her ear. It was something Achilles had seen many times and he smiled to himself. Only Phoenix can talk with the animals. The horse was now working its way in a circle to where Achilles sat with a dozen Epirot tribesmen all enthralled by Phoenix's horsemanship. She still bucked and protested but something in her eye told Achilles that she was ready to give in, to appease this two-legged violator. She paused and gave a low groan but then took off sprinting at speed out of the stableyard over the dunes towards the low valleys. The beast was broken but for Phoenix this was the harshest test, his thighs sore and aching as he pressed them hard into the muscled flanks of the colt. Phoenix felt alive though his throat was parched and his limbs ached. But he knew this fine Magnetian was his. I will take one more and perhaps another from the stable. Then the words of Triades returned to him and the phrase that he had twice used, 'your king.' His world fell apart and he swung the colt around,

"Fool!"

Everything happened very quickly. Achilles felt a sharp tug on his hair and in a moment he was half walking, half being dragged towards a fenced off field. He heard jeering and the voice of Triades,

"Great warrior? Saviour of Greece? Let's see how you do against this enemy."

Achilles tried to gain a footing as he passed the back of the stables where Balios and Xanthos were tied. And then Achilles knew. He knew he was in the midst of an enemy. He knew they had been tricked. He knew he was alone.

129

Danae's betrayal stunned Orpheus. Helen's betrayal broke him. He thought of his early years, poisonous musings on his mother's foibles, his father's distance. The emotions condensed and were intoxicating and yet he still dwelt with himself, clutching at his thoughts with an inward capricious horror. The full weight of his loneliness would leave him gasping for air as he groped blindly for a centre. He began to repeat Helen's words but they made no sense tumbling from his cluttered mind. The other soldiers thought him strange. And yet sometimes a human contact would send the fear fleeing, a touch or a smile. But then a glance at the stars would reveal the hole in his soul, the emptiness that guided his volitions and hollow madness. And so he careered into self destruction. One night he fell to his knees and prayed to farseeing Zeus but the prayer remained frozen on his lips. The soldiers had laughed at him and taken him to the old whore Chrysalis who sang alone in a high clipped voice, slumped forward lazily tapping out a beat on a finger drum. In his mind she coalesced into the rarified delights of Helen. Like a caterpillar yields to the beauty within this old woman spawned a butterfly of exquisite colour in his mind's eye. Orpheus ate from her hungrily feasting on this succubus whore. Afterwards he felt elated then disgusted. There had been no music. There had been no truth. There had been no Helen. He had fooled himself. But before he left he bought a phial of bee juice and placed it on her lips,

"Lips smeared with honey have the gift of eloquence."

Chrysalis cackled and counted the copper coins in her darkened room as the soldiers jeered.

130

The sacred Apis bull worshipped by the Cretans and further south by the cult of Isis was ebony black. Checked by Triades that morning a single white hair would have rendered him unclean. But the beast was flawless and now turned to face Achilles.

"Your friend Achilles" laughed Triades, "he will guide you to Hades."

Phoenix's words returned to him,

"Two battles to fight boy. Your fear and the enemy."

Achilles looked up. He would at least stare death in the face. The bull pawed the ground and eyed him uneasily. The muscles in his neck showed a raw strength that could toss a man high in the air. The scent of Achilles reached his nostrils. Who dares to enter my domain? To the east a wolf howled. Achilles tightened his grip on his short sword tossed to him by Triades. The Epirotes looked on and yelled,

"Your sword will bounce off him. Are you ready to die prince?"

He looked into the eyes of the bull and saw no fear in its eyes. He took a step forward his movements as soft as a shadow. He imagined Phoenix at his side,

"Your gaze will be steady boy. Do not tilt your head or furrow your brow. Stay as strong as water. It is awareness of yourself that is your hindrance. Have no thought of yourself and victory will be yours."

As the land grows silent when the owl swoops so a hush descended as the brute reared and tensed, the inevitable prelude to battle. Twenty paces now separated man and beast. Achilles' hair glinted. The drowsy sea birds took to the heights climbing to feel the fading warmth on their wings. Achilles felt a conflict in his young heart between his desire to not disappoint his mentor and the fear he felt for this massive creature. Was it wrong to feel fear?

"Fear cannot hurt you any more than a dream Achilles."

It was habit rather than intent that moved him nearer to his newest challenge driven by a force he didn't yet understand. The winds fetched from the plains of Mysia hurried over the landscape and cooled his brow. The bull charged silently and swiftly and was on him before his sword was raised. Achilles spun and moved to his left feeling the rush of wind from the creature as it brushed his body and turned ready to charge again. Still Achilles had no time to raise his sword as the bull bore down upon him. Is this my moment of departure from sweet life? In that breathless moment his soul was elevated into a strange twilight between life and death, a shadowy half life where his short years passed before him. He crouched and thrust his sword upwards feeling the blade move through chest and heart as the warm blood showered him and his youth fragmented. Childhood's end. He vaulted the fence and quickly cut Xanthos and Balios free before racing through the stable yard where Phoenix reappeared at speed,

"This way. To the cliffs."

Spears thrown by the Epirotes landed to the left of them and Phoenix's new mount reared. He fell but in an instant was off the floor and on the back of Xanthos. The spears were joined by arrows but Achilles and Phoenix were now clear of the camp. Triades was quickly in pursuit. The short sharp shrieks of the men from the western isles flew through the air and pierced them like arrows.

131

After a short ride it was clear Triades was gaining. Arrows landed near them as they retreated ever closer to the sheer drop of the cliff. Far, far below a chaos of rocks deadlier than any sword. In front of them Phoenix saw a group of men closing in slowly. To their left their way was blocked by a similar number of fighters. Their small round shields and long beards gave them away,

"Pirates. Phoenician. So Agamemnon has them in his hand. The Epirotes are in league with the pirates."

There was no escape. He pulled up and cursed himself for not seeing the obvious before it was too late. Why had he brought the boy here? Was he old enough to fight? Of course not. They would be cut to pieces. Achilles understood his mentor's mind,

"I can fight sir."

But before Phoenix could answer and prepare the boy he felt a black arrow fly by him and pierce Achilles' heel. The boy yelped in pain and fell to the ground. The Pirates on seeing the boy collapse screeched and closed in. Phoenix was down by the boy in an instant and pulled off his tunic which was already stained with blood. Tearing it into strips he prepared to remove the arrowhead. Triades, eager to show off to his men now threw his spear and broke into a gallop eager to have the blood of the Thessalian prince on his sword. Agamemnon will surely reward me! Phoenix started to remove the arrowhead but it was the best he could do to break off the shaft at the point of entry. Achilles stared into the eyes of Phoenix as he ministered to him. He secretly hoped the tip was not poisoned, a favourite trick of the pirates on the western shores. Triades' spear had landed close to them and Phoenix knew the end was near. Calmly he spoke to Achilles,

"I have no time to remove the arrow now. We haven't much time until they're upon us. I can fight three possibly four but there will be twice that upon us and soon."

Even with Achilles healthy Phoenix knew they had no hope. As for Achilles he bravely stood but when reaching for his dagger and hilt his leg spasmed horribly. But much braver to die with sword in hand than be dashed on the rocks below or meekly submit. The rocks below? Phoenix knew there was another way, an idea that had lain dormant and which he had not dared consider. A slim chance made even more desperate with Achilles injured. But as the Epirotes drew nearer the idea became more fertile and grew in his mind. Phoenix knew now it was the only way,

"Achilles, we have one chance. A way that will save us if you can hold your wits and do as I say."

"I can sir."

Phoenix then lay and looked over the cliff edge.

"Are we to jump?"

Achilles, injured and in pain felt light headed as he followed the gaze of Phoenix. Now on the edge of delirium it didn't seem the strangest suggestion.

"There is a goat's path here, the width of a man's foot that snakes to the ground."

Phoenix pointed to a ledge about ten feet below them. It was the start of a small track maybe a foot wide that crumbled and curved its way along the cliff face then seemed to double back gradually making its way to the sea a league below. Long ago abandoned even by the goats it was a refuge for the thousands of sea birds that sat along its edges before launching themselves on the winds and breezes that stirred the ocean. Achilles remembered watching the birds only the day before.

Looking outwards the shining sea lay spread before him, waiting as still as a pond showing not even a ripple perfectly reflecting the blue face of the heavens. But time was short. Phoenix lowered himself down over the edge feeling for the ledge with his feet. Phoenix kept his eyes forward and focused on the cliff face then slowly moved to his left to allow room for Achilles.

"I will catch you and hold you as you come down."

Achilles knew it to be a slim chance but it was a chance all the same. Better than standing and dying, valiant as it may be. There was no shame in this – how can I fight anyway disabled as I am?

"Throw your sword and weapons lad – they'll only hinder us."

Achilles lifted out his sword and scabbard and threw them high into the sky. He briefly saw the silver handle of his father's sword glint as the dying sun caught the bronze blade. The pursuers seemed to pause at this. What trickery now? Are they to fight us bare handed? The pain in Achilles' heel was now so great he feared he would not have the strength to even lower himself down. This coupled with the dizzy height made fainting a real probability and for a moment he thought it may be better to face Triades rather than be dashed on the rocks below. Phoenix sensed that Achilles was hesitant,

"Quickly boy. Do what you can and I will steady you."

But Achilles was unsure and scared. He looked at the path that was narrow enough at the start but then dissolved drastically into a mere thread as it descended slowly down the cliff face becoming so thin in parts that even the gulls struggled to perch and launched themselves forward into the void. The Epirotes were fast approaching, Achilles felt the ground shake as the horses galloped closer. The voice of Phoenix was clear and measured and stiffened his resolve,

"It is now or nothing Achilles. Look towards the cliff, never down."

Achilles, with his leg disabled and much weakened by the loss of blood sat down,

"Sir I am a hindrance to you. You stand a better chance alone. It is me they are after and they may spare a boy. Go alone."

It was as if Achilles had never spoken. Although Phoenix heard the words they were dismissed out of hand and never considered although his heart warmed at the bravery of Achilles. In truth he knew the Epirotes were in the pocket of Agamemnon and would not spare him. He would be paraded then tortured and killed. And with the Thessalian heir out of the way it made Agamemnon's position much stronger.

"Achilles. We can do this. Keep your eyes closed. They will not follow us on this path. There is no other way unless they ride around and back which is half a day lost. But you must close your eyes Achilles. I am here to ease you down and then you can shuffle forward on your knees and hold my calf with your left hand. But always lean towards the cliff face."

Achilles held his breath and did as he was bid and soon he was stood on the tiny ledge facing the cliff wall with his eyes shut. It was better for Achilles to make the descent blind. And so they began a steady shuffling descent which took them quickly out of view of the Epirotes. At the top of the cliff they screamed and clashed their spears but none dared follow. Phoenix knew that to increase their pace would lead to their doom. So he focused his mind even more shuffling forwards on his knees feeling the path ahead with each hand in turn. Achilles stayed silent not wanting to distract Phoenix. His heel seemed to hurt less but a part of him felt unreal as if he wasn't there at all. His head felt light and for one moment he wanted to sing and dance. The wind blew hard and the gulls rode the currents staring at these mad wingless birds who invaded their territory.

Out at sea Caresses watched from his fishing boat in disbelief as two figures made their way slowly down the face of a sheer cliff which he knew to be impossible to descend,

"Hey, Aantes, Pattia, quick, look."

Soon, all three fishermen watched open mouthed at the desperate figures on the cliff that now shone deep red in the level sunset.

132

Achilles couldn't remember a time before the cliff. *Have I been here forever? Was there any before and will there be an after?* His face was white with abject fear as he clung to the calf of Phoenix with his left hand his right leg trailing uselessly. *Will I die here in this far off place? Will this sky be my shroud and the sea my grave?* He thought of Lyria and Orpheus; a shadowy penumbra, a mad mélange of memories. But mostly it was Lyria who filled his head. He prayed for her now and to be rid of the breathless sun and the wild waves that broke far below him. His mind surged and soared. He felt himself spinning and gripping the calf of Phoenix so tightly that he broke the surface of the skin and Phoenix grimaced.

"Sir, I can't go on. I can't."

It was then that Achilles opened his eyes and saw the footless chasms of air below him and a nausea overwhelmed him so he knew he was to fall. He wished for it, anything to relieve the delirious sickness in his stomach that the great height brought. He cried out so that Phoenix, knowing the peril, swung his left arm out and behind him so as to press Achilles and wedge him against the wall at the same time crying out for him to shut his eyes and so he did. Phoenix's problems had now doubled as Achilles threatened to pull them to their doom as his stomach churned and his head swam.

Caresses and the fisherman watched breathlessly as one of the men fell from the cliff face. He seemed to reach out to take the other with him but he fell alone, his brains dashed on the sharp rocks below, his body horribly still and bent before the sea took it for the fish to pick at. Caresses then shouted out his orders,

"Toward the cliff. As close as we dare."

133

Achilles had shut his eyes as Phoenix had ordered but not before he caught sight of Triades wild eyed and desperate miss his footing then slip and scream a hollow scream as he fell into the void. Then the voice of Phoenix pierced his brain,

"Climb on my back and I will carry you."

But the fear that had paralysed Achilles did not lessen. He faced the cliff, his eyes shut, his body fatigued beyond exhaustion. He hadn't the heart or will to carry on. The gulls conspired with the winds and whispered for him to be done with the matter and fling himself onto the rocks to join Triades,

"We must move forward Achilles."

Phoenix who still had his arm levered against the boy's body now tried to gain a grip and pull the boy towards him but he hadn't the strength. He then spoke gravely in measured tones which seemed at odds with the winds that blew around their ears. But Achilles heard every word,

"Achilles, if we are to die we die together. Either we move forward or tumble downward. But we'll stick together boy that I promise you. I'll leave the choice to you."

The words resonated with Achilles. It was one thing to die alone but he wouldn't be responsible for the death of his friend. For the first time he realised he must move to save Phoenix not just himself. So summoning the last vestiges of a strength that should have long ago dissipated he dragged himself slowly over the legs and onto the back of Phoenix who now moved forward at an even slower pace. Shortly after the path became a little wider, enough for Phoenix to rest a little. He hadn't the luxury of closed eyes but still kept his gaze fixed firmly on the ground as he crawled whilst continually exhorting Achilles to keep his eyes shut. No words were now spoken. The greatness of the height stilled their tongues. Achilles with his blood loss had lost consciousness soon after he had placed his arm around Phoenix's neck. Phoenix took it as a blessing for although the boy was a deadweight he was a steady one and he made his progress without the worry of sudden movement or panic from his passenger. But at the back of his mind he knew that the boy would die if he didn't receive help soon and this gave him the heart and resolve to keep forging ahead as his strength began to fail him. The jagged coastline was now darker but still glittered where the sea dashed the rocks and the spray reached out for the light. As the sun set deeper the cold crept in but Phoenix hardly noticed as he made his way slowly and with infinite care, not looking forward or behind, up or down, knowing this would mean disorientation, dizziness and death.

134

Later as the ship made its way around the coast Phoenix looked back. On the top of the cliff he could just make out two helmeted figures seemingly identical, their armour shining and still bright in the moonlight. They stood side by side, expressionless and arcadian, their waxy white skin tightly stretched under their blonde shaven heads. Holding hands they stared out to sea proud as Poseidon looking for a sign. They turned to each other simultaneously as if coming to a decision then walked away, their step and gait in perfect symmetry. A short time later the boat came to land,

"We will moor here. Look, your horses."

Sure enough Balios and Xanthos waited obediently. They had easily outpaced the pirates and galloped up the coast looking for their masters. Caresses refused any talk of recompense,

"My trade has been threatened by Agamemnon's bullies. If you are who you say you are then go with my blessing."

Caresses then helped lift Achilles who remained unconscious on to the back of Xanthos, the sturdiest of the two with the broadest back. Phoenix took to the saddle swiftly then they were off taking the same route they had walked only a day before but this time with greater purpose and speed. He galloped over a sea of fallen pine needles and their scent rose as thick as honey wine so the mayflies meandered drunkenly in their wake. The oak woods of Epiros were reviving but its breath was still cold and stilted. Phoenix knew there wasn't much time. The face of Achilles was already bloodless and white. He thought of the ointments and dressings he had already prepared and in his imagination he ministered to the boy whilst he rode. Their valley soon came into view. Phoenix tethered the horses and took Achilles in his arms. But how to carry him up the sheer rock that led to the entrance to the cave? His mind was so focused, his thoughts so desperate that he didn't question the gentle hands that took Achilles' legs and eased his burden. Taking the listless Achilles between them they soon had him laid on the cave floor.

"Fetch the breads girl from outside the cave. I've left them in the sun."

Phoenix hadn't the time to question the extraordinary appearance of Lyria but he recognised her as a friend of Achilles. Lyria quickly left to fetch the bread.

"But it's green."

Phoenix didn't answer but pressed the aged loaf to Achilles' wound,

"Hold it in place."

Phoenix didn't understand how this mildewed and mouldy bread worked. He just knew it did. Another gift from Asclepius and his son Apollo.

135

The arrowhead was deep. Phoenix knew this from the size of the swelling around the entry. Phoenix had long since broken off the body but the head remained embedded. The arrow was barbed so to pull out the fletching would be difficult. He knew he had to work fast or the infection would spread. He had already prepared powdered opium tempered with mandrake root to act as a sedative but too much would render the boy unconscious permanently. He mixed some vinegar with the opium and gave the mixture to Lyria,

"Keep this under his nose so he breathes it in."

Lyria nodded. Phoenix then carefully widened the wound using a marble scalpel he had cleansed under running water,

"Be ready with the bandage once the arrowhead is clear."

Phoenix then teased the head left and right feeling for the best possible exit. Achilles stirred but remained unconscious. Finally it was out. The honey soaked linen stemmed the bleeding and packed the wound. Yarrow helped the blood to set but Phoenix knew the next day would be crucial.

Achilles' head swam as in a punch drunk dream. Lyria took his hand and he leant forward somewhat clumsily to kiss her. But she knew his mind and drew back shyly.

"Don't move Achilles. You must rest."

All was still but for Lyria's eyes that danced with such an exuberance that Achilles decided at that moment to leave her. For a short time he just stared at her contemplating his next words. A moments clarity.

"I'm not frightened that my life is ending Lyria. It's just that it never had a beginning." He could see the girl was gone so he sighed for the lost years and fell into a deep sleep. The opium was doing its work. Outside the cave the moon farmed the night and yielded a crop of stars. Sickling the darkness she ploughed down through the purple hours until finally, exhausted, she leaned low to touch the flushed forehead of Achilles who lay in a daze his mind fishing for stars. His lips were full and red and his body drenched in sweat and hot to the touch but still he shivered. His tunic clung to him as if to squeeze his life out. Although his eyes were open they swam unseeing, blue and impotent. He awoke a short time later but he was under the Aegean by the shining rock. The face that stared at him was the face of Poseidon. He knew he had to swim away but it was no good. The face followed him. So he screamed. For Lyria it was the merest of whispers. She spoke softly,

"I am here Achilles. You are safe."

136

Lyria sat cross legged eating figs and vetches. Phoenix stared at the young girl,
"I've seen you with the prince. There is another boy too. Why are you here?"

Lyria took her hand from Achilles' forehead and stood.

"I've come to be with him."

There was nothing else she could think of to say. It was the easiest answer and the most truthful.

"Your name?"

"Lyria."

"Of Lesbos?"

Phoenix then saw his old friend Philon in her eyes and he drew her too him. And then Lyria knew and the pain was so great she fainted. At that moment spring came in the valley and the woods awoke to the birdsong and the snowdrops. The yellow cowslips embroidered the hillside in a patchwork of colour.

137

Every night she lay over him, listened for his breathing and mopped his brow. The breathing was faint but it was there. She felt for his pulse. It was barely perceptible. But Achilles was hanging on showing a fight that surprised Phoenix. That Achilles had not succumbed by now was testament to a will and spirit that he had not witnessed fully in training although it had shown itself on the cliff face.

"I will have to stop the poppy. He must fight the pain alone. The flower will overwhelm him. If it's a fever from the swamps it will break in three days. If not then he will die."

And so the pain surged back. Achilles lay whilst Lyria bled him and cleansed him, lingering over him as good as any wife attending a dying husband. But young as he was there came a time on the fourth day when his body could take no more. The pain left him, he felt calm and relaxed and a warmth overcame him. His body was surrendering. Achilles was dying.

"The Gods have cut him loose Lyria."

"The Gods have cut him loose."

Through the mists of his wounded dreams Achilles heard these words and stared at the stainless skies. But the sky and the earth were dwarfed by Hector whose breath drew the wind and the waves to his side. Then the vision and the wisdom of the centuries of Troy that had been passed down to Hector became part of Achilles as he crashed to the dry earth. The noise filled the whole world crying to an outside unseen. Mighty Achilles can you tell us what it is like never to have existed? The world grew silent and blind for dying Achilles but he heard Hector approach. Out of the view of the weeping Andromache he knelt and kissed his dying eyes and whispered to the weeping prince,

"My brother, cross the river."

And where he lay the dry tides were swept aside and the sands turned to flowers when the rains came. Tell me Achilles, is your slumber the true sleep of death? Tell me brave Achilles whilst the world is still young. Is this darkness a dream that you dreamed all your life?

"Cut me loose have they?"

His heart surged, his spirit woke and the pain returned. I'll be cut loose when I decide. Above him Phoenix and Lyria held hands as they cried over his prostrate body.

138

Achilles' transformation from fever to relative contentment had been so quick he hardly knew himself. A short period without nausea, a morning when the pain eased, noticing the sunlight on the ferns of the cave for the first time in days. But all the time the presence of Lyria, a dream, a smell he faintly recognised. Now, emerging from the shadows, his preoccupation with his wounds and agonies ceased. Finally to look outward! Phoenix had been impressed with the skills of the young girl and was not naïve enough to pretend her affections and attentions were merely perfunctory. And so now he drew back as Achilles recovered. Lyria crouched by him and held his hand and wiped his brow as she had many times for many days,

"Are you well prince?"

Achilles sighed and turned his head. He was smiling.

"Come closer. Let me see your breasts like rosy apples."

Lyria smiled,

"You are healthy."

139

The next day was fresh. Rain in the night had woken up the earth. Gone was the dank smell of stale blood and disease which had seemed to fill the cave. Achilles felt clear headed as soon as he awoke. As usual Lyria was the first person he saw,

"Thank you for everything you did for me. It was kind."

Lyria said nothing. Her deep green eyes looked downwards. Achilles, his head in his hand looked at her, she felt her pulse begin to quicken,

"And what I said yesterday?"

Lyria blushed,

"Well it was wrong of me."

"I'm surprised you remember."

"It was clumsy."

"I would have done it for anyone – please don't apologise."

"Anyone?"

Lyria sensed his disappointment,

"Well you were ill. It was my duty to help."

"Why did you come here?"

"I've come to help you."

"Alone?"

Lyria couldn't answer. She looked at Achilles but her mind was elsewhere. She sometimes felt as if she couldn't control the images that flitted across her mind. The way he held his head, the line of his nose, his tousled hair,

"Come. I need to check your leg. Try and sit up please."

140

His strength had returned quickly. Despite her protestations he was soon up and eager to leave the cave. He showed Lyria the nooks and secret places he was now so familiar with, the jutting rock to the left of the cave that acted as a marker, the bend in the river where the bream gathered and were easier to catch, the pansies and peonies in the meadow, the hyacinths, the owls den. Achilles delighted in showing her the valley and sharing the knowledge he'd gained from Phoenix. They sat by the river staring at the fish gathering in the cool depths,

"Look! Loach, it's smaller than the other fish. When Phoenix catches the small ones he throws them back till they're bigger."

Lyria smiled and dragged her hand in the water enjoying the contrasting sensations of the sun on her back and the water cooling her forearm. Achilles was happy, as happy as he'd ever been. The next words he spoke tumbled from his mouth before he'd had time to check them. Such is the measure of all boys as they wrestle with their emotions and sit on the cusp of young manhood. But Lyria couldn't answer.

141

The next day Lyria awoke and decided to walk down the slope of the valley to pick figs that she knew were ripening. She had observed them for days, the green clusters dripping with dew and swelling with every sunrise,

"Achilles shall be the first to taste them."

But first, pursuing a whim, she walked down to the river's edge where the bank was low and the sedge grass grew from the muddy silt. She decided to swim and throwing off her tunic ran through the weeds that fringed the banks and waded into the river so that soon it was over her knees and up to her thighs. She could feel the pebbles now on the riverbed and wished she had kept her sandals on. She lay on her back and drifted enjoying the feeling of the sun on her naked stomach, letting her red hair fan out behind her. She thought about Achilles. She imagined him holding her, kissing her, the feel of his body, his eyes and the way his mouth curved when he smiled. Achilles, out of sight watched her. His thoughts were much the same. The delirium had passed from his brain, the dryness from his lips. It was a delight to be alive. He bathed in the stream. The water was infused with colour and light so like liquid gold it healed his skin. Beyond the bend in the river on the fringes of the orchard Phoenix watched them both and sighed, his face a mixture of sadness and resignation.

"Puppies paddling in pools. I will see to it that Achilles doesn't swim out."

142

They sat together on a piece of raised ground where daisies and dandelions grew freely in the day and slept at night. Achilles sought her hand then lay back to look at the stars but they were hidden.

"I cannot see any stars" he said disappointingly, "can you?"

Lyria looked hard searching between the cimmerian coloured cloud for a winking pinpoint,

"I can see one" she squealed. "Perhaps it is yours Achilles."

"What do you mean?"

"Everyone has his own star. Didn't you know? A star appears when you are born and goes out when you die. As you grow older it fades and gives off less light."

"Do you believe that Lyria?"

Achilles stared intently at the one star that was visible. Despite the cloud it was easily viewed, bright white and bold. They remained silent for a short while before Achilles spoke,

"And what of a shooting star Lyria?"

There was a silence. Lyria felt sad. Her breath left her and she felt weak,

"Please be gentle. I shall fall down."

Achilles kissed her. His hands wandered tentatively. Then desire came over Lyria in waves of dizziness,

"I'm sorry. My hands. It's like I'm swimming."

And then by the cave tender as a tear she kissed his forehead. Shaking with excitement she traced the outline of his mouth with her forefinger as a child paints a picture. Her body was firm, febrile and sentient. She lay on the grass and welcomed him, aware of the moonlight and the dark blue sky. She faltered. Achilles without knowing how or why was tender and fierce. When the time came she screamed, the sweetness opening up, digging her nails into his hips to take him with her. Her whole world was now in that place. Later they lay together and stared upwards,

"Achilles, will you do something for me?"

"What is it?"

Lyria instinctively set the folds of her chiton, adjusting it more gracefully across the shoulders, tying the belts and laces. Achilles was confused.

"It will be a comfort to me Achilles if you do this."

She took off the pomegranate ring.

"Here. Wear it. My father gave me this. He told me it was mine to give to someone who...." She paused, "it has been blessed by the oracle at Pella."

Achilles took the ring carefully and examined it.

"Pomegranate? Demeter?"

It was now Lyria's turn to blush.

"Yes, it means you will live to have children. Demeter will spare you to this end."

Lyria's voice was now shaking with emotion. She watched as he placed the ring on his finger. His blue eyes shone with a kindness making his face even more beautiful. She turned back to the cave. Lyria knew it had been a special day so she closed its eyes with care and gently smoothed its brow folding the grey thin hands of twilight in the half light of her memory.

143

Lyria enjoyed looking for cyclamen and mint as Phoenix had taught her and searching under old logs for mushrooms. Phoenix enjoyed Lyria's presence for as she cleaned the cave and prepared the meals it gave him more time with his charge, to teach Achilles a new defence or spend more time with his medicines. Achilles grew stronger every day, more poised, gone the gawky awkwardness of boyhood, his legs now firm, his arms fuller, leaner. But still that lack of selflessness crucial to all fighters. Phoenix knew that victory was for the fighter who has no thought of himself.

"But always balance" he told himself. "Too much self consciousness is the greatest hindrance in battle. Too little and the senses lack an edge like a blunt blade. It will come for the boy."

But now Phoenix noticed a change in Achilles. He lost focus a little too quickly, he was too pleased when the sessions ended. Phoenix wondered.

144

They liked to walk by the river and through the woods passing the hives, the milky moonlight soaking the ground before them. Now Lyria found his hand and they strolled towards the pulsing stars. She knew she loved Achilles. She loved him from the inside out, blood entrails and all. Her finger would trace his face as he slept. She wanted to please. As for Achilles he was happy to accept these easy affections, to wander lazily with her solicitudes, to be adored by one so beautiful. He was typically Greek and made love without guilt or deceit with no time for reflection. He felt empowered the more they coupled, the closeness faded from kiss to kiss. It was a delicious thrill. He knew there was a chance he could accept never seeing her again. The responsibility of love irked him. He knew he possessed her and this at once delighted and disgusted him. A part of him pitied her and pity punctures the very heart of love. Ah, to avoid the bungling iterations of love. Finished! Ended! So his perceptions of love took on an odious aspect; an insidious mutation that pulled him in a different direction, a fear of intimacy and closeness. Ambivalence. As for Lyria she was hopelessly young, too young to substitute passion for reason. Too young to mock the language of love and its empty endearments. Her spirit openly played out its colours on her young face that held no secrets. At once shy, quizzical and merry there were no shadows between the emotion and response so a myriad of meaning fluttered over her features every moment as her eyes danced, her head tilted searching for signs of the summer. Achilles looked at her. Just woken now, smiling a warm smile and stretching out to the sky, drinking in the morning colours, her fingertips stroking his skin then sinking again with this dew drenched flower.

Achilles has fifteen summers. Phoenix's charge, Phoenix's warrior boy, raised by his hand. For his mornings the tutoring, hunting, setting traps, herbs and medicines. For his afternoons the sword and shield. For his eyes and ears the discipline of Phoenix's drive. A drive born of love as Achilles' spirit worked its way into his heart. And now Phoenix feared this love lest it should compromise his task. He gazed down at the sleeping boy knowing he was on the edge of greatness. Sometimes in the early hours he would stare at Achilles and wonder,

"Here is the child, the father of the man yet to be."

He sighed. To the childless the whole world is a folly without resonance. What will I ever know of love until I have a son? He shook his head slowly. In his mind he rehearsed the words he would speak to Peleus on their return; 'the task was onerous to begin with Lord Peleus. Done from fear and obligation. I started with misgivings but I finished with love.'

Achilles awoke and half asleep embraced his master as if he had heard the words. Phoenix threw a small log on the fire and the flames leapt up blue and green from the salt soaked oak.

"What of Agamemnon?"

"I hate the stinking guts of him. I will enjoy killing Myceneans."

Phoenix looked at him sharply. The words didn't suit him, the words of the boy dreaming of the man.

"Do not speak of things of which you do not know Achilles. Know about things of which you cannot speak. Caution and temperance are advisable in battle." He paused, "and in love too."

Achilles looked up sharply. Phoenix placed his hand on his shoulder,

"But don't fear love Achilles. You may as well fear life."

At that moment a dormouse scurried down the arm of Phoenix coming to rest on his palm where he turned and looked up at his master his black eyes blinking.

145

Lyria lay back on the moss content. There was no past and no future. Each moment was being lived as its own entity. A beautiful precious thing. No other time or place just the wonderfully exquisite here and now. To think that such a short time ago I had been at my chores in the palace. She heard the voice of Phoenix outside the cave,

"I will gather some wood for the fire."

A short time later the shadows were dancing unevenly on the cave walls and casting strange hues and shades on the instruments of war that hung there and further to the back of the cave the jars and pots of medicines that Phoenix delighted in creating. Later after they'd eaten Lyria listened drowsily as the boys spoke of fighting and battles,

"It is said that at Quadesh Ramses the Great was alone and surrounded by a hundred Hittite warriors. His generals had forsaken him, his army scattered."

Achilles imagined for a moment what it would be like to be in such a predicament. Perhaps not so different from the one they had faced on the cliffs.

"And what did he do?"

"Ramses is the sun God to his people. The sun God helped him and shone so brightly that his enemies were blinded by the single reflection from his shield. His generals saw it and used it as a guide to reassemble their divisions. The battle was won. Ramses celebrated his victory and then personally beheaded his generals for cowardice."

Lyria listened but found herself overcome with a terrible

weariness, the inevitable prelude to sleep and soon she wrestled with Morpheus. She was woken by Phoenix who crouched over her, his hand on her shoulder. His face seemed sterner and when he spoke his voice was harsh and serious although not threatening.

"I understand why you are here Lyria and I take no umbrage with that. But you must know Achilles' destiny is not his own to choose. He will learn and one day fight and lead the Greeks. This is spoken by Apollo. And anyone who perverts or defies this course will have to answer to him."

Phoenix still gripped her shoulder as he spoke, but now his tone softened,

"So you may cook and tend and clean and watch. But I beg of you, for his sake as well as your own do not let yourself love him, nor him you."

Phoenix disappeared into the blackness. Lyria, flushed and very much awake stared into the cave. It was some time before sleep overtook her again but the words kept going round and round in her head. He is too late! He is too late!

146

Macedon looked around him. Antigonus slept. Sniffing the air Macedon knew that what he smelt was new to him. As a slave he had ploughed and farmed, toiled the dry earth of the southern islands before being sold to the eastern masters at Troy. In the salt pits there had been no spring, no sense of a beginning. Winter instead turned into summer and her breath was harsh, choking the life from the land so the roots missed their youth and turned pale too soon. But here on the peninsula the breath from the sea saved the soldiers from summer's overripe carcass. It cooled the worried brow of Antigonus, who, now awake turned to his friend and pointed to the guard who approached them and saluted,

"Macedon and Antigonus. Greetings. You are summoned to the tent of Meriones."

"And if we refuse?"

Macedon had no intention of refusing. At last something to do to relieve the boredom. But he didn't want to make things easy for this impudent young Greek. The soldier faltered much to Macedon's delight. It was all he wanted to see. Putting his arm around the guard he laughed,

"Come, show us."

Antigonus sighed and followed.

147

Achilles walked. The valley was cupped in evening's fragrant palm and the breeze that was distributing the blossom was like warm velvet. The smells were so rich that he reached out to touch his childhood and wear its invisible cloak. A cloud of short lived gnats now hung before him like a shroud,

"A single day is enough for you. Maybe I've lived too long already."

The wind changed direction and the smells became suddenly stronger, fertile and sweet, lemon trees, citrus and coriander. To the north out of view Anubis lay and watched him as the rest of the wolves rested. Twilight came and Lyria came looking for her lover.

"How long should this last?" she asked.

"A moon? A lifetime? Why speak of that Lyria? You may as well trap the tides. It had no beginning or end. It just was. It just is. Do now. Now is all there is."

Lyria recognised Phoenix in his answer. She squeezed his hand but his words had unsettled her.

"Love is when we learn from each other Achilles. When soft fires burn in the heart. I want a love that will never yield to habit or circumstance. I'd prefer loneliness."

"I've heard of this love. I think I'll know it when I see it."

Lyria's heart sank,

"Or when you've lost it."

Lyria walked slowly back to the cave. Achilles' words had stabbed her heart.

In the cave Phoenix was preparing to leave. Seeing Lyria was upset he put down his sword and faced her.

"Dear Phoenix. I'd be glad to give you my heart in another time."

"And I would be glad to accept it Lyria because it would be gentle and strong."

They embraced, Lyria with a visceral tenderness and Phoenix with a ghost of a passion that once he'd known. But he felt something else pass through him as he smelt her hair. He hungered for something he would never taste, the scent of a flower, the sound of ice melting and the turning of a key in a lock. And then she was alone.

"I will say goodbye to Purdy."

With an infinite sadness she leaned forward to hug the kid one last time but, as if sensing Lyria's melancholy he ran to the back of the cave beyond the shelves where Phoenix worked on his medicines.

"Purdy, come here. Don't worry. Your beloved Phoenix will be back soon."

Purdy cocked his head to one side at the mention of the name Phoenix and looked around expectantly. Lyria smiled. The kid then began to wander miserably around the cave clearly disgruntled that Phoenix had left him behind. Lyria felt tired and tearful and she lay down and closed her eyes. Her tears had exhausted her. Purdy watched her for a short time then trotted over to where she lay and licked her cheek. Lyria woke with a start,

"Purdy. Please."

She put her arms around him. Purdy lay down with her and placed his head on her stomach. The green ferns that hung at the entrance to the cave kept it cool and diffused the light. They looked an incongruous pair as they lay there. Lyria with her golden hair spread out on the mossy floor embracing a small goat – both bathed in a curious green light.

148

It was morning when Lyria finally woke. Lachrymose and wretched, the rocks in her heart weighed her down as she thought about Achilles. She was angry at herself for having slept for so long. Seeing that she was alone she called out for Purdy. The cave was exactly as it had been when she lay down.

"Phoenix? Achilles?"

It was not unusual for them to stay out all night. Sometimes they would track a deer and sleep on the valley floor. The fronds at the front of the cave were undisturbed. As her senses returned she noticed that Purdy was missing. 'He must be at the back of the cave' thought Lyria. She raised herself quickly. If Purdy had tampered with any of Phoenix's medicines he may make himself ill. But Purdy was nowhere to be found and all Phoenix's precious potions lay undisturbed. Just at that moment Lyria heard a noise which made her jump. It seemed to come from beyond the back of the cave. A strange scraping noise. Lyria didn't like it at all and began to feel nervous. Where is Purdy? Lyria was desperate to leave before Achilles and Phoenix returned. Gathering her courage she lit a torch and slowly walked to the back of the cave beyond Phoenix's workshop. The air became cooler and the walls and floor were moist so Lyria slipped more than once. The second time she held onto a ledge that jutted out and saved her from falling. She lifted the torch over the ledge which was the height of her shoulder. She was surprised at what she saw.

"Why, it's a hole. I bet that's where Purdy is. The scamp. He must be scared."

Lyria clambered up and onto the ledge and with no thought of what lay beyond lowered herself into the hole and was surprised to find herself in a tunnel. The scraping noise stopped but in the distance she heard a muffled sound almost like a distant roar. Perhaps it's the Cretan minotaur waiting for me. The walls were slimy and evil smelling. Lyria was glad of her torch. Her curiosity was greater than her fear so she took a few steps forward but suddenly without warning something hit her knees and she collapsed to the floor in a heap as the creature whizzed by.

"Purdy, I've found you. Come. You can protect me. Let's see where this leads."

Walking forward slowly the tunnel widened out into another cave.

"Stay close Purdy."

"Purdy, Purdy, Purdy."

Lyria nearly dropped her torch at the voice that repeated itself and surrounded her. And then she was suddenly excited.

"It's Echo! Echo, where are you?"

"Where are you?" replied Echo.

Lyria lifted her torch higher expecting to see the beautiful Echo perched on a rock. The cave was so large she couldn't see the roof. Echo could be anywhere! Lyria knew that Echo was a mountain nymph punished by Hera the wife of Zeus. She would distract Hera by talking to her whilst Zeus seduced the Oreads.

"So she took away your voice. Dear Echo."

"Echo, Echo, Echo."

"And now all you can do is repeat the voices of others."

"The voices of others. The voices of others."

"Poor Echo. I forgive you."

"Forgive me. Forgive me."

Lyria was beside herself with sadness and sat down and cried for the lonely young maiden. Echo cried with her whispering her tears to the invisible corners of the cave. Lyria sat still for some time gazing at the lumbering shadows cast by her torch. She was reminded of the tombs her father had shown her as a small girl. She heard the voices of her dead ancestors calling her as she walked slowly around the cave looking for a possible exit. Presently she came to another tunnel. It was quite narrow but Lyria squeezed through easily with Purdy still following close at her heels unwilling to stray too far. Again the distant roar. The tunnel led upwards and was very straight and smooth as if worn through by some great force. The floor was slippy so even Purdy lost his footing splaying his front legs and landing on his tummy. The roar was much louder. If it is a beast of some kind it doesn't even pause for breath. Perhaps I should go back. But Lyria's curiosity again drove her on. The roof suddenly got much lower. This seemed to amplify the booming noise even more. Lyria's inquisitive mind worked at a pace. It's the noise of Hephaestus's workshop! He is fashioning a shield for Athena. This truly is the valley of the Gods. First Echo and now the blacksmith God. The noise was deafening, Purdy cowered and crept forward slowly at Lyria's feet. Then the passage turned and Lyria drew in her breath sharply at what she saw,

"The waterfall."

The passage led to a stone ledge that came to an abrupt stop directly behind the waterfall. Lyria's face was covered in a fine spray from the tumult of water that fell in front of her; a sheer wall of liquid unbroken as it fell a great distance then smashed on the rocks. Lyria was awed by the sight. She stood as close to the edge as she dared. The rock formed a natural ledge which ran the whole width of the waterfall. It was possible to look around the side of the water to the valley far below. It was impossible to get to the ledge apart from through the mountain. Anyone who tried would surely be dashed to pieces. What a vantage point. What a view! Lyria looked toward the valley and saw Achilles making his way slowly towards the cave. Her heart was glad but she was angry with herself for having not left already. Am I kidding myself? Can I really leave? But then her blood ran cold. A short distance behind Achilles two helmeted figures were following. Surely he must have seen them? But Achilles hadn't seen them. She watched helplessly as the pair closed in on him. She had an idea. Moving to the side of the fall she jumped in the air waving her arms high above her head hoping to distract the soldiers. Achilles didn't see her but momentarily the soldiers stopped. It was as if they hovered over the ground. The looked in the direction of the waterfall. Lyria knew there was no way they could clamber up. Half of her hoped they would try. By this time Achilles, still unaware, had parted the ferns and entered the cave. Lyria continued waving and screaming until her throat was sore. Finally the two men turned and slid away and she ran back through the tunnel with Purdy at her heels. Echo was breathless and frightened as Lyria ran through the cave. She fell but the pain didn't bother her. Meanwhile Achilles had arrived and was surprised to hear a noise from the back of the cave. He drew his sword then put it back puzzled as he saw Lyria and Purdy emerge broken and bleeding.

"What are you doing?"

Lyria quickly explained where she had been and the danger that Phoenix was in. Purdy sat with his head cocked looking around for Phoenix. And then without warning he ran from the cave to look for his master. Lyria instinctively followed but Achilles held her back.

"Leave him."

"Where is Phoenix?"

"Half a day from here. Tracking."

Slowly and methodically he began to dress as if for battle. First his grieves then his battle tunic. All the while Lyria watched silently.

"I'm just learning to be strong. It's what will keep me alive."

"It's what will keep you alone."

Lyria's voice was raised. It was unlike her and Achilles looked up surprised. Lyria already knew that love delighted in self recrimination. She knew that some women were born to love those who wounded them the most and that a malignant despair will destroy all affections.

"Return to Thessaly. Tell Peleus what has happened here. Tell him I am safe."

He paused,

"See that Orpheus is well."

They stood both looking through each other before Lyria finally spoke,

"This thing you have stirred in my heart there is nothing greater, there are no words. But I do not care that I leave now as I saw happiness and felt it with you."

She made no attempt to stop him as he pulled back the ferns and left her.

149

Meriones, obdurate and contrary, was indiscriminate in his loathing. He hated everyone equally. But he inwardly spat at the two peasant Greeks who entered his tent. 'Bring me two men of no consequence or rank' had been his command. And so it was that Macedon and Antigonus stood before him. Meriones despite knowing he may be sending these men to their deaths failed to muster any cordiality. He stared blankly at the pair. Antigonus, increasingly nervous, looked downward. Anything to avoid the stare of the powerful Meriones, leader of the Perrhaebi. Macedon however was of sterner stuff and met the stare of the general. The cold sneer Meriones received from the soldier told him his guard had chosen well. He stroked his fat chin and stared Macedon up and down. Macedon continued to return the stare. His impudence began to insult Meriones who had only known servility.

"Do I know you? Where are you from soldier?"

"I worked the farms of your southern lands then toiled in the copper and salt mines of Kyprus and Anatolia."

"Toiled?" sneered Meriones, "did you serve at the table and touch little boys?"

Macedon knew it was a time to stay silent. And yet...

"I've heard of you Meriones and seen you with the sword. I have always wanted to fight you because I love my life and want to live long."

Meriones' eyes flashed. Antigonus in utter horror uttered a short soundless prayer. He knew now they would not leave the tent alive. But Meriones knew better.

150

As they left the camp Zeno of Soli spoke to them,

"Be careful slave. The two Perrhaebi they sent haven't returned. Probably caught and mutilated."

Macedon walked on though Antigonus paused. At least they had the pick of the horses. They rode out of camp unheralded and unnoticed. Gathering pace Macedon let loose his braided hair, a sure sign of his slave pedigree, and rode freely. The goats on the hills scattered before them and the shepherds looked away scared incase they looked on the emissaries of Agamemnon. Meriones' words echoed in the head of Antigonus,

"You are my new *Hequetai*. You will spy for me and bring me Agamemnon's plans."

They left the lowlands just as the dawn broke lighting up the distant slopes of Parnassus and beyond that the Delphic oracle shattered and bruised after the slaughter. They passed Chaeronea pushing their horses hard. Sometimes their saddles creaked as they raced across the plains their heads rolled back laughing at the sky. Sometimes the wild flowers bloomed blue and yellow as the butterflies skitted amongst them. And now slower their hooves rattling and skidding on the shale ground of the stone valley as the sun set behind them.

"We must be cautious Antigonus. Agamemnon will have boundary scouts. We will have to pass them unnoticed. If we are seen we will die. We will sleep here."

A short time later Antigonus, wrapped in blankets looked down the valley behind him and traced in his mind's eye the route they had taken that day. 'I hope I get the chance to retrace my steps' he pondered. The valley seemed ominous and silent to him as if it held a secret. Whilst his friend slept he stared into the twilight and then inevitably the darkness. A short distance from where they lay two of Agamemnon's men sat silently waiting for the spies to continue their journey.

151

The next morning Antigonus awoke early and seeing his friend asleep walked up the gentle slopes that formed the foothills of Mount Parnassus. Antigonus once again had not slept well having taken great exception to the snoring of Macedon. He had punched him in the ribs continually to end the torrent of noise only for his friend to smile and dream. He had stared into the sky eating dates and spitting the pips at his friend as he slept. But now the birds suddenly emerged from their secret places and sang full throated. Antigonus looked up to the sky and then into the dark horizon. The sun yolked and spread herself over the yellow valley breathing life and light into the day. He walked a short distance and gazed at the wild silence. For a moment he felt uneasy, exposed and anxious. He thought about his wife and the son he hadn't seen and missed them. Without warning a hand came over his mouth whilst another powerful arm held him tight. Antigonus was powerless, in the grip of a strength so much greater than his own. A voice whispered close to his ear,

"Antigonus I love you but I swear if you ever wander off like this again I will slit both our throats to save Agamemnon the bother. We are less than a day from the enemy and you are wandering around like a boy in a brothel."

Macedon released his grip,

"Now come, let's eat."

152

One was armed with a short wooden club and had the markings and brandings of a slave. The other clutched his long sword anxiously. So Macedon and Antigonus made their way across the plains under the stinking sun so their throats were cracked with thirst sending their pennants of dirt high into the air. This was the terrain Macedon preferred as their dusty tracks were soon blown away. It pleased Antigonus too for there was a growing unease in him that they were being followed. And so Macedon and Antigonus lay near the outposts of Agamemnon's camp. The early morning mists still crowned Mount Helicon to the south,

"So why did he let us live?"

"He hasn't. He's sending us to our deaths. He expects us to die like all spies. I intend to surprise him by staying alive."

"There's nothing you can do now to surprise me Macedon. But I'm with you. I'd like to stay alive. Just another day would be good."

"Shh, then stop your prattling."

Macedon could see two guards only a hundred paces away. To be caught meant instant execution. Beyond them Agamemnon's army could be heard, the laughter of the generals, the tedious drills of the rank and file. It was clear that the men were well organised and confident of victory.

"How much longer?" whispered Antigonus. "We have lain here for two nights."

"Till we have learned something. We have to return to Meriones with information or not return at all."

Antigonus for a moment considered the last option but then dismissed it. To not return would mean they'd be hunted by two armies instead of one. Macedon suddenly lay flat and pulled Antigonus with him who exhaled sharply as his chin hit the frozen, leaf strewn ground. The two guards had turned towards them. They paused and began to inspect the outer stockade walking up and down the dykes, thorns and trenches, typical Mycenean fortifications. Macedon considered the pair. One was evidently of high rank judging from the elaborate wrought armour similar to that of Meriones with its filigree patterns. Antigonus recognised the guttural tones of the Myceneans from the traders who had passed through his farm selling pots and tools. After a short time the two men wheeled around and returned to camp. Macedon and Antigonus turned to each other and nodded. Only when the moon set over Mount Helicon did the two men dare to move.

Castor and Pollux strode on. Entering a clearing near the cliff edge they chose to sit in the branches of a yew tree that commanded a good view. All around the ground was blood red with the fallen waxy berries. They waited and watched. Night fell softly but the moon retched as she looked down on them. A week before the twins had killed a kid and dragged it to the tree. They now took great delight in staring at the corruption and taking choice bites from the festering flesh; wiping the blood from each others mouths with their identical cloaks. Later they would pick at the bones. As one slept the other cast his eye over the cowering landscape. Then without a word or nod the other took over. All the time holding hands, their helmets shining in the moonlight. Motionless they turned to face each other. A soft hiss could be heard as they spoke simultaneously,

"We"
"Shall"
"Find"

"Him"

"Here"

They slithered to the ground as the air shuddered around them.

153

"Soon we will arrive at back at the forward garrison of Meriones. He expects us there."

Macedon could only think of his stomach as it rumbled and groaned,

"And when is our next meal due?" he asked.

"Yesterday."

Macedon and Antigonus had run through the day side by side. Macedon's sheer size had meant that Antigonus often had to wait on his friend who had long since discarded his sword so he could run unencumbered; now a short dagger was his only weapon. They forded rivers, drank from lakes and sheltered in ravines. On the second day they rested in the early hours under a sweet smelling pine which had held on to its scent despite the cold. The men huddled together for warmth and looked up at Mount Orchomenus. Clouds scudded by dark and ominous. A hawk landed near to the men as they shivered and stared too cold to speak. Its bright beak shone in the pale light of the moon as it stared back at them unblinking and proud. They both fell into a fitful brief slumber. Antigonus was woken by the screaming of the gulls. But it was Macedon, his terrors mimicking the seabirds. Antigonus held the head of the slave in his lap stroking his madness as he yelled out,

"Where is my father and brother? Darkness!"

Antigonus kissed the brow of his friend. These ravings were unfamiliar to him although he had heard of quiet men who had bitten throats to the bone in battle only for the memory to overtake them and torture them. Where had this man come from with his night terrors and bright eyes? He held him as his body shook just as in the raddled hot hours of desire he had seen him tremble. And Macedon woke and looked up at Antigonus smiling,

"I am well now."

They fell to sleep again. Antigonus woke a short time later. A greenish hue to the east told him the day had begun. He carefully escaped the embrace of the bear like Macedon so as not to wake him. Looking down he saw the hawk at his feet, still. Its claws and feet were curled around its exquisite face, frozen to death.

154

It was Macedon who heard the noise first like the gurgle of a stream. The man appeared in the half light crawling and slobbering in the dirt of the road. He had no left hand just a bloody mass of sinew and flesh. But he spoke quickly and with clarity knowing he was dying.

"Agamemnon won't wait for the spring. He has with him Menelaus and the Spartans. Many more wait in Euboea."

"And you?"

"I was seen and nailed to the tree. But one of my hands they nailed loosely. When they slept I ripped it away."

In the throes of a death agony he pleaded,

"Now, help me die."

Antigonus, tearful, passed him his sword,

"Help me."

So Antigonus held him as Macedon drove the sword into his chest and kissed his cheek even as the blood covered him,

"Go to sleep."

So died Philon of Lesbos, brother of Lyria.

155

Meriones was a clumsy man uneducated in the social mores of Peleus's court despite his Penthelid origins. Uncultured and unsubtle he cut a swathe through the fancy rituals shouting his presence to the men, drinking hard, his armour worn clumsily, his favoured short sword hanging to the knee. Any opinions or pursuits that didn't concern him or further his ambition he had little time for. Pragmatic and self serving the prattle of the Thessalian courts passed him by; administrative and political gossip he treated with indifference. When in the company of generals and visiting dignitaries he made a habit of saying the opposite of what he thought purely from boredom. So to some he seemed frivolous and contrary, to others arrogant and bellicose. But Peleus knew him for a brave fighter, incalcitrant but tactically brilliant so he listened on the night of the slave's return to his plan. The two spies had done well. It was clear Agamemnon favoured the higher plains of Parnassus with its hidden ravines and clear views afforded north to Thermopylae and south to Delphi itself. Peleus disagreed at first with the plan more from bloody mindedness than any tactical acumen. But as the wine took hold so did its plausibility. In the morning at first light Antigonus and Macedon were woken by the officers and found themselves marching eastwards along the sea coast north of the Kalapodi valley with its flurries of sea showers and muddy passes. Thereafter the second army led by Peleus headed south to Delphi. All day Peleus marched the men quickly over the yielding ground until the mist rolled from the plains. At his side Meriones, leader of the Perrhaebi rode grim faced and thoughtful tugging his beard with his fingers. He turned to Peleus,

"This strategy of the Penthelid. It stands to win the throne of the Mycenean if executed well."

Peleus knew what the general wanted.

"It would see you and your people well Perrhaebi."

156

The sun rose and Phoenix saw it though his eyes bled. He had been stripped and nailed to the tree. They had mutilated him, cutting off his ears and nose until his skull filled with their laughter then fell away in a vacuum of inaudible agony. Then the pain had woken him and wracked him and his tongue lolled and his eyes pleaded as he spat and yelled. And the sun became his pain as it arc'd and wheeled so one moment became many days. But with the vision that comes to doomed men he knew that death would visit soon. And yet it didn't. It circled suspiciously like the crows overhead and prowled and tore at his flesh with the wolves until he shrieked and screamed and they fled. He prayed for death. Phoenix had seen men nailed to the tree. In the dark pools of his childhood he remembered their carcasses as they shuddered and swelled and then fell to silence. So the cadaverous crows watched and waited. They knew he lived as his body twitched and groaned as he cursed the cold moonlight. In the morning Phoenix still had life. The day was young and below him lay the moving mass of the western sea, the mists still laid heavy on her like a shroud. The ocean sizzled as the sun rose shooting an orange path of flame across the swollen water. And then for a final time Phoenix raised his eyes in an ecstasy of pain and saw Achilles strong in battle. He saw a mighty Trojan warrior and through the ocean haze a woman with hair like yellow sunlight.

157

As the soldiers marched they told each other of the black heart of Agamemnon who was in league with Hades himself – the desecration of Delphi, the farms and cattle slashed and mutilated, the statues defaced and smothered in excrement. The anger rose in their hearts and their stride became stronger. Peleus knew most of the stories for lies but was happy to countenance the rumours as he knew it put fire in the hearts of his men if not actual food in their stomachs. Peleus led from the front riding on a giant of a horse that despite its size trod surely with its red rimmed mane and tail. Behind him, rank and file strode the soldiers. How could they lose with Apollo on their side? Macedon enjoyed the marches as he strode in front of his friend Antigonus. He was tireless and always had a smile upon his lips. Antigonus soon learned why. Macedon was an inveterate farter of Herculean proportions. Ten rows behind him battle hardened foot soldiers sniffed the air and examined the soles of their feet,

"Macedon. This must cease. My clothes are wilting and my sense of smell is now paralysed."

The soporific atmosphere, the dank air, Macedon's emissions, the forced march; they all combined willfully to produce a torpor in Antigonus that was close to delirium. Macedon, grinning wildly, marched on. That night Antigonus was unforgiving,

"Must you?"

Macedon turned to Antigonus,

"Must I what friend?"

"You know well what I mean. You're an old scrote and well overdue for cremation."

"I prefer burial at sea to cremation and both to your cooking" mused Macedon

"You have the manners of a pregnant boar" retorted Antigonus.

Macedon turned his back on his friend and chuckled to himself hugging his sides like a child before lying on his side and falling asleep where he dreamt of stoats. Antigonus lay back and smiled at the moon. He wondered whether the Gods were looking down and if so were they smiling on him?

158

Sometimes his memories of the Minoan girls overcame him with their long trimmed flaxen skirts of crimson, the curls in their scented hair, but best of all their bodices open to the waist. Peleus's heart grew heavy at the memory and his mouth dry because of lost summer days and nights. Then his mind would wander eastwards to Colchis and his doomed search for the golden skin of the ram.

"I was a fool to follow Jason" he muttered.

The love that Jason had borne for the priestess almost deprived him of his reason. Peleus had never trusted Medea who had betrayed her own family for nothing but her own ambition. They had set sail from Iolkos but there had been no golden fleece, only the women who smelt of the sea as they sailed eastwards past Lemnos. Moving north of Troy and Priam's country they had entered the dark sea with its high waves crashing on the Korcasa mountains. Then the old familiar faces would haunt him; Hercules and Acastus, Polydeuces the swimmer, Phineas with his tireless spirit. Peleus ached for those days, his head dizzy with nostalgia and the pain of loss. But Jason's quest had succeeded in its own way, his journey had been honourable and he knew the days of his young manhood had been the days of his glory. Peleus cultivated his memories and held them close. Like an old song he played them over and over. Were they now out of tune they were played so often? Were the strings missing like an old lyre? It was then that Peleus wished for his old comrades so he could play the tunes and have them sung once more. But in public his demeanor remained courtly and measured, a swan like control as he gave out orders. For it was his own private hell. What was I before and what have I become? Was I a wandering fool amongst men? Did they love me as I loved them? Were those things that we achieved an echo sounded out by the Gods? Did that same sweet wind caress them as it blew us westwards? Have I yet woken or was it a dream that I dreamed all my life, an untouched stair, a stone making not a single sound; echoing to an outside unseen…? And then with a fear that struck him to his core he reached out and saw that there was no reason for the sun, a simple ball of flame two leagues in the sky and The Argo was just a dream.

159

Phoenix's corpse sagged and stank. After two days the flesh had sunk into the bones following the patterns of the flanks and ribs, the eyes staring into a frozen nightmare. The air was still and labored like a dying breath. So the day sweated. The sky and the earth pressed against each other to squeeze out the living air when Achilles found his mentor. Anubis lay at his feet, by her side Purdy lay dead his throat cut. But the vultures stayed away wary and puzzled by this she wolf who protected these corpses. On seeing Achilles she raised her hackles and her head at this new intruder but soon settled as his familiar scent reached her. Xanthos muzzled his dead friend. Achilles fell forward his breath heavy as if he'd been punched in the stomach. And he wept that he would never hear the soft, wise voice of Phoenix again or feel his hand on his shoulder and turning, see his smiling face. The sun's strength was now spent as it set over Epiros. Achilles watched through his tears as endless rays were shot from Apollo's bow into the vast arena of the cerulean sky. They arc'd and fell tinting the light cloud with golden shadows. It grew cold but he stared as the ghostly hands of dusk spun a web of twilight around the moon and the stars. There was beauty in the air. It grew colder still as he raised his hand and gently stroked his mentor's skin one last time. Anubis watched and guarded, a friend to no one but Achilles. Then his tears ceased and he began the pyre.

160

The next morning Achilles sat and stared without seeing. From one moment of life to the next and then equal with those born a thousand years ago. His passion and bile rose in waves and he cried again for his old friend and mentor and the creatures who had loved him and died with him. For Purdy with his cut off tail, the twitching dormouse, Lyria the lizard with her broken foot but still as quick as fire with an eye of amethyst. Achilles saw their shadows on the pyre. Bruised and breathless with pain he went down on one knee and gasped at the anger that pulled at his ribs. His soul was suddenly weary but his spirit was honed and trembling as he clenched his jaw and planned his revenge. As he rose something caught his eye. There in the ashes of the pyre was a small ring. Puzzled Achilles examined it closely then placed it in his tunic.

"Come Xanthos. North."

161

Achilles moved on sometimes sleeping as he rode. At Chyton he worked the plough in return for beef and wine. Now north toward Chaonia, Pindar to his right. The smells and vegetation were unfamiliar to him. The figs pushed their fleshy leaves between the humble grey, green myrtles, the over ripe lime green pomegranates that Phoenix had loved. He picked one and bit into the sickly flesh his fingers covered in sweet juice. North of Aous he was followed by a girl who begged him to take her with him. Mica, a house servant was buxom and handsome. Intoxicated by the romance of his imminent departure she lay easily in his arms but Achilles now knew how easy it was to leave. She was delicious with a laugh that reminded him of soft water. An aura of chastity despite her well practiced proclivities; she fought hard to win his affections. Her movements spoke of light and laughter and for a short time nothing else mattered. The sweet consolations of sex.

"I'm looking for someone. Perhaps you've heard of Skirantes?"

But at the mention of the name Mica took to her heels and was gone.

162

Lyria recognised the wood where she had fallen and Cerebus had saved her – from who or what she still didn't know but when she had awoken he was dead by her side. She remembered the kindness shown her by Claryta, wife of Antigonus who had lost her child. How sad she was to leave her. And poor brave Cerebus who protected her till the end. She had buried the flower where it had fallen. Celandines marked the spot. She saw the north star and remembered. She kept silent and thought of her old friend. The most sacred of all anniversaries are those unspoken; the secret anniversaries of the heart. She thought of the past year. She thought of Achilles. She knew she loved him. As a child on Lesbos she had loved the playful ponies. Seeing the still child in his eyes mixed with the poise of the warrior prince. Oh the fickle manchild! It is never the father who first sees the woman in the child – some say he never does. It cannot be checked by calendar dates, only a word or the touch of a hand. Then a gladness born of pride and fear, a new stronger nature emerges and the child vanishes like a dream at dawn. Lyria like all young lovers was not happy to let things lie. Time and again she explored the fragmented nuances of their courtship for new meaning that would elevate it to an even higher plane all the while not realising that a cold analysis infects all passions with a cancer that will eventually destroy love.

163

Achilles was tired and lost. He longed to feel water on his face not the sun on his back. The dust had worked its way into his teeth and toes all summer. Winter was late. He thought of him stirring the seas and the trees to cool salvation. He closed his eyes but still saw the dark wounded sun shimmering in his brain. To his left the sea was a deep bowl of dust coughing up the dry days, the ground unforgiving on the cracked hooves of Xanthos. Must go forward. His thoughts, desires and purpose coagulated so he was no longer sure where he was or who he was.

164

Agamemnon son of Atreus and Aerope. Agamemnon, ruler of Mycenae the powerful centre of the Argolid region with its fertile valleys watered by underground streams. He sat in his huge canvas tent and brooded silently watching the flies which he would sporadically catch and hurl to the floor. The tent was dark. He would often invite his generals to a darkened room then serve them black olives and show them black slabs of stone and inform them of their cause of death. He found his generals agreed to his plans more readily afterwards.

"We could do worse than trade with these barbarians from the east."

Agamemnon looked doubtful,

"The Phoenicians?"

"They have built cities at Tyre and Biblos. They navigate well by the stars selling their cloths and cedar to the Kush."

"They are still peasants" replied Agamemnon, "lighting fires in caves and wearing animal skins."

"If we make on the deal what does it matter?"

Ganymede, prince of Ida had much to gain from a trade agreement and waited nervously whilst Agamemnon considered his reply,

"You are right. And we need the wood for our bows."

Agamemnon then ordered his generals to his quarters. He sat as usual in the darkness his sword at his feet,

"Where is Peleus?"

"Our reports have him marching towards Parnassus."

"As expected. And what else?"

"His camp is ill equipped, they don't drill their men, they are unorganised."

"When will he move?"

"After the winter."

"Good. That gives us time to secure the pass."

"And the spies misinformed?"

"Yes my Lord."

Agamemnon had long suspected that Peleus would not engage until after the winter. So he prepared for this. Supply lines were in place. Great wagons had been constructed to carry their fuel and food. Women were brought for the sole purpose of cooking and amusing the men. So the camp became a homely place, the smithy fires flared all night, the sounds of the wheelwright mixing with the laments of the sleepless newborns. Men hammered their shields into shape and sharpened their blades whilst the women hung flowers and boughs on the huts drawing elaborate images of the Gods to bless their warriors. Agamemnon looked westwards over the pass. The sun rose and parted the mists so the world shone; washed clean by the night rain. Making camp at Orchomenus by lake Copais would provide game and refreshment for his men and was only a days march from Thebes where extra men could be called upon. On a clear day Mount Parnassus could be seen just north of the desecrated Delphi. Winter was approaching. Agamemnon was confident of gaining the pass – the ridge that fringed the valleys was half a day's march away; this held the key to the higher ground and would give him the advantage.

165

Arriving at Orestis Achilles stared unblinking and sightless into the inner sanctum of the temple. He attempted to dismount but fell heavily. Nephele the young priestess who had never seen an entrance of such pathos rose from her prayers. Infinitely bored with the endless routine of worship she made her way over to the broken manchild. She moved silently like a ship in full sail. Voluptuous and desirable she moored at the side of Achilles. He at last began to gain some clarity firstly through his nose as he smelled her perfume and then through his eyes as he took note of the gold bracelet which gleamed on her ankle. And finally through his cock which shivered like a lyre string as he noticed her fine leg – and then more as she bent over and his eyes were drawn to a necklace of obsidian quartz and amazonite which rose and tumbled on her bosom like a jewel on a midnight ocean. With a faultless grace she began tending to him.

"Thank you." Achilles mumbled the words

"It was an interesting entrance."

From the corner of her lips a smile slowly evolved and then spread with an indescribable beauty to her eyes.

"I will take you to my father. But first…"

166

Nephele's father took him in. He fed him and told stories only some of which were true. Nephele was a frequent visitor. Achilles listened to the old man after he'd spent the days sleeping and gaining strength. The stories oozed from the grey folds of his memory and lapped at his feet like the waves of the Aegean filling the air with sea salt and half truths. His uncle eaten by sparrows, his brother living with the Amazons, his first wife dragged off by leopards in the land of Kush. All his tales were delivered with brevity his eyes bloodshot and reddened by the wine which he drank copiously. His smile was as unpredictable and crooked as his stories owing to an unfortunate collision with a Dipylon shield whilst fighting for Peleus. His sinus was thrown out of line thus his smile appeared from anywhere and spread across his face in random quixotic spasms – only the most tenuous tad of skin separated the bone from the grin. Achilles looked up sharply at the mention of Peleus,

"Were you happy to fight for him?"

"Certainly, he paid well."

The old man gave a half smile,

"But he had a temper and sometimes his orders were vague and simple. We just ran at the enemy. No lines, no instruction." He paused, "like at Leuctra."

Achilles listened as the old man continued,

"We lost so many men, the tactics were restrictive, we fought on higher ground, the rains had been. It was a quagmire."

He paused and took some more wine. It was good to have

company for a change. And this young man had manners and listened.

"The oracle says his son Achilles will be a good fighter and lead us. I don't see it. He is a puny specimen they say but this Agamemnon worries me."

"Why?"

The old man paused for a few moments then gave his answer as Achilles bent forward,

"He has destroyed Delphi. Some men are capable of nothing but pain, no arguments can appeal to them apart from the sword. Unless Agamemnon is stopped we are doomed. The man is a monster wearing a human disguise."

Achilles sat back,

"What is your name old man?"

The old man stood and for the first time Achilles was struck by his bearing and noble stature.

"I am Skirantes, leader of the Chaones. Still loyal to Peleus. And you are?"

167

A fractious truce prevailed within the army of Peleus as they slithered south and he knew it. He knew that if the winter was harsh the Perrhaebi would not stay long under his command. They marched with slung shields their sullen sword hilts protruding from their damp cloaks. Shepherds and freemen watched uneasily as the snake went by. Some joined eager to fight this man who had defied the Gods. How could they lose? So the snake grew fatter and longer. The Perrhaebi sharpened their swords and looked on whilst the *Periokoi* of Thessaly tested their slings moodily. Peleus set the men to regrinding the metal on their armour and swords so they balanced evenly in the hands. The Perrhaebi placed boars tusks on their helmets and bull tails on their shields to invoke power and courage. Macedon simply leered at them.

"Macedon, you are tired and sick. And your feet smell. If you took a bath once a year it would be a start. Even the whores in Piraeus turn you down."

Antigonus was tired and his temper was once again being tested by Macedon's pungent body odour. All Macedon could do was grin,

"Never. Never wash. Washes away the soul you see. And what do you mean by 'sick'?"

"You bloody well know" replied Antigonus. "The way you looked at that goat this morning. You didn't want to eat it that's certain."

"It's a lie!"

"It is a lie" interjected Paroxes, an old soldier from Corcyra who had been listening to the conversation with mild amusement, "he prefers cows like Poseidon's bull!"

This was enough provocation for Macedon who leaped at Paroxes who was still guffawing at his own joke. The sudden lunge of Macedon caught him unawares and he was soon head first in the dust apologizing whilst Antigonus urged his friend to let go which Macedon duly did,

"I submit to insults from no one. My father always taught me to fight often and fight bravely."

"You certainly do that Macedon. Now here, have some wine and sit still awhile. Here Paroxes. Sit with us. I am Antigonus of Thessaly, famed breaker of horses. And this is Macedon of Crete famed breaker of wind."

Paroxes accepted the invitation rubbing his jaw and spitting blood and dirt from his mouth. He would think twice before insulting Macedon again even in jest. But one man looked at Macedon with bile and loathing. Simonis was a Perrhaebi and senior soldier loyal to Meriones. Belligerent and intolerant he turned to him and smiled,

"From Crete? How lovely. Did not Daedelus build a fake cow so your Queen could copulate with a bull? Tell me if I have that wrong."

The fight was long and bloody. But finally Macedon stood whilst Simonis lay at his feet broken and bleeding. Macedon's stock was rising amongst the men.

168

As they marched the harsh winter bit at their heels. Now the ground was higher and the sky grew greyer so the wind blew harder bringing great swathes of snow drifting where the woods lay thickest. Some flakes landed on the eyelash of Antigonus as he gazed around in wonder and for a brief moment the world was slashed with the colours of the rainbow, the gleaming mesmerising landscape of the Gods and he ran through the snow quickly feeling the full force of Macedon's skill as his snowballs hit their target with unerring accuracy. The snow glinted white and grey. Day after day they awoke to its bright welcome until Antigonus tired of it. On the low plains of Thessaly the snows rarely came so the men held out their hands and opened their mouths to collect the flakes. Others were frightened thinking it the work of a malevolent God. But the free men from the northern slopes of Mount Pangeus in Thrace smiled and remembered the cold dawns of their homeland. Now the mornings came white with frost and the men shivered and huddled together watching the swallows that flew south to Kush. Fishing through holes punched in the ice to entice the frozen fish to bite. But even they shivered in their shoals keeping to the depths of the river where the water was warmer. The cold stung Antigonus and his bloodless lips thinned and his knees trembled so Macedon held him tight. The hoar frost cut into their sandals and the cold winds blew west over the Boeotian plain and through the high passes. This same wind chased away the mists that hung around the neck of Mount Helicon to the south. But the cold didn't worry Macedon or his brethren many of whom had left behind the mines of the Portico's. Agathenes preferred the march to his endless toil in the fields. Barratae who had rowed the Phoenician galleys smiled at the wind. And Aethalides (who brought with him his sister Anticlea with whom he lived in incest) chuckled and garnered her hair with chaplets of dead leaves and flowers marvelling at this new freedom where no one whipped them and laughed at their screams. Macedon looked around and savoured this egalitarian company, to not be judged by the colour of his hair, his price, where he was captured, the port where he was stripped and sold. And Antigonus who spoke to him with grace and love thus bestowing a verisimilitude in his life that had been stolen from him when he and his brother were enslaved and marched east long ago. And where was his brother now? Macedon gripped Antigonus tighter and put it from his mind.

169

At night they trudged on mocked by the laughing moon that followed their slow progress casting her white light in picaresque patterns over the troops so their pallid faces shone and their shields shimmered. The men rarely spoke so their silence merged eerily with the silver shadows thrown into the sockets and caves of the valleys so to any onlooker they appeared as a phantom army making their ghoulish progress under a bilious moon. Then in the day the pungent prostitutes charmed the soldiers and slaked their thirst squeezing the monies from the fleshpots, impenitent when coaxing out the age old desires. Blue skinned negresses from Nubia, golden haired Spartan girls, the old flesh wrapped around the new bones, the snowdrops in their souls crushed long ago when they learned their art with sober tears as children in the meat houses of Argos and Nemea. Now passing the great swamp lands of Arcanania where the flooded plains caused the men's feet to fester and stink with disease. Peleus warned against desertion – hunger had driven some to stray and loot the small holdings that had been deserted stuffing their tunics with fruit and old corn heads. The rain came in torrents and the army dragged itself and plodded wearily until they were in sight of Parnassus. It was here that Peleus halted. The men needed rest and shelter. Only the great mountain range separated them now. Agamemnon would want me to march on Mycenae itself. But that won't happen! He will have detachments as far south as the Isthmus. It would be foolish to attempt these passes in the winter. Peleus looked southwest. The skyline was mountainous and intimidating, a jagged horizon. Beyond lay Phocis and Boeotia and the armies of Agamemnon. He turned to his generals,

"We make camp here."

170

Antigonus walked from the camp to escape the noises, the drudgery and smells of the makeshift huts and shelters. The camp resonated with the sound of the carpenters and blacksmiths, the smell of the trades reeking to the sky with the smithy's smoke. The men sat, some attending to their armour or sewing their tunics. The eastern slaves bought and sold on the trade routes through Samos and Miletus licked their putrid feet and wounds thinking it would heal them as they'd seen with the horses they worshipped in the lands of the far isles. Antigonus watched their faces. As he left the camp behind and the silence overcame him he saw that his life was short and that he had come from the earth and would return to it. Perhaps soon but almost certainly in the spring when the armies clashed. He looked up at Parnassus. It looked forbidding and seemed to promise nothing but pain and death. He turned away and was surprised to see Macedon at his shoulder smiling,

"Thinking of leaving us?"

Antigonus smiled, pleased to see his friend,

"Come Antigonus. I've half a lamb on a spit. Let's eat and drink and bore each other with old tales."

Antigonus put his arm around the broad shoulder of his friend as they returned to the light and warmth of the camp. Macedon was antic and brutish in many ways but he knew Antigonus well, recognised his moods and, like all true friends, knew when his presence was needed and more importantly, not needed. Antigonus remained thoughtful as they prepared to eat.

"Perhaps there is just the one God in whom all others reside. I've heard the Hebrew tribes speak as much."

Then silence as they sat and ate corn and the flesh of a kid served to them by the wife of a Perrhaebi spear carrier who had joined her husband on the march. Eventually Macedon spoke,

"The Hebrews? Barbarians. I've seen them bury their dead in the earth. And then to add to the shame they erect a stone for all to see. Perhaps this Perrhaebi will lay with me later."

Macedon had a unique talent for lowering the level of conversation and soon the air was filled with smoke, curses and laughter.

171

A familiar angst had captured the heart of Peleus. He remembered his young manhood when friendships came easy and choices were simple. The shadows of Thetis filled his head. Did I treat her too harshly? He remembered their courtship. He had worked hard to pleasure Thetis. He had dreamed of her. Her pleasure had been paramount, the juice from her garden would prolong his life and ensure a boy child.

"I dreamed of you Thetis."

"What of it?"

"Zeus spoke to me. He wishes me to take you."

"I'd rather be drenched in piss and faeces and plough an endless field."

But the days had passed and she had weakened. He feared her virginity had been taken. Her bed manner and the look in her eyes allayed his fears. After a while there was peace. Peleus seemed happy to her and she was glad.

A groan, long and guttural brought the guard into Peleus's tent,

"My lord?"

Peleus reached out putting his hand on the guard's shoulder, "Find Thetis for me."

Outside the moon slipped out from a cloud and sailed into view but it wasn't the moon that Peleus had once known as it pitched through the night ocean. He walked the perimeter of the camp checking the sentinels trying to forget his past. The sun had long ago set and the earth was black and grey, the soaring mass of Mount Parnassus etched in darkness. The air felt suddenly fresh to Peleus, full of sweetness and light. Then seeing the moon edge slowly upwards he called for the watch to sound their horns and signal the curfew. He saw himself in ten years time maybe sooner, his bones creaking. His voice faltering and dying into silence until all that is left is a faint pulse until even that fades. And what then?

"Old age is the one disease I don't want to be cured of."

"Lord Peleus."

The guard's voice sounded surprised, almost excited, "What is it?"

"Your son seeks an audience. Achilles. Prince Achilles!"

172

Antigonus and Macedon listened to the horn and stared at the night sky,

"Do you think there will be a time when men don't fight? Sometimes I wish we were of another time."

Macedon grunted,

"We must accept it. It is our path, our time."

"I knew this would happen. Last spring Hermes sent me a dream. Agamemnon was a bull with a man's body. His army of wolves ate us then ate themselves."

"A cheery dream then eh? You're full of them. Too much red meat."

And then suddenly without warning the sky spat shards of fire across the sky. Both men sat up and gripped each other,

"Look, the stars are racing."

The stillness of the night was loosened as the belt of Orion unbuckled and sped south. The camp became lit with starlight as one after the other the stars buzzed the sky so the two men held their breath in fear. The soldiers turned to one another,

"What does it mean?"

"An ill omen. It has to be."

But Orpheus didn't think so. His expression was sad as he stared upwards motionless and unmoved. He knew that sometimes the stars died and threw themselves to earth and it had no bearing on the destinies of men. The Myceneans saw the same sky and shivered in fright turning to Agamemnon whose words soothed them,

"Our star leads us to victory."

Thetis looked up and laughed then bit her nails till the blood ran. Melantho, a slave jailed for sheep stealing and awaiting execution stirred then howled thinking she was saved. The whores in Corinth gathered and pointed in awe at something true and full of hope then returned to their filthy flesh pots just as their star waned and died. Agamemnon curled his lip and sneered,

"The stars fall just like Peleus."

Telesippa, a young woman from Lesbos raised her head and saw to the north, shining and straining at their yoke, the ploughing cattle led home by the north star. The moon was waxing so her silvery gossamers threw a thin veil of white light over her hair. For a long time she looked and wondered then closed her eyes and faded fast in her arms.

173

Achilles entered. When he had left he had seen pride and strength in his father's eyes. Now just sadness and a greying beard. He remembered a strong Peleus placing him on his shoulders. So long ago. So powerful was the memory that he knelt on one knee and shook at his father's feet. Peleus, seeing this as an act of supplication was gratified and flattered. The real reason for his son's subservience would have destroyed him.

"We go to war then in the spring."

Achilles stayed on one knee,

"Do you want war father?"

"Who would want war Achilles? Who would want his son to fight? It's the way of things that you should see me over the Styx not the other way around."

Peleus looked at his son. Achilles could see his eyes widen. Was it pride that flashed quickly across them?

"You are older son. You look it."

Achilles said nothing. Peleus noted his straighter broader shoulders and the musculature, his carves and biceps set in stone. Achilles in turn looked hard at his father who had never burdened him with affection. But despite this he felt close to him, admired him. But more for what he'd been than what he was; something in his eyes made him pity his father. He was about to step forward when Peleus spoke again hesitantly,

"And me. Do I look any older?"

174

Macedon was happy. Full of mutton and wine he smiled and blinked in the midday sun like a basking lizard. When there was no battle to be fought his idleness was preternatural in its scope.

"When do we fight? Does nobody know anything? I grow fatter daily."

"I'm glad you've brought the subject up."

"So when do we fight?"

"No, about your stomach" said Antigonus grinning and reaching over slapped his friend's belly,

"That will be rippling for a week. Look at that blubber. Some soldier will find you easy meat."

"Ha! I'm not finished yet. There's enough of me to finish off a few of Agamemnon's generals before I bite the dust."

"Enough of you? For once I agree friend. You need to chase some goats for a few days. If you sit around here any longer we'll need ropes to hoist you up. Your shadow alone covers half the camp."

Macedon lay back and grinned. He wouldn't have taken these words from anyone but Antigonus or his brother who now most probably lay dead in a Greek ditch. Macedon reflected on his lost sibling but not for long as it wasn't his way to let himself become maudlin. But he knew he missed him. He knew this from the dreams sent to him by Hermes. Antigonus knew because Macedon spoke in his sleep. Despite his jests he knew what a formidable fighter his friend was whether fat or thin. He gazed at Macedon who was smiling. 'He's thinking of his next meal' thought Antigonus. But he was wrong. He was thinking of the whores long ago in Eretria who'd smelt of leather and lillies.

175

Achilles pressed Peleus for a response but none came, "Your stockade is not enough father. Agamemnon may not wait for the spring. He will take the higher ground. Do the soldiers know their divisions? They must fight in formation."

Peleus merely shrugged.

"We have enough men. And remember the Gods are on our side."

"Are these the same Gods that helped the Phocicians when Agamemnon called?"

Achilles was now exasperated.

"I will train them father. In your name?"

Peleus nodded. Achilles set about the men who were now aware of their roles and their immediate superiors. They knew their tactics; their weapons bristled, their senses sharpened. No time now for soporific tales told drowsily by the fire. The men were drilled. The Thessalians raced their thoroughbreds, the Arcanians boxed. The bronzed men from southern Aetolia bent and primed their bows and calmly mixed the poisons for their bronze arrowheads. They all watched in awe as the Minoans wrestled in oil, their naked limbs glistening in the bright sun. Rivalries were punished, arguments forbidden. Standards were used to denote rank and file. The blacksmiths worked ceaselessly producing axes and blades, their fires pulsing through the night. Daily battles and drilled scenarios were endlessly re-enacted. As for the men they were happy to obey, dreaming of a free Greece without the tyrant Agamemnon – but mostly they dreamed of his gold that they would take home.

"This armour is heavy. Years out of date. Send the seamstresses to me."

Achilles put the women to work so the old cumbersome bell corselets were replaced with lighter flexible materials; layers of stiffened linen reinforced with metal plates. As for the helmets boars tusks were used, carefully cut into oblong plates, pierced and sewn into a leather cone.

"All soldiers are to wear chin straps and neck guards."

But Meriones, the leader of the Perrhaebi was unhappy,

"You work them too hard Achilles. You confuse them. My men are fighters. They know their enemy. What else is there?"

"Bravery alone doesn't win battles. Training and tactics. A cool head. Show me an army that is all heart and I will show you a defeated one. It is not enough. You will organise your men Perrhaebi and drill them. Once I was a child but I no longer suckle my mother's breast. I learned. The world moves on."

And Meriones returned wearily to his men.

176

Peleus and Achilles sat and listened whilst Meriones spoke. "It's the Greek way to advance slowly gaining ground step by step banging the shields in rhythm."

Achilles shook his head,

"No, no. We run at him. Smash through his defences. And we need more chariots."

"To carry the weapons?"

"No, to hold two people, the driver and the archer. The wheels must be made of bronze. Strong enough to carry two. It's a weapon not a wagon."

Peleus was astonished and impressed in equal measure. Where had these ideas come from? In his youth chariots were merely a way of conveying people to and from the battlefield.

"The chariots will take us to the field of battle quickly. And further."

"How do you mean?" asked Meriones

"Ride them into the enemy like a battering ram. They'll be manned by two people. An archer and a driver. Make the wheels out of bronze. If there's no bronze then elm or willow."

Achilles looked to his wheelwrights who nodded,

"Make the wheel and central axis midway under the chariot. Give the charioteers the best protection, the cuirass made of bronze. They'll have a better chance of surviving. Tell the men anyone who mounts a chariot wins my favour and will be *Periokoi*, a free man of Thessaly."

He looked to his father for approval. He nodded and the orders were given.

In Thessaly winter was old and dying. He leaned heavily on early spring looking for strength and solace. But spring did not listen. She stretched skywards and the green leaves in the groves and woods turned from opaque to lime. Childlike and joyful they reached out growing and breathing in their mirth. The grass trembled with hope and anticipation humming and singing with the high blue sky. It was a harmony of colour, light, life and fire that spoke of creation and a new beginning.

177

As winter waned the soldiers became more nervous.

"What do you know of the Myceneans?"

"Animals. They wear no clothes in battle, their eyes are always blue."

Macedon cut in,

"That will be the inbreeding."

The man continued,

"Their legs are short and muscular, they have no need of clothes."

Airetes, a wool maker from Lemnos spoke up,

"That's right, they smear their bodies with pig grease and the juice of the mastic plant so blades slide off them. My father lived and traded in Mycenae for a year. When the men get older they take themselves away in the night and slit their own throats just to save fuss. They can't be beaten in battle."

"Well I can save them the bother of slitting their own throats" said Macedon. "Naked in battle? Well if I don't die by the sword I'll die laughing."

Antigonus turned to the wool maker,

"What is your name?"

"Airetes sir at your service. I only tell you what I have been told in faith. It was rumoured that he had a forest cut down in Macedonia and transported to Mycenae so he would have enough timber to execute the Greeks, to burn us alive in a gigantic pyre."

"You are fun to have around Airetes. Remind me to never invite you to my symposiums."

And so the old myths and stories continued worn smooth as

sandstone. They gorged on stew and fat and wine. Antigonus no longer felt a stranger. He warmed to the men around him. He felt more comfortable here than he ever had at home but he still thought of Claryta and hoped he would one day return to her.

178

Macedon and Antigonus listened intently as Achilles spoke.

"Their shields are small and rounded, less cumbersome. But they have no shoulder strap on the left arm see? Just a hand strap so it can't be slung around the shoulder. Most will wear it on their left arm."

Achilles demonstrated,

"So their right side is always vulnerable."

Achilles knew that the main weapon of the Mycenean foot soldiers was an eight cubit spear tipped with bronze and spiked at both ends for balance. Many would be equipped with a short stabbing sword for close fighting. The elite warriors would have their swords inscribed and boast bronze plated armour. The phalanx would move forward in columns of eight with the rear ranks favouring composite bows with obsidian or bronze arrowheads some dipped in poison.

"The momentum is always forward. They are vulnerable to attack from the side. A jab in the ribs and they'll lose their formation. When that happens they will lose their structure. Their rank and file is strong but predictable. Agamemnon expects us to throw stones and scatter. But there is a way to beat his machine. You, pass me your spear."

Macedon handed his spear to Achilles who looked it up and down closely,

"They need a stronger base, pull the metal collar further up the shaft – slightly top heavy. And you practice every day."

"Poisoned?"

"Wolfsbane. Slow but deadly."

Macedon nodded. Later Antigonus questioned him,

"This young prince. He seems knowledgeable. A good man to lead us Macedon?"

"Perhaps. I will let you know when I've seen him fight."

179

Spring came quickly. Lamps were lit. From cold clouds came green and golden days scattering the scent of gorse and blossom. The streams tepid, the fish faster, keener. Helen knew from the smell of the hyacinths which seemed to come earlier in Thessaly. The smell stalled her and for a moment she was a child racing through the gardens of Sparta stumbling and collecting olives for her mother. Her thoughts came quickly as she tried to remember the names of the flowers that made the special potion. She knew her mother, Leda, would test her that afternoon when they walked in the hills to look for herbs. She giggled at the strange shape of the saturian and xiphion leaf then looking down she noticed some cyclamen with its distinctive red flower. She remembered her mother's words, 'now this will make a woman fall in love with a man.' Just at that moment Leda appeared, her long hair held with a pin. She was finely dressed as always in a white robe held with a crimson braided sash around her waist. A string of pearls from the sea of Propontis hung around her neck. Helen always thought her mother should live on Mount Olympus, she walked with such poise and was so beautiful,

"Look mother, I have cyclamen which will make a woman fall in love."

"Only if it is mixed with powdered periwinkle and earthworm" answered Leda, "and the effect will only last for one moon."

"Are there any herbs which will make a man fall in love with a woman?"

"No Helen." Leda could see the frown on Helens face and knew what she would ask next. Ever since she was weaned Helen always questioned and seemed to disagree with the order of things.

"Why can't a woman woo a man?"

Leda sighed, "it is for men to woo and chase and for young women to gracefully decline. Where do you get these strange ideas from?"

"Can a man and a woman not love each other equally?"

"Darling daughter, there will always be a lover and a beloved. A man's love is for him a thing of little consequence – but it is a woman's life."

Helen shrugged, "then I shall never love a man!"

Leda laughed. She loved her daughter's lack of convention and was already looking forward to sharing her foibles with her future husband. The sun was now dipping into the ocean, the twilight vapours laid delicately on the seas surface. Then she swooned and breathed her last.

"I have someone here who wants to meet you. He has come a long way."

Theseus came from Athens, his hands were rough, his breath smelt of stale wine. She had bitten but he had persisted. Her mother walking away. Were the Gods unhappy with me? They must hate me. As time passed the memory sank deeper. There was the time before and the time after; her life now neatly sundered by one event. Two blocks of light that circled one eternal darkness. The inky fugues of her unconscious mind honed her appetites and pulled her convictions towards a new destination just as a bird of prey is blown off course by a strong current but finds new meat on a darker continent; her shallow beauty perfectly camouflaged the dead fish of her soul. Amatory, predatory and wretched her true pleasure was now taken in sucking dry the virtues of others. But the more she fed the hungrier she became, the events of her childhood now neatly sublimated into subterfuge and vitriol. Her spirit was sick and a sick spirit cannot be bandaged.

180

Achilles could find no sleep and so he rose and went out alone, walking through the camp and listening to the men as they spoke of the great and grave deeds they were going to perform the next day. Some recognised Achilles as he passed and so puffed out their chests and tightened their grip on their swords. Achilles smiled. In his heart he felt bitterness and disgust but also a wild delight at the freedom he still yet held and shared with those around him. He cursed Agamemnon but tempered his hate for he knew it was cold indifference and tactical acumen that would win the day. Not blind fury. He looked to the outer camps of Meriones and his Perrhaebi. What he saw filled him with surprise then anger and he stood paralysed.

181

Antigonus too could not sleep so he left his tent and stared blindly into the long grasses that spoke quietly of the summer breezes yet to come. Will I feel them? He thought of home. The scent from the earth was powerful and left him reeling as he was taken to a time when he named the night birds and wrestled with his brother whom he had loved and who had become weak overnight. The same plague took his mother too and he had watched again as the light died in her eyes as the morning whitened. He prayed that he would see them again in some Elysian fields. Hearing a noise he looked to the east and thought he heard thunder,

"False dawn, east storm."

Macedon, dozing behind him heard it and looked upwards to the moon that was hidden behind clouds that were barely discernible against a dark blue velvet sky. Half asleep he muttered an age old prayer,

"Oh Zeus. I will gladly sacrifice a hundred bulls at your altar if you give us this victory and scatter the entrails over the temple walls with rivers of wine."

182

Peleus heard the same noise and wondered if a storm would favour him or Agamemnon. Alcaeus of Parthos heard it and looked out on the night sky and, thinking of his daughter Alexa, instinctively felt for the twisted gold bracelet she had given him before he left. He lay back entombed with a lover who had stayed with him for the long march. In this woman he channeled his angst so she awoke each morning bruised and shamed. Yet she always returned craving the darkness he opened in her pulling her desires towards their malevolent beginnings. Sniffing at the air for a dawn that wouldn't come he returned to his rest. The *Periokoi* heard the noise as they dreamed of the soft winds of Thessaly and the welcoming women, the wild horses and the wilder nights. It was a sound which came from the earth itself as if the dawn had taken up arms and even now marched towards them. Then the fragrant dawn did come as did the spring and the fitful Thessalians remembered the dull distant noises of the night and understood where they came from. The fires burned low as first one voice then another shouted out,

"Meriones has gone"

"Meriones has deserted."

"He has taken his army to Agamemnon!"

183

Agamemnon's army shivered with the cold dawn as they descended the dark twisting roads which snaked the slopes of Parnassus. Then tramping through the dead grass which still waited for its rebirth they met with Meriones. So the armies conjoined and walked forward, grim faced and confident of another easy victory. Meriones rode with Agamemnon,

"These Thessalians are animals. Peleus himself eats excrement and worships horses. They paint their faces and polish their teeth with arak wood so their grins are green."

"Don't worry. They won't be grinning tomorrow. Look."

Meriones shielded his eyes and looking up through his fingers saw the carrion birds gathering. They circled in the hot air watching the armies draw dry breaths from parched lips.

"The earth is a wound Meriones that must be healed. They play their part by picking at the bones. Tell the men to make camp here tonight. We will have our war tomorrow."

184

At dusk Agamemnon rode silently and looked at the Thessalian lines of defence. He wondered. The earth was piled high from the freshly dug trenches; the rain had turned these trenches into quagmires into which pointed stakes had been placed every three paces. Then beyond them sentries, their helmets gleaming watching for any movement of the enemy. Peleus looked towards Agamemnon. So the great men saw each other across the vast plain. Agamemnon's crimson cloak was wrapped tightly around him but he suddenly let it loose so it floundered and blew in the breeze covering the flanks of his horse. Agamemnon recognised Peleus and his charger, the great Bucephalus so dear to him, the filigree bronzed armour. Above them the sky pulsed. The clouds bled and limped across the sky then faded fast into a bed of crimson. Agamemnon well beyond arrow range turned and cantered back to camp. Something was troubling him. Peleus watched him disappear then turned to his flanking guard,

"He should enjoy this night. He doesn't have many left."

Anubis lay by Achilles and remembered her cub. Dear heaven how he had purred and gambolled, how he had cocked his head!

185

The army of Peleus waited. All down the lines of soldiers silent prayers rose like orisons to the blue heavens. In the bowels of the battalion the men stared vacantly into the sky, fear and expectation of death conspiring to produce a languid torpor. Men hugged, gave final instructions to their friends, looked to the sky and to the ground. Aello of Marathon thought of his *agrimi*, the wild Cretan goats he had bought to support his family. Would they be enough if he didn't return? He spoke to his friend Cottus,

"Do you believe in an afterlife Cottus? That people dwell in Hades? Without Meriones it is not if we will die but when. Perhaps Agamemnon will be merciful."

Cottus, a short man of limited means stared ahead and cursed his comrade's ill timed enquiry. Having spent the morning trying to procure a pair of decent sandals Hades was far from his mind. Anyway he had spent most of his twenty years in the Hittite salt mines so Hades held no fear for him. He turned to his friend,

"I don't really care. I'm planning on living forever."

"Me too" replied Aello. "So far so good."

Five rows behind stood in the bowels of the left flank Dioscuri wondered how he had ended up about to fight the greatest army ever assembled. Only three moons ago I was tending horses on Scyros and riding along Perissa beach. He gripped his spear tightly and thought of his beloved horses. Iacchus who stood at his shoulder gripped his arm and spoke in loud whispers,

"You will know when the Myceneans shoot their arrows. They cover the sun and the world goes dark. I've heard

Agamemnon swims like Polydeuces and runs like Hermes."

"And fights like Aphrodite" said Dioscuri who had put up with his woes and bleak predictions for too long. He made a silent vow to strangle Iacchus with his own hands if he got through the day alive. Orpheus reflected on the shallow pools of his experience. To peer into those pools was to see his bloodless face and nothing more. What do I really know? Where have I really been? He spoke silently to himself not wishing anyone to hear,

"Life has been a mystery to me. A great surprise. Who is to say death will not be a greater one?"

Macedon shuffled at his side. He had heard Orpheus. But he had no time for philosophical musings.

"It's too hot to moralise. Lead me to the enemy."

Macedon was strong enough to use a full bronze tower shield coated in Cretan oxhide that he'd won in a bet. From the hollow of this shield he produced a piece of goat's cheese the size of a fist and took a large bite out of it. He turned to the bewildered Orpheus,

"I always get hungry before a battle."

The Myceneans advanced. Then they halted as first one then another looked to the north where silver shards of light glinted off a host of shields. Fresh standards and armour suddenly sent sharp shadows along the ridge of the valley and they hesitated. Some recognised the standards,

"It is Skirantes. The black banners of the Chaones."

The Thessalians cheered. Achilles nodded and raised his sword in recognition. Skirantes did the same and marshalled his men.

186

The front fighters of Agamemnon with only linen and leather for armour struck their huge animal hide shields as they walked. The elite warriors with their inscribed swords and bronze plated armour hung back, their rank signified by the transverse crest on their battle armour and their braided hair. With their breastplates, grieves and boars tusk helmets they felt invincible despite this late appearance of Skirantes. The long haired Spartans under Menelaus jostled and elbowed their way to the front line hoping to catch their leader's eye. To lead a charge meant greater pay. Agamemnon, imperious in battle, rode between the rank and file reminding them of their great victories over the Opeans and Phocicians. He wore a coat of mail over his leather cuirass. Skillfully woven into its weft and mesh were links of filigree gold, a fine prize he had pulled from the body of a Phocician prince. Only a man of his strength could carry it into battle. As he rode he promised riches and honours and the men believed him marching forward to a drumbeat of gold and jewels; an easy life in the rich whore houses of the southern ports. Behind the rank and file and flanking them the horses pranced and stamped whinnying and wild eyed waiting for their war. Both armies were well in view of each other now. Agamemnon knew that Peleus would charge – it was the Thessalian way to move forward without form and cohesion. This was the way all primitive armies fought. It would be easy enough to absorb this charge and close in around them. Cool and calculating he dispatched two cohorts to deal with Skirantes. Still a short day's work. In the Thessalian ranks the generals followed the orders of Achilles whilst Peleus watched,

"Stand firm, let them come on! Spear their horse. Thrust at their legs. Then the men will fall. The horses first!"

The armies then drew nearer. Agamemnon noted the reticence of the enemy to charge and scatter and put it down to cowardice rather than tactics. One strong horse charge will have them fleeing. So with his standard raised he gave the order for the horses to lead the lines. At the same time in the front line of the Thessalian ranks Antigonus turned to Macedon,

"Well my friend. If we live through this we will have earned our keep tonight. We can drink to your fat belly and the Gods."

But Macedon hardly heard him. Already in the grip of battle fever he held his sword tighter as he saw the horses and chariots thundering nearer. Turning to Antigonus he shouted,

"We will stay together like the wolves in the hills. If we stray and scatter we will be picked off. Now down on one knee!"

Antigonus on hearing his friend and seeing him kneel followed suit. Macedon who had by now gained much respect amongst the soldiers turned and shouted,

"On one knee and thrust upward!"

And so all the army followed like a giant wave. Some swirled their blades in the air with a yell. Their swords and shields caught the early sun that rose over Parnassus and peeped uneasily through the pass. And so it seemed to the charging Myceneans that the enemy knelt in obeyance and prayer with a flourish of light, a foe slashed with colour so great that some put their hands to their eyes though the sun was at their backs. All yelled as they rode, the mountains resonating with curses and oaths. Antigonus blanched as the horses approached and the ground shook before him. Three rows behind him Alcaeus of Parthos held onto his spear and thought of his daughter Alexa. The gold bracelet he had given her for her birthday now wrapped around his dagger hilt. He trembled and choked at the air that was suddenly thick with the stink of sweat and faeces as some men lost their bowels along with their resolution. Prince Lycomodes with his pockmarked face thought of Thetis. Leonides the wheelwright thought of his wife and lover, his land and livestock. He muttered a prayer to Ares but it was barely audible spoken through dry lips. This was Agamemnon, undefeated in battle. Descended from Hercules himself so they say. Son of Atreus!

187

Agamemnon's men were unsure as they saw their enemy kneel. Their opponents had usually fled on seeing a thousand charging horses. Eratos of Lesbos, agent of Agamemnon, murderer of Parmenion, complained of the heat as he stood in rank but something wasn't right. His voice trailed off into a childish gurgle and blood poured from his mouth as he fell forward. There was one arrow in his eye and two in his neck. His comrades pointed and laughed but then a great shadow passed over them and they looked to the sky. Achilles had ordered his archers to let loose their arrows so five hundred arc'd and fell and more blood was spilt. The Thessalians then took heart from this. So they bleed! They fall from their horses! Macedon suddenly grew in stature though he had needed no reminder of the enemy's mortality. With a wild cry he thrust forward his spear then wheeled and spun so three of Agamemnon's riders were unseated. Macedon fell on them and slit their throats. This stirred the bones of his comrades and they took up the charge their courage returning. Agamemnon was surprised at the resilience of the front lines of Peleus but unmoved. Raising his arm he summoned his army forward as his horsemen retreated.

188

Now the blood of the Myceneans was up and they fought like wild animals with little thought for tactics. Agamemnon ordered his men to stay in line but many ran forward screaming wildly only to be hacked to pieces by the enemy as they stood fast. Achilles ordered his front lines to attack then retired them after a short engagement so a fresh line could take over. The tactics proved supreme and the Myceneans fled and were pursued without mercy. And now Agamemnon saw that his army was losing and for the first time doubt edged into his mind. The Thessalians hadn't been swallowed up. They hadn't charged wildly or fled. This was no disorganised rabble. He looked again at the ordered ranks of Peleus, the riders flanking and to the rear, the foot soldiers and archers well positioned to protect their slow advance. He gave new orders and the generals nodded.

In the Thessalian ranks Macedon, knowing Antigonus to be of a fanciful disposition kept half an eye on his friend fearing he would break ranks. But he needn't have worried. Antigonus was stern faced. The sight of death had focused his mind and he set to his task with a stoic determination. Caresses who had rescued Achilles from the cliff bit at his arm to try and ease the pain of his lost hand. Gnawing at the stump like a mad dog he licked the gaping wound before the pain sent him into a blessed delirium and he fell unconscious and bled his way to Hades. At the same moment Macedon's shield was hacked from his arm, leaving four of his fingers sliced clean off. His scream of pain was swallowed up by the butchery that surrounded him and he fought on stronger till a Mycenean club felled him and knocked him cold.

189

Agamemnon could see that his army was made up of mercenaries and slaves by the way they fell on their enemy. One young man, a nobleman from the court of Peleus looked to the sky as he was torn apart. Agamemnon watched with amusement as they sawed at his head and cut off his ears whilst the soldiers shouted encouragement. The salt and copper slaves bought from Lydia had never been shown mercy and were not about to dispense it. Denied the sun and the taste of wine for so long they delighted in their task of mutilation long after the young man was dead. So died prince Lycomodes with his pock ridden face who had loved Thetis but never knew her. But the armies of Peleus showed equal savagery when their chances came, bathing in blood and pulling the entrails from still living bodies. One of these was Orestes, ruler of Lesbos and puppetmaster of Agamemnnon who now lay dead, mutilated and shamed. But the Myceneans were now killing for pleasure and great shouts went up as they wielded their weapons with a raw delight. Finally in desperation the Thessalians turned outward to form death rings which the Myceneans struggled to break. But it was only a matter of time. Meriones had taken their battle plans and nearly half their men. This was a mortal blow that even the brave Skirantes and his Chaones could not heal.

Already beneath his feet the dead legions clammered for a breath of wind. Lycomodes now impotent to act amongst the feckless hosts, the numberless and undefeated, the ever expanding army of the dead. Screaming for vengeance and clawing at the light. Quick as a dream, waking their pleasure from memories in the hollows of Hades. Icarius, lizard lipped and cruel knew where he was. Reaching through the shadows his eyes stared sightlessly through the soft light of Stygian gloom and he moaned. The dagger wound in his chest now strangely painless, just his soul screamed. At the great banquet he tapped his old friends on the shoulder but when they turned no one knew him or recognised him. Above the ground Achilles felt a tremor in the earth. He paused and shuddered then strode on.

190

Agamemnon saw the day was won yet he hesitated. What if these retreating hordes were leading him out of touch with his rear flank so as to leave a gap south to Plataea and Megara? Where was Peleus? The Chaones were fleeing. If this was a ruse then it was well executed. He watched as three times the Thessalians turned to face the advancing Myceneans. The women from Cretan Cydonia now fought alongside their men bare breasted and wild swinging axes and swords with little skill but accounting for a good many of Agamemnon's men. But not all wished to fight. Achae the sister and lover of Melos, heavily pregnant, ran through the belly of the battle unnoticed until a Mycenean short sword cut her down, the unborn foetus spilling out on the soil. Agamemnon watched unmoved. The Thessalians fell backwards their retreat now blocked by a lake and like a wounded animal the routed followers of Peleus limped around its perimeter. Alcaeus now stood and he fought with a fury that only comes to those with no hope until he too was speared and spat on; his last thought was to hold on to his daughters bracelet to carry him through his death throes into easeful slumber. But Merakiles of Sparta denied him this. He stood over him and ripped it from the dying man's hand and smiled before placing it in his leather salt pouch and gouging out the eyes of Alcaeus whilst he still breathed so as to give him clearer vision in the battles to come.

191

Water was the only sound as Thetis approached the temple. Two men, acolytes and servants to the priestess stood silently at the door. Their heads were bowed yet their stillness was malevolent and menacing as if even now they searched for auguries with the dead. The priestess prayed to Hera and Hecate and brought incantations and amulets.

"Child of Paphian, daughter of the evening star. My lady we thank you for the corn and the grape and the light of the sun and the moon."

Every week the rituals were repeated and every week the Gods were agreed,

"Achilles, little Achilles, Greek hero who sails for Troy. Who fights for Agamemnon."

The Priestess paused and looked up,

"He will not return."

Helen waited till Thetis had left then, pulling off her veil called in Eurypylos,

"Follow her and report to me."

192

The night drained the battlefield of all its ghoulish sights, the shields and swords that a short time before glittered and danced in vainglory now a soft hum of trembling death; the corpses recumbent leaving a sombre progress enjoying their first watch in the legion of the dead, their bodies bloodless, their bowels emptied so the air stank. Light bathed the face of old Skirantes, his crooked smile now forever fixed. The golden pallor gilded the furrow in his brow but the grey hairs at his temple splayed horribly, his head cleaved in two by a Mycenean axe. But the birds still sang and swooped over the deadlands creating a bizarre juxtaposition of sound and sentiment. The earth was shaken, raped by the storm of men that had torn the land. The bloodstained air heavy as a sigh. Even the mist had a reddish hue. The sun set and crawled away for once happy to send in the shadows and let the night steal the light from this saddest of days. So she set with a shudder as the *Periokoi* lay dying.

193

The morning swung swiftly over the Aegean. At Elis the old men awoke eager for news of Peleus and Agamemnon. In the ruins of Delphi the ground still smouldering, the birds still silent. The young women of Thessaly thought of their husbands. The older women thought of their children with fear in their hearts. Claryta worked the fields and thought of Antigonus whom she now knew was with the army of Peleus. She missed him, she grieved her lost child buried now in the grave her husband had dug for himself; her back bent in two as she raised the plough and fed the oxen. But the whores who had followed the army of Peleus secretly laughed. What fools for thinking they could defeat Agamemnon! Many were still young so their hearts were filled with hope that they'd be spared. So they cleaned their bodies and painted their faces waiting with high hopes and half smiles. Peleus awoke to darkness. With a raging thirst he felt around and dipping his hand in a puddle of water sipped from it then fell unconscious. When the sun rose fully and the light woke him he saw he had drunk from a pool of blood. Furious he had not died in battle he looked around for an enemy soldier. He didn't have long to wait. Agamemnon now walked the battlefield breathing in the sweet and rancid odour of blood, bile and faeces. The smell excited him. Battle and death were the only things that restored his equilibrium; his source of joy to see a soldier breathe his last, better still a kingdom. A shadow passed over Peleus and he looked up to see Agamemnon. His sword inscribed with lions swayed in its kidskin scabbard. Drawing it he threw it on the ground beside Peleus.

of Agamemnon as if he were dreaming. Or drunk. Or mad. In his mind again a traveller on the Argo. Never looking outward, careering into himself, scrutinising the smallest detail. Was the prow repaired with ash or oak at Cannakale? Was the shoreline sand or stone at Propontius? Tapping out the beat of his heart with the stroke at Chalcedon where he saw the oxhides and fleeces hung out to dry in the heat and it had seemed to him that they had all glinted gold in the late autumn sun and that somehow this had given him the right to take what wasn't his. Finally he looked up.

"I took the Golden Fleece! Yes. But it was for Thessaly. Medea, the priestess at Delphi, she knew. She was the only one who did. So she had to die. I had no regrets, the Gods wanted it. She never loved Jason. The Delphic oracle? Apollo was a mere servant of the moon Goddess. He betrayed Selene. It was not a desecration at Delphi but a liberation. Ha, what do I care for Apollo and the new Gods? The world blames Agamemnon."

"Do you hear this prince Achilles?" Agamemnon roared, "do you hear the noble Peleus admit his guilt? This is the king who invites hubris. It is Peleus who sneers at the Gods and makes war on oracles. It was he that destroyed Delphi. Not I! No man that is false can win in battle. So it is shown. Why else would you send a peasant with a saddle full of stones to negotiate a peace? Did you think I'd let Dion live? You sent him to his death. It's a peace you never wanted!"

Agamemnon now left Peleus and summoned Achilles. Achilles turned away but Agamemnon persisted,

"Could you serve me? Could you love me as a brother? Could you love me as you loved Phoenix?"

Achilles stopped.

"What do you mean?"

Agamemnon now took his hand,

"The pomegranate ring you wear. It belonged to Phoenix. I gave it to him and now you wear it. The other I gave to his mother Danae. Yes, Lyria's mother. He was my son. If you loved him as a brother then accept me as a father of Greece."

Achilles, stunned, stared as Agamemnon raised his sword to finish Peleus but his sword dropped and he fell as Anubis brought him down biting deep into his leg. Agamemnon screamed as the blood gushed from his thigh and puddled the muddy ground. Anubis had her revenge. Achilles looked between them then slowly, wearily, walked away. He walked through the torn men, the broken men dying around him. Laying in heaps under the clear skies they cried for their mothers and unborn sons. The soldiers ministered to Agamemnon and took his instructions as they tried to stop the bleeding,

"What of Achilles?"

"Leave him be. One day he will fight for me. Light the fires at Elias. Go to Larissa. Helen rules through me."

"And Peleus. The eels?"

Peleus waited for Agamemnon's judgement knowing the best he could hope for was a quick death.

"You will be paraded in dishonour. Tell your soldiers they can return to their homes. I need them to work the land. They fight for me now. Any still here by sunrise we will finish."

194

The long march back to Thessaly began. The men staggered home wrapped only in the shivering moonlight gazing ahead with shallow smiles made of nothing but skin. Amongst these were Otus the sea captain and the furtive Copreus, friend of Parmenion. But also Orpheus saved by Acristes whom he had comforted years before after Icarius had cut off his ear. Acristes remembered little from the battle, only the knife he had plunged into the chest of Icarius. Orpheus walked with his head bowed wracked with guilt at what he knew was a betrayal of his dearest friends. He had wielded his sword with little skill, protected fiercely by Acristes and the large man with the goat's cheese shield. Peleus gazed at the wounded men left behind, then turning to his commanders gave his orders. Immediately the soldiers tended to their comrades, stroked their hair and joked. But it was to no avail. They had heard the order. Some cried and wept, some tried to run but many bared their throats after first giving final messages to their families. Most agreed, better to be slain mercifully than torn apart by the birds or Agamemnon's men. Already the Myceneans were picking the bones of the battle throwing the choicest finds onto their chariots, the bronze breastplates, the ibex-horn bows. Macedon who lay dying spat at them as they went by. His face now white, both legs shattered by a chariot's wheels. Antigonus took him in his arms and stroked his hair.

"I see you are here to save me friend."

Macedon handed him his dagger. As he did so a small tear ran slowly over his cheek.

"There will be no pain dear Macedon."

Antigonus stabbed him cleanly through the ribs and upwards to the heart. The blood ran slowly as the heartbeat was faint. Macedon didn't react immediately, just a tremor flowed freely across his face, the slightest spasm, the briefest flicker of the eye before he whispered calmly,

"Where is my brother? Fetch the fool here."

Antigonus laid him down with infinite care, his head cradled in his arms,

"Macedon, Macedon, my dear friend."

"Forgive yourself. Forgive me. Now go home."

"The brother I lost. He…"

"Don't go overboard eh? By all that's mortal stop your squeezing boy, you'll take my last breath, now where's your hand?"

Antigonus had his arms about Macedon and was squeezing him tightly as if to stop the life from leaving him. But finally his great leonine head sagged and Antigonus felt the full weight of it as he lay him on the ground and closed his eyes. So died Macedon. Far to the south in the Gulf of Pagasae the dark blue sea pulsed calmly like the heart of a sleeping lion.

195

Achilles kneeled at the feet of his mother,
"Peleus is defeated. Agamemnon now rules Thessaly through Helen. Come with me mother. You aren't safe here."

"I am not safe anywhere dear Achilles. From myself least of all. I cannot come with you. Please do not think of me as someone who is denying herself something in life. My solitude does not deprive me of anything nor am I fitted to be anything other than I am."

She remembered her passionate affairs when she had come with the storms and counted the crimson tides.

"I am who I am. I will not resort to sophistry or word play. By nature or nurture I am made and there is no forgiveness."

She faltered and looked beyond her son,

"But there is something else Achilles."

She beckoned her son to the next room. Achilles followed. In the corner almost covered by a blanket lay Lyria. Thetis knowing her son's mind held him back.

"No. She is not well. She must rest."

But Achilles broke free and knelt at the side of Lyria and took her hand.

"Now I can nurse you Lyria."

He spoke the words excitedly, overjoyed to see her. Lyria too, invigorated sat up and embraced him.

"I will stay here with you till you are well enough to go. We will return to our cave in Epiros."

But he noticed, as their high spirits waned and the heat

gave way to the early evening coolness, that the air provided no refreshment for Lyria. Her face was pallid, her movements insipid and soon a burning rash on her forehead rendered her helpless. The next day she lay naked for she couldn't bear to have any clothing touch her skin. Achilles knew of this new terrible disease that marched through the body visiting the head then chest leaving each infirm and disabled with a mortal coldness. Today the enemy was camped in her chest and she coughed and spluttered searching for a breath that wouldn't come so she bucked and panicked like a stranded fish. Achilles stayed but was mindful of exhausting her. The moon was just a sliver of ivory peel when she began to fall. A powerful vomiting began which he ministered to but all he could do was watch as the enemy took more ground. Lyria was no longer coherent but Achilles was careful to speak with the same hope in his voice of their plans, the games they would play, the places they would go when she recovered. Then the corner of her mouth quivered and her hand trembled so he held it. Yet he now dreaded any signs of coherence for with it came a terrible pain. Uncaring of advice nor mindful of contamination he now lay beside her to pass on the warmth of his body to hers and he hoped more besides. Through the night he lay with her until her hand became stronger one last time. Lyria thought of her earliest childhood and recalled just sunlight – sunlight and Orpheus on the brow of the afternoon, mottled on the dawn. Achilles was the first to speak.

"Is it any comfort to know that you will live with me and I will weep for you every day?"

She closed her eyes,

"No, because I will not see or taste your tears."

Then summoning the last of her strength she turned,

"Do not forget me completely Achilles when I'm gone. Though I to you was just a passing fancy to me those short times were my life's course and fulfilment. But I am not sorry for this. I know you never loved me Achilles but I loved you the more for never telling me this."

"You are wrong Lyria. That love you spoke of. I know it now. Here."

Lifting her penitent hand he placed the pomegranate ring on her finger,

"May your deeds dance wildly in a golden bay."

Lyria looked to Thetis,

"I know a part of you was always sorry for me Achilles but now see your loving son and know him for your own."

Thetis passed the newborn child to Achilles and Achilles saw the boy just as surely as he saw himself.

196

Under the timid moonlight the Penieus stretched out into the distance till it became just a fine silver thread spun by a careless hand. For Achilles all the beauty and ugliness of the world lay in Lyria's face. Her lifeless body drove away his hope. He knew instinctively that he had died a little inside.

"What more is there to give?"

He lifted her body with infinite care. It was the end. Lyria lay still, her skin still flawless for the dead don't bruise. Her smile now only slightly faded as if she had just fallen asleep which of course she had. But death hadn't yet changed her face, her features soulful, the workaday woes melted, the flowing hair graced her pale cheeks with a royal flourish taking away deaths rudeness.

Outside the air became sweetened by the scent of the cypress and the newly dead. The flowers turned to the sun and their colours brightened. Lyria's body grew stiff as the blood set cold in her veins. Sweet blood that now stained the Styx. Time passed. Then the moon crept out from behind a black cloud and the world was white. Achilles wept as he held her tightly. Stroking her hair he kissed her sad eyes. But Lyria was silent. He pulled her into the question mark of his body.

"What treasures do you have Lyria? I have ostrich eggs from Egypt and ivory from Syria. I have dyes from Crete and copper from Kypria."

All her breathless loveliness returned to him and overwhelmed he fell to the floor and as the tears left him so did his mercy. Half dressed and shrieking oaths to the sky he mounted Xanthos and galloped towards the palace at Phalanna.

197

Helen, ruler of Thessaly sat surrounded by her symbols of wealth. The carnelian and amethyst from her lesser admirers, the gold and silver from princes and kings. But never satiated, a festering soul always craving more. Despite himself Achilles was again struck by her breathtaking beauty, her breasts deliciously hidden within diaphanous blue robes stitched with gold and inlaid with faience. Full of grief, full of vengeful thoughts he looked around for a sword but was disappointed.

"Don't blame me for the girl's death. The plague can strike anyone. You want to take me Achilles? Not very wise with a phalanx of bodyguards a shout away – and you with no weapon. And anyway you should thank me."

"For what?"

"I'm not the enemy you think I am. It was me who saved Lyria from her mother on Lesbos and put her on the boat. Agamemnon mistrusted Danae, thought Lyria may well have been of use. She was. And it was me who saved her from the clutches of Leodes. But it was the bastard boy Orpheus I was protecting. Agamemnon may still have plans for his illegitimate offspring."

"Orpheus is the son of Agamemnon?"

"Yes, and Danae. She was ordered to abandon him. Phoenix too."

"What do you know of Phoenix?"

"He paid the price for deserting his master. It was the Libyan who ordered his death. Castor and Pollux were sent to spy, to follow. Not to kill. It was them that released the horses to save

"Why not take it Peleus like you've taken everything else?"

Achilles sat on his haunches a short distance from his father and watched as Peleus took the sword and stood.

"Better to die with sword in hand Peleus like your army."

Agamemnon took the sword offered to him by Anexos and stood back. Peleus the *myrmidon* bristled and lunged at Agamemnon. But Agamemnon knew better. He was expecting a quick and easy kill but his heart grew light as he realised the fight would be drawn out. Flushed and angry Peleus pressed again spinning so the air was cut and spliced with clashing curses. Peleus felt his knees and wrists tiring and the wrist is the heart of swordplay so he fell back. Agamemnon now knew he was the fitter man. He'd always known he was the greater warrior. Peleus now kneeled, beaten and breathless. But Agamemnon held the final blow and whispered to his enemy,

"A quick death for you Peleus if you tell them. Tell your son. Tell them what I know. Tell them what you did. It will be better for Thessaly. Make your peace with the Gods Peleus."

Peleus looked up and paused as Achilles and the generals pressed closer.

"You wanted this Peleus."

Agamemnon now shouted,

"Where is the fleece? Do you hear Thessalians? Prince Achilles? Tell them! Why did you do it?"

Peleus bowed his head.

"Remember Peleus. Tread carefully through your knotted memories old man – or let me untangle them for you. Where is the fleece? The golden fleece you stole. I want it. For the men you betrayed. The Gods want it for the priestesses you murdered at Delphi."

"I can't. It will lead to chaos."

"I don't care. I don't care if all Greece descends to Hades and the seas boil over."

It was as if the graveness of his thought was a leaden weight that pulled him down into himself. Peleus stared over the head them from the wolves. They killed these men and got this information. They avenged Phoenix, they didn't murder him!"

Achilles stepped forward. Helen rose and reached for a dagger but her hand passed over it. He was unsure. Her pernicious beauty perturbed him. Her profound control irked him and he paced anxiously stealing sideways glances. But then a fury overcame him that blinded him and he lashed out so she fell to the floor. Whispering and stroking her face, he kissed her cold lips till he gave in to a lust that sickened him. Helen gripped his arm,

"Rule with me Achilles. Be at my side. We can be more powerful than Agamemnon. You have a son, we have an heir. Orpheus too. Find him. Thessaly will grow again, we will wait then strike."

She stared at him with a look that was beautifully absent, an utter lack of depth which spanned from her scented hair to her embroidered toes and painted nails. Achilles left without a word,

"Where will you go? Your kingdom is lost. You need me!" Helen yelled. From behind the crimson arras Danae listened with interest then stole away to inform her master.

198

Thetis, sea girl, mother of Achilles made her way to the ocean. She hid herself from view when she rode only appearing when the moon was sliced. Set in her solitude, a solitude from which she gained self efficacy and affirmation. The sea was silent. From the ridge she looked down at the boats in the small harbour. They stood motionless with their sails tied to their masts. She lay back on the warm grass and breathed the air that spoke of summer and all its heady delights. Then she turned to her side to shield her eyes and fell asleep. She woke to watch the swallows skitting on pinking skies. Night lay watching and waiting then sick of the suns sin she raised her cloak and the world went black. The colours died to reveal the twinkling stars.

"The stars are enough" she murmured.

She remembered the stars of her childhood and how the wind blew in through her dreams. Thetis had known her son's fate long before it had been whispered to her by Helen with her pale almond face, pleading and apologetic. The dew lay heavy with the dawn as the realisation took a grip on her senses as a serpent coils its prey. In the days that followed Thetis did not fight the waves of her mounting despair nor seek distraction from her gloom. Farmhands would see her clutch at her heart as if to rip it out. Lost in reverie she became young again, buoyant and brave as a leopard with Achilles at her breast. So the sea became the pendulum which swung her heart plunging her into the vagaries of reflection and regret. Its vulgar swells pulled her thoughts towards the dry tides, borne away licking her wounds, the fragments of her life washed up before her. A shell. What was left of her sullen aniline beauty ebbed and left her and, tossing and turning in anguish, a hostage to her dreams, she thought of self destruction for the first time. With her mind dull with despair a mothering, smothering, soulless pain entered her and inward, downward she careered until there was nothing. And so it was that she stared at her ocean but saw nothing, wading to the waist she felt nothing; whimsical and welcoming the prospect of oblivion she whispered her son's name as the sea took her and drowned her with a sigh.

199

The murmur began with the foot soldiers then spread quickly. Agamemnon had the victory but the soldiers spoke excitedly as they returned to Mycenae.

"I looked westward and saw a figure lit by the morning sun" said Thanaxos, "a solitary still figure on horseback gazing at all before him. His legs hairless, his shoulders not broad like Hercules. A beardless lad barely past puberty. But no fat on his limbs, his arms and legs knotted in iron and sinew."

"Anubis stood with him. The man eating wolf" said Olistes a flag bearer.

Some said they could see his face, a grim face with a clenched jawline. The mist had cloaked him imperiously giving the vision a sense of mystery. His ice blue eyes showed no emotion as he eased himself forward in his saddle and returned to his army. It was only then when the sun glinted on his golden blonde locks that they had guessed and turned and spoke in hushed tones. Achilles? Was this the cowardly boy they had heard of? But one man remembered better than any. Thanatos was a foot soldier of Agamemnon mercifully knocked unconscious and mistaken for dead before he faced the young prince,

"If it hadn't been for Meriones's betrayal it would have been us paying the boatman. I saw him before I was hit. His feet moved but we didn't see them. Instead it was the world that rushed by. Then everything slowed for him killing men at ease as they waded through honey but he was light as air. Nothing around him lived, his face as still as marble, his enemies as slow as stone. His sword passed from hand to hand sending them to Hades cursing and spitting blood faster than an arrow in the hot southern winds."

200

Taking the pomegranate ring from his finger he placed it in his tiny left palm. But the fingers wouldn't bend so he gave the ring to Claryta,

"Give it to him when he is of an age. His left hand. Nearest his heart."

Claryta bowed,

"And his name?"

Achilles smiled,

"You decide."

Claryta considered.

"I will call him Patroklus, the glory of the father."

"It's a worthy name."

Achilles mounted Xanthos and headed east. Behind him trotted Anubis.

"We will find Orpheus Anubis. You see, together we make both halves of Apollo."

The sun set with a sob and the refulgent rays expired. Now a dark red jewel. The poppies heavy with seed. The ripe pomegranates ripped apart by sparrows, the chattels of Aphrodite. Achilles knew that neither his family, nor his lovers or his Gods would ever be as important to him as his honour or his glory. He determined at that moment to lock the thought and feeling deep down inside so that it would never leave him. He knew as he gazed at the heavens that this was not the fanciful whim of a likely youth but the fierce destiny of a man and in that second he swore by almighty Zeus to fulfil it.

A few days later Antigonus returned to Tricca. Claryta stood with her arms crossed,

"Forgive me Claryta. I was a little distracted."

Claryta smiled,

"The things you will do to avoid hard work!"

"And the child was born?"

She nodded nervously. Antigonus took the child in his arms and was glad. Secretly he would have liked to call him Macedon but thought it prudent not to incur his wife's anger,

"Now for an easy life. Let me tell you of my adventures. Anciles bring the wine!"

THE END

ACKNOWLEDGEMENTS

Thanks to Dawn and Kelly "mad dog" Mueller for their invaluable assistance. And to my sisters Alison and Melanie for their much appreciated help and support.

simonbriancartlidge.co.uk